W9-BJE-835

RECONCILIATIONS

RECONCILIATIONS

Elizabeth Klein

April 27, 1982
To Gene and Irene
With friendship and
good wishes,
Elizabeth Klein

Boston

HOUGHTON MIFFLIN COMPANY

1982

The author would like to thank the Ragdale Foundation, Lake Forest, Illinois, where a portion of this novel was written.

This novel was partially supported by a grant from the Illinois Arts Council, a state agency.

Copyright © 1982 by Elizabeth Klein

All rights reserved. No part of this work may be reproduced or transmitted in any form or by any means, electronic or mechanical, including photocopying and recording, or by any information storage or retrieval system, except as may be expressly permitted by the 1976 Copyright Act or in writing from the publisher. Requests for permission should be addressed in writing to Houghton Mifflin Company, 2 Park Street, Boston, Massachusetts 02108.

Library of Congress Cataloging in Publication Data

Klein, Elizabeth.
Reconciliations.

I. Title.
PS3561.L345R4   813'.54   81–19192
AACR2

ISBN 0–395–32048–8

Printed in the United States of America

V 10 9 8 7 6 5 4 3 2 1

This book is first
for
Michael.

It is also for
Carolyn, Jonathan and Daniel,
who were there from the beginning,
and for
Naomi,
who arrived in time for the end.

Once you know in back of every parent, there's another parent, you have to forgive everything.

— Susan Fromberg Schaeffer
Falling

Rabbi Zusya said just before his death: "In the world to come they will not ask me, 'Why were you not Moses?' They will ask me, 'Why were you not Zusya?'"

— Hasidic tale

SILVERSTEIN FAMILY TREE
December 1972

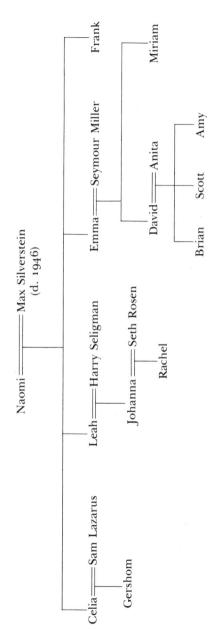

RECONCILIATIONS

I

~~~~~~~~

NAOMI SILVERSTEIN suffered mostly from weak eyesight and poor feet. She wore thick glasses to clear her sight and custom-shaped shoes to ease her corns. At the moment, however, her glasses were fogged, having just come with her from the cold outdoors to the heat of her daughter Leah's apartment, and her shoes, still incased in heavy plastic bags taped at the ankle, could carry her nowhere without staining Leah's dark red Persian rugs with gray New York slush.

"Cold out. Goes right through to the bones," she said and began to shed her layers of covering, passing coat, hat and sweaters to her son, Frank, still in his own coat, who stood behind her accepting them. He did not move until Seth Rosen, Leah's son-in-law, brought the chair he had gone to get for her to sit on.

"Let me help you, Grandma," Seth offered, going down on one knee, but Naomi put her hand on his shoulder and said, "When I'm an old woman, Seth, you can do that. Take the presents if you have to do something." She laboriously bent over and pulled off her shapeless, improvised boots.

Frank, hanging coats in the closet, gestured helplessly at the several shopping bags filled with boxes wrapped in Christmas paper, ribbon, and tinsel plumes. Seth added the packages to the massive pile already stacked beneath a Christmas tree heavy with fine threads of silver tinsel and multicolored glass balls.

Naomi made her way to Harry Seligman, who was seated on the couch, reading a picture book to a tiny girl dressed in light blue velvet.

"Harry, you've got Johanna and Seth's little *maideleh* there. Hello, sweetheart."

"Mother," Harry stood up and kissed Naomi's cheek mechanically. "You're looking well. Rachel, say hello to Great-Grandma. You know Great-Grandma, don't you?"

"Greatgramma," Rachel said agreeably.

Naomi leaned over precariously to kiss the child's head. "She has a shining spirit. A sweet child!" She carefully lowered her short heavy body onto the couch beside Rachel.

"Frank," Harry thrust out his hand. "How are things?"

"Not bad, not bad. How's yourself? Where are the girls?"

"In the kitchen getting things ready. Girls? Girls!" he called in that direction and after a minute, Leah, with short steps, leaning as if into the wind, came followed by her daughter, Johanna.

"Mother! Frank dear!" Leah's eyes were wide with greeting. "Is the weather awful? Frank, please put your galoshes in the boot tray. Not there. Near the closet. Rachel, did you say Merry Christmas to Great-Grandma and Uncle Frank? Isn't she gorgeous? Johanna dear, please tell Elise to check those cheese puffs in the oven so we can have something warm to offer." She ran her hands smoothly down her gold wool jumper over her small waist and glanced with a smile of pleasure at herself in the mirror near the entrance.

Buzzing from downstairs. "Seth darling, Frank's umbrella is wet. Do you think you could put it in the maid's bathroom? Thank you."

"Sit down, Leah," said Naomi. "Already you're fidgety. The day's just beginning."

"I'm not fidgety, Mother." Softly: "Harry didn't sleep too well last night. I want things to go smoothly for him."

Doorbell ringing. Johanna coming back from the kitchen. Seth opening the door.

A slim young woman with an unlined, slightly freckled face burst in, her red coat and fur collar wet with melting snow. "I'm here! Merry Christmas! Now the festivities can begin." She tossed her head back, pulling off her coat, her eyes sparkling as she laughed with the force of her own enthusiasm. "Seth, let me give you a cousinly kiss." She grazed her lips against his cheek. "Umm! Sexy aftershave! You're a lucky woman, Johanna. Uncle Harry," she said and kissed him warmly and handed him a bag of gifts. "Do you mind adding these to the pile?"

"I'll take care of it," said Leah, taking them from her husband. "Harry has enough to do with getting drinks." She unpacked the bags, piling the boxes out from under the tree against the marble mantel from which hung four red stockings. "What lovely wrappings, Miriam. You must have spent hours doing them."

"Had some free time the last few days." Miriam beamed. "It was great fun. Grandma." Her smile softened as she went to embrace Naomi. "I'm so glad to see you. You too, Rachel." But the child had already scrambled away toward her mother.

Naomi reached an arm around Miriam's neck just missing the short red-brown curls and pulled her granddaughter to the place Rachel had just vacated. "Sit down, talk to me." They began to speak softly as Harry rolled in a leather-trimmed mobile bar, parked it before a floor-to-ceiling textured collage in grays and silver, and began taking orders for drinks.

Bell. Seth threw the door open. "Look at that! What a system. All the Millers arrive at once. It's Emma and Seymour with David, Anita and the children." He took the bags from them as they came in. "My quartet could do with a little of your coordination."

"We just happened to meet outside the building," said Emma. She nodded toward Miriam, "Oh, Mimzie, you're here already."

"Just got here, Mom," she said, standing up.

Anita, the younger woman, held a baby wearing a pale pink

snowsuit who peered at the assemblage with big eyes and began to cry. "She's scared by strangers right now. It's that stage. It's all right, Amy. There's a love."

"It's all family, baby," said Emma. "You have to get used to them."

Johanna led Rachel to Brian and Scott and the three children stared uncomprehendingly at one another as both boys were peeled of outerwear.

More gifts.

Johanna urged everyone into seats as Elise passed the tray of warm cheese puffs.

"Take *one*, Brian," Emma cautioned.

"He's not doing anything, Ma," said David.

"Yes, David, he was touching the ones other people are going to eat." She sat down next to her mother on the couch. "How are the feet today, Mamma? I'll have a whiskey sour, Harry, please."

"They're feet. As long as I don't have to stand too much, it's not bad." She gestured toward Miriam across the room with her chin. "So, she's still seeing him. I don't understand. Where does his wife think he is when he's with her?"

"In New York. He has his own place and only goes home to Connecticut on weekends anyway."

"But he stays with Miriam. How can he get away with that?"

"He has a phone extension at Miriam's. His apartment number."

"I didn't know you could do that."

"You can do anything if you have enough money."

"One of the troubles is he has too much money."

"That's never a trouble! Look, Mamma, I really don't want to discuss it now. Leah," she called, "you look marvelous."

Leah's hands raised almost inadvertently to her cheeks, her gold, green and silver chiffon sleeves bobbing like full sails. "Thank you. Did Harry get your order? The baby is precious."

"Oh, yes. After two grandsons, it's nice to have a granddaughter. I see Rachel and the boys have found each other. That's quite a dress she's wearing — hand-crocheted cuffs and collar, I'm sure. You must have gotten it for her."

"At Saks. It's a grandmother's prerogative."

"Anita likes clothes that wash easily for the children. I try to buy things to make her life a little easier."

"Here comes Seymour. Good! I haven't said hello to him yet," said Naomi.

"Mother." He had gray rings under his eyes and a vague boyish smile. "How are you?" He leaned over and kissed her.

"Fine. Fine. How are things at the store?"

"Could be better."

Emma poked her mother in the ribs. "Mamma, not on Christmas. He has to worry about it the other three hundred and sixty-four days. Seymour, do get me a cheese puff over there, please. One for Mamma too." As soon as he moved out of earshot, Emma shut her eyes and said softly and quickly, "He's had a few good weeks what with the holidays, but not good enough to make up for the fall. Let's not talk about it."

Seymour trailed back with cheese puffs and Harry with drinks. "Seymour," said Harry, "I have some information about a new tax law that should save you hundreds. We can discuss it tomorrow at my office. Things will be slow. Can you come about . . ."

Leah's lips pursed and her hand trembled slightly. "I wonder," she said, interrupting her husband, "where Sam, Celia and Gershom are. It's nearly three-thirty. I hope they're not having trouble getting here. Celia's already nervous today. I called this morning just to remind her about the time and apparently she'd had some sort of fight with Gershom. He was sulking in his room."

"Will Celia Lazarus be able to endure her son Gershom's sulk? Will husband Sam be able to get them to her sister Leah's in time for Christmas? Tune in tomorrow," said Harry with amusement and moved away.

Leah followed him with her eyes. Then she continued. "She

really dotes on that boy. I understand, you know, having an only child myself, but his every movement makes her vibrate. She's been upset lately because he's been talking about possibly moving into the dorms or getting an apartment. It's just an idea but she's frantic — as if he were already moving out."

"Sam pampers her," said Emma in a disposing tone.

"Celia was such a nervous child. She could hardly eat sometimes, she would get so excited." Naomi shrugged. "Once I remember, I took her to a labor rally. She must have been about two and a half. Leah was a baby and I was pregnant with you, Emma. When she saw the signs waving and the policemen on horses, she got so frightened I couldn't do anything with her. She bellowed and screamed so hard, I had to take her home and miss most of the speeches. Terrible! I couldn't even calm her down at home. It's hard to change that kind of disposition."

"Emma made up for it. She has nerves like steel," said Seymour.

Buzzer downstairs.

"I don't know if I like that," said Emma.

"I meant it as a compliment, Em. I don't know how I'd manage if you weren't so tough."

Doorbell. Gershom in first, looking pained. Sam and Celia together behind, Celia's mouth drawn up in the twisted hook of a smile.

"You're here. You're here. I was getting worried." Leah tripped across the room, arms out. "But now we're all together. All here."

*   *   *

The distribution and opening of gifts was postponed until everyone had had a drink and something warm to eat.

Gershom moved among his family and swayed like lanky and tenacious ivy toward Johanna and Seth, who were standing to one side of the tree.

"I must admit you're right — that pile of gifts really is oppressive," Johanna was saying.

Gershom trembled slightly, his eyes black points sinking under dark brows. He clenched his fist and released it to an open palm several times.

"Don't worry, Johanna, I like your family anyway." Seth rocked toward her and put one arm around her shoulders, his head of unruly blondish hair bobbing close to her dark one. "Here's a family member I especially like. Hello, Gershom. We missed you this week."

"I thought I'd come down yesterday, but I got involved helping my mother wrap gifts. When I'm home it's hard to get out." He passed his hands above the gifts in an ironic benediction. "Just to keep in the spirit of things, last night, on impulse when the guys I was supposed to meet didn't show" — he paused, almost as if forgetting what he was about to say — "I went to mass."

"It's a good show," said Seth, "really beautiful, though I used to like it better when it was in Latin and I couldn't understand it."

"You know how I felt? Like a foreigner in a country that seems closer than his own. That Catholic music was more my music than anything I've ever heard in a synagogue."

"Well, more familiar anyway," said Seth.

In the kitchen, where Elise was unmolding the cranberry Jell-O, perhaps too soon, Celia, her tight curls defying the hot moist air, was standing against the cupboards, Kleenex in hand, and addressing her sisters Leah and Emma in a mucousy voice, sharp with imperatives.

"He *must* learn to protect himself better. It kills me to think how he must have waited last night for those bastards who never came. I can see how they hurt him. I heard him in his room, crying. I've said to him so often, 'Bring the boys home. I'll make a dinner.' And sometimes he does but rarely anyone of his caliber. Like that Jesse Bruen he got mixed up with in

high school. Oh, my God, when I think of how I worried about
him being with that creep who used marijuana I'm sure, and
the girls. You know once Jesse wanted to bring a girl to our
apartment while I wasn't there. You can imagine what he was
up to! I thought that when Gershom got into a fine school
like Columbia, he'd at last make friends who would be appreciative of him, people he would have things in common with,
but so far, whether because he doesn't live in the dorms or
because he's so shy I don't know, he doesn't seem to have
found anyone decent." She passed the Kleenex across her eyes,
a shadow moving.

Emma folded her arms in front of her chest. "Celia, it seems
to me he's just going through what many boys go through
during their adolescence and perhaps you have to give him a
little room for growing, even getting hurt, which, after all, can
teach too."

"Sam says that. But Sam, my Sam, he too. Such a brilliant
man, so perceptive, and what does the world do to him?
Sometimes I really ache. We saw an article in the *Times* recently about his old classmate Bernard Katzman. There's a
man who used to come to *Sam* for advice on his college papers, who wasn't half the student Sam was, and now he's touted
by all the literary people — 'a brilliant novelist,' 'a brilliant critic.'
He had one stroke of good luck. He didn't have to go over-
seas during the war, and while he was stationed in Texas doing
whatever it was they did there, he wrote a novel that might
never have been published at another time. It hit the public
in a vulnerable moment though and made him a fortune, so
he didn't have to go to work right away afterward the way
Sam did. He was able to go and get his Ph.D. And there's
Sam, with all his ability, stuck teaching those animals in that
horrible high school. Well, my Gershom is intelligent but
doesn't push himself forward just like his father and I don't
want the same kind of thing to happen to him."

Leah softly advising Elise on the condition of savory-smelling delicacies cooking on the stove, turned and patted Celia's arm. "Dear Celia, I know you worry but it's really too early to guess what his life will be like. He's a nice boy. Johanna and Seth think so much of him and . . ."

"They are the high point of his life," moaned Celia. "I'm eternally grateful they live near the university. I think he feels closer to them than to anyone."

"They say," continued Leah, "that he's doing splendidly and I think he's fine."

"He was crying last night when some no-good boys didn't meet him. He was so unhappy when I tried to comfort him, he actually said shut up to me." She seemed near collapse.

"Celia, you must stop this carrying on. We will have a perfectly miserable day if you don't get a hold of yourself. Don't ruin Christmas for us, please." Emma pulled at Celia's elbow.

Leah shook her head at Emma. "She'll be all right. Don't be hard on her. Come, darling, we'll go in now." She began to steer them like amusement-park cars, her energetic efforts turning them slowly in her intended direction.

"Not a word," said Celia, "not a word about it, please. He mustn't know I've been talking to you."

Leah in the lead, they bled into the living room toward the pile of packages, a defiant mass of color. Outside the light was failing, the gray of winter afternoon slipping into dusk, the sky obscured in the window by the sides of buildings, grayness reflected in their windows, in one or two of which Christmas lights flashed like beacons.

"It's time for presents, get the children." Leah's voice was high-pitched, vibrato. "Come on, come on. Harry, you want to take over? Elise says dinner will be ready in half an hour and we have all the presents to open."

Miriam got up and went for the children, who, after several furtive snatches at the pile, had been sent into a back bedroom where Leah had toys for Rachel — a rocking horse and little table, blocks and dolls — prominent in an otherwise adult room. She looked in at Rachel, Brian and Scott, all playing alone, ignoring one another and for a moment stood captured by their self-sufficiency. "Presents," she said gaily. Brian leaped up, his shoes off, and went racing toward the living room, leaving Scott and Rachel still occupied. Miriam picked up Brian's shoes and put them under her arm. "Come on," she urged, "or I'll tickle." But she touched each head protectively.

As she returned to the living room holding each child by the hand, her Aunt Leah smiled at her, looking briefly at the topaz-and-pearl pin she wore, one of her Christmas gifts from Arthur. She squeezed the children's hands before letting go and put down Brian's shoes. Then she cupped her hand beneath the pin as if to support its weight.

"Who'll be the Christmas elf?" asked Harry, laughing. "Scott, this year is your turn. Maybe we need two, Brian. Maybe we need three, Rachel." The family collected near the tree, seated mostly, Johanna and Gershom on the floor near the mantel. Gift-giving was a little drama to be played upon a public stage: the mock surprise as gift-tags were read and the expansive display as each gift was opened were the hallmark of Silverstein family Christmases. Harry leaned over and took the first gift from the pile. He read the tag. " 'To Uncle Sam, Much Love, Miriam.' Here, Scott, give that to Uncle Sam. Over there."

Sam took the package from the child and unwrapped it with all eyes on his heavy hands. A book with a gray and red dust jacket appeared. "*Accusations and Dreams,* Bernard Katzman's new book. Thank you, Miriam," said Sam. He got up to kiss her cheek. "You know, I knew him at school. An old friend, he is."

Celia grimaced, then forced her lips into a tortured smile. "Sam and he were very close once."

"Years ago," Gershom muttered. "She knows. That's why she gave him the book."

Celia looked at him, her eyebrows arched; then, sucking in her cheeks, she looked away. "Very nice, very nice."

At first each gift was opened with singular attention, but after a while, the three elves were each giving out gifts at once, in between opening their own, and the debris of ribbons and paper, the crumpled end of effort, lay heaped on the floor. Anita was exclaiming over a little blue dress, a much simpler version of Rachel's, for Amy. "Oh, Aunt Leah, she doesn't have anything like this. It's gorgeous." Everyone was admiring Johanna's handmade pottery and sketches. The children were playing with Russian nesting dolls from Naomi, who was herself squinting at a book of photographs of the Lower East Side before 1920. "Takes me back to when I came," she said. "I can remember these scenes, those poor people, clear as anything." Clothing, books and toys glutted the room. "The pin I got you is from Tiffany's," said Leah to Miriam, "but I can see it doesn't compare to the one you're wearing."

Gershom, sitting by himself on the piano bench with a pile of books intended to encourage him to think about law as a profession, held in one hand the glazed chalice from Johanna and Seth.

"Don't be fooled by our calling it a chalice," whispered Seth from behind. "It's a Kiddush cup, though I can't get Johanna to admit it in her parents' house on Christmas. But that's what it really is, I think."

"It's a lovely Kiddush cup," said Gershom, "the only ray of human feeling in this exchange."

"You forget your mother's knitted gifts, your Aunt Leah's choices, all expensive, but all chosen with the greatest of care and love. What about Miriam's offering to your father?" Seth laughed and put his hand affectionately on Gershom's shoulder. "I can't escape the fact that year after year I object to this celebration, but when it actually comes I enjoy having my principles sullied by all these goodies."

Gershom barely smiled.

"They love you and one another in their way," said Seth. "Do you really doubt that?"

Gershom did not answer immediately. He opened the cover

of one of his books and ran his hand down the crease of the binding. The book smelled of binding glue, a dry tingling smell that scratched his throat. The end papers had pictures of maps: dark red lines on raspberry. He laid it down, grazing the keyboard with his elbow and shrugged his shoulders at Seth. "The way a boa constrictor loves its prey perhaps."

"You don't mean that."

Gershom shrugged again. "Perhaps," he said thickly. "Perhaps."

Elise, changed, her round Irish face ruddy above a black dress with white apron, came from the dining room and rang a little brass bell held in the mouth of a flat brass dragon. "Dinner is ready."

The table was set and glittering with tall red candles in handsome silver candlesticks, already lit and flickering waves across the white plates with gold and black flowered edges. The silver gleamed at each setting and flashed, reflecting in the crystal. Rolls — crisp, warm, brown — peeked from beneath a napkin cupped in a basket. Golden slabs of butter filled scrolled silver butter dishes at each end. Two tall decanters of cut crystal filled with pale amber and rose wines and one opaque gray clay pitcher, clearly Johanna's work, dominated the middle of the table. Around each candlestick, a circle of small pine boughs and holly berries had been carefully laid out on the white damask tablecloth.

Emma sighed and turned toward Leah. "You do set a beautiful table. Always elegant." The hostile edge to her voice was restrained.

Leah moved to seat them all. "Thank you, Emma. I'm just sorry about the plastic on the floor but Harry and I were afraid with the children . . ."

"Mommy," said Johanna, "don't apologize for goodness sake."

They slipped easily into their chairs and Harry moved about the table serving wine, followed by Elise carrying a tray with soup bowls steaming with cream of mushroom soup. Harry patted each person on the shoulder as he passed, filling glasses, and offered juice from the clay pitcher to the children. He reached the last person and looked down at her.

"Miriam, you look lovely today. Didn't I mention it before?"

"Mimzie always looks lovely," said Emma smoothly.

Harry laughed a hearty studied laugh. "Always does, Emma, but especially today. Could it be love?"

"Harry," said Leah, her voice strained with warning.

Miriam blushed slightly as she looked up at her uncle with a wink. "It's that Christmas spirit, thanks Uncle Harry."

"Miriam has more than a pretty face," said Naomi, dipping her spoon in and out of the soup without taking any. "She's a bright girl with a well-paid, responsible job. Independent."

"To what do I owe all this attention?" said Miriam. "I thought only children got praised in their presence." She raised her glass, spilling a bit of wine on her plate as she did.

"What an idea!" Leah interjected hurriedly. "Is everyone enjoying their soup?"

"Grandma," David was speaking, "you really fit right into the women's movement these days. I bet there aren't too many eighty-year-old women's libbers around."

"More than you think," said Naomi. "After all, we were already grown, mothers, before women got the right just to vote in this country. Maybe in a better system, it wouldn't be so important." She looked off over the candles.

"It's interesting," said Sam, his round face reflecting the candle glow. "I can't think of a single major American novel about women's suffrage. I've been trying to collect a list of books on social movements that might interest my students and I noticed that most women's books are about sexual awakening or dissatisfaction with marriage, but nothing notable about suffrage."

"You can imagine how his students will take this list he's been working over all fall," said Celia, wiping her lips delicately with her napkin. "I wonder that those nig — I won't say it — can read at all. He works so hard trying to get them to pull themselves up by their bootstraps, and you should hear what they say about Jews."

"Celia," said Sam, patting her hand on the table beside him, two furrows forming above his brows, "Celia darling, you shouldn't. They live hard lives, I've told you. It's not easy to teach them as it is. They have very little, sometimes not even the bare necessities. But even when they do, as Lear says, 'Allow not nature more than nature needs, Man's life's as cheap as beast's.' If I can't persuade them I'm offering that something more, something they can give their children, it's not altogether their fault."

"Aunt Celia, I think you don't appreciate their point of view," said David carefully. "They see Jews as successful and rich. The fact that all of us aren't rich doesn't register with people who have to live in rat-infested tenements, lots of them owned by Jews."

"This is a country in which lots of poor people have made their way. What did either Papa or Mamma have when they came here? When I think how Papa made the Liberty Press a good business out of nothing!"

"Celia, sometimes I wonder that you're *my* daughter. Even though Papa loved the place, most of the time he had to work like a dog just to keep it going. And to get started! When I met him and even a little while after we married, he worked at two jobs setting type — one Yiddish, one English — struggling to collect a little something. He didn't even have a day off. If this country was really free, if everyone started out with what they needed without having to kill themselves or take welfare like a dirty gift, it would be better. There wouldn't be such bad feelings."

"Uncle Sam, don't you think things are improving?" Johanna's voice was gentle as she moved her hands around the clay pitcher from which she had been pouring juice, an echo of her movements in making it.

"I always hope," said Sam. "I always hope. Each year there's somebody who shows promise, who reads and wants to write. Immigrants, at least Jews, knew their own language, so to learn English wasn't so difficult, but these poor children speak a language that isn't a language . . ."

"Listen to that saint," groaned Celia.

"All the writers about black English," said David, "say that's a prejudicial point of view, that their English is a dialect — regular."

"Well . . . ," Sam said, looking skeptical, "and there's also the problem of the Spanish speakers who want to make a bilingual society instead of mastering English."

"I had to hire a Spanish typesetter at the place recently. I didn't want to keep having to turn down Spanish jobs," said Frank casually, almost as if speaking to himself.

A crease appeared between Leah's eyes. She spoke slowly and deliberately, as if trying to restrain her words. "How could you do that, Frank? You know how Papa felt about the press, about English. He dreamed once it would publish great English books. He would be appalled at the idea of Spanish pamphlets."

"Business." Frank shrugged, nervously rubbing one finger along either side of his pencil-line mustache, and he looked down into his plate.

"It's not the language that's the big problem," said Harry. "It's not being able to get work even when they've got simple skills. For educated blacks it's actually getting easy, but for the people at the bottom it's still hard. And you can be sure we haven't helped that situation any by just reelecting Nixon. Besides, there's this business of drugs."

"That," said Seymour, breaking through his own silence, "is why I have to close up the store with gates every night. Sometimes I even get nervous when I'm alone there during the day. Dope!"

Celia put her crushed napkin on the side of her plate, watching Elise clear the soup plates, as Leah rolled in the turkey on a teacart. "It's the drugs in that damned ghetto school that make me so afraid for Sam sometimes."

"You know, Aunt Celia," said Miriam, "it's not just black kids who take drugs."

"I remember," said Harry, absent-mindedly standing to carve the turkey, "you worried awfully about some high school friend of Gershom's, Celia — a nice Jewish boy who took marijuana." He peered at the turkey. "Some bird, don't you think?"

Gershom had been seated, his shoulders hunched forward, eating quickly or shifting his silver quietly throughout the conversation. His impassive face suggested nothing, a look calculated to prevent a too easy reading of his feelings. When he heard his name, his head rose and he sucked in his breath like a diver about to plunge again beneath a sea alive with unnamed monsters. He looked around at the children sitting near him.

"Harry," Leah was again in a hurry, "you really bring up ancient history."

"I don't want to talk about that, Harry," said Celia, stiffening, glancing at Gershom down the table from her.

Seymour laughed and said to Frank, "Your sisters all worry. Gershom, don't give it a thought."

"You've been known to worry about things," said Emma shortly.

"Gershom, surely a college freshman occasionally meets someone who takes marijuana these days." David nodded at his younger cousin across the table.

Gershom spoke into his lap. "My mother worries that the world will bruise me like a piece of ripe fruit."

"Gershom, your mother wants the best for you," said Leah sternly.

"Mommy," said Johanna.

"Let's not discuss this now," Emma crowed. "How about a round of 'Jingle Bells' while we're waiting for the turkey. 'Jingle bells, jingle bells . . .'" No one joined her except Scott, with whom she sang one chorus quietly.

Gershom smiled, his eyes two smoldering pieces of coal. Celia gestured, shaking her head very slightly in Leah's direction, her hands agitated butterflies. "No more, Leah."

"So," said Frank with simple curiosity, "do the boys you know smoke pot?"

"Some probably do," said Gershom.

"Have you ever tried any?" Seymour's question.

Gershom did not answer. He swung his chin down and took Rachel's hand. The child sitting between him and Johanna put her head to one side. "Mommy makes pots," she said. Everyone laughed.

"Gershom," said Seymour, "you don't say much, and now you've got a straight man working for you."

Laughter again. Hot steaming food coming to the table.

"Seymour, leave him alone," said Emma.

"He's a big boy," said Seymour irascibly. "Tell us about Columbia anyway, Gersh."

"It's all right."

"Just all right?"

"I don't know it well yet," he said, shifting uneasily in his chair.

"What do you mean, well? You go there, down on the subway each morning. Do you like it?"

"Sometimes."

"Seymour," said Emma, "don't pester him."

"I liked it when I took a General Studies course," said Frank. "I made some good buddies there — guys I still see."

"Look, the turkey is mostly carved," said Leah. "Let's eat."

"Gershom," Seymour lifted his hands and the glow from the candles made the hairs on the top stand out like luminous threads, the weavings of a psychotic neon spider. "Gershom, why are you so quiet? What do you know that you're not telling? Don't you want us to keep in touch with what's going on?"

His hands jerked, meaty chops now. Gershom closed his eyes.

"Nothing," he said deliberately. "I know nothing."

"He can't be expected to speak for his whole generation."

Seth's instinctive, protective gesture was swallowed by Seymour's voice, thick, raised by the swampy mixture of Scotch and wine. "But you know *people.* What do they have to say?" "Please, Seymour," said Emma urgently. "He isn't feeling his best today." Gershom's head came forward with a little thrust, his shoulders coming up on either side. "What do you know about what I'm feeling?" he said to his aunt. Not a question — a denial. She colored and hurried into explanations. "Just your mother said you weren't happy last night, had a bad time. Let's forget it. Have some stuffing." She shoved the plate at Gershom with a fearful laugh.

Sam moved, stirring cautiously, his wife beside him, electric with terror, her fingers taut, telegraphing panic. His son looked darkly out of a tortured angularity, every soft line departing his face.

Gershom stood up. "She's right," he said. "I feel rotten — like I'm smothering."

Sam stood up too.

"Gershom, dear boy, sit down, please."

"I don't think so," he said. "I want my own life," his voice quivered.

"Gershom," said Emma, "I didn't mean anything. Please, I hardly said anything to upset you so. Hardly anything."

Johanna whispered over Rachel's head, "It's nothing. You know they can't help talking."

"Oh, they can," said Gershom. "I can." He moved away from the table as Celia clasped her hand across her mouth to restrain the whimper that escaped around her fingers.

Leah, her quick steps lifting her like a sailboat moving through choppy water, bobbed to his side. "You're not going to let this ruin our Christmas, are you? It's only once a year and we're all together."

"Shall we all take off our clothes," said Gershom sharply, "and show off our wounds? This is, you know, the birthday, some say, of Jesus Christ, the Father of Mercy, not just another feast day, so we've got no business celebrating it any-how. And don't tell me it's just an American holiday because it's not. Maybe because we're Jews and our Father of Mercy hasn't shown us much, we don't know mercy or privacy. Do you know that's the greatest mercy? Privacy. My torments ought to be my own. If I want to lie on my bed and howl like a banshee, I'd like to be able to do it without my cousins and their spouses and lovers and all my aunts and uncles commis-erating. You don't know anything about my life, my lousy life." He looked at the table where heads rose as the family stood to pull him back. He moved away, backing out of the dining room, just beneath a beribboned sprig of mistletoe in the archway.

"Privacy," he muttered. Johanna came toward him, now on the same side of the table as his retreat. "Don't tell me, Jo-hanna." He faced her, one hand out, a traffic policeman's ges-ture. "Don't tell me when I get out of the house it will be any different. You don't think I hear every detail about your baby's diarrhea, and what pot you're making for the woman who lives five blocks uptown from you and is so interested in your work, and how Seth and you have such a lovely mar-riage, and how my cousin Miriam has too many men, or now a married one, or . . . ?"

"Shut up, Gersh," said Miriam, getting out of her seat. "Don't go spilling your vomit on me."

"What a dreadful thing to say," Emma, visibly paled, turned toward her daughter, a diversion.

"And to think how I have trusted you, Johanna," Celia was moaning, "and all the time it was you encouraging him to leave his home. Gershom . . ."

Sam had come over to his son and touched him. Gershom moved back. "You're out of control. This business with your mother this morning. It isn't worth this. You know she loves you and wants you to be happy. Your happiness makes her life."

"What right has she to make my happiness her life? What

if I'm unhappy? Do we sink together? Does the whole family sink because one is drowning? 'Hold on to me, I'll pull you down.' " Mockery. He still backed up. "And everybody knowing everybody else's business." His voice raised to a falsetto, " 'But don't say a word about it.' So no one dares utter anything like truth in the open or, if by some miracle they do, all those alarms go off — names said in a 'significant' tone. And these rotten gifts most of us can't afford, to celebrate what? The birthday of somebody's savior, but not *our* salvation or even the chance of it." He stumbled backward toward the coat closet.

Celia rushed out of her seat, running across the room to where he was pulling his jacket roughly from its hanger, knocking other coats to the floor. She grabbed his shirt, clutching the material in her hands and pulled at him. "Where are you going? You can't go! I won't let you go! Where are you going? Sam, help me, help me! He can't go!" Drops of perspiration rose on her forehead.

There was a flurry. They were all in the living room moving toward him, except the children, eyes glowing, like oncoming traffic. Seth put his arm around Gershom's shoulders and tried to catch his eye, then feeling the shoulders receding, withdrew. Leah took his hand but he pulled away.

"Please, Gershom, your mother is very upset. Whatever happened before, don't humiliate her now. 'Let us be true to one another . . . ,' " Sam said quietly, intending this for his son alone.

"Cut the goddamn quoting. Can't you ever just talk without quoting some poet? Anyway it's lovers who are supposed to be true."

A flash of pain passed over Sam's face, but his eyes fixed on Gershom, anxious and ready as he began to move toward the door.

Celia fell to her knees screaming, "You'll have to step on me to go. I won't let you." She crouched down in front of his feet, embracing his ankles.

"Get out of my way, Ma." Gershom's voice was unrecognizable. "You're the one stepping all over me. You're strangling me with all your adoring words."

Sam's voice roared, "Don't talk to your mother like that." He raised his fist in Gershom's face and shook it just below his nose. "What kind of maniac are you to talk to your mother like that?"

Celia, still on the floor, whimpered and Johanna stooped by her, whispering, "Please, Aunt Celia, let go of him. It's not fair."

Gershom suddenly pushed forward, nearly tripping and falling on Celia. There was a great jostling of arms, Harry and Seymour pulling, holding Gershom by the elbows when, suddenly, Sam said, "Let him go."

He did not even turn but raced toward the doorway, Celia crawling after him on her knees. She collapsed, heaving sobs at Sam's feet as Gershom slammed the door.

"No, no," Sam began to stroke her hair, her tight curls under his heavy hands. "He'll be home later. Don't worry, don't worry. Come, my girl, come. The children are frightened."

"Oh, the children," she sobbed, and struggled to her feet.

He rocked her against his shoulder, murmuring soft indistinguishable words, then, "Almost 'Poor Parnell. My dead king!' eh, love? Come, I know he's grown but I won't let him talk to you like that again. Come."

2

*A*FTER DINNER, which despite all had continued through a plum pudding with hard sauce, Sam and Celia were driven home. Brian and Scott snuggled comfortingly between them in the back seat of David's and Anita's car. The locked downstairs door in the vestibule of their apartment building had many panes of glass veiled by a gauzy white curtain through which figures could sometimes be seen, moving like ghosts on the lobby side. Tonight there were none. Celia, her hands agitatedly smoothing her coat, pressed her face against the glass while Sam fumbled with the key, then entered the musty smelling lobby, empty except for a Christmas tree surrounded by piles of polyester snow and trimmed with strings of flashing colored lights. She gave a frightened gasp and clutched Sam's arm.

"He's probably upstairs," said Sam. "I'll give him hell for frightening you so." He rang the elevator bell. "Did you really think he'd be waiting in the lobby?"

At their apartment door, Sam paused, then opened it slowly. In the foyer, the overhead light was on. He pushed the two shopping bags filled with unwrapped gifts inside the door and went in calling, "Gershom! Gershom! We know you're here." Celia crept behind him, calling in a tiny voice, "Gershom, darling? Gershom?"

In the living room, stillness stretched before them, the air stirring like heavy curtains disturbed by their movement. An accumulated odor of Lysol and furniture polish rose from the corners. Nothing moved. Even the plants, waiting before the windows in speckled pots, seemed webbed with secrets. The sound of their footsteps filled the room. Celia was now taking off and putting on one glove, over and over, pressing the glove down between the fingers with the index finger of her other hand. Her lips pressed together in her evident struggle not to scream.

"Well, he's obviously been here," said Sam, throwing off his coat. "The light's on. We didn't leave it on when we left this afternoon." He stepped into the little hall to inspect the two bedrooms and bathroom and returned to Celia, putting his hand on her shoulder. "Take off your coat, Celia. He's a big boy."

They were standing near Celia's harp, its golden pillar stretching upward into the neck like a column before an ancient tomb. In the semidark, the gold of the harp and the russet of Celia's coat blended, both nubby, curlicued; even the tight curls of her hair a part of the texture. She leaned back lightly against the harp and it rocked gently. Sam unbuttoned the top button of her coat and pulled out her scarf. He leaned forward and kissed the corner of her mouth, then unbuttoned the next button, and the next. Then he led her back to the kitchen silently, where he switched on the light, pulled off her coat and seated her in a chair with tender pressure. At the stove he turned on a flame, then filled the kettle with water and placed it on the burner. Returning to the table, he reached for her hand still swathed in black doeskin.

"Celia, Celia. We'll have some tea. Please, he's fine."

"I shouldn't have said anything to Leah and Emma. I couldn't help it," she was whispering.

"Who knows what set him off," said Sam. "He was very disturbed today. But we really have to forget it. These things happen, but they are best left to die naturally. You know he's had an adjustment to make to college this year, and he's sensitive. It's hard." He rocked slightly.

"I blame Johanna for some of this," said Celia. "When I realized she and Seth have actually approved of his idea of moving out, possibly even suggested it, I saw things clearly." She whimpered slightly but the whistle on the kettle absorbed the sound.

"No," Sam was at the stove. "No, you didn't." He moved the kettle to a cool burner and flicked off the gas, prepared tea bags, their tails hanging over the tall white cups, and poured water steaming away toward the ceiling.

"I'm sick," she said flatly. "I should be serving you."

He quivered, his shoulders winging out, then relaxed as he realized Celia was not talking about her health. He removed the tea bags and brought the cups to the table where she still sat motionless, her gloved hands stretched out on her thighs toward something unseen. "Take off your gloves, darling." He reached for her fingers and pulled the soft fabric gradually from her hands.

"Maybe we should call the police," she said in a little voice, piping, like a child.

"What would we say to the police? That he isn't home? That maybe he went to the movies?"

"I would never do such a thing to my parents," she said as if she had not heard him. "No note. Did you look for a note, Sam?" She sat up, lively.

He shook his head. "I don't think there's a note. He would have left it here. He'll be back in a little while anyway. We must ignore this. He got upset but he's a good boy."

"I once came home late from a concert at the Brooklyn Museum. The trolley made a terrible clanging all the way home, saying, 'Your papa's mad, your papa's mad.' He was a great worrier, Papa. He nearly whaled me. 'You'll come back on time,' he said. I still remember how I was shaking in front of him, and crying. Oh, God!" She closed her eyes and put her hands around the warm cup, her fingers drumming. "Sam, you ask next door if they saw him." She looked up with frightened eyes. "Go, go."

He stood up and heard, as he often did, his life intoned as if in the pages of a novel: "For Sam, it was a moment of crisis, not wishing to expose his son and wife to the curious eyes of neighbors. A heavy man with a white crew cut, he made his way to the kitchen door." It was involuntary, this narrative habit from his youth.

"You're sure you want me to?" he asked gently. "I know he'll be back soon."

She said nothing, looking into the steam, her eyes glazed. He sighed, putting his hand on her head as he went out.

In the hallway, where the walls were painted a mustard brown, Sam moved to the orange door at a right angle to his own, and rang the bell. Inside it chimed, and he waited, hearing shortly the expected shuffle. The trap on the peephole clicked and the door was opened by a short woman with dyed red hair. She wore scuffed fuzzy pink slippers on her feet.

"*Mis*ter Lazarus, *how are* you?" Her voice ranged upward, a friendly hoot, almost a song. "Come in, come in."

He stepped inside the dim foyer lighted with a forty-watt yellow bulb. An elephant's foot, hollowed as an umbrella stand, stood dustily by the door.

"I can only stay a minute, Mrs. Appel. I'm coming only to ask if you saw Gershom this evening."

She peered at him, twisting her brow in a puzzled grimace. "He isn't home?"

"No. We thought maybe he went out to a movie or something."

"I didn't see him. Such a lovely boy. Always so polite. If I saw him, I would tell you."

"Thank you," said Sam, and turned to go.

"You're worried about him? You ask because you're worried?"

"My wife is a little concerned." Sam bobbed his head, hoping to finish the conversation.

"There's plenty to worry these days," said Mrs. Appel, blocking the door. "My nephew was just going out of his own building with his wife when some Hispanic type comes up from behind, hiding in the lobby, and puts a knife to my nephew's throat, and another grabs his wife and knocks her down. All this for twenty dollars, and my nephew's watch. Didn't even take his wife's engagement ring which was *worth*," her voice ascended, suggesting immeasurable value. "I don't know where it's gonna end." She paused, contemplating her fingernails, then looked at Sam, her eyes blinking bafflement. "Whatta you think happened to Gershom?"

"Nothing, nothing," said Sam. "He just went out and we were a little surprised. That's all. He was upset about something and we were just wondering if someone saw him, knew when he left."

"Oh, Mr. Lazarus, I'd be the first to tell you if I knew. I'll listen for him. He should get home safely." She nodded sternly, then patted the doorknob with a large flat palm.

"Did you know Mr. Violas, Three-D, is very sick? They took him to the hospital yesterday and he's in intensive care. Didn't even know his wife today. Such a nice man. And you know," her voice got lower, a confidential tone slipping around the words, "they're Catholic. For them to have sickness on Christmas, it's very bad."

Sam shifted and moved sideways toward the door where she still stood, hand on knob. "I'm sorry to hear that. Please, I didn't mean to bother you. I just thought maybe you heard Gershom. I need to go back. My wife doesn't like being alone too long."

"Give Celia my good wishes," said Mrs. Appel, moving away from the door. "I hope he comes home soon and in one piece."

Sam moved backward out of the door, nodding. "Good-night. Thanks." The hall was glaring after the shadow of Mrs. Appel's foyer. He stumbled back into the brightness of his own apartment and went toward the kitchen. "Celia? Celia?"

She was not at the table any longer and he hurried back through the living room toward the bedrooms. She was stand-ing in the doorway of Gershom's room, one hand on her head, the other clutching her throat. Her cheeks sagged. "He's gone, gone!"

"What are you talking about?" Sam came toward her. "It's only ten. He's hardly out unreasonably late."

"No, I mean he's gone. I looked in his drawers. His gray sweater and his favorite striped shirt and a few pairs of un-derwear. I know. I just washed yesterday. The little duffel bag he uses for school books is gone. I know his room, to keep it right for him. I know his books, his clothes. Everything is dif-ferent, even the things that aren't moved." She closed her eyes and thrust back her head. "Sam, Sam, you call the police. I tell you he's gone. God knows where he's gone."

"I won't call the police," said Sam. "I won't have him col-lared like a criminal when he may be thinking better of the whole thing and be home in an hour or two. Did he take any money?"

"I don't know." She was swaying dangerously, the skin of her knuckles white over gray bumps of bone. "I don't know. He kept a little money in his desk drawer, under the stapler. A few dollars."

Sam went in to Gershom's room, where his bed with a smooth mahogany headboard was spread with a boyish plaid cloth. The desk rested, oddly neat, a blotter carefully covering the center. Sam hesitated, a pause before he brought his hand down and opened the drawer. Inside, a clutter of writing im-plements rattled as he pulled it open. He shuffled the con-tents desperately, but there was no money anywhere: under, or beside, or in. He slammed the drawer and crossed the room toward the bathroom and medicine chest in which there was a Band-Aid box filled with folded bills. The box was still there, heavy with money. Sam counted it and sighed. "He took ten dollars from the kitty too. How far can he go on eighteen, nineteen dollars?"

Celia did not answer. She was leaning against the wall between the bedroom doors, her eyes closed, her hands clasped between her small breasts, like a ripped poster buffeted by wind to total stillness. Sam could feel her tension radiating toward him, pulsating: an aura of pain. He touched her shoulder and she shrank away. When he tried again, she turned her face to the wall.

"Celia, darling, please, he won't stay away. He was angry and unhappy. I can't believe such a little thing would make him run away. He'll calm down and come back. After all, he has his school work and the end of the semester coming. He's not going to abandon everything. Come. 'Screw your courage to the sticking place.' He'll be back." He rubbed the back of her thin shoulders with the tips of his fingers, and although she did not evade his touch this time, her back curved in a position of desolation, a special aloneness he could not hope to reach. For a few minutes they stood in the hall in a stifling silence broken only by the rattle of the refrigerator coming from the kitchen, and the ticking of a clock. Finally, Celia turned and walked past Sam toward the kitchen without looking at him. He followed and watched her take a glass and fill it with water from the faucet. After drinking, she put down the glass and said in a flat, strained voice, "You must call the police, Sam. Perhaps they can find him."

"I won't, at least not yet. He may come back any minute. You know that." He felt he was cajoling a child and strangely as if he were pacing down some avenue with Gershom, not talking but walking together. Like a double vision, the image set upon the scene, his mind oscillating between the real and the imagined. "Let's just take things easy for the next few hours. We'll read. If you'd like I'll read aloud to you." He looked at her hopefully. She did not move.

"How about some short stories? De Maupassant maybe?" His voice lilted over the words, "Or perhaps some poetry. 'Leaves of Grass,' or Edna St. Vincent Millay?" She still said nothing. "Where are you, darling?" He came toward her. She was pale, her cheekbones covered by a waxen skin, and her blue eyes like chips of ice. "I couldn't sit still. No reading," she muttered and began to walk from kitchen to living room to hall, turn, to living room to kitchen, turn, to living room to hall, turn, pacing, pacing a steady ringing kind of walk. Sam turned on the lights in the living room and sat down in a bentwood rocker beside a round table with a tall gold lamp. He sat watching Celia, his heart beating with a persistent noticeable thump, then got up, breathing deeply, and went to the shopping bags filled with Christmas. From one he took Bernard Katzman's book and returned to the chair. He opened the cover, which crackled stiffly, and turned to the preface. It was difficult to connect the printed words with meaning. Celia continued to pace, her hands twisting tissues, or rubbing one another, two lost companions in some natural waste, her feet shuffling. Sam was acutely conscious of the sound.

I must stay calm, he thought and forced himself to read.

At midnight, he looked up. She was standing beside him, her lips laxly open, unattractively, he thought, then banished that judgment with a flush of shame.

"If you don't call the police, I will," she said, her voice dry and hollow.

"First, can you think of a friend he might have gone to?"

"No. No one whose mother wouldn't have called."

Sam shifted slightly. "What about Johanna? Do you suppose he went there?"

"You can try. If he's there, and they didn't call, I'm finished with her." The words shot out with a fine spray of spittle.

The phone rang several times before Seth answered. Sam

liked Seth but something held him back from discussing this matter with him. "Is Johanna there?" he said oddly. "It's Uncle Sam. I know it's late, but I'd like to talk with her."

"Of course," said Seth and left the phone. No, thought Sam. No, he's not there.

Johanna's voice, sleepy, came across the wire. "Uncle Sam? What's wrong?"

"It's nothing really," he said, Celia coming beside him and breathing in short heavy breaths. "It's just that Gershom isn't home. I mean he was home, but before we got here. He took a few of his things and a little money, and he hasn't come back. I thought maybe he was there."

"Oh, no!" she said, gasping the answer in exclamation and response. "No."

"All right," said Sam," I didn't really think so. Aunt Celia's very worried and I just thought I'd try."

"I'm sure he's fine," Johanna's voice came steady, now awake, on the line. "I'm sure he'll be back. He probably just wanted to get away to think about things."

"Yes," said Sam. "Yes."

"Keep me posted," said Johanna. "I'll let you know if I hear from him."

"Yes," said Sam and he hung up.

"Police," demanded Celia.

Sam tried to put his arm around her but she sprang back. "He's not a criminal, Celia."

"Police," she shouted again. "Now! I can't stand this anymore." She pounded his chest with her fists and then fell against him crying, burying her face in the curve of his neck. He rubbed her back, and stroked her arm with the other hand. "Police, you must, you must. I'll do it. No, you must." He patted her gently.

"Celia," his voice soft, pleading. "Celia."

"I'll die. I'll throw myself out the window. I swear it." She was now rocking against him frantically.

"I think it's a mistake," he said, but lifted the phone from the hook.

Ten minutes later, two young, tired-looking policemen appeared at their door and, with their uniforms, brought organization into the living room. Celia was weeping quietly and dabbing her eyes with a tissue.

"O.K.," said the first, a sandy-haired tall man of about twenty-three. "What's the complaint?"

"Our son is" — Sam paused uneasily before saying the word — "missing."

The policeman who had spoken opened his heavy-covered notebook with a snap, and took a pencil from a case on his belt.

"How long is he gone?"

"Six, seven hours." Embarrassment for Gershom flooded Sam.

"You mean he was expected here six or seven hours ago?" The officer was writing as he talked. "Did you tell them this was the complaint? They don't generally send us for missing persons till seventy-two hours."

"I didn't say how long," said Sam. "Just that he and some things were gone. We were somewhere else, cross-town, and there was a little family difference. He ran out and apparently came back here, took the things and left."

"What sort of things?"

"Some clothes, money."

"You want to charge him with theft?"

"Of course not," whispered Celia. "It's all for him."

The officer looked up; his partner shifted slightly and began to walk quietly about, inspecting the room.

"Well, what's the charge?"

"There's no charge. He's missing! We want to find him. We want him to come home."

"O.K., as long as we're here. How old is he?" The policeman's voice sounded scratchy, like he had been singing too hard.

"Just eighteen. Eighteen and two weeks," said Sam. "He's a freshman at Columbia."

"Name."

"Max Gershom Lazarus, but he's called Gershom."

"Gershom — G-E-R-S-H-O-M? Right?"

"Yes."

"Description? Any distinguishing marks?"

"Tall," said Celia stuffily. She had stopped crying.

"No, darling," Sam interrupted. "Tall to you, but he's not really tall. He's about five-ten, has dark brown hair, brown eyes, acne on his cheeks. It's rather noticeable. He was wearing a blue duffel coat and gray slacks with a white shirt, maroon tie and gray plaid sports jacket."

"Glasses?"

"Only for reading."

"Got a recent photo?"

Sam took out his wallet and hesitantly removed Gershom's high school graduation picture. "Must you take it?" he asked as the policeman snapped it shut in his book. His tongue felt very dry. What kind of file was he starting for Gershom?

"Look," said the policeman, yawning, "he's a runaway, clearly. I can't tell you how many there are. We really don't catch too many of them unless they get involved in criminal acts. They just run away, and sometimes they come back themselves after a few days. Now when they're minors, the law has some jurisdiction over them. But he's not a minor. He's eighteen. He'll probably come home by himself but we'll keep our eyes open." He yawned again and his partner came forward, zipping up his heavy jacket.

"Is that all?" said Celia, getting up and shredding the tissue she had been holding as she came over. "Is that all you can do?"

"Mizzuz Lazarus, if you want to charge him with theft, maybe we could do something, though unless he tried to fence the stolen goods we would probably have trouble finding him.

But, as it is, we can just report him as a missing person and
make our standard morgue and prison checks." Celia visibly
shuddered. "Since he's not a minor, we can't make him come
home even if he does turn up. Morgan," he turned to his
partner, "do you have any leads?"

Morgan merely shook his head.

"You gave your phone number to the attending officer when
you called? O.K. We'll be in touch if we hear anything." The
policemen started to walk toward the door. The note-taker
turned. "And if he comes home, please be sure to let us know
so we can take him off the books." They walked out and
slammed the door.

Celia hit her head with her fist. "The morgue, Sam! Bastard! He didn't even look at the picture." She began to sob
long heaving sobs.

"Please, Celia, darling." Sam, his own hands shaking, caught
her fingers and kissed the palm. "Please, please, we have to
be strong and rational and consider all the possibilities. He's
really a good boy."

She did not answer but sobbed again, this time shrieking at
the end in a high-pitched tight scream.

*　*　*

They lay beside one another through a long night. Pipes in
the old building thumped, the floor above creaked. Sam became aware of an occasional humming, which he realized, after
the second time, was the elevator in use. Why had he never
noticed it before? Sometimes Celia rocked slightly and whimpered but when he would creep his hand toward her to touch
the dry skin, she did not respond in any way. Once at about
three o'clock, the refrigerator rattled on again in its old auto-
matic rhythm, and Sam thought for one moment he heard
the door. His head came abruptly off the pillow as he listened
desperately, then fell back like a stone. After five, Celia fell
asleep and he crept from the bed to the kitchen, where the

darkness of a long winter night still blackened the window. He turned the flame on under the kettle and stood beside the stove until the whistle was about to blow, then turned off the gas. He poured himself a cup of tea and walked back to the table, rolling the cup between his big hands. The warmth of the cup was comforting.

Seated, he tried to make some order of his thoughts, to lead his mind like a pilgrim among tales and poems accumulated for years against a danger, and he recalled, almost without being able to term it memory, the sensation of safety he had felt standing between the stacks in the neighborhood public library he went to as a boy. He would lean back against the shelves behind him with an open book in his hands and race into a world of adventure and discovery, seduced farther and farther from his Yiddish-speaking home by his romance with literature: the English language, his street language, transformed and magic. What was there in this memory to comfort him, to call his son back? He considered where his son might be running, what escape route he was choosing, and from what. A door slammed somewhere and, startled, he half stood, inadvertently saying, "Gershom?" then sat back again and muttered, "Fool."

His skin prickled as he noticed the slightly sticky quality the newly waxed floor had against the roughness of his slipper bottoms. His hand fell on his knee and he was aware of the slight bumpiness of his flannel pajamas beneath his fingers. The uncommon acuity of sensation conjured up a writing assignment for his junior English students: "Describe the way a paper bag, a piece of leather or a key feels in your hand. Pay attention to texture, temperature, shape . . ." No. They wouldn't like it, or even do it. Some might hand in obscene descriptions: "Her tits under my hand were like hot pieces of shit . . ." He banished the idea.

Often he asked himself why his students in recent years seemed unable or unwilling to escape their dismal lives, to run as he had run into a world where thought and fantasy could exclude unpleasantness. He had felt many of them actively push away what he offered as an alternative to street life and almost certain trouble. He blamed their resistance partly on television, partly on a lack of good adult models, but mostly on the absence of love in their lives. That *they* should want to run away would make sense to him but they never seemed to, in fact seemed chained to their front stoops, able to move the distance of the tether but not to break it. He had compared them often, unfavorably, to Gershom, who read a great deal, much as he himself had done, who was nurtured with as passionate a love as any child he had ever known and who was a successful though not brilliant student.

There had been moments though, secret moments he would not have shared with anyone, during which he had wished Gershom had some of his students' misdirected energy: the energy that erupted often in violence and rage, but sometimes more sensibly in athletic feats or musical performances. Not that he wished Gershom to be a jock or a rock musician, but he had noted that Gershom's travels into books, his success in high school, a fine high school that admitted students on the basis of preadmission tests, and, certainly, his new opportunity at college seemed to lack vitality, even the suggestion of a hidden life.

He had tried to open the subject with his son but always ended sounding pedagogical; and then, he noted, his own life was a model only in the deepest recesses of his mind, in the stirring passion he still felt for literature, and the tender love he felt for his wife. That last would hardly have been called passionate by contemporary critics, who abjured sentimentality in word or deed, and yet Sam knew it was a passion although not an ordinary one. He thought of Gershom married someday and wished him a bond as strong, though perhaps less dependent on dependence, and at that point he would always stop himself. His wife was more fragile than any person he had ever known.

His father-in-law, who had died several weeks before they

were married, had deeply approved of their match. The knowledge of his approval had allowed Celia to go ahead with the wedding, but throughout the first year of their marriage she had suffered a blinding grief that softened only very gradually, long after her mother, sisters and brother had recovered from their loss. When Gershom was born nearly seven years later, a gift — for by that time Celia, who conceived only with great difficulty and was now in her late thirties, had miscarried three infants — she could never bring herself to call him by her father's name, Max, which was the first name they gave him in memory of his grandfather. She cried bitterly through the first two weeks of Gershom's life each time he was referred to by name and, finally, Sam had proposed they call him by his middle name, for Sam's father about whom Sam's own emotions were unclear, perhaps nonexistent, and whom Celia had never known.

He reflected on the past as the black window facing the air shaft grayed and the grind of garbage trucks and clatter of cans announced morning, the day after Gershom's departure.

When Celia woke, she looked gray, a sleeping beauty grown old during her slumber. She moved about the apartment in her pacing step of the night before and after an hour, still disheveled and undressed, dialed Leah.

"You didn't call this morning," she said angrily into the phone.

"I was just about to. Everything's all right now, isn't it?"

"Didn't Johanna tell you?"

"Tell me what? Johanna doesn't tell me everything, you know." Leah's voice was tinged with resentment.

"Gershom's gone."

"What do you mean, *gone?* He hasn't been home?" Cautious concern permeated the tone.

"He came home, took his things, and left." She began to sob into the phone, her words muffled. "He hasn't come back. God knows where he is!"

"I can hardly understand you, dear. Didn't he say where he was going?"

"Nooooh," she was moaning. "We never saw him."

"Celia, oh my poor girl, I can't hear what you're saying when you cry like that into the phone. Please. I'll come right over if you want."

"Yes, he — policeman — said, oh terrible — check morgue — wanted us to make a charge." She threw the phone down and the receiver simply hung in the air as she sobbed into her arms, Leah's voice saying, "Celia? Celia? Celia?" loudly. Sam picked up the receiver.

"Leah, she's very upset. I can't help her much."

"I'm coming," said Leah. "I take it Johanna knows."

"We thought maybe he went there."

"She likes to protect people by not saying much. Strange protection, she didn't call me." Anger shifted to comfort. "I'm coming right away." Click.

Minutes later the phone rang. It was Emma.

"I hear there's a problem," she said.

"Yes," said Sam. "The boy's gone." He turned to Celia. "Emma."

"I won't speak to that bitch. It was her and her husband pressing him who drove him away," Celia screamed.

"I heard that," said Emma. "Sam, you can't imagine how terrible I feel, and sorry that Seymour or I said anything to encourage this, but, truly, I don't think you can hold us responsible. The boy obviously has difficulties that have nothing to do with us. I'm being straightforward with you because I know my sister and I know how she can be. I don't want to subject my husband or myself to her hysteria even though we would like to help in some way. Have you called the police?"

"Yes. They can't be of much help. He's not a minor anymore and we didn't want to charge him with anything. I'm afraid they'll only be of use if something awful happens to him, God forbid." He steadied his voice. "I expect him back today, really. Once he's gotten over being angry."

"Do you suppose he could have called Johanna?"

"We already tried."

"Mimzie? David and Anita? I'll try them."

"Thanks."

"Does he have friends he might go to?"

"Not many." Sam felt his tongue stiffen with the answer. "He's really a very solitary boy. I'll try one I can think of who *maybe* . . ."

"I'll talk to you in a little while," said Emma. Then, "Tell Celia to calm down. It's not possible to act sensibly in such a state."

As he put the phone on the hook, it rang again. Naomi.

"Sam, I'm coming right away. I called Frank at the place and he's coming back to get me. Let me talk to her."

"It's your mother," said Sam.

"Mamma, I'm dying," Celia was beating her temple with her fist. "I need you."

*　　*　　*

By afternoon, Celia was no longer crying. Her frantic throaty moans were now dissolved in deep sighs. Sam was able to pat her hand occasionally though it felt limp and cold. Indeed, the apartment seemed cold but when he checked the radiators he found they were working. Leah had prepared lunch while Sam called Gershom's high school friend, the infamous Jesse Bruen, and with great embarrassment asked his futile questions. Naomi had sat stolidly, just where Frank left her, in the middle of the green couch with wooden arm rests, urging Celia to consider all the children who had left home for a time and survived, while Celia, dressed but disheveled, occasionally plucked a string of the harp to sound a mournful drone. Each time the phone would ring she would sit forward, eyebrows raised, but sink when the caller was identified.

"Your father was sixteen when he came to this country,"

Naomi was saying. "And he came to a new country, didn't speak the language, without any family except Moshe, a good man, may he rest in peace, a cousin he hardly knew. And look, alone he survived. Fifty-eight when he died. It wasn't so old, but it wasn't so young either. He's old enough to take care of himself, I'm trying to say."

Again the drone.

"Celia!"

Leah came in from the doorway where she had been standing with Sam.

"I think he's being inconsiderate," she said, standing behind Celia. "He could let her know where he is. Papa didn't just walk out of his house one day and not say where he was going. He's being selfish, Celia, no question." She put her hand on Celia's shoulder but Celia did not acknowledge her gesture, so she removed it. "I'll be glad to comb your hair for you, dear. Your curls are going to be matted if you don't comb them out."

Drone.

Leah sighed and sat down beside her mother on the couch. Silence closed over them like a blanket, even the plants seeming to droop beneath its weight. The phone rang and all three women started, an anticipatory ascent as Sam hurried to answer.

He picked up the receiver eagerly, then held it for an anxious few seconds before saying, "Hello?"

"Uncle Sam?"

"Johanna, hello."

"Have you heard anything?"

"Not a word. You?"

"No. I've stayed close to the phone all morning. Then I called Mommy, and Elise told me she was with you. How's Aunt Celia?"

"Not too well. I think the police upset her. She insisted I call them last night, after I talked to you."

"Uncle Sam, Seth and I have talked about this, and we feel

he may stay away for a while. Sometimes we would talk with him about the family, about his feelings. Forgive me. He said he felt confined . . . that wasn't the word he used . . . locked in, I think he said. Only once. He's not very good at putting his feelings into words but he and I always understood each other. Always understood how difficult it is to be the center of your parents' vision. I think he wants to get out of focus for a bit." She stopped, her voice still rising as if in mid-sentence.

Sam waited but she didn't continue. Yes, he thought and the acceptance lay like a stone in his belly. "How long do you think 'a bit' will be? A day? A week? The rest of the Christmas holiday? He doesn't have much money."

"Well, he could always get a job but I think he'll be back before school starts again, perhaps. You know he might send a message to you in the *New York Times* public notices. He loves to read them."

"Oh?" said Sam, startled. Should he have known?

"You could send a message to him that way if you wanted."

Sam held his breath. Then he exhaled heavily. "I'll keep it in mind, Johanna. Really. I appreciate you and your friend-ship for him. I sometimes pass him for days without talking about anything more than who should take out the garbage." His voice broke, and he thought hurriedly, No! No! Don't do this, and recovered himself. "Johanna, do you want to talk to anyone? Grandma's here too."

She hesitated. "Can I talk to Aunt Celia first, then Mommy?"

"Sure," he said. "Celia, Johanna wants to talk to you. Will you talk to her?"

Drone. "No," Celia said. Drone.

"She doesn't want to talk, Johanna."

"She's really upset!"

"Yes. Leah?"

"Oh, so she wants to talk to me. That's good of her." Leah sat petulantly on the couch for a few seconds, looking into the kitchen where Sam was standing holding out the receiver. She got up and came to take the phone.

"Well, so you're finally going to talk to your mother. That's nice."

"Oh, come on," said Johanna. "Things are too serious for this."

Sam had gone out to the living room and taken Leah's place on the couch. Leah took the receiver and walked as far into the dining alcove of the kitchen as the wire would permit her to go, and began to speak in a barely audible huskiness just above the level of a whisper. "I don't like to be exposed like this before my mother and sister. Why didn't you call me?"

"Uncle Sam called after twelve last night, and I thought I'd just wait and see if Gershom turned up this morning."

"It was very embarrassing for me when Celia called and expected that I knew."

"I'm sorry. I'm sorry I'm always saying I'm sorry, but I didn't feel it was necessary to start putting up warning flags. Once the word got out, it really got out. I've had calls this morning from everyone in the family but Grandma. How's Aunt Celia? Uncle Sam says she's very upset."

"Terrible. She's just terrible. What would you expect? I offered to comb her hair but she wouldn't let me. She's not talking much. I don't know how she's going to be if that selfish young man doesn't start thinking of someone other than himself for a change, and call his mother."

"He doesn't usually think of himself at all. In fact he's very restrained about himself. That's the trouble."

Leah's whisper rose a little. "*You* would say that, Johanna. We'll see how you'll like it when your precious little daughter shows as little concern for you as he is showing for his mother now, as you show for me."

Johanna sighed. "Listen. David asked Anita to stay close to home in case he should come to New Jersey, and Miriam thinks maybe he'll come to her place. She was angry at him, but now she's quite calm."

"He only said what was true about her," interposed Leah. When Johanna did not respond, she continued. "What are you going to do?"

"Wait here. Are you going home to have dinner with Daddy?"

"Yes. Before his Democratic Club meeting."

"I'll call you tonight. Will you tell Uncle Sam that I'll do anything he feels would be useful?"

"Yes, that's good. I'll tell him. Goodbye, dear. Give Seth and Rachel a kiss for me." Her anger spent, she hung up the phone and delivered the message.

"Celia." Sam's voice was soft. "Everyone is so good. What can I get for you, darling? Coffee?"

"No."

"Maybe you would like to go for a walk. Leah and Mother would be here to answer the phone."

"No."

She plunked the one B string again, then drew the music stand toward her, turned to the harp, and began to play from memory Dvořák's *Humoresque,* the music lilting, quick notes, and continued with the singing harp parts from Mozart's concerto for flute, harp and orchestra, and Inghelbrecht's sonatina for the same two instruments. She had played all these pieces publicly at one time long ago, and now a remnant of her stage presence emerged. She took out her music and moved on to Liszt's *Liebestraüme* and then through a variety of popular songs including "Ebbtide," which she played twice, her eyes set, luminous, yet hazed. As she finished with them, she piled music books and sheets beside the music stand and she played on: Renié, Mendelssohn, Schumann, "Londonderry Air."

At first, Naomi and Leah listened, while Sam, now in the rocker, moved back and forth in a rhythm unrelated to his wife's fingered melodies and glissandi across the strings, but when the concert, an enforced musicale, had continued for a long while, they began to talk quietly to one another, a steady murmur beneath the fluid sounds of the harp.

The doorbell rang with no urgency. Celia barely blinked her eyes. If Gershom was to come home, he would come in, enter and be there. No ring! She hit the strings harder. The notes vibrated in waves across the room.

Outside, Mrs. Appel whispered to Sam, "Have you heard, Mr. Lazarus?"

He shook his head.

"Terrible, terrible," she said, pushing her slippered foot back and forth over the threshold. "I don't wanna concern you, but you read such awful things, mass murders, boys mugged by homosexuals." She looked up at Sam, who was only a few inches taller, as if he were a giant. "Could I see poor Celia?"

"She's playing the harp now," he said hesitantly, but Mrs. Appel was already pushing by, and stood in the archway of the living room listening and nodding her head. As Celia came to the end of "Canadian Sunset," she said quickly, "Celia, you O.K.?"

"Yes," said Celia stuffily and continued to play.

Mrs. Appel stood for a few minutes nodding and sighing deeply until Leah got up and said softly to her, "I don't think it helps to stand here. Come. She's playing her whole repertoire." She linked her arm in Mrs. Appel's and firmly led her to the door. "Thank you for coming," she smiled graciously.

"Terrible," said Mrs. Appel. "I only hope he comes back alive." She faded back into her apartment.

"I hope she's not going to trouble you," said Leah to Sam as she closed the door.

"She can't help herself," said Sam. "Seneca says, 'Calamity is virtue's opportunity.' She means well." He sighed and rubbed his hands together. The downstairs bell announced Frank. He came up, the knot of his gray and green striped tie pulled down, and nodded to his mother and sisters. Then he pulled Sam by the sleeve and motioned him back toward the bedrooms. The harp went on, Leah saying loudly to Celia as they went off, "You're really taxing yourself. This is too much, Celia. Your fingers will be ruined."

"What's happening? Anything?"

"No," said Sam. "Frank, we've known each other such a long time — such a long time." He sighed. "Your sister is a wreck. She's playing, playing and inside she's hysterical, really hysterical. It frightens me."

"What can you do?"

"Nothing. Wait. It's horrible. Even though I'm sure . . . I believe Gershom's all right, I'd like to scream. Not that it would do any good and I have to calm her if I only knew how. Nothing I do seems to help. Her mind is fixed on him and she suffers so! You know that. I remember the first time you ever mentioned her on our way to Europe during the war. You told me about her going to Paris for that harp competition — how the whole family had gone to meet her when she came back and found her weeping because she had disappointed all of *you* by not winning anything. It really moved me, that story. Right then, I wanted to meet her. Do you remember?"

"It must have been our being on that transport ship made me tell you. Because she'd gone and come on a boat." Frank looked bemused.

"It's really true that the things and people she loves the most cause her the greatest pain. 'Ay, in the very temple of delight, Veil'd Melancholy has her sovran shrine . . .'" He shook his head and pressed the heels of his palms into his temples. "Frank, what do you think?"

Frank stood motionless. He turned his head shyly, cocked to the right, and took Sam's hand between both of his as he said, "Sorry. You know I don't understand women. I guess she'll be better. He may come back tonight. I think he really may. Where is he going to go? Look, I'll take Leah and Mamma home and you can order some food in from a Chinese restaurant and watch a little television, or what. Then by ten, maybe he'll be here."

"And maybe not," said Sam. He turned sharply and glared toward the living room. "I wish she would stop playing."

Bundled in coats, Leah and Naomi stood over Celia. "Please," said Leah plaintively. "Please stop playing and say goodbye to us."

"Goodbye," said Celia but she did not stop.

"Gershom is a good boy," said Naomi. "He's just trying out his wings. You be calm. It's hard for you, I know. You don't have a peasant's strength or toughness but you don't need to play the fainting woman."

Celia continued to play "Way Down Upon the Swanee River."

"I'll come back tomorrow," said Leah. "If you need me, call. Harry and I will be home. Well, I will."

Celia nodded, her curls bouncing slightly.

Leah looked at her mother, raising her eyebrows and folding her lips together. They turned, the bundles of their coats like wadding, insulated walls between them and the musician whose fingers were now clearly red, the skin broken in places. "I'm sorry I didn't make any dinner, Sam," said Leah.

"It's all right. I'll call the Chinese place. Frank suggested it. Celia?" He waited and when she just played on, he continued. "You like that, don't you?" Her arms were beginning to sag and she was playing with her elbows resting against her waist.

He ushered them to the door, and as they left, a bitter flavor rose in his mouth and he suddenly felt the needling isolation the ringing of the harp created between him and Celia.

Only after the food had been delivered did she stop, playing the last notes with her palm on the middle of the strings, a haunting harmony, then a last run, and she sat, her arms hanging down, looking into the hall toward the bedrooms, blood purpling the tips of several fingers around the little pads of callus.

Sam patted her back. "Go. Go wash up. There's some liquid

skin in the medicine chest, darling. Put it on your poor fingers."

"Yes, Papa," said Celia in a little voice, then stood and seemed, despite all, herself suddenly. She returned from the bathroom, sat down at the table, leaned against the chair's back and began to eat without waiting for Sam. He was startled and tried out a narrative by way of explanation. "She wondered where her son was eating that night, and forgot her husband in her misery at the thought her boy might be hungry." No. He sat down with her and silently ate the wonton soup, the egg rolls, the moo goo gai pan, watching her, not daring to speak until, at last, he ventured, "Do you feel better?"

She blinked but did not answer.

He watched her rise, collect the plates, put the remains in paper cartons in the refrigerator. She left him his teacup but took the dishes to the sink where the splash of water and groan of pipes abrasively broke the stillness as she rinsed the dishes. Then she turned and walked back to the living room, her curls now damply sinking toward straightness. He felt his breath catch in his throat as the silence buzzed in his ears.

"Celia," he called, following her, raising her name like a standard.

She was sitting in the living room in a green and gold brocade chair, looking in front of her, and she nodded slightly as he came in. "Celia?"

Silence. She did not answer, and his heart began to beat more rapidly as he sensed, in what way he could not have explained, the silence around her, encapsulating and palpable. "Celia?"

She barely smiled.

"Celia? Won't you answer me?" But he already knew, pierced with that knowledge as with a knife, that she wouldn't.

3

*A*FTER CELIA went to bed, still silent, her hair unset, Sam
went out. He rushed to the little newsstand by the entrance to
the subway on Broadway that never seemed to close. It was
lighted, and inside, in a space only big enough for one person
to sit, was a silent old man with a maroon balaclava helmet,
peering out into the night over his assortment of papers and
magazines. Sam, a regular customer, nodded, acknowledging
their acquaintance as he thrust down the coins before grabbing the top paper off the pile of the next day's *New York
Times*. It was snowing slightly, a slow flurry of little flakes,
which wet the paper as he opened it desperately and turned
to the last pages, ripping it as he did. Under the greenish
glow of a streetlamp, the snowflakes falling on the paper like
gray tears, he found only that Simon Richter would no longer
be responsible for his wife Delores's debts, she having left his
bed and board, and that the class of 1947 of Washington Ir-
ving High School was planning a reunion, would members call
. . . He folded back the newspaper in quarters, his pain enlarging, put it under his arm and turned up the block toward
his home.

The next morning, just as Sam feared, Celia rose silent as
she had retired and sat like the eye of a storm, oblivious, it
seemed, to the frantic activity her stillness caused. After a week

of nightly runs for the paper, a week that lasted longer than
any Sam had ever known, Gershom seemed farther away than
any distance might have placed him, and Sam, feeling inarticulate and ashamed, asked Johanna to place an ad in the public notices. "He might answer you. It won't seem so much like
pleading," he said, wincing as he spoke. Standing in the im-
personal cast of the green streetlight on the second night of
the new year, he read:

Wednesday, January 3, 1973
PUBLIC NOTICES

> My wife, Emilia Ramirez having left my bed and
> board, I will no longer be responsible for her
> debts. — Pablo Ramirez
>
> Gershom — Your mother is so upset, she won't
> speak. Are you O.K.? Please call. — Johanna
>
> Study being prepared on overweight problems.
> Anyone more than 50 pounds overweight,
> ages . . .

Sam had learned a great deal about the force of silence that
week, the noise of it, which rose above the chatter of Leah
alternately sympathizing and coaxing, and above the voice of
Naomi lecturing Celia on the subject of independence. It even
could be heard above the nursery rhymes Rachel sang to entertain them on the day she came to visit with Johanna.

Emma, the first to abandon hope, would not come to see
them though she spoke to Leah or to Sam on the phone regularly.

"Look, I'm busy now with buying the spring and summer
lines both for the store and for the Lorelei chain. And Seymour needs me in the store too. Besides, you heard Celia in
one of her last speeches. I'd like her to speak but I don't want
to have to act as target for her anger." Then softly, "I'm sorry,
Sam. *You* don't deserve this."

"So I'm to be the responsible one, as usual!" said Leah fiercely to Johanna after one of these calls. "Sam has to go back to teach soon and we just can't leave her alone."

"Why not?"

"Because she's sick, mentally injured. Don't you understand that? Well, of course she's disturbed. How could she be otherwise? Somebody has to be with her if Gershom, that selfish no-good, comes back."

* * *

On Monday evening toward the end of the first week that the notice had appeared daily in the paper, Seth and Johanna left a college student in their apartment to answer the phone and care for Rachel, and went to see Sam and Celia with Seth's father, Gabriel, a professor of neurology, originally at the University of Prague.

Gabriel was a tall, dignified man with thick white hair that rose in bunches from his head. His skin pulled across his cheeks and forehead tightly and shone above dark brown eyes and a full, white, wiry beard. He had long ago adopted the fashions of his new land and now dressed in a formal style stamped with his own particularity — a fondness for paisley ties and pale blue shirts. At home, he wore a little, black velvet yarmulke, the skullcap of an observant Jew, but left it in his house when he went out in the world, considering his relationship with God a private matter. He was still teaching, though past the age of ordinary retirement. Johanna had once gone to hear him lecture on the effect of neurological disorders on the work of certain artists and had been impressed. When he moved in that lecture hall, she had told Seth later, he vibrated like a good performer, and his students responded with perfect attention and rapt expectancy. "Now I know where you get your cool before an audience from," she had said, but Seth had laughed. "And here I thought I developed that myself."

Sam greeted them at the door, coming from the room that hummed with Celia's silence. He looked dazed.

"Gabriel, my friend," he said. "Johanna, Seth, please come in. Celia? Seth and Johanna have brought Gabriel to see us."

From the vestibule, they could see Celia seated in the living room on the green and gold chair, her hair tightly set in rollers, a task Leah had performed that afternoon before she left. Her hands hung down through the arms of the chair, her palms slightly flared outward, as if she were waiting for something.

Johanna went in without taking off her coat, kissed her aunt on the cheek and sighed with relief when Celia did not turn away. When she had come previously with Rachel, Celia had refused to look at her, turning always to the window, walking with her back to Johanna, deliberately and expressively. This time she merely accepted the peck, and Johanna lifted and stroked her left hand, feeling words she could not say clotting in her throat. There was such a temptation to yell, to accuse Celia, of what? Of being self-indulgent? Of being crazy? Of causing them all additional pain? No. Probably her aunt could not help herself, was winding herself in the comfort of quiet. Johanna turned and went back to the coat closet where she gave Sam her coat.

"I didn't know if I should come," she said softly, "because I knew Aunt Celia was angry with me, and because perhaps Gershom would call. But I thought, since the sitter is no one he knows, he'd be willing to call back if he decides to telephone."

"I'm glad you came," said Sam, and he leaned forward and kissed her cheek again, seeing in his mind the four-year-old she had been when he first knew her.

Gabriel walked into the living room and went to Celia. He held out his hand and said, "Celia, good evening." She smiled at him and took his hand, nodding.

"Are you well?" His voice was husky, a deep rasping voice inflected with a dim central European accent.

She turned her face downward and raised her eyebrows in two arcs.

"I am well," said Gabriel, as if she had asked for his health.

As Gabriel moved away, Seth leaned over to kiss the top of her head, and then sat down on the floor beside her and took her hand in his. She did not pull away and he just held it, as silent as she.

Gabriel was now seated on the couch. "I understand, Celia, that you are distressed, but you know Gershom is not wild. He's a sensible young man even if that act seems wild. You have taught him how to take care of himself. Have confidence in that."

She nodded with the barest movement of her head.

"And of course, you have your work, the house, Sam and your meals to get. Sam's distressed too. He needs your care."

She looked shocked, as if he must be foolish to say such a thing to her. Then the expression faded and she stared back across the living room toward Johanna standing near the plants and stroking, absent-mindedly, the furry leaves of the picka-back.

Gabriel followed her eyes and looked at the array of green leaves, apartment-raised avocado and grapefruit trees, beside a rack of philodendrons, ferns and violets. His husky voice began again in a lilting manner. "I understand you have shown great care for your plants, and I see they thrive. Do you play the harp now?"

"She hasn't touched it," whispered Sam, who had come to sit next to Gabriel on the couch. "Not since *that* day."

"Celia?" Gabriel gestured toward the harp. "My dear, will you play for me?"

She neither shook her head nor moved, but her eyes glanced toward the harp and closed for a moment.

"Do you fear for the boy?" asked Gabriel.

She did not gesture, blink or smile. Nothing. Seth lifted her hand, still in his, and put it against his cheek gently. "He's fine, I'm sure. He's fine."

She looked down at him, again only the bare movement of her eyes.

"I tell her," said Sam, "I tell her he's fine, having an adventure somewhere. Not that he ought to be having a good time, but he's always been a good son and I want to welcome him home when he comes." But he added softly to Gabriel, "I can forgive his anger, his going, but doing *this* to his mother . . ."

"He had no idea," said Johanna, "no idea. He was just stumbling, I'm sure, without thinking what would happen. How could he have known?"

Sam stared at her as if about to answer, then shook his head and looked away.

"He should be in our prayers," said Gabriel. "I pray for him and for all of us that we may be in the care of the Almighty."

Celia shivered, an inadvertent trembling.

"My dear, I am saying we must have faith. We are like leaves buffeted by the wind except for that eternal part of ourselves, and it can save us. The world is full of horrors but it is also full of miracles and I urge you to turn your heart to the miraculous."

She closed her eyes and breathed in deeply.

"Abba," said Johanna to Gabriel, "the miraculous is sometimes very far away from us. It's not all that easy to set your heart toward God."

"No," said Gabriel, "not easy." He smiled.

"Aunt Celia, I played at Alice Tully Hall last night," said Seth. "We did one of those late Beethoven quartets you've always told me you like. The ones he wrote when he was deaf."

A smile breezed her lips but she did not look at him.

"We must get you some tea," said Sam, standing up.

Immediately, Celia got to her feet and turned toward the kitchen. She walked out quite naturally, and they heard her fill the kettle with water: first the hollow sound of the stream in the empty metal, and then the further swish; the little click of the gas jet as it burst into flame; the sound of the cupboard opening; the clink of plates as she moved about her tasks in the workroom of her life.

"What do you think?" Sam whispered to Gabriel.

The tall man shifted, raising one leg across the other, his shoes polished to an even dull gloss. He looked at Sam for a long moment, and Sam returned his glance, eyes wide, his hands resting on his thighs.

"She has undergone a trauma, it's clear, but in some senses she still functions normally. She seems to have chosen to observe rather than participate, to wait, and I think we should let her. Has she done anything unusual in an active way?"

"No," said Sam. "Oh, except for not setting her hair, or having to be led to the shower."

"She's withdrawn," said Gabriel, "to allow whatever will happen to happen."

"One other thing," said Sam, his voice thick as he looked down with embarrassment. "You know I was at one time very close to Bernard Katzman, the critic, though I haven't seen him for years. Celia has always felt, in her special loyalty to me, that he had opportunities I should have had. Of course, it's madness. Well, anyway, Miriam, you know, my niece, gave me a book of his for Christmas, and shortly after Celia stopped talking she took the dust jacket of the book that had his picture on it and cut it up in little pieces."

"That's all?"

"That's all."

"That's nothing compared to things I've heard her say about him," said Johanna.

"It's such foolishness," whispered Sam almost to himself. "Such foolishness."

"Perhaps," Gabriel's softly accented speech reached out like a warm arm, "this act has eased her anger. She will have to shed her anger if she is to improve. Even if Gershom comes home now, she will not necessarily begin to speak again."

They began to discuss her reading habits: just skimming,

nothing from beginning to end. And Gabriel stood to contemplate the bookshelves, removing the Bible he came upon and laying it on the table near Celia's chair.

"Uncle Sam," said Johanna, "I called the school today, just thinking maybe Gershom had gone to classes, and was somewhere around the campus. He isn't. The dean's office checked with all his professors, and one called me, a Mr. Toledano, his history instructor, very upset. He apparently is very fond of Gershom and thinks he's an excellent student. He said he would do anything he could to help."

"What can he do?" asked Sam as if to himself.

Celia reappeared at the door of the living room, carrying a tray filled with cups, a large red teapot, and a plate of cookies.

Sam stood up quickly and took the tray from her. "Sit, darling, I'll give people tea. Celia made the cookies just today."

Celia resumed her seat, and Seth again took her hand.

"I'll tell you about the concert," he said. "Brendon, you know, the violist, was wild last night. His tempo threw us off during the Beethoven — the F major — and before we recovered the balance, I had an awful moment when my cello seemed like the only instrument playing."

Celia did not respond, and they all lapsed into the wave of her stillness. The ticking of a clock from off in the bedrooms seemed magnified.

Then Johanna said, "Mommy tells me you went back to school this week, Uncle Sam."

He laughed quietly, a mouse amused by his trap. "Yes, but I wonder more than ever if Oscar Wilde wasn't right when he said nothing worth knowing can be taught." He stopped then turned to Johanna. "Your mother has been wonderful. She comes every day at seven-thirty so I can get to school by eight-fifteen, and she stays till I get home, has a dinner ready that Celia can heat up. She takes Celia to the store, to the park. She's being more than a sister really!"

Johanna laid down her cup. "It's her way. She's very concerned."

They finished their tea and got ready to go. Celia acknowledged neither their goodbyes nor their embraces but sat, trancelike, observing the plants.

At the door, Sam pressed each of their hands and kissed Johanna on the cheek.

"Sam," said Gabriel, "pray for her but don't be afraid."

"Do you think a doctor — a psychiatrist — would help?" Sam asked warily, his voice betraying his dread.

"Might," said Gabriel. "But he might also do some harm. For the moment, I'd wait."

"How long do you think?" He was ready to make plans, hope illuminating his face.

"I can't say. She has some health in her. It would be best if she passed through this valley by herself. Just keep things as normal as possible so she doesn't feel the rest of her world slipping away. I'll stop by now and then. Call me if you need to."

"So," said Sam, "she comes to Aiken's 'shoreless shore of silence . . . seeking in all that joy of things remembered one image, one the dearest, one most bright . . .'" He sighed. "Keep running the ads, Johanna. It's something. You can change the message, maybe each Sunday." His eyes filled with tears and he opened the door to usher them out.

In the street, they walked through the stiff hush of cold air toward Broadway.

"What do you think will happen with her, Abba?" asked Seth.

"She is in pain. Her love has been a kind of gluttony and now she suffers the torments of that. But just like an obese person has a healthy thin person hidden inside the flesh, she has a normal loving self hidden in her. Do you think the boy will come back, Johanna?"

"Not for a while." She took Seth's arm. "I thought he would come back before school started but now that he hasn't I think he may stay away a long time. The Mr. Toledano I talked to today was very kind. He was really upset, almost like family.

He said he had felt Gershom was troubled, especially the last month, and that just at the time other first-year students seemed to be adjusting, he seemed to be more frenetic. Poor Gershom. He's never known how to say no to his mother in an ordinary way and he finally exploded, I guess. If I could just feel sure he's all right, I think some defiance might really be a good thing for him."

"Do you think after he has made his angry statement, he will return to his parents?"

Johanna was silent.

Seth looked at her and then at his father. "Not to the way things were, I would hope. I feel for him. I would have run from that oppression too."

Johanna was shaking her head violently but it was Gabriel who spoke. "You say that with glorious illumination of hindsight. There are far worse oppressions and a few weeks ago you probably would have said so too. Even though Gershom is young, resilient, I hope he won't encounter some of the oppressions the world can offer." He was walking quickly, ahead of them, to the bus stop. "But Celia troubles me. I see in her eyes a blankness I know. Your mother, Seth, began to decline the day we left Prague with nothing but a day's change of clothing for you and Rifka."

They had come to the bus stop and waited, Johanna staring at Gabriel.

"What's the matter, Johanna?"

"I've never heard you say anything like that," she said. "Never."

"Well, I'll say more. I knew the Germans were coming. I should say I believed. Everyone knew but not all believed. She did not believe. By the time we got to our friends in Oxford, Czechoslovakia was gone, but she wished to go back — with a six-month-old infant and a little girl to go back to the lion's den. Months, we stayed in Oxford, months we spent walking through the colleges, looking at monuments to martyrs — all from another world, another age with different goals — waiting. I remember roses. They bloomed all the time we were there. But she saw nothing, began to fail before my eyes. Not so dramatic as Celia but in little ways. In the year, we came to New York. She tried to make Prague in our apartment. It wasn't to be." He was not looking at either of them.

"She had ten reasonably good years after that," said Seth, "and only one bad one. You know what would have happened if we had stayed. Anyway, Celia's situation is altogether different, Abba."

"Loss is pernicious. Unless the loser gives up willingly, it can be killing. She has to learn to let go."

"What if he comes back?" Johanna posed.

"Especially then," said Gabriel.

*   *   *

Seth and Johanna came back to their apartment, where the baby-sitter was sitting cross-legged and surrounded by her books on the floor in the living room. Seth opened the door and Johanna slipped in ahead of him.

"Hello, Barbara," she said, standing in front of her. "Did anyone call?"

"Hi, Mrs. Rosen. Your mother called and a cousin." Johanna stiffened then relaxed as Barbara continued. "I think she said her name was Miriam. And a lady about a pot. She said she'd call back. The messages are by the phone."

"Thank you," said Johanna, taking money from her purse to pay Barbara. "And Rachel?"

"Slept all night."

Seth helped the girl on with her coat and left to take her home. It was only a few minutes after ten, the clock in the kitchen with its big hand like an arrow, silent in its electric dream when Johanna picked up the phone to call her mother.

"Did you take Gabriel up?" said Leah first thing.

"Yes, and he says just what we thought, that a doctor might

help but might not and that she may be able to pass through this herself."

"Well, I'm grateful he isn't ready to write her off. It's just what I tried to tell Emma." She paused. "What was your impression of her tonight?"

"I really could only think about what she's putting Uncle Sam through. I feel so sorry for him."

"She? It's what Gershom is putting her and Sam through. Don't forget Gershom's part in this little drama." Leah's voice was prickly.

"Mommy, I've tried to explain to you that Gershom is doing his own suffering."

"So he wanted to make everyone else suffer? Is that it? Well, I told Sam today not to look forward to his coming back. He'll have to start from scratch as far as I'm concerned. He'll have to turn himself inside out. I only want him to come back to ease her pain. I said to Sam, 'That boy has lost all my respect, and I don't know if I can feel the same way about him again.' "

Johanna sat down and put her chin in the cup of her hand. "Do you think that helped Sam?" she said softly.

"He's got to see the boy straight. You don't have real sympathy for the parents, I know. Parents are parents and children bear up with them, that's your attitude."

"I wish you wouldn't tell me what I think."

Leah paused and gave a little snort. Her voice turned a corner. "I have other things to tell you. My sister Emma, and I use the word *sister* advisedly, will do nothing to comfort Celia and Sam. Tonight she called up and went on at great length about how Sam would help everybody if he put Celia in a hospital. As if she's being inconvenienced at all! She even got Mamma on the phone and went on about it. And my mother, who at least has her decency left to her, finally said, 'I'd better not get senile, Emma. You'll put me away.' "

"Did they both tell you that?"

"The very words."

"Aunt Emma just can't stand unpleasantness. She likes life to go on smoothly."

Leah's voice intensified, the phone like a magnifying glass, enlarging the tremors of emotion. "Do you think that excuses her? All she cares about are appearances, and it goes so deep, she can't recognize what's genuine. She actually told me I'm doing what I'm doing for Sam and Celia because I like to look noble, that that coarse husband of hers thinks, says, though I don't know who he'd speak to, that I'm playing Joan of Arc. Self-centered people!"

Johanna switched the phone to her other ear. "What does Daddy think?"

Leah's voice dropped to a whisper. "I don't want him to know I'm talking about him. He feels, I think, that Emma ought to share some of the responsibility. I've been getting up at six A.M. to be there by the time Sam has to leave and I think Daddy feels I'm being greatly burdened. Well, you know he feels that! At the same time, I think he considers this whole sequence of events a confirmation of my family's volatility, instability, I don't know, whatever it is the Seligmans say to one another about me. It's difficult for him to really understand."

Johanna said nothing.

"Are you there?" Leah's tone was sarcastic.

"Yes."

"Have you nothing to say?"

"What do you want me to say?"

Leah paused just long enough for Johanna to regret having asked the question. "If you don't know, I can't tell you. I can only say I would welcome some unqualified support and I'm certainly not getting it from you."

A familiar tightness fairly closed her throat as Johanna considered all the possible responses, and old conversations filled her mind, like background music in a 1940s movie. She longed to find the right words but they eluded her. At last she said,

"Don't abandon the rest of your life to this, Mommy. I know you are doing something very good but perhaps there are other ways of handling the problem."

"And I thought I could count on you," said Leah with disgust.

"Why do you always turn on me?" asked Johanna sadly. "What should I do?"

"Nothing," said Leah, her voice intending pretense. "Give Seth my love." She hung up.

Johanna put her face in her hands, resisting the temptation to scream. She felt Seth's hand around the back of her neck, kneading, rubbing the place where a sore inflexibility was settling, spasms of comfort coursing through her from his fingers.

"My mother sends her love," she said into the kitchen table.

"Difficult?"

"Very. So much I never heard you come back."

"She wants what?"

"I'm not sure. A lot of the themes are old ones — Emma's irresponsibility and Seymour's coarseness, what my father's family thinks, being one up on Emma with Grandma — but she's angry at Gershom in a way she's never dared be angry with anyone but me before, and she's smoldering at my father though she's not saying that exactly. I think she's even angry at Uncle Sam. There are a lot of things going on and, as usual, I'm getting her emotional garbage."

"You don't have to listen."

Johanna didn't answer. Exhaustion blanketed her.

"When I came in, didn't I hear you telling your mother not to abandon her life to this problem? Such good advice! You ought to take it yourself. In the last two weeks, you've spent so many hours on the phone, or nearby, it's been as if you were chained to a switchboard. You can't go on like this. You have to detach yourself somehow."

She pulled away from him wearily. "Seth, things can't go on

being this hairy for long even if I go on running the ads. I'm used to listening to Mother."

He smiled with a look of skeptical amusement and ran his hand through his hair so it nearly stood on end. "And of course you need to stay in in case Gershom calls, to support your Uncle Sam, and occasionally listen to your grandmother, the villainess Emma, maybe even to Frank. And let's not forget your cousins David and Miriam!"

"Oh, Seth, cut it out!"

The phone rang. It was Miriam.

"Johanna, how are you and how's that handsome husband of yours?" Miriam gave a playful giggle.

"Fine," said Johanna. "And you, Miriam? I was just going to return your call."

Seth gave a little mock bow and left the kitchen.

Miriam cleared her throat. "You know, Johanna, I don't usually get involved in these family things but this business is a little different. My mother and I have been on the phone a ridiculous amount for two people who don't own a share of AT and T between them. It's not so much that she's worried about Gershom — I mean, he's not a child anymore — but she does feel terrible that she and my father, especially my father, had anything to do with getting him so upset. (He must have felt really awful, Johanna.) And since his running away set Celia off, she feels guilty about Celia, which your mother doesn't help by playing Lady Bountiful. You understand what I mean, don't you?"

"Yes, I do," said Johanna, "but there's nothing I can do about it."

"I didn't call you to ask you to do anything. The way the Silversteins are skewed, you'd have to be something of a wizard. Even Grandma. No." Miriam paused. "I don't really feel I know what's happening and I thought you could tell me."

"As well as anyone can, I suppose."

"You know my mother!" Miriam sounded as if that knowledge could only be amusing. "She was convinced to begin with that Celia was putting on an act, looking for attention, sympathy, but now that she's convinced it's a breakdown she thinks Celia ought to be in a hospital or under medication at least. She runs that by me at least twice a day. The whole thing makes her very uncomfortable, especially the prospect of having to explain a silent sister to people without some medical term to make it authentic." Laughter permeated Miriam's voice. "She tells her friends Arthur has an 'open marriage' — Eileen should just hear that — because she so likes having names for things."

Johanna, cradling the phone between her shoulder and ear, had gotten up and walked about the kitchen. Near the stove on a counter, she found a can of her daughter's Play-Doh — red with bits of yellow in it. She took the blob and began to mold it even before she was seated at the table again, her fingers moving deftly through the medium of clay. The curiosity which Miriam's last remark sparked, smothered in her lassitude. She suddenly realized there was a silence on the phone, Miriam waiting for her to respond.

"Yes," she mumbled.

"Johanna, have you seen Aunt Celia?"

"Of course. We were there this evening."

"She's really gone crazy, hasn't she?"

Johanna's fingers curved, a funny, fat-bellied Buddha swelling out from her finger tips.

"Seth's father came with us. He says she's going through a storm. I don't think it's going to pass quickly and I don't think Gershom's coming home would speed it up because his leaving wouldn't have done this to her if she had been truly well before. She's always been angry and dissatisfied about something. Or frightened. Maybe she'll pass through this, like through a tunnel, and come out different."

"Or maybe the same," said Miriam.

Johanna pushed her Buddha in the stomach. She rolled the

Play-Doh in a ball and began to shape it again. "The person I feel the worst about is Uncle Sam. He's such a gentle man and, despite all her craziness, he loves her very much. You know, my mother once told me that when they first met, he would bring her poems that he had written out in a fancy calligraphy, and chocolates, and they would sit for a whole evening while he held skeins of wool for her to roll. He gets so little satisfaction for someone who gives so much. He goes to that dreadful school — I'm sure he must be afraid a lot of the time — teaches English to students who couldn't care less if he were teaching them Sanskrit, and he and Celia don't have many friends, or enough money to do anything outrageous and pleasant, even to take a vacation somewhere, and through all that he remains affectionate and devoted. Marvelous."

She paused, the Play-Doh now in the shape of a tiny pleading red hand. Several seconds passed, a muffled sound oddly coming across the line. "Miriam?"

"Uncle Sam," she heard Miriam whisper huskily and as if she were addressing him. "I'm sorry. Oh, I'm so sorry."

4

Sunday, January 28, 1973

PUBLIC NOTICES

Gershom — Your mother's silence continues. Aunt
Leah with her days. Worried. Please call us. — Johanna.

M IRIAM WORKED in a large office building in midtown
Manhattan near wholesale jewelers. She often spent a little
time after lunch admiring the stones and settings in the windows along the side streets and imagining this necklace or that
pin on a stylish outfit hanging in her closet. She loved clothing
and since Christmas had indulged herself with visits to Bonwit
Teller's. Among other Christmas gifts, Arthur had given her
the store's charge card in his name with a note that read: "For
your future use." Wondering what future Arthur might have
in mind, she had asked coyly, "Does this make it permanent?"
He laughed, reaching out to touch her breast with an insin-
uating pressure, and said, "As far as I'm concerned, puss, we
can go on this way forever." She had run one finger along his
collarbone and said, cocking her head, "Until now, I've liked
paying my own way." "Consider this just another present —
one that gives me pleasure." And he kissed her with an open
mouth.

He could well afford her usual abandon in the shops, but
despite a lot of window-shopping, it was weeks before she used
the card. She bought, then returned, an artificial leopard-skin

jumpsuit, realizing it could hang in her closet for months, perhaps years, before an appropriate occasion for wearing it might turn up. She used the $275 credit to buy a bikini and beach ensemble with the expectation that Arthur and she might get away to St. Thomas when his wife went to visit her family in Seattle with the children at Easter time.

She never considered buying jewelry, disliking even first-class costume jewelry, her tastes honed on the diamonds she admired in the stores near her office and on the good gold and fine stones of Arthur's choosing.

It was on one of her lunchtime excursions in mid-January that she had first noticed a red-bearded young man in the long black coat and wide-brimmed black hat common to Hasidic Jews who made their living in the diamond industry, standing near a corner and stopping passers-by. He talked to them politely for a few minutes, then sometimes gave them a leaflet, sometimes merely raised his fingers to his hat.

Miriam was accustomed to people distributing literature, as the blocks near Fifth Avenue were often crowded with them, but there was something different and disturbing about this man. He looked about the street with an intensity and she felt the energy radiating from him even when she passed on the other side of the street.

She noticed him again as she came out of her office one late January day to meet her mother for lunch, this time stationed at the very corner of her office building and braving a cold wind. She was relieved that she did not have to pass him since her destination was in the other direction.

Her mother and she met at a particularly good Japanese restaurant in the Fifties. Emma, on a downtown buying trip, was dressed in a fur-trimmed beige coat, her hair neatly shingled and her wide mouth and eyes heavily made up, just short of too made up Miriam thought, behind large pale-blue-rimmed glasses. They kissed, hung their coats in the coat room, and glided after the kimonoed waitress through a dark bar to a back room, and a small table with a hibachi built into the center. In the background soft oriental music piqued their attention without holding it, chimes, woodwind sounds.

They ordered drinks, Miriam ordering "Chivas with a twist," her hand flipping back over her auburn hair, with the assurance, learned from months with Arthur, that naming a particular brand of liquor marked a sophisticated drinker. Emma looked across the table at her daughter and laughed a throaty little chirp.

"You look nice. Purple's a good color for you. It's in this season. I just bought a whole batch of spring coordinates, for Daddy's stock, in different shades."

"How's business?"

"Awful. He works like a dog, twelve hours a day, and whether it's because business is off generally, or Queens Boulevard is not as good a location as it used to be, he struggles. If I didn't do this extra work for Lorelei, I don't know how we'd manage."

Miriam braced herself against the contempt she heard in her mother's voice, but then the drinks arrived and they were asked to order their lunch as the waitress flipped on the switch to heat the electric hibachi.

"You order," said Emma brightly. "You know this kind of food better than I do."

The waitress, her bright sash shimmering, smiled submissively as she took their order and shuffled away on her tiny clogs. Miriam took a long sip of her Scotch.

"Have you and Daddy ever thought of closing the store and maybe managing someone else's business?"

Emma stirred her drink with the pink plastic swizzle stick as if gazing at the ice cubes.

"Daddy wouldn't do well in that atmosphere, I'm afraid. He works so hard, poor man, but he's not an imaginative businessman, and I think he wouldn't like having to be responsible to anyone else. He likes to gossip with the women from the neighborhood, have friends drop by, and he would have to pay much more attention to the management end of it if someone were always looking over his shoulder." She continued stirring, the cubes hitting the sides of the glass with a dull clink.

"How many hours a week are you there now?" asked Miriam, a question she was accustomed to asking because the answer was always changing.

"Fifteen, I'd say. And I spend another ten or twelve buying, more like twenty in the season. My week's busy what with the housework, and going out to see the children and help poor Anita when I can."

Miriam looked directly at her mother but the darkness and drink kept Emma from meeting her look head on.

"Have you seen Aunt Celia lately?"

"No." Emma's voice fondled the word. "I just told you how busy I am. The whole thing is *so* unpleasant."

"Talked to Uncle Sam?"

"Yes, I talk to him. He puts up with a great deal from my sister. It hurts me to say it, but I don't know how many men would put up with this so-called storm. (I can just imagine what your father would do.) Of course, Sam, who adores her, though I hardly know why, has always let her get away with things just the way Papa did. Pampered! They never had much money, but he wouldn't let her work, except to give harp lessons from time to time, and then only to the children of friends who didn't pay much. And when Gershom was a child Sam would never cross her, though she acted as if Gershom's dinner hour, his chicken pox, his art lessons, were the only important things."

"Sensitive," said Miriam. "That's what Grandma calls her."

"It's been indulged, I'm afraid." Emma looked squarely for the first time at Miriam, her big eyes peering in the dimness. "She carried on for years after Papa died. At his unveiling she lay down and sobbed on the ground. The rabbi wouldn't even go on until she got control of herself. And always so angry. For somebody who's sensitive, she has some tongue. You've heard her. She throws 'bitch' and 'bastard' into her conversations the way other people use pronouns, and she said some dreadful things about your father and me just before this almost merciful silence descended. I was furious at her."

"Are you still?"

Emma looked away again. She did not answer immediately.

"No, I guess. You know me. I'm not good at holding grudges," she said at last. "I guess I just have to accept the fact that her problems are always top of the agenda." She swallowed the remainder of her drink.

Miriam tapped the rim of her glass with one manicured pearl fingernail. They sat briefly occupied by their own thoughts. Then Miriam said, "Aunt Leah is spending every day there, I understand."

Her mother's eyes narrowed. "Aunt Leah has the time no one else has since she doesn't have to work. It's good of her, of course, but as I told you there's a large element of feeling noble on the public stage."

"I didn't think she was doing it to publicize herself. When I told Arthur about it he said, 'Well, there are still some selfless people in the world.' "

Emma leaned against the back of her chair and gazed across at Miriam. "I'm surprised you discussed this with Arthur," she said.

"Why?"

Emma eyed her daughter, then retreated. "Well, your Aunt Leah does many things that appear selfless, but really have the intention of highlighting herself. She likes everyone to think her life a model, so substantial — her money, her marriage, her child. She discovers artists so when she talks about them she can give the impression of having all sorts of deep insights. It's pathetic really." Her voice was taking on a kindly sympathetic tone which Miriam recognized as far more deadly than the raw anger of the words.

Emma continued, lowering her voice as if the other diners were trying to listen. "When she married Uncle Harry, I think she really believed his family with all their old connections and money were going to embrace her and she would enter their world bringing the rest of us with her. As if any of us cared one way or the other! Well, I'm sorry she found them not quite so receptive and then, she was terribly disappointed that Daddy and I got married before she and Harry did because it diminished her glory. I think she still holds it against me."

"I can't believe that," said Miriam, irritated with her mother. "After all, you had known Daddy a long time. It was perfectly natural for you to get married then."

The conversation halted as the waitress came to check their drinks and only resumed after she had turned to go to the kitchen for their food. Emma spoke quite softly. "Well, it's true, but we didn't get engaged until after Harry and Leah did. We had talked about it, of course, and Daddy had wanted to get married, but we weren't actually engaged until after they were because I'd been a little uncertain."

Miriam shifted slightly in her chair. "So, why did you get married first?"

"Well, you know they had to wait till the end of the spring term so Harry could finish law school. And your father had dropped out of school by that time and didn't have any reasons why not, and I decided if I wanted to finish college I could do it married, so we just went to Papa and said we wanted to get married in the spring. He and Mamma were already planning Leah's wedding. She was always his favorite, and since Harry's family was Harry's family, it was going to be the biggest wedding Papa could afford. But I guess he realized he couldn't do less for me than he did for her. After all how would it look? And, just the year before, the whole family had scrimped to send Celia to that fool harp competition. So we each had slightly smaller weddings, shared the wealth so to speak. Your father's family, of course, hardly knew the difference. I suspect Leah, who has never had to do without anything since, has always felt she would have had a bigger affair if Daddy and I had waited, but there was really no point in waiting."

The waitress arrived with two lacquered bowls filled with a clear soup in which delicately sculpted pieces of carrot floated, and a platter of raw beef to be prepared on the hibachi. Emma smiled up at the waitress brightly as she watched her lay the meat across the iron grate. "How clever! You do it at the table. What's in the sauce?"

Miriam knew at once that their conversation was suspended. Her mother never discussed anything personal in the presence of others. Besides the waitress was a charming diversion for Emma to flutter against, while Miriam sipped her soup and considered the implications of what her mother had been saying. In the background she heard her mother's voice, high, gay, laughing, over the sizzle of meat. "So you call those clogs *geta*. How interesting! What do you call that marvelous orange sash around the kimono?"

The waitress giggled softly. *"Obi,"* she said and deftly turned the meat with chopsticks.

"Oh, is that it? Do you have to learn to tie it specially, or is it already tied when you put it on?"

"Special way," said the waitress. "Is sa soup good?"

"Wonderful. Don't you think, Mimzie? Tell me, where are you from in Japan?"

The girl was now just standing by the table, performing the hostess role. "Kyoto."

"Really? A very good friend's nephew just spent his junior year abroad in Kyoto. He's majoring in Japanese culture. He wants to teach Japanese."

"Arthur once visited Kyoto on a business trip to Osaka," said Miriam, mimicking her mother's gay tone. She saw the clouded look telegraph her caution: "Not here, not now," but she chose to ignore it. "He says that most of the women wear western dress these days. Is that so?"

"Oh, yes," said the waitress, beginning to fill their plates with the barbecued meat beside mildly pickled vegetables. "Western dress much more simple." She put another round of meat on the burner, took their soup bowls and departed.

"It's not wise to mention Arthur in a place like this, do you think?" Emma whispered, raising her eyebrows.

"I suppose there must be four or five thousand Arthurs in New York," said Miriam with amusement.

"And how many of them have been to Osaka on business?"

"Some," said Miriam and took the teriyaki with her chopsticks.

"I realize it's hard to have to be so discreet all the time." Sympathy and understanding.

Miriam gave in. "Maybe we should talk about Gershom instead. I wonder where he is."

"I'm afraid as far away as he could get," said Emma. She turned to the food. "My, this is good!"

*   *   *

When Miriam returned from lunch to her office, she was preoccupied with her thoughts, which wandered through the dingy (yes, *dingy* was the right word) store on Queens Boulevard, and to her sluggish, distant father who lived in a perpetual rain of bills and shipping orders, who made bad jokes about the naked manikins, and who spruced up on Saturday nights to visit with a tight circle of old friends. Her mother was really quite different. Miriam had often wondered how a person who cared as much for propriety and the appearance of things as her mother did could have married someone who cared as little as her father did. They had always seemed mismatched, though at times affectionately bound to one another. And her father was clean, which meant a great deal to her mother, as did his bluff congeniality. But the something, the peculiarity that had joined and mated these two, had always stayed just outside the periphery of Miriam's vision, stirring, present, but unable to be seen.

She was so deeply engrossed that she did not notice the young man with the red beard standing inside the outer lobby just on the other side of the door, stamping his feet impatiently and blowing on his fingers, his little pile of leaflets heaped beside him in his respite from the cold. She opened the glass door still looking down, and nearly ran right into him. He leaped back, scattering the pamphlets all over the floor.

"Oh, I'm sorry," said Miriam. "I just didn't see you. I'll help you pick them up." She got down on one knee.

The sharp blue eyes caught hers for only a moment and he put up his hand like a prophet of old and said in an oddly inflected speech: American English, New York, but not ordinary, with short bitten-off words, "Don't touch them, please. I cannot take them from you."

She drew back and stared at him with surprise, recalling the fear she had skirted each time she passed him in the street. As she stood up, he faced her directly, looking slightly, intensely, above her head, and said, "Are you a Jew?"

The shock of the question and his intense eyes kept her from answering immediately. Inadvertently she shuddered, then struggled to be civil, "Yes, I am."

"Do you observe the *mitzvos* a woman must observe? Do you light the candles on Shabbos?"

She could hardly believe his questions. Her Jewish education consisted of two years in a Sunday School held at a Jewish Center in Rego Park, from which she remembered mainly learning Israeli dances and songs. The word *mitzvos* was familiar, but puzzling, yet she hardly dared ask this strange red-bearded Hasid what it meant. As for the candles, no one on the Silverstein side of her family lit Sabbath candles except Celia on rare occasions to satisfy Sam's nostalgia, and lately, she suspected, her cousin Johanna. On her father's side, the Millers, some of the women covered their eyes before flickering flames on Friday night with the quality of savages before a totem god. "Superstitious. Aunt Lil is just superstitious about things like that," Emma would say in her special embarrassed-kindly voice. "It makes her feel better to do it."

Miriam realized she had not answered him, but was still standing there, staring. She pulled herself up, standing straighter, and said in a cheery flirtatious tone, "I'm not especially religious. It's the nineteen seventies, you know. Excuse me, please." She took a step forward.

"Do you think the Divine Spark in man is absent because the calendar changes?" He was not smiling.

She did not answer but already he was asking another question. "Do you know what it means to be a Jew? Our people have been given a special place, unique in the world, and many abandon it without even understanding it."

"For some people, it just isn't important," said Miriam. She could feel herself getting angry, irritated and embarrassed too, by the stares of the people entering and leaving her office building. "I'm sorry I startled you, but I think I had better leave now."

As if he had not heard her, and she was not really sure he had, he proceeded on. "Our lives are intertwined as Jews. What one does affects another. I offer you a door to your true self, to perform the duties of a Jewish woman, to be blessed like the Matriarchs, to be one with your people as *Ha-Shem* has intended us to be one. In the light of the Shabbos candles glows peace and holiness."

"For me, they would just be candles, nice decorations," said Miriam, and she moved to one side to enter the inner lobby. He took one of the leaflets and held it out to her. "Decorations can become more than decorations. Read this."

"I don't want it." She was steaming.

"How can you know?" He was not actually blocking her way, but she somehow felt incapable of moving past him without taking his pamphlet. She reached out and felt it fall in her hand.

Suddenly the bearded cheeks rose with a lively smile. "This is the beginning," he said. "Mazel tov! Push the *yetzer hara*, the evil spirit, down and restore yourself." Her heart began to beat quickly. Without another word she stuffed the leaflet in her pocketbook and fairly ran into the building.

In her office, an inner office without windows, she hung her coat on a coat tree and tried to calm down. After a few minutes, she went to the office next to hers, where her good friend Cynthia Levertov was laughing gaily on the phone, and waited until Cynthia plunked down the receiver.

"Did you see a ghost?" said Cynthia with some amusement. "You look unstrung."

"Have you ever seen that red-headed orthodox Jew who gives out pamphlets around here?" asked Miriam, her voice uncertain.

"Oh, him!" said Cynthia with disgust. "There's a movement that really wants to put Jewish women in their place." And she made a Bronx cheer.

*   *   *

When she left for home at five o'clock, Miriam noted with relief that the red-bearded man was no longer around, and she began to walk gaily to the crosstown bus and, passing Saks Fifth Avenue, gazed with interest in the windows. She winked at the bus driver, who was a familiar one, as she put her token in the box, and jostled with packed passengers down several streets to Second Avenue, where she transferred to another bus and continued on downtown. In her building, on the avenue side, there was a bakery that specialized in wicked napoleons, cream puffs, custard tarts, the sorts of pastries no girl who wants to keep her figure should indulge in, but all the same she thought it would be fun to bring something home for her and Arthur to share for dessert and, joking all the while with the owner, a tall man with blond bushy eyebrows, she selected a chocolate frosted seven-layer cake as an appropriate indulgence and had him cut a slab. "Not too big," she

said, laughing, "but not too small either." He roared and she
demurely put her head to one side, all in the game.

Just as she was leaving the shop, a young man arrived at
the door, about to enter. He was taller than she, dark-haired
and had acne, and for one moment she caught her breath,
thinking, Gershom, but then realized he really looked quite
different, broader, less stoop-shouldered, and she made her
way out, having hardly hesitated.

In the apartment, Arthur was already seated in her sling-
back red canvas chair, reading the paper and sipping a Scotch-
and-soda. She came up behind him, put her hands over his
eyes and said in a nasal voice, "Guess who?"

"Who!" he said. "I knew it was you." He took her hand,
pulling her around onto his lap. "How's my girl?"

"Fine," she crowed, and gave him a wet affectionate kiss. "I
can taste Scotch."

"Have some more," said Arthur, kissing her again, and as
she got up, he stood up too. "I'll make you one, puss."

She took the box with the seven-layer cake into the kitchen
and opened the refrigerator to get the pork chops she was
going to stuff with truffles and breadcrumbs. She planned
broccoli with hollandaise sauce and baked potatoes. A good
meal.

Arthur followed her in, carrying her drink, and stood in
the doorway.

"So what happened to you today? Anything interesting?"

"I worked on a new lipstick campaign. We need to put out
some really flashy copy about Rose Blush." She trilled the name
as she opened the pockets in the pork chops.

"Sounds rosy," said Arthur, sipping his drink, and they both
giggled. Almost a head taller than Miriam, he was big-boned
and balding. His hairline had receded, leaving a U-shaped
patch of skin that was freckled as were his temples and forehead. The ring of brown hair remaining was just long enough
to fit the current fashion, but not so long that he looked un-

kempt. He was an oval-faced, sharp-featured man, and his eyes, green and rather large, gleamed with amusement over his handsome pointed nose. Unlike most of the men Miriam knew well, whose excess flesh offended her, he was truly trim. His belly was flat, the muscles toned by three hours weekly spent on the squash courts of the New York Athletic Club, and a session now and then in the weight room, and he carried himself with a youthful jauntiness, as if daring age to catch up with him.

She was mixing the breadcrumbs, onions sautéed in butter, parsley and truffles from a small red can in a little mixing bowl and she said, her voice high-pitched, "I had a strange thing happen to me today. I was coming back from lunch with my mother when a Hasidic Jew who is always giving out literature outside my office building asked me if I was Jewish and gave me a lecture on my people and my religious life, I guess, and insisted I take a pamphlet. When I told Cynthia about it she said he's part of a movement to bring Jews back to Judaism. They don't try to convert anyone, of course — only talk to Jews — but it's like a mission. Really strange."

Arthur clinked his glass on the counter. "Oh, God, they're like those born-again Christians, I bet. My son has a friend who got involved with *that* group — only fifteen years old and he acts like he has a pipeline to heaven. He leaves tracts around the house and he's always after Bruce to come to meetings and be saved. I'm not against a little church-on-Sunday religion, but this movement is out to make every moment of the day palpitate with God. This kid wears a wooden cross around his neck the size of a book. Makes *me* cross as hell." He winked at her. "Got into it through a teacher at school, too, advisor to some club. Well, I say they should roll out that holy roller." He finished his drink.

Miriam passed close to him to turn on the oven, and he pinched her bottom and rubbed the flat of his palm over her backside. "Come on, puss, dinner can wait. Let's go inside and listen to a little music, have another drink, give each other a kiss or two."

She coyly turned her head and said, "I'll just stick the potatoes and chops in. They take about an hour anyway."

They wandered back into the living room and Arthur set the record player to provide them with an hour's worth of music. The first record was *Hair* and they exchanged a private smile. They had seen the show early in their relationship, not exactly together — Arthur with his wife and Miriam with a man from her office — but coincidentally on the same evening. They had stared at each other across the lobby during intermission and somehow managed not even to smile. She and Arthur rarely went to the theater together and perhaps for that reason especially, they liked to talk about the show and that particular performance, spiced as it was by their daring exchange of glances. Now, as the music filled the living room, the memory of Eileen, whom she had seen only that one time, her bright red hair pulled back in a French twist, her laugh closing in a smoker's cough, arose in Miriam's mind. To clear it, she turned to Arthur, as they sat down on the couch, and kissed the rim of his ear.

He pulled back and looked at her with surprise. "Before dinner?" he said and slipped one hand between her thighs.

"It's comfortable just like that," said Miriam, holding his hand still. "Remember all those naked bodies?"

"None as nice as yours," said Arthur and took her hand in his. He began to tell her about the board meeting he had had to sit through and the luncheon afterward with some of the people from the international car-sales division, where they made "natural jokes about those environmentalists who can't stand the exhaust because they don't like anything to compete with the hot air they're producing naturally.

"But the best thing today was a small transfer of funds. I walked into the big boy's office and said to that pretty blonde secretary, 'Here's a little something to buck you up,' and handed her the check for two million. You should have seen her face. She'll remember that someday in her tidy subdivision house with kids running in and out, and it will make her feel she was really somebody once." He smiled, pleased with the thought.

The first side of *Hair* was finished. Frank Sinatra, Arthur's favorite, had come on and they got up to dance. Rocking against him, she nuzzled her face in his neck while, in a low bass voice, he echoed the record lyrics in her ear until the timer on the oven rang, calling her away to uncover the baking chops and start the vegetables.

As she returned to the kitchen, she was surprised by a catch in her breath, almost as if she were about to cry, and a sadness creeping into her chest like a cat, stealthy and sleek. Her stomach just below her rib cage was aching the way it had when, as a child, she had felt the pain of someone else's sorrow, or seen an animal injured. Her family had always called her soft-hearted, a quality all right in a woman, though unacceptable in a man. Her brother, David, was not allowed to cry. "Boys don't cry about things like that," she remembered her mother saying brightly to him when one day his best friend had moved out of New York to San Luis Obispo, California. "You can write to him." David, of course, had never seen him again. But anyway, this memory seemed irrelevant. What was causing this dull ache that threatened to become fluid and frantic, she had no idea. Dinner was coming along smoothly. Arthur was in good spirits. Nothing sad had happened to her after all. Perhaps it was seeing the boy who looked like Gershom. She pondered that for a minute, her knife poised above the fresh broccoli she was cutting into delicate flowerets, her cousin passing through her mind as if on a moving track so that although he ran, he seemed to get nowhere. She almost envied him, running. Who knew where he might be, what adventures he might have, and yet, and now the pain grew worse, there was her poor Aunt Celia, hysterical and silent, and even sadder, Uncle Sam, who had told her such wonderful stories when she was a child.

She began to melt the butter for the hollandaise sauce, and tears welled in her eyes from some fountain of sorrow buried in her, a secret source. Arthur had turned off the music and put on the television news. He was involved in watching Walter Cronkite, and she felt grateful to have the next twenty minutes or so to herself in the kitchen with the excuse of having to set the table, make the rest of dinner, to keep her private. She wondered sometimes if marriage demanded being always perky, and wasn't sure she could take it if it did.

Her mind tided back to her aunt and uncle, whose loss seemed so devastating. Was Gershom's disappearance and their anguish the real cause of all her apprehension? She sensed her family floating apart like ice floes in a lake touched by a February thaw. The dissolution was mysterious, as was the feeling she had had at lunch when her mother had exposed something she had never known about the past, her own past in some way, the significance of which she had not really assimilated.

And there was the unexpected anger. Her aunt's silence certainly troubled her mother more than Gershom's absence, for runaways were not so uncommon, you read about them in the paper, but *silence.* That was another thing. How could one tell what silence meant? She knew silence when she was alone in the apartment, but it was not a deep silence so much as an omission, and besides she played records and the radio, watched television, talked on the phone a lot. Only sometimes after she had gone to bed could she hear the stillness of something absent. It was never the same when Arthur slept there. Perhaps Aunt Celia was playing out, as a mime might, what she felt about Gershom's absence. As Miriam set the table just on the other side of a dividing counter, she heard the word *absent* ring over in her ears — *absent . . . absent . . . absent* — like an echo.

Arthur had come in and had been watching her for a few minutes before she noticed him.

"You're lost in thought, beautiful," he said gaily. "Didn't think you were going to come to." He kissed the top of his finger and put it on her nose, a gesture she usually found endearing.

She made an effort at laughter but it wouldn't come out, and thought to turn it to a joke but could think of none, so tried honesty. "I guess my family is on my mind. I had lunch with my mother today, and I'm just unhappy about how things are going."

Arthur sat down in his place as she put out the wineglasses. "Is the boy still gone?" he asked.

"Yes, and my aunt is still silent."

"Strange lady. Sounds like she needs a shrink."

Miriam, wearing red and gold oven mitts on her hands, was bringing the sizzling pork chops to the table on a white platter. "I don't know if that would help. My mother thinks my uncle shouldn't 'indulge' her, as if he could bully her into talking. He's such a sweetie. He's the one suffering doubly. In a way he's lost both his son and his wife. My mother just compounds the situation by washing her hands of the whole thing and leaving the job of caring for Celia to Aunt Leah and my grandmother who's not able to do much and is, well, in some ways, tough like my mother."

She brought the plates with broccoli cooked perfectly, a bright green, topped with the yellow sauce flowing over it. On each plate she put a brown potato.

"Aunt Leah's still going every day, huh? That's sisterly devotion. I can't imagine one of my sisters doing anything like that." His sisters were well-known Los Angeles socialites he didn't see too often.

She sat down at the table as Arthur got up to get a bottle of red wine from the small wine rack in one of the lower kitchen cabinets. Miriam actually felt tears trip over her bottom lids, her hand propping her chin. She felt them roll down her cheeks and fall on the table as a second set began.

"I feel terrible," she said stuffily. "My mother is politely vicious about Leah, accuses her of all sorts of ulterior motives, and she probably thinks worse things than she says. My poor Uncle Sam has to go on with his drab life, even drabber than ever. My cousin obviously must have hurt a hell of a lot inside to have run off like this, and I never knew or did anything to help him. I've been so wrapped up in my own life. God knows what's been happening to him."

"And He won't tell," said Arthur, who had been sympathetically thumping her back.

"And then at lunch my mother, going over old complaints she likes to drag out when occasions like this arise, told me about how she and my father came to get married when they did, or maybe to get married at all. She wanted to make sure my Aunt Leah didn't have the glory of getting married first. Well, she didn't put it quite that way, but that's what I think it meant. When Leah and Harry got engaged, she accepted my father and insisted they get married right away, before Harry and Leah anyway, who had to wait till Harry graduated. I had this funny feeling as she was telling me about it, that she would never have married Daddy if marrying him hadn't given her that opportunity."

Arthur's hand passed over the back of her head in a paternal gesture. He laughed slightly and coughed. "Well, puss, most people get married for reasons no better than that. Are you shocked?"

"No," she said, her breath catching, and she wasn't. "It's just that Harry and Leah have always rankled my mother, and she claims my father would have done better without Harry's legal advice all these years, which he took because it came free. I don't know why it bothers me so." She wanted to go on, but stopped, feeling Arthur's hand stationary, waiting for her. "Sit down," she said.

He moved to his seat and poured the wine. "You know marriage is just an arrangement between two parties, like a contract, and even when it starts out with lots of feeling it gets routine after a while."

Miriam took her fork and began to eat the broccoli. "Doesn't everything?" she said. "Somehow I once thought people's relationships changed because the people changed, not just because they got locked into some sort of two-step. I guess I was pretty naive to have believed that."

"Maybe so," he said. "But some relationships are better than others. Let's drink to ours." He lifted his wineglass.

She clinked hers against his half-heartedly, and said, after a sip, "Why did you marry Eileen?"

His eyes opened wide, amazed; then he smiled broadly, his forehead wrinkling up into his bald U.

"It was a typical fifties marriage. She gave me her virgin body, quite willingly I might add, and then made it clear she was ruined for anyone else. She was a cute kid and not as snotty as my sisters, who couldn't stand the sight of a Roman Catholic, let alone a Jew or black. I thought, 'Why not? She's as good as the next.' "

Miriam rubbed the rim of her wineglass with one finger. "Oh."

They both ate for a few minutes in silence, Miriam feeling the swell of stillness closing over her, swelling like her Aunt Celia's silence.

"I can't help wondering about Gershom," she said. "I wonder where he went, or if he'll come back."

She was not looking at Arthur but she felt the vibration of his annoyance as he shifted in his chair. "Let's make a deal," he said. "Let's put your family in the freezer for the moment. I know they're on your mind, but we can talk about something else for a while and you'll feel better."

She nodded without looking at him.

"Are you going to do both the magazine copy and layout for Rose Blush?"

She could hardly remember what he was talking about for a few seconds, but they soon drifted into a cosmetic conversation and it drew them through dinner, the seven-layer cake, the coffee, and into bed, which Arthur said was the only sensible place to be at eight-thirty.

At nine-thirty he was naked, sitting at the edge of the bed and smoking a cigarette, while he fondly stroked her shoulders and breasts with his free hand, when his phone, which he had just replaced on the hook, rang. It was the extension of the one now ringing in his own empty intown apartment.

"Can't answer it yet," he said, smiling, though he was sitting right next to it. "Three rings so she won't think I'm hanging on the phone for her call." Miriam got up from the bed as on the third ring Arthur picked up the receiver. "Hello?"

She tiptoed out as she heard him say, "Hi, honey," in a lively earnest tone. "Is it snowing in Connecticut? How are the kids?"

Standing in the bathroom, she could hear his voice, though not each word, rumbling, the rhythms familiar and friendly, and she looked at herself in the mirror, noting her eye make-up was smudged and her hair tangled. She took her robe from the back of the bathroom door and slipped it over her head, its synthetic softness falling in folds over her breasts and hips. Her head emerged and she closed the door, took a bottle of cold cream and cleaned her face. Then she ran the warm water and washed, dried her face, and looked at herself again. She wrinkled her nose and squinted. "Who the hell are you?" she said to the reflection.

She quietly opened the bathroom door, and hearing Arthur's voice still rising and falling in a pleasant male roughness, she went to the kitchen where her own phone was located, and dialed a number. Sitting on a step-stool, she leaned her head, hair uncombed, back against the refrigerator as the phone ringing on the other end graveled signals to her.

"Hello?"

"Uncle Sam, hello."

"Miriam! How are you?"

"Fine. How are things with you?"

"The same. Aunt Celia seems to be well. She keeps the house in order, reads a bit, and while I go to school Aunt Leah takes her for walks, goes shopping at the market. But things are the same."

"No word from Gershom?"

There was a pause. On the other end of the phone, she could hear Sam's breathing, even and heavy. "No," he said. Then: "Grandma was here today and we were talking about you."

"Why me?" Despite herself, Miriam began to grin, an affectionate vision of her spectacled grandmother, her feet swaddled in shapeless shoes, passing her inner eye.

"Grandma is proud to have her granddaughters working at their own professions. She thinks your job is a good one, and she was boasting about it."

Miriam's inner and outer eyes fogged. I'm getting sentimental in my old age, she thought and pinched the bridge of her nose, placing her thumb and forefinger in the corners of her eyes. She heard her uncle go on. "She asks herself all sorts of questions now, more modern than some younger mothers, about Celia and whether she has something to do with this . . ." He did not finish the sentence, which hung in the air like a balloon on a stick, quivering.

Miriam moved her voice to the edge of the fence containing her thoughts. "Does Grandma think this" (again it remained unspoken) "has anything to do with anything but Gershom's going away?"

He cleared his throat, and spoke softly into the phone. "Miriam, you are a young woman now and surely you must know our deeds hang one on the other like grapes in a cluster. If he comes back, please God, she might (I say 'might,' I don't know for sure) greet him as Lear spoke to Cordelia: 'When thou dost ask me blessing, I'll kneel down and ask of thee forgiveness.' *I* might say that. Your grandmother says that, I think, to Celia herself. When Freud gave children the right to be angry, he neglected the suffering of the guilty parent who tries to say at some point, 'My child, you are responsible for your own life,' but always wonders, 'What should I, could I, have done differently?' It's not easy."

"No," she shut her eyes tightly, patterns of whirling geometric forms flashing against her closed lids. "May I come to see you this Saturday?"

"Of course," he sounded ebullient. "Please, please."

"All right. I'll be there and bring lunch for you both." She waited, then breathlessly said, "Give Aunt Celia a kiss for me. I love you."

"Love is a *mitzvah*," he said, and she came forward from the refrigerator abruptly. "A good one to follow. We love you too."

"Yes. Goodnight, Uncle Sam."

"Goodnight."

She hung up the phone to see that Arthur had come into the living room wearing his robe, and had propped his feet on the glass coffee table before her couch. "Oh, puss, come here. Who were you talking to?"

"My uncle."

He raised his eyebrows with a twinkle, then said, "Let's have a brandy," and she knew she was not being invited to go on.

She brought two snifters to the coffee table and filled them with topaz-colored liquid from a decanter that he had brought from his apartment. They sat silently, each cupping a glass with curved palms.

"Come on, Miriam," he said after a minute. "You are usually such a light, happy girl. I've just spent half an hour listening to the most picayune details about Bart's college applications and Bruce's plans for the summer to go to some whitewater canoe camp that his religious friend goes to. Eileen's all upset about it. I just want to enjoy all that's right with us."

"All's right," she said and smiled a tentative smile, not sure what wasn't right.

They turned on the television and watched through the eleven o'clock news, one lurid death in the city morgued above another, and after the weather Arthur began to kiss her hungrily like a teen-age boy sitting in the movies with his girl. With his arm around her neck, he began to unzip her robe, and reached his hand in down toward her breasts. She suddenly withdrew from his grasp and stood up.

"I'm not in the mood now, Arthur. Couldn't we just go to sleep?"

He took her hands in his and kissed them. "You sound like an old married woman, beautiful. It's not like you. Maybe we should take a shower together." He chucked her chin up and kissed her neck. "That will put you in the mood."

She knew it was a battle she did not want to win, and turning off the set, obediently followed him to the bathroom, wondering as she went whether he could lather out her pain.

*   *   *

Later, Arthur lying snoring in the bed beside her, she lay awake contemplating the pale shadows on the ceiling cast by the streetlight glow four stories below through a crack between the drapes. They moved as the drapes stirred in a cold breeze, as shadows in dark seas mysteriously break before the diver's eyes. As silently as she could, she rolled on her right side and rose from the bed, tiptoeing through the dark again to the bathroom for her robe, and out to the living room, where windows, facing the same side street her bedroom windows faced, undraped, exposed a dark whiteness. The cold of the day, bitter and bone-aching, had turned to snow that fell shifting, illuminated from below, a single lighted window in the building across the street framing the fall. She pulled the sling-back chair toward the windows, and sat down facing them, staring into the luminous dark. Within the walls of the room there was the presence of something she recognized as *nothing*, and within her own walls, her flesh, absence. She sat watching the snow fall, feeling swollen with absence, absence, but she could not have said of what or whom.

5

Sunday, March 18, 1973
PUBLIC NOTICES

Gershom — No change. Miriam with your folks
Saturdays. Mr. Toledano still concerned. Miss
you. — Johanna.

A LTHOUGH LEAH was sure Harry would not like her absence at dinner, she had agreed to stay late this Tuesday so Sam could attend a late teachers' meeting. It was after nine-thirty. The electric clock over the refrigerator spun its second hand soundlessly. The evening television had been turned off, and Celia was already in her robe.

Leah took rubbing alcohol and poured it onto a small rag, part of an old undershirt, and rubbed viciously at the blue stain, food coloring that had transferred off a supermarket price sticker to the Formica in Celia's kitchen. The blue faded reluctantly under Leah's abrasive hand. She turned to her sister sitting in a chair against the wall and smiled.

"See, I told you the alcohol would take it out without ruining the finish. Emma taught me to do that. Once in a while she has something useful to offer."

Celia said nothing.

"Are the curlers all right? I didn't make them too tight, did I?" She walked over and smoothed the back of Celia's head with her hand. "Well, dear," she said, "Sam's meeting should be over and he'll be home soon. If he wants a snack later, there's cold lamb in the refrigerator. I'm sure you'll find it."

She dabbed at a smudge on the stove with a large gold sponge. "Did I tell you Harry had a meeting tonight too? Very convenient, really. He had some sort of conference with the president of the district Democratic Club and several district leaders. He's always up to something with them. Not that I'm sorry." She stood back and squinted at the smudge, then attacked it again with the sponge. "Men like Harry are needed just to keep government responsible. He has such integrity, and when I think how demoralized we all are by what's going on in Washington, I realize he could make a valuable contribution, but at the same time I feel he has so little time for himself, and this attraction for public life is sapping a lot of his energy, to say nothing of just hours . . ."

Celia stared straight ahead, her palms curved at her sides.

Leah giggled girlishly. "Do you remember Mamma yelling that Papa spent too many evenings at the theater? 'He doesn't have time for anything but his precious English.' She didn't mind the Yiddish theater though."

The sound of Sam's key in the lock and the door opening silenced Leah. Celia stirred though she did not stand.

"I'm glad you're home." Leah came toward Sam in the hall. "But please, dear, don't take off your coat. I want you to take me down to get a cab. I'll be ready in a minute."

Sam merely moved his head in Celia's direction with a questioning expression. Leah shook her head and lowered her eyes.

He nodded. Walking around to the kitchen, he said loudly, "Hello, darling. I brought you a little box of peanut brittle. I know you like it." He pulled out a white unlabeled box from the pocket of his rubbed brown tweed coat, and put it on the table before her. She did not touch it. He opened the box, took out a piece and put it in her hand. She raised it to her lips and sucked it like a child.

Leah, back, her camel-colored coat with a thick black fur collar neatly belted, her black fur hat crowning her head, said to Celia, "I have to go now, Ceil. Sam's just going to take me down to get a cab. He'll be back in a minute, and I'll be here tomorrow." She blew a kiss from the doorway.

In the elevator, Sam rubbed his hand over his chin, which was sprouting a white stubble. "Thank you," he said. "Thank you again. The union meeting was all about safety precautions for the teachers. Everybody should stay in pairs — no one alone in the halls, or in the offices. Not even in the toilet. What a mess when you have to live in dread of your students." He turned to leave the elevator. "One child threatened to blind another with a penknife today. Terrible!" They went through the lobby toward the street.

"I wish you could be assigned to a less dangerous school," said Leah. "God forbid something should happen to you, and where would Celia be?"

"Nothing will happen," said Sam. "Did she eat today?"

"As usual: not a lot, but enough."

"Miriam brings up delicatessen on Saturdays. You should see how she eats then, my poor girl." He sighed heavily.

"You're a saint, Sam," said Leah.

Sam shook his head. They saw a cab coming with its numbered yellow light on. He ran toward the curb to hail it. "If Gershom comes back, I'll have to learn about being a saint."

"Don't even mention him," said Leah, about to get in the cab. "If he doesn't want any part of us, we certainly don't need him. Just take care of yourself and Celia." She got into the cab, and leaned toward him from the seat. "Just take care of yourselves. You don't owe him a thing."

Sam didn't answer. He slammed the cab door and waved wanly at her. And then the cab moved away.

*   *   *

Before opening the apartment door, Leah took out her sculpted gold compact and a lipstick. Under the hall light, she carefully traced a deeper red along her lips, pressed them together, and squinted her eyes to catch an impressionistic view of her image in the compact mirror. She snapped the compact closed like a castanet.

As she opened the door with her key, she could hear voices humming in the den, a throaty woman's laugh rising above the other sounds. She closed the door softly and, without taking off her coat and hat, walked across the living room to the den door. Inside, Harry was serving drinks to seven people of whom only Edward Gregor, the district club president, was someone she knew. Edward always looked like a young man about Washington, though he was a New York stockbroker with thinning blond hair. His charcoal gray suit was impeccable, the jacket buttoned even at this late hour, and his smile always displayed even, polished teeth. The other three men were less fastidious; one, wearing jeans and a Scandinavian ski sweater, stood next to Edward Gregor and punched his arm for emphasis as he spoke. Two of the women were young with loose long hair and expansive gestures. The older woman was perhaps forty-five and wore her hair in a Dutch-boy, curled under slightly, a few streaks of natural gray, highlighted by a frosted streak across the top. Her voice was the throaty one and she kept her hands tightly clasped around her glass as she talked.

Leah stood in the doorway, taking them all in for several seconds before Harry saw her. He beamed and came to lead her in, helping her off with her coat, which he put carelessly across the back of an unoccupied chair. "I'm so glad you're here. I'd like you to meet these people." He turned. "My wife." He introduced them all to her, their names mosaically fitting in the puzzle Leah kept in her head labeled "Politics." Except for Edward, and the older woman, Freda Ornstein, the female district leader, she had never heard of any of them before. Harry looked radiant, she thought, actually youthful. "These people" clearly pleased him and he moved among them like a lion in his pride.

One of the younger women, a girl called Sandra, leaned in her direction as conversation resumed and said, "Mrs. Seligman, this is such a beautiful apartment."

"Oh, thank you," said Leah, trying to determine the intent of the compliment. She looked the girl full in the face and noted she smiled back openly.

"Harry showed us some of your magnificent paintings when we came up, and tells me you selected them. I'm really impressed with your choices."

Leah smiled stiffly. "Mr. Seligman helped choose them too," she said. "He has an excellent eye for art."

"Leah, dear," said Harry, his voice jocular and unfamiliar, "would you like a nightcap?"

"Just some brandy," she said, and when he gave it to her, she merely swished it around in the snifter enjoying the warm, pungent smell.

She and Sandra continued a little private conversation which she followed obliquely, responding only to key words as she struggled at the same time to make out what the others were talking about. Against the curtain of loosely woven words — "strategy," "canvass" — she learned that Sandra came from Portland, Maine, and had been an art history major at college. She was working as an editor at a publishing house that specialized in art books, but, she confided, "politics is getting to be more and more my main interest. It's *people.* Art is so abstract, no pun intended."

The men were laughing, the other young woman got up and patted Harry's arm affectionately after he made a disparaging joke about political turncoats apparently aimed at the mayor, and now Freda Ornstein's laugh sounded loudly, a baffleboard for their conversation. Then Edward stood up and said, "People, it's time we let the Seligmans go to bed. Harry, we thank you. Mrs. Seligman, your husband is a fine fellow and we all appreciate him."

"Hear! Hear!" said Freda Ornstein, holding up her glass.

"To future successes." The others murmured and lifted their glasses, most of them empty.

Leah moved toward Harry tentatively, her warning system on full alert. Whatever Harry was a part of must include her and she beamed at their guests, her eyes shining.

They all moved toward Harry, the men shaking his hand, the women delivering chaste kisses on his cheek. Sandra clasped his arm and said, "Harry, this has been a wonderful evening. I can't tell you how much it has meant to me." She blushed as he gave her another peck, laughing in forced little puffs. "You're a dear, you're a dear."

Leah moved closer and extended her hand, almost between them, and said to Sandra, "I'm so glad we were able to get acquainted. I'd love for you to meet our daughter one day. You share many interests."

Sandra shifted and pumped Leah's hand enthusiastically. "Thank you for everything. It was just lovely to meet you." Her eyes glittered with an unstifled pleasure.

As the rest of the party gathered in the hall by the elevator, Edward Gregor stood at the door, exchanging a few whispered words with Harry. He finished and made a grand gesture in her direction. "Mrs. Seligman, we'll be seeing you soon, I'm sure." He straightened his velvet-collared coat and disappeared into the hall as Harry closed the door.

When he turned around he was smiling, his eyes crinkling at the corners, and he rubbed his hands together in a gesture Leah recognized as delight. His voice was trembling slightly.

"Leah, darling. They are pretty sure they want me to run for Congress in 'seventy-four. Of course, there will have to be a primary first, though maybe not — the old guard seem to have given up on this district — but what with the strange goings on in Washington, despite Nixon's big win, and the fact that I'm fairly well known in the other Assembly districts, 'A name to be reckoned with,' Freda says, I have a very good chance of winning."

He was so excited, he hardly looked at Leah. She rocked slightly on her heels and then went toward him with her arms out. "Harry, I'm so proud they want you, and I know you deserve everything." She hugged him and felt his arms go around her with an old affection, something they carried from their youth like a jewel. Then she drew back.

"Will this involve a lot of activity now?"

"Some entertaining, of course. Nothing is definite yet, and I expect you and I will have to make a number of appearances at political gatherings. But the real push won't come till later. I would like to have at least one dinner party soon though with a few of the old notables. I'll make a list. Most of them are people we've met and been entertained by at fundraising parties." He spoke, pacing nervously in the living room, while Leah watched him without smiling.

"I can't now, Harry. I know you want this very much, and God knows I want you to have it. Nothing could give me greater pleasure than to see you recognized, but I can't do anything now."

He turned toward her, visibly surprised. "Why not?"

"Why not! You mean you don't know?"

"Your sister? You have another sister who could give a little service. Your mother could be left alone with her once in a while. We could even pay to have a nurse come in, if that's the issue."

Leah looked down at her hands.

"It's not just a question of who stays with her. It's the way this whole thing has affected me. I'm not up to entertaining an illustrious crowd just at the moment. Political life is very demanding, and I think, Harry, that perhaps you ought to ask yourself if, my problems aside, you really want to do this."

He stared at her. "I'm not hearing you right. Don't you realize I've been thinking about this opportunity for years?"

"Have you?" she said weakly.

"Look, I know you've been upset. It's quite understandable.

You're not just an ordinary sister. But let's be honest. Celia may stay the way she is for a long time. Has it occurred to you that Gershom may never come back?"

Leah closed her eyes and said nothing.

"I mean realistically now, he's been gone nearly three months, Johanna's been running ads for two months. Children disappear and never return — it's an old story. Are we going to have to tailor our lives to your sister's sickness for the next twenty years?"

"Until now, I haven't asked you to tailor anything."

"You're asking me now to give up something I want very much."

"I didn't know you had ambitions of this sort, but even if I did, even if I shared them, why should we have to start all this social business now? Couldn't it wait till the fall, till next winter?"

"Leah, I'm talking about one or two dinner parties and an occasional night at someone else's affair. You wouldn't even have to come to all of those."

"I'm sure," said Leah.

"What do you mean by *that?*"

"I'm sure some of the ladies I met tonight would be glad to go with you."

"Leah, you're out of your mind. Those women are club workers, members of the executive board. I don't think the girls are as old as Johanna."

"Your daughter," said Leah.

"And Freda Ornstein is . . . This is outrageous. Let's drop the subject. Are you going to flatly refuse to do these things for me?"

Leah paused, her breath shallow. Then, "Maybe you should consider whether it's really necessary — even if you do run eventually. What if Celia's problem existed in your family?"

"It wouldn't," said Harry. "My family has a little self-restraint."

"It's bloodless, that's why."

"It's not hysterical, that's why. God damn! Your sister torments her son until he quite sensibly decides not to take it anymore, and then she punishes everyone else in his place. She's manipulating you and your pity, don't you see?"

"What would you do if your daughter disappeared?"

"*If* she did, I certainly wouldn't impose my problem on everyone I knew, and if you acted like Celia, it would be off to a mental home you'd go."

"Gabriel says a home would be damaging to her."

"Gabriel is something of a nut himself, if you'll forgive me. He's just telling Sam what passive old Sam wants to hear."

"Sam is a decent, patient, loving man."

"Sam is a jerk, a nice jerk, who lets life wash over him, who is so used to being abused he doesn't even know what's happening to him. You don't think a different man would have gotten a different job, stopped his wife from carrying on like a maniac about him and his son years ago? You know, it's a very subtle sort of put-down she does of him: 'Bernard Katzman wasn't nearly the man Sam was, and look at him. Tch! Tch!' " His voice was falsetto. "I like Sam, but he's a jerk."

Leah's face had become quite red. Under her make-up blotches, pink patches, began to appear, moving in a line up her forehead. She struggled to compose her face.

"I'm not going to defend Sam, although he deserves it, but I think it's some sign of your feelings about me that you can't even imagine keeping me around if I were mentally disturbed."

"What do you want from me, Leah? We have to live our lives. I've been very understanding until now of the days there, the early morning hours, the endless, absolutely endless telephone conversations, but I'm not willing to sacrifice my own life, or my wife indefinitely."

"How would you run if I dropped dead?"

"Differently, you can be sure, but then it wouldn't matter if those doe-eyed young girls looked at me with interest, would it?"

Leah clapped her hand over her mouth and looked at him through narrowed eyes. Then without another word she went to the bedroom and locked the door. Inside, she gathered his pajamas, robe, clean underwear, socks, a blue and gray striped shirt against which she held a handsome gray, blue and red paisley tie, his toothbrush and hairbrush from the bathroom, and his slippers. At the door, she listened for a moment. Hearing nothing, she opened it and put the little pile neatly outside in the hall, then locked the door again and sat down on the bed, deciding it was too late to call her daughter. She ran her hand over the fine satin of their bedspread and began to cry softly — exasperated tears.

In the morning, she prepared his breakfast without speaking, and when he finally broke the silence saying, "Do you suppose we can discuss this matter more rationally this evening?" she nodded, stiffly, drawing her lips together as though in pain.

That evening, he brought home a basket of flowers: daffodils and irises with a few lilies of the valley, delicately arranged in a wicker shell. He held it out to Leah, who took the bouquet and looked at him questioningly.

"A gift," he said, and turned to hang up his coat.

She reached around and kissed his back, and briefly they held each other. Over the dinner table and above the basket of spring blooms they talked insignificantly about their day.

"I know Celia is not an easy person to be with, even when she's talking," said Harry after Leah's account had finished. "You've really been marvelous. I just wonder though, now that it seems clear she may be like this for a long time, if you can't consider making some other arrangement for her."

"Sam can afford nothing," said Leah petulantly. "What's more, I don't feel that I would trust some stranger to take care of her properly."

"Leah, are you willing to let her craziness rule your life, to make you crazy with her?"

"I know you want my attention, Harry, and I normally love to give it to you. You know that. Nothing gives me more pleasure than your pleasure, but I ask you this one time to put me first."

He put his forehead on his fist above an elbow propped against the table and closed his eyes.

"I'm not asking you to forget the whole thing," she said, her voice higher pitched than before, "but I don't feel able just now to be a charming hostess for people who are prominent, perhaps, but not really friends and never will be. I hate having to smile sweetly at a lot of coarse men I really want nothing to do with, but I would do it for you at any other time."

He did not open his eyes, or move when he spoke. "You're turning a minor matter into a federal case. Elise prepares dinner anyway. You're home weekends. You would have to make the most superficial noises toward some rather interesting people on one or two Saturday nights, and you're acting as if I'm asking you to do some obscene thing with them."

"Harry, you are disgusting. What have I said to suggest anything like that? Just consider my position."

"You just consider mine," he said. "Am I to understand you're not willing to socialize at all with my political associates?"

"Perhaps in a few months, but not now." Her lower lip and chin quivered like a child's.

He stood up, his face dark, and his back unnaturally straight. "Your family has held you by the throat as long as I've known you. I've asked myself over and over why a grown woman would feel it necessary to call her mother and sisters daily, or why she would want to involve her daughter in the same insanity."

"We are not discussing Johanna!" Leah's voice hardened.

"No, we're discussing *you*, and you say you want to be put

first. You're always complaining that no one puts you first, sometimes at the very moment you're insisting on devoting yourself to them whether they want your services or not. Here you have a chance to put yourself first instead of being absorbed into a psychotic's illness."

"So, I should change her psychosis for yours? I should imagine myself at Washington dinner parties again? I had a taste of that scene when Johanna was a baby."

"Good grief, I was a lawyer doing government work during the war. That's a different ball game, Leah." He was standing by her now. "Will you talk about this reasonably? If we postpone the social activities as long as possible to still let me assure myself the nomination, will you be willing to campaign with me, or even not to campaign, but to accept my winning, if I win, and my running whether or not I win?"

"I'm not sure."

"Why?"

"Well for one thing, you have given no consideration to my feelings, never asked what I felt before you made this decision."

"What do you think I'm doing now?"

"I think you're coming to me with a fait accompli, something you've cooked up with those shiny-teethed jet-setters in that fashionable political club, and that you have never discussed before with your family."

"I've discussed it at length with my brother."

Leah raised her chin belligerently. "And, of course, Belden never said 'Consult your wife,' did he?"

"No, he didn't."

"Have you talked to anyone else before me?"

"You think Sam, or Seymour, or even dear brother Frank would be wise advisors? What is the matter with you, Leah? You want to be inside my skin. I shouldn't burp without your approval."

"What are you talking about, Harry?"

"Sometimes you aggravate me. It's always 'the family this,' and 'the family that,' but that's just your way of saying 'me, me, me.'"

"I can't believe you're speaking this way to me. You have been the center of my life — everyone else knows that, even if you don't."

"You're my *wife* with all the opportunities that come with it, including nodding to people and saying 'Harry comes first' when it suits you."

Their voices grew louder and Harry pounded on the table.

* * *

Seth and Johanna had just sat down to dinner with friends when the phone rang. Johanna answered and heard her mother's voice, heavy with significance, say, "Johanna, dear?" At eight-thirty on a Sunday night, most unusual! "Will you be home tomorrow afternoon?"

"Yes."

"Will Seth be there?"

"He's out recording tomorrow until five-thirty. He'll be back about six."

"I wanted to see you alone. How are you feeling?" She shifted tone so quickly, Johanna could hardly grasp it. She was newly pregnant and her mother had, for the past few days, roller-coastered between concern for Johanna's condition and distress with her own.

"Well. Come when you leave Aunt Celia."

"Can you talk?"

"Mommy, the Holseizers are here for dinner. I have moussaka in the oven about to be overdone, and everyone is waiting to begin."

"Oh, darling, forgive me. Go have a wonderful evening." Her voice became buoyant and artificially gay. "Have you talked to your father since he made his little announcement to you? Just tell me that."

"No. Have you suggested that he talk to me again?"

"I haven't suggested *anything* to him."

Johanna's heart began to pound. She said, "I'll talk to you tomorrow, all right?"

"All right. Give my love to everyone."

Click.

She stood in the kitchen, her heart racing, and closed her eyes.

As she brought plates with cold stuffed grape leaves to the table, she said, "My mother. I'm sorry." She thrust down the dishes, dropping a few grape leaves on the tablecloth. "I'm sorry I'm sorry. She makes me nervous sometimes."

"I become frantic when my mother calls," said Rita. "My whole personality changes. My voice gets high and I start talking in superlatives. Don't apologize."

"Well, I'm always a little that way but this is different," Johanna said. "I don't know why I feel so uncomfortable. Pregnancy lowers my emotional threshold, I guess. Usually, I feel as if I could get control of myself if I wanted, but this time . . . I guess the whole family mess has turned me to mush." She shuddered slightly, her shoulders curving.

"Have you heard from your cousin?" asked Oren.

"No, no. I think he's probably seen the ads, but . . ." She did not complete the thought.

"I'll tell you an odd thing about that," said Seth. "A teacher of his, at Columbia, has become very upset over his disappearance. He calls us regularly, comes over a lot. Mr. Toledano, a history professor about our age. We can't quite figure out his interest — Gershom had never mentioned him to us. Lately he's wanted us to take him to see Gershom's parents, although we've explained how they are . . ."

"And my mother is really against it, so we've put him off so far," said Johanna. She had stopped eating and put down her fork. "There must be something wrong with me. Here I am, past thirty, and most of the time all I can think about is what my mother wants or feels. Crazy!"

"These grape leaves are fabulous," said Rita.

"Oh, I'm glad you like them. It's all Greek tonight . . . Even a minor Greek tragedy for your entertainment and edification, *madame et messieurs*," she said with a slight smile and an ironic wave of her hand toward the telephone. But she did not join in their laughter.

* * *

At the sound of the doorbell on Monday afternoon, Johanna opened the door to see her mother standing in the hall holding a blue suitcase, her face tense as she tried to smile.

"Hello, darling." She leaned forward to kiss Johanna. "How are you? Tired?"

Johanna was still wearing her work smock, damp with clay she had been using. She merely accepted the kiss without returning it and pulled away. "Wet," she said as Leah looked hurt, and gestured toward her smock, a protective armor against something she felt was dangerous about this visit. Leah stepped inside the apartment, directly into an alcove off the living room which faced west, and was filled with the light of a dropping sun.

"It's my darling Rachel," said Leah, going to hug the child who was absorbed with figures on the television screen.

"Stand up, Rachel. Give Grandma a hug." Johanna heard her voice, though surely not her self, speaking to her daughter. She recognized the tone: one she hated, had quivered at in childhood and sworn never to use.

Rachel stood up and vaguely acknowledged her grandmother while keeping her eyes on the screen. "Oh, I'm disappointed. No big kiss?" said Leah with a performer's pout. Wearily, Rachel turned her head to kiss her, then sat down again. "Darling! She reminds me of you at her age. I had such fun with you!"

"Come on," said Johanna. "I'll make some tea."

"Seth isn't here?" said her mother brightly.

"I told you he wouldn't be."

Leah let down, the inflated quality of her arrival disappearing instantly. Her face, carefully made-up, aged. "I don't want to be exposed before my son-in-law," she said.

"He knows all about your differences with Daddy."

"Well, he'll have to, I suppose." Leah sat down at the kitchen table and stared at the blue and yellow plastic salt and pepper shakers, almost neon beside the brown ceramic sugar bowl. "I've decided to leave your father. Don't you think I should?"

Johanna did not move as she ran those words over through her mind like a slow-motion instant replay on a televised football game. She did not look at her mother even as she heard her saying, "Well, don't you?"

"Why are you asking me? You've decided to do it already, haven't you?" She leaned forward against the stove for support.

"Well, really yes. I just thought you might have something to offer about this."

"If I say I don't want you to do it (and I don't) you'll go back and in a few days tell me how awful everything is, but that you went back for me. Forget it."

Leah bit her lip. "Johanna, please don't scold me. May I stay here for a while? I could stay in your studio. I won't be any trouble. Days I go to Aunt Celia, and weekends and evenings, I can help you. Especially now that the baby is coming, you need help." She stopped as if in midsentence, more a plea than a statement.

Johanna could feel her nerves at the very surface of her skin. This scene had been a recurrent fantasy, one she had generally subdued with her optimism, a quality that led her to open herself to her mother's secret suffering again and again. She had struggled with her fears over much of the last week as her mother's anger had escalated over her father's proposed ambitions. Strange. Her father had told her about his opportunity in even, untroubled tones; it seemed quite reasonable, a logical outgrowth of his many years of law and politics, if anything a chance come a little late for he was in his middle fifties. Now, she felt impotent, unable to answer her mother, or even to turn, so she concentrated her attention on the kettle, and finally said, "Of course, if you want to stay for a while, it's all right. I think it's a bad idea, and I'm surprised you're so strongly set against something Daddy wants so much, but I understand your conflict. What else can I say? Is there anything?"

"What will Seth say?"

"That it's all right, I suppose."

"Do you really think this idea of your father's is reasonable?"

"Yes."

Leah shifted heavily in the chair and gazed at her daughter with rage. "Under the circumstances? I don't really talk about what it's like to spend days with that silent, beaten woman. I have not mentioned it, even, to any of our friends. It's just too painful."

"What do your friends think you do during the day?"

"Oh, they know I see her, that she's sick over that horrid son of hers, but they don't know about her silence. How could I explain it? We'll just say it's a family secret. Do you suppose you could look at me while we're talking?"

The tea was ready and provided her no more excuses. Johanna turned, choosing her words carefully.

"If you want to stay here, you should know that all our friends know just what's wrong with Aunt Celia. I don't want any pretending in this house."

"Well, you can do what you want with your friends, and I'll do what I want with mine. I would, however, prefer that you didn't mention that your father and I are separating." As she used this word, the weight of it oppressed her and she began to sob.

Johanna let out her breath with a loud puff.

"Mommy, what do you suppose I will *need* to say if you are

going to live in my studio? The fact will speak for itself." She watched her mother, whose make-up was beginning to run, her shoulders hunched over, asking for an arm to hug them, asking for protection. She felt her embraces restrained as by a straitjacket, years of attempts to comfort someone who could never be comforted properly, never loved enough. Inside, from the living room, she could hear the lilt of her daughter's television program singing, a rhythmic child's pattern, against which her mother sobbed irregularly. Johanna put down the teapot she was carrying and, fighting the restraint she saw could only offer her temporary protection, walked over to put her arms around her mother. She had barely touched her when Leah began to sob quite desperately. Johanna stroked her mother's hair but said nothing. Rachel came to the kitchen door and peered in.

"What's the matter with Grandma?"

Leah pulled herself from Johanna's embrace and reached toward Rachel, struggling to talk without her voice trembling. "Come here, my little love. Grandma's going to come and stay for a while with you. Won't that be nice?"

"Yes," said Rachel without much feeling. "Is Grandpa coming too?"

"Grandpa," her voice quavered precariously, "is too busy with his politics."

Johanna grasped Rachel's shoulders and turned her toward the television, where another show was beginning. "Look, Rachel, your favorite."

The child looked at the television screen from a distance with a vague curiosity. "It isn't," she said, looking up at Johanna, who said rather sternly, "You must go anyway. Grandma and I are talking." Rachel wandered back into the living room.

"Mother, she's only three years old. You must not involve her."

"How can you even suggest such a thing?" Leah recovered in her anger. "What kind of person do you think I am? In your eyes I'm always in the wrong. Would I do anything to hurt that child, whom I love more than life itself? Sometimes you really shock me, Johanna."

* * *

"Of course, by letting her stay here, it's going to look as if you're taking her part." Seth's voice was steady against the tremulous violin music from the stereo, as he and Johanna sat side by side on the couch, alone in the living room while Leah gave Rachel a bath. They had, the four of them, had an extraordinarily ordinary meal, talking of many things. Seth, having come from a day in a recording studio, described the electronic clutter. Leah, in her most exuberant voice, talked about plans to take Celia to the museums now that the weather was getting better; Rachel volunteered information about the nursery school gerbil; but Johanna said very little. Almost nothing. She was still quiet now when she and Seth were briefly free to consider what was happening to them.

"Johanna," he said, "I've never seen you so still. You do know you don't have to agree to this arrangement, don't you?"

"If you say no, she doesn't have to stay."

"Do you want me to be the one to make that decision?"

She looked straight ahead, but she could feel his eyes on her and imagine his curly light hair catching the glow of the lamp as he bent his head toward her.

"No," she said at last, "unless you have your own reasons."

"Well," he said, "I can think of lots of surprises I would have preferred coming home to. Having your mother-in-law move in with you is not considered an American ideal. And I do think she is altogether wrong, but she's your mother and if you want her here, I'm not going to make a fuss."

"I don't *want* her here." Johanna's oval face seemed almost a tear.

"But you're not able to say no."

"I'm not willing to say no."

"O.K.," said Seth. "I hope this separation is short, perhaps an evening. If she asks me, may I tell her what I think, or are we pretending I have no opinions?"

"That tone of voice makes me god damned mad, Seth." Her long hair swept along the sides of her cheeks.

He took her hand and kissed the palm. "I don't mean to make things worse for you, but you have to face up to the fact that you are going to have to explain to your father why you are willing to be a party to this battle, and *you* are going to have to live with her. Are you ready for that?"

"She says she doesn't want me to take sides."

"The hell she doesn't."

"You don't understand. She's come to me because she knows I'm safe and no matter what she says, I won't think ill of my father."

"Knows that!"

"Yes."

"She never seems to know you won't think ill of his 'old-German-Jews-but-no-character' family, or that she won't convince you the Silversteins are jealous because she was her father's favorite."

Johanna pressed her hands together. "You don't understand. She likes to believe because she loves me we share all the same feelings even when it's perfectly obvious we don't." The lines on her face hardened. "It's wicked, I know, but sometimes I really understand Gershom running. I felt like running a thousand times when I was younger. Sometimes I think the real reason I got married was to escape in a respectable kind of way, even though I loved you. We were lucky. It could have been a disaster."

"Never," said Seth, and he kissed her hand again. "Well, you may have to learn how to say no if she stays a while. Not to run, but to stand your ground and say no."

"How do you say no to a whirlpool? Well." Johanna sat up straight. "I've got to think about Daddy now. I think I ought to call him."

"Ever the negotiator."

She looked at him squarely. He was smiling, and with a fist, gently prodded her chin. She longed to be able to throw him one of her mother's wounded glances, the kind of withering hurt look that had charged her guilt so many times, but all she could do was nod in recognition of herself.

"Always," she said.

The downstairs bell rang and Seth started to laugh. "If it's your dad, and he's come to carry her off, that will make her happy." He got up and went to the house phone. "Yes?"

"Raphael Toledano," the voice over the intercom rang in the room.

Seth raised his eyebrows and ticked the buzzer. He turned toward Johanna and shrugged with an exaggerated lift of his shoulders. Johanna shook her head slightly, looking away.

"What could I do?" Seth whispered.

"Nothing," she said. "It's all right." She got up and went to the bathroom where her mother had Rachel wrapped in a large green towel and was combing the child's damp curls with her own tortoiseshell comb.

"Aren't we nice and fresh?" said Leah.

"Mother, Mr. Toledano is on his way up. I just thought you ought to know."

Leah removed the comb from Rachel's fine light hair and thrust it in her own, turning her head to catch a look at herself in the medicine chest mirror.

"Maybe you want to call Daddy before you come out and meet him."

"No," said Leah. "He knows where I am. I left a note. I'll go get Rachel ready for bed. Come on, sweetheart." She walked out of the bathroom, leading Rachel, as the front doorbell dimly rang.

By the time Johanna reached the living room, Seth was taking a dark blue toggled coat from a slight man with a neatly trimmed black beard and a full head of curly black hair. He was very thin and wore blue jeans that seemed suspended on his hips, a wide hand-tooled brown belt, and a rust-colored turtleneck. His face was very gentle, and he smiled with a childlike openness, his eyes lighting as he caught Johanna's hand.

"Forgive me, I'm always doing this to you. I just was passing by, and I thought I would drop in to see if you had heard from Gershom."

Johanna shook her head.

He put her hand down, the light in his eyes fading. "Oh, I feel terrible." He seemed momentarily lost in thought. Then he looked up. "How are his parents? Is his mother talking yet?"

"No," said Seth, coming behind him. "She's closed."

"And the father? He's still doing all right?"

Johanna gestured for him to sit down and they all took seats a little stiffly.

"My Uncle Sam is an unusual man. He's very enduring."

"He's not so unusual," said Seth, "but he has a lot of love in him and that keeps him going."

Mr. Toledano stared at the floor and passed a very pink tongue between his lips from one corner of his mouth to the other. For a few seconds they listened to the rich violin, still a low background. "I think about them very often," he said. "Gershom was, is, such a fine kid, but so inside himself. I keep asking myself if I couldn't have done something." He looked up suddenly, wide-eyed, first at Johanna, then at Seth. "I suppose it may seem strange to you, but you know Gershom reminded me of myself at his age. Sometimes he would say something in class, you know, really perceptive, but then he would never follow up on it, never argue his side to the end."

"Have you ever had a student disappear before?" asked Seth tentatively.

"No, not that I know anyway," he said and smiled a crooked little smile, "but I'm an expert at disappearing myself."

At that moment, Leah arrived with Rachel in a pink and

white gingham quilted bathrobe, pink-flowered footed pajamas covering her tiny feet. Johanna stood up.

"Mr. Toledano, this is my mother, Mrs. Seligman. You remember I told you about Gershom's teacher." She gestured in his direction. He got up and walked over to Leah, his hand extended.

"How do you do?" They shook hands. He looked down at Rachel and smiled widely. "And how do you do, Miss Rachel?"

"Nicely," said Rachel and they all laughed.

"I'll put her to bed, Mother," said Johanna. "Sit down." After a minute of elaborate goodnight rituals, Rachel was led off to bed, and as Johanna tucked her in she said, "Grandma is going to read the real *Peter Rabbit* to me tomorrow. She said."

Johanna felt the memory, briefly lifted, of her mother's reason for arrival fall over her again.

"Say your prayers, Rachel." She listened through a long list of "God blesses" and whispered "Amen" with Rachel at the end, kissed her several times and crept out. In the living room, she found Leah describing Celia's emotional state to Mr. Toledano in the most careful, compassionate terms, explaining that despite a nervous disposition, nothing in her past could have prepared them for this reaction. Sitting down, Johanna watched her mother with a familiar amazement that the tearful pained being of the late afternoon and this self-possessed cordial woman could be the same. Over and over, like a magician's stick with different colors on each side, her mother seemed able to shift character with the flick of a wrist.

Leah beamed at the young man. "Where are you from?"

"New York. Just down the street."

"No, I mean where is your family from. Have you always been a New Yorker?"

"I lived with my aunt in Springfield, Illinois, from age ten. Before that I was from Verona, Italy. You know, *Romeo and Juliet.*"

There was a brief lull in the conversation, a momentary

processing of data, but Leah, her voice sprightly in its obscured nervousness, asked, "What brought you to Springfield?"

"My aunt lived there already. It was after the war. She had tried to find out what happened to my family and discovered me. My history is short enough. My father was an engineer, Italian, working in Belgrade, Yugoslavia. When the war came and the Nazis started to round up Jews, I guess he may have hoped we would be safe because he had an Italian passport. Anyway, we were still in Belgrade in 1942, my parents and sisters and I, when the Nazis came to our place and my father ordered us to hide. I climbed out on the roof through the skylight and when they searched the apartment they found everybody but me. I hid among the chimneys and heard my mother tell the officers I had gone to Verona to be with my grandparents. I sat out on the roof until they were gone a long time, and then climbed down. I was six, but not an innocent American six, you know, and I knew my parents meant for me to go back to Verona, so I did. That is a story too, I won't bore you with it, but it took me many months, and when I got to Verona, I could not find my grandparents, nor any of my relatives, but a non-Jewish neighbor who had known my family took me to a convent near the center of the city and the nuns kept me through the war. After the war was over, my aunt managed to locate me and bring me to Illinois, where she was living. She had been what you might call a World War One war-bride, but her husband was dead by the time I came to live with her, and she worked as the manager of a dress shop. I was the only one left of all her family. My history." He stopped abruptly, as if this story so full of unanswered questions could only be left suspended, as they were, in the air.

"Like you," said Seth hoarsely, "I was a near miss, except that my family and I got out from Czechoslovakia together just in time."

Johanna stared at her husband. She had thought she knew his story as if it were her own, but now it was thrown into relief by the new tale, illuminated as if by a spotlight for the first time. She trembled slightly.

"Yes," said Mr. Toledano gently. "There are many stories. You were lucky you came with your family." He pushed his fingers through his thick dark hair until it stood on end.

Leah leaned forward, extending her hand toward him, as if to touch him. "Did you stay in Springfield?"

"Yes, till college. Then I went not far away, to Urbana to the University of Illinois, and then to Chicago to graduate school." The phone began to ring. "By then my aunt had died and I haven't been back."

Seth stood up to get the call.

"You like the city?" Leah, still salvaging.

"Yes. The university is a lot like Chicago and the tempo of the streets keeps me feeling alert, not always in a positive way, but alert."

Seth had come back and leaned over his mother-in-law's chair. "It's Harry, for you," he said softly.

Leah's face changed instantly, her eyelids lowering and her high color changing delicately. She excused herself with a nervous laugh and retreated to the extension in the bedroom. Seth hung up in the kitchen and came back. He sat down, then rose again to offer some sherry. Before he had finished, Leah reappeared.

"Daddy would like you to join our conversation," she said to Johanna and turned back down the hall.

Johanna looked desperately at Seth who raised his eyebrows but said nothing. She glanced at Mr. Toledano. In the presence of this stranger, she felt awkward. "Excuse me," she whispered and stepped inside the kitchen door to the phone.

When she lifted it, she heard her mother's voice, composed and formal, in midsentence, ". . . need some thinking time without me around. I left word with Elise that she's to continue to do everything as usual, so you'll be taken care of."

Her father exploded, shouting into the phone. "I don't like being strong-armed into anything. I don't even like the attempt. You must realize what an antagonistic act your little departure is."

"I'm not the only one capable of antagonistic acts," said Leah.

"And why the hell did you go to your daughter?"

"I'm here," said Johanna, but her father continued as if she had not said anything.

"You have a mother with a home big enough to accommodate you."

"I would have to travel in every day from Brooklyn. What's more, I'm not ready to discuss this matter with my mother — she's not always been my most ardent supporter."

Harry's voice was now so loud Johanna had to hold the earpiece away from her ear and his voice sounded into the room with the odd distortion of a voice on a short-wave radio. "So you've tried to enlist your daughter."

"No one's enlisted me," said Johanna softly.

"What in hell does she want from you? The kind of subservience you can't get from me? I tell you, Leah, that lunatic sister of yours has infected the whole family, as if they weren't loony enough already. Even Seymour. He came to see me today about his taxes and went on about Celia and how upset Emma is."

"I'd like to see some sign of *her* concern."

"I said, 'How come she can't come in once in a while?' but he got very defensive, said she couldn't." His voice had softened. "Leah, please come home. We'll work out the entertaining. It doesn't have to be this month, or next even. I want you to support me in this project. Won't you be reasonable? Consider the long-range picture."

"Perhaps," Leah said archly, "you should support me in my projects."

"Oh, good gods!"

"This isn't a permanent move, Harry. I just feel I ought to be out of your way now."

His voice became very flat, a sarcasm inflecting it. "So you said. All right. Take your time. You might do some thinking too, while you're away. Now, Johanna, I'd like to speak with you."

"Why, Harry?" asked Leah.

"She's *my* daughter too. You've had your turn. You have to hear my side of this, Johanna."

"Of course," said Johanna. Her jaw was so tense she could hardly speak.

Leah raised her voice. "Don't try to use her."

"You don't think she's being used already? Some daughters wouldn't have let you in, not that I would like her to be that kind."

"Please," said Johanna in a whisper so Mr. Toledano would not hear, "will you get off the phone, Mommy? I'd like to talk to Daddy alone."

Leah grunted, then, "All right. Goodnight, Harry. Don't forget your dental appointment on Wednesday afternoon." She hung up.

"Daddy," Johanna said, her heart pounding. "I'm sorry. I had no idea why Mommy was coming here today."

"Well, I don't want to make this situation more difficult for you. I don't think I'm the ogre she's painting me. I'm flabbergasted that she's unwilling to give me her help."

"You took her by surprise."

"Come on, Johanna. Were you surprised?"

"No," she smoothed her hair, which felt rough and knotted beneath her touch, and breathed in heavily. "Not at all."

"Do you think Aunt Celia is worth your mother's whole energies? More than I am?"

Johanna raised her foot over the floor, as though testing thin ice above a lake. "I think she identifies with Aunt Celia, and we could talk about the reasons some time, but I don't think she can help herself. I realize that puts you in an awful spot though and I can imagine how you feel."

"Well, since you're *so* objective, perhaps you'll be my hostess for a political dinner party, if your mother won't. Does your neutrality extend to that?" His annoyance pounded through the wire.

Johanna's throat prickled with dryness. She could feel every function of her body, it seemed: the blood coursing, digestion, the cells reproducing themselves. "If I must. Elise would help, I'm sure. I hope you won't need me though. Why don't you give Mommy a few days. I think she'll get over this."

"I wonder," said Harry. "She wants cities to fall at her word."

They said nothing, then Harry spoke again, calmly. "I'm not blaming you, honey, don't worry. I'll talk to you tomorrow. How's my bunny rabbit?" He meant Rachel.

"Fine."

"O.K."

"I love you both, Daddy. You know that, don't you?"

His voice was resigned. "I know. Goodnight."

"Goodnight," she said and hung up, her hand over her eyes. She drew her fingers together across her eyebrows, pinching the skin together, and went to rejoin the others in the living room where her mother was absorbed in listening to Seth and Mr. Toledano, who were having an intense discussion about America's role in World War Two.

By ten-thirty when Rafe left, he was no longer "Mr. Toledano," and they had agreed to take him to see Celia and Sam on the weekend.

"I hardly know myself what I can offer them," he had said, "but perhaps if they know that someone else shares their sense of loss, or at least regrets it, cares about it, maybe they won't feel so helpless."

Then shyly he had bowed his head and left.

Now, with Leah in her studio, a converted dining room entered through French doors from the living room, Johanna carefully lifted sketches that had been laid across the day bed, covered with an Indian throw, that her mother would sleep on. She emptied two drawers in a small unpainted dresser on top of which she piled the sketches, putting bottles of glazes, ceramics magazines, and sculpting tools on the end of her work table. Holding sheets and pillow case pressed to her breast, Leah watched Johanna move like a dancer as she touched her possessions with love — a lightness that lifted through the strange shapes, irregular vials and sticks, and radiated through the papers.

"I'm sorry to put you through this, darling," Leah said. "Can't I do anything to help?"

"No, I have to move everything myself to keep track of it. Here." She pulled back the throw. "I think it's ready, Mommy. Let's put the sheets on. You can put your clothes in these drawers, and hang anything in the front closet."

They began to move in a tired unison, fitting the sheets to the bed, Johanna bending and bobbing as Leah moved in steady waves at the bottom, until snug and tight, russet heavy wool blankets defined the bed and changed the aspect of the room. They sat down together, and Leah reached for Johanna's hand. Tears stood in her eyes like extra lenses before falling. "I'm sorry."

"I'm sorry too."

"You haven't done anything."

"No, I don't mean it that way." Johanna almost inadvertently pulled back her hand, as if she could slip from Leah's grip. She felt the corset of her girlhood settling over her, binding her chest and waist, a now expanding waist, as if the child she bore, the responsibilities of her adult life could be compressed into the shape of her early days when she and Leah had sat just so on the bed in her red and white room. She knew their bond was like a restraining garment to which her compliance gave form, and she felt her teeth begin to chatter as if she were cold, an old symptom.

"Do you really think your father is right?" Leah asked, snuffling, a baffled childish tone.

"I don't think it's a question of right or wrong. He wants to do something and you want to do something, and the two just don't mesh."

Leah straightened, preparing her defense. "I don't *want* to do what I'm doing. It isn't exactly a frivolous activity. If I knew what it meant, all that silence, maybe I would say, 'Let's get a nurse,' but can you just imagine some starchy I-don't-care-just-give-me-your-money caring enough to try to understand what's happening. Gabriel said it was a storm she was passing through. Well, storms can be very destructive. How can I let her be pulled apart? How can he ask me to let that happen? My other lousy sister tells me how upset she is, but doesn't come near Celia. I don't have much else to say for her daughter, but at least Miriam comes once in a while. And Mamma? Mamma comes and gives Celia lectures on how this could never have happened in a truly liberated household. Can you imagine what Celia makes of that? Frank might do something if he had the time, but he has the business and Mamma to look after. He's really a wonderful son!"

"I could go more often," said Johanna, "if I could take Rachel . . ."

Leah interrupted before she quite finished. "No, no. You have more than enough to do. No, the one who's left is yours truly." Her voice escalated as she spoke, a spiral of anger rising. "And it's not as if when I'm busy being the dutiful sister or the dutiful daughter, I'm not the dutiful wife."

"Don't forget the dutiful mother," said Johanna, her hands hanging helplessly between her legs.

"How can you be sarcastic to me!" Leah's face was brushed with pain, and she began to cry, using a ripped tissue to wipe her eyes.

Johanna reached over to pat her mother's back, stroking her from a distance, and wondering with pain if Rachel would one day want to keep her own preserve this way. "Look," she said, "I don't want to get between you and Daddy. Everything you've said is true, but he's not asking you to abandon Celia. He's only asking you to do the very sort of professional socializing you've always been delighted to do for him, except that this time it's not for his practice. I know you've never been wild about his political activities, but be honest. If he were suddenly to ask you to entertain some board chairman he wanted to represent, you would do it. Right now."

Leah looked up at her daughter from a bowed position. "Do you know those political people swarm about him like flies to honey — lapping young lawyers who want a nice contact, and women, young girls, younger than you, who pat his arm and laugh at everything he says whether it's amusing or not?" Her eyes were wide and sparkling with fight.

Johanna laughed. "You sound like a jealous wife."

"*No!*" shouted Leah. "Of course not jealous. I don't for a moment think there's the slightest danger of your father having a romance, if that's what you're suggesting. It's just that they flatter him to use him — all of them, and you watch him wear down through a campaign, tired out even if he is elected, which he probably will be, and they will suck what's left of him like the leeches they are."

"You sound like Aunt Celia." Johanna closed her eyes. "Look, Mommy, do as you want. You're welcome to stay if you feel you must, but I hope you'll go home and try to work this out with Daddy." She patted her mother's arm.

"My father was always doing just what he wanted without considering Mamma, but Mamma was the same way, a different kind of wife than I've been. I always felt I'd be with my husband, a helpmate, a companion, but that in return he'd consider me." She stared off for a minute. "No decrees from either party, that was the rule I started my marriage with. We would complement each other."

"And you have, mostly," said Johanna, but she knew her

mother's consideration to be a demand as shrill and strident as the fiercest revolutionary yell. Hollowed by her own polite deception, she stood up to leave. Her mother, suddenly looking frightened and older, stood too. They faced one another in the room lit softly by a single lamp and waited briefly as if their stand-off could express something they were incapable of saying. Leah put her arms out and Johanna could not escape. They embraced awkwardly, Johanna holding back to keep softness from enmeshing her. "My darling," whispered Leah, and Johanna, horrified, felt Gershom's feet stirring in her own, wanting to run from all the dear people in her life, the frail and the noble, her truly beloved, even from the child she carried in her womb, to run, to run and run.

6

Sunday, April 15, 1973
PUBLIC NOTICES

Gershom — Mr. Toledano comes regularly. With Folks next weekend while Miriam away. Other problems. — Johanna.

"You can't imagine how strange it was," said Miriam, rolling over on her stomach on the green-and-gold striped beach towel under the clear Caribbean sun. "He came in dressed in old jeans and a blue work shirt, not at all my idea of a Columbia professor. Right after he met me he went in and sat down near Aunt Celia, took her hand and said, 'Mother, little Mother,' in this funny kind of voice. Not Mother like she was really his mother, but like soldiers in a Russian movie I once saw called an old lady whose house they were staying in Mother. Then he sat with her, holding her hand and talking to her about Gershom, and what a good student he was. She watched him every minute, even nodded a little when he called her Mother."

Arthur was lying face up beside her, his eyes covered with reflecting sun goggles, his violet bathing trunks lower on his right hip than on his left. He rocked toward her as he spoke though his face was directed away. "Did he say anything to your uncle? I mean he sounds like an odd bird. *This* is what's educating our kids these days."

"Well, he *was* strange, but gentle too, and when he did talk to Uncle Sam they got into a big discussion about attitudes toward Communism in the nineteen thirties, the last thing you'd expect under the circumstances, and then they started to talk about what they called proletarian literature. It was like they were in another world. The truth is that I haven't seen my Uncle Sam that drawn into a conversation about anything but *the* topic since December."

"So they like this guy."

"Yes. So do I. He isn't like anyone I've ever met, vaguely foreign, delicate for a man, but I think he really did them good. Then there's another thing." She rolled on her side so that she was facing him. "I think my cousin Johanna has her own problems. No one has said, but I've got the distinct impression that her mother has moved in with her. It's hard to imagine that the family lovebirds, Leah and Harry, aren't making it together, but something funny is going on there."

Arthur didn't respond. She took a little sand, white and hot, and sprinkled it a few grains at a time on his shoulder, then leaned over to kiss the place. With his far hand, he reached across his chest and tousled her hair.

"I like you," she said.

They had come to St. Thomas two days before for a fleeting long weekend on clean warm beaches. Five days in a world where she could feel free to hold his hand in public and they could talk with other couples, or eye each other moonily and privately over wineglasses in restaurants. In the bar of their hotel, drinks of rum mixed with exotic fruit juices were served with orchids or hibiscus blossoms clipped to the lips of frosted glasses. The air in the bar was slightly perfumed, but so was the air outside. From a height, their room overlooked an expanse of turquoise water, white sand, and green and brown palms. In the evening they would sit on their balcony, watching the sun set in a brilliant display of neon pinks and rose. As she lay beside him now, hidden from general view by a dune and dimly aware of sailboats with striped sails passing in the water many yards from shore, a warm affection crept over her without warning, easing like a bandage over the dull sore that emptiness had worn in her over the last months. She could never remember another time when her laughter and sense of the absurd were unable to disguise, if not destroy, the nagging of introspection. But those qualities had failed her lately and, unaccustomed to feeling low, to asking questions of herself she could not answer, she had become weary with the effort of bubbling on for Arthur's satisfaction, and oddly relieved on weekends when he disappeared into Connecticut and she could discard her smiles. Just before this trip, he had insisted she go shopping, and she had returned with, among other things, a low-cut see-through dress fastened with wraparound ties. He had watched her model it braless, and said, "Every man in that hotel is going to get tight pants when you make the scene," and lunged at her, really quite hard, knocking her head against the wall as she fell to the couch. Of course he was sorry and awkwardly solicitous while she rubbed her head and laughed through tears that had smarted to her eyes from the pain. "Maybe I'd better take it back, if it's going to have that kind of effect," she said stuffily and then signaled him that she was better by lying down on the couch and holding out her arms.

He admired her; she never doubted that. And more than just the way her body looked, or the way she moved at one with him, when they were in bed. He admired the fact that she held a good job with a first-class advertising agency, and that she was free, as he put it, to be herself.

She had begun to wonder about that, however; not his belief in her freedom, which was grounded in the convictions that banter and a mild contempt exposed people's *real* feelings, and that total sobriety was at best an affectation, at worst self-indulgence, but whether in fact she was free at all. Sometimes lately she had looked at the copy she handled advertising some item — generally cosmetics or liquor — designed to cover things as they are, and felt a nagging despair. And then she had wondered in a quiet inarticulate way, as if she dared not put in words the uninvited thoughts she entertained, what she could expect from her future if she spent the present disguising things. Arthur and she lived, after all, in a shadowed world, but it was more than that she sensed standing between herself and her freedom — a veil she could not define.

"Well, puss," Arthur said, "I think we had better get out of the sun. I don't want to have to explain a peel to Eileen." In preparation for this trip he had been taking sunbaths at his club, to avoid suspicion when they returned.

Miriam smiled slightly and stood up, pulling at her red and pink bikini bottoms where they were cutting into her leg just below the seat. "It's time for lunch, anyway. Why don't we go change?"

He took the beach towels and tossed them in the cabana they had been assigned, red and blue striped, just on the other side of the dune, then came back and put his arm around her shoulders.

"You're a beauty, girl," he said. "I'm mighty proud," and he kissed her. She giggled and slipped her arm around his waist.

They started a slow walk back toward the hotel, carrying their beach jackets and singing together in the style of the steel drum calypso bands that entertained them each evening in the hotel. "We ought to get some records of that music to play back in the city," Arthur said.

"And I can dress up in my bikini and we can throw down a beach towel in the living room, pull over a potted plant and pretend we're back in the islands." She turned her head coyly at him, but felt only a dull grinding sensation in her neck.

"That's what I love about you," he said. "You're able to make any place you are into a paradise. That takes special talent . . and imagination."

"Do you?" she said vacantly.

"Do I what?"

"Do you love me?"

He started to laugh and hugged her. "Of course I do. You've made me damned happy, Miriam."

"How?"

He stood still and pushed her away, looking at her with amused surprise.

"Well first of all," he said trying to keep his voice gruff as a racing motor, "va va va voom," and made a gesture with his hands in the shape of a woman's body.

"Oh come on, I don't mean that. You wouldn't stick around all this time if I were just a good lay."

He passed his tongue between his teeth and paused as if composing what he was about to say, though Miriam knew that gesture as one of embarrassment. She waited.

"Look, puss, you are a bright interesting woman with a life of your own, and a lot of wit, and you keep me laughing. In addition, you *are* beautiful and a good lay." He waited for her reaction and when none came, he added, "I live a very pressured life most of the time, lots of responsibility, lots of money power — that makes a man lonely, you know, a pillar of the community, as it were, and with you I can relax. If I say something foolish you're not going to throw it up to me like my dear wife would. I feel I'm important to you without being needed as a crutch or used as a stepping stone. I don't know. What do you want me to say?"

"I don't know either," said Miriam. "That's good enough, I guess," though she thought it sounded like something out of a soap opera.

He looked at her, shading his eyes with his hand. "Something's eating you."

"Sometimes I feel empty, that's all. It's not your fault."

He smiled stiffly. "Here? Now? Maybe you're unwinding. You live a pressured life too, you know. I'm here and I want to help you unwind because I care about you." His smile had become more natural. He pulled her toward him, and she rocked forward on the balls of her feet as he kissed her hair.

"Lunch?" she said brightly. "Maybe that's why I'm empty."

*   *   *

That evening she wore her see-through dress to dinner in
the main restaurant of the hotel, and was ogled by most of the
men in the room, even by the bus boys and waiters. Although
she had been prepared to attract attention, the quality of those
looks and the unabashedly curious stares of the women actually embarrassed her, just as they excited Arthur, who suggested they go skinny-dipping after dinner in a little cove they
had discovered, out of view from the hotel and beach. When
they got there, however, three boys no older than fourteen
and a girl about the same age were already splashing in the
dark water. Arthur found a sheltered spot in the curve of the
low bank that rose gradually from the water, and they sat
down, propped against the wet sand, waiting.

"Good thing we stopped to change," said Miriam, running
her finger down the side of Arthur's trunks. It had been her
precaution, not his.

"Damned kids," he grumbled, "always in the wrong place.
My younger boy's about that age, and can he make a riot!"

"Do you like him?" Miriam spread her fingers before her
eyes like the ribs of a fan taking on the sheath of the moon
which hung, a pale egg yolk in the night sky.

"Sometimes. He's not a bad kid, all told. He's got that friend
now who's hot and heavy for his accepting Christ and I get a
lot of static about that from him and his mother, but he'll get
over this phase too, I suppose, just the way he got over wanting to be a professional football player. He was so fixed on
that he used to come to the dinner table with shoulder pads
on. Wanted to practice every spare minute. He's like that. His
brother is another kind, takes things in stride, lots of interests,
lots of friends, but everything in proportion. Bart'll be a hard-
working man who'll know how to enjoy himself. I can count
on him to do well at college but not knock himself out. I wish
my other kid would be as well rounded."

Miriam closed her fingers, closing out the moon, and pushed
the sand with her toe. "Do you want your boys to be like you
when they grow up?"

He laughed a cracked laugh and gestured toward the splashing foursome. "Mostly, I want the noise to calm down. I can't stand the racket. I hope they'll know how to make a good living."

"Marry?"

"Sure. If they want to." He took a shell protruding from the sand and moved it in soft lines along her back, where it felt cool and smooth.

"This place doesn't seem real," she said. "It's so beautiful and still. Even those kids seem magic, but I wonder. All the time these days I keep feeling that there's more to what's underneath than we ever let ourselves see — good and bad. Sometimes things look bad and under it all there's something substantial, while all the things we spend such a lot of time on, or even things like this place, that seem natural, cover up a lot of rot."

His forehead wrinkled. "My God, I'm hooked up with a philosopher. It's your serious side, Miriam, whatever's left of your Jewish blood that hasn't been diluted by life in the outer world." He lay back and looked at the moon, his skin grayish in its light.

"Why do you say that?" She didn't look at him.

"Why not? Oh, puss, you're so damned earnest. Where are you? I know you're a bright cookie but please don't try to see through surfaces. In the end, that's what we have to live with and if we concentrate too much on what's on the inside and not enough on what's on the outside, we've got a product nobody buys."

"Some nobodies," she said, "but not others."

"The nobodies who count."

She stared off for a long while, her arms around her knees.

"Can I tell you something?" Her voice was high and tremulous, childish to her own ears. "Something about my childhood?"

"Sure. Surface or underneath?"

"Good question." She sighed a little. "My mother always

wanted things to look nice, I mean not just pretty, but pleasant, and she had a way of twisting the truth so that things that
weren't pleasant came out sounding all right. She still does
that. Well, when I was about eight and my brother was twelve,
he had to write a family history for school because they were
doing a unit on immigration . . ." She paused and laughed
slightly. "If a teacher assigned that in your part of Connecticut, she might get some very old stories, Mayflower, etcetera,
but there in Queens in the early nineteen fifties practically
everybody had a grandparent who came from somewhere else.
Anyway, David went to my grandmother, my mother's mother,
and she's quite a character, I've told you. I really love her,
she's got so much spunk, though she's sometimes a little self-
righteous, and she told him this incredible story about how
much she had believed in the Bolshevik revolution and how
she wanted to stay in Russia to see it all come true, and how
she only came because, when her brother had come back to
Moscow with their passage already paid for, her sister wanted
to go. So she came to the United States dreaming of revolt
and made a lot of friends, communists who wrote Yiddish
tracts about it and plotted to return to Russia. Then she met
my grandfather, who had other ideas, and when they married, her friends drifted away from her. For a while she was
enthusiastic about the labor movement and then about the
suffragettes. And, of course, she was caught up in the family.
In her heart though, I think she has always remained a communist, at least her idea of a communist. Well, David wrote
this essay about all of that, about how sick she was crossing
(she's always said the Statue of Liberty is green because she's
seasick from standing in New York harbor), and my mother
read it, and said that David couldn't hand it in. Those were
the McCarthy days and people were a little crazy, I suppose,
but David wanted to hand it in anyway. He thought it was
very interesting and they got into a fight about it, not shouting but like two bulls standing off. A twelve-year-old doesn't

have much chance against an adult. She shredded it, all the while standing there talking calmly to him, and then she made him rewrite it, telling more about our grandfather, who loved everything about America and the English language. He spoke English perfectly though he didn't learn it till he came here at sixteen. She said he could write about our grandmother but only about *how* she came, not what she felt. I mean she dictated it to him. I remember that: sitting at the table, watching him crying and writing down what my mother was saying. Every so often my mother would say, 'David, you must stop crying. Are you a baby? If you're going to cry I won't help you.' Can you imagine? Here she was forcing him to do something and threatening him not to help him do it. As young as I was, I knew there was something wrong. What's that? Surface or substance?"

He said nothing.

"When my father came home, David started to tell him what had happened, and my mother got very angry and told him my father was tired and he shouldn't bother him. But David got enough out so my father got the idea and he started to argue with my mother, I don't think because he cared about the story, but because David was so upset. Then my mother said something I've never forgotten. 'Seymour, you're a man who isn't exactly a roaring success. You're a very nice person, but perceptive about the world you're not.' I've heard her say that sort of thing thousands of times since to him, about him, but that was the *first* time. My father was standing there with his hand on David's shoulder. He had such a look on his face — old almost. He said something like 'I support you,' and she said, 'Ha!' She sounded like a witch to me, and David backed up against the wall. She said, 'It's my family's story. It's none of your business anyway.' And he said, 'David is my business,' and David began to cry so hard he threw up. Then my parents both got very busy cleaning up and yelling that it was the other's fault. It's amazing I should remember it so clearly, but that was the first time I saw the underside, maybe because they forgot all about me — everything happened as if I weren't there. I thought then I wanted things to be nice. Just happy and nice. I didn't ever want to watch them crumble again." She was silent.

The boys and the girl had come out of the water and were drying off. They began to walk over the dunes, singing together, and Arthur waved at their backs, "So sorry to see you go, guys." He looked at Miriam, who, unmoving, still stared out at the water.

"Puss, that's quite a story. Your mother was probably right about not letting your brother hand in the composition. In those days, your grandmother might well have been visited by the FBI. We all have these memories that frighten us because we didn't really understand what was happening. You were scared because of the fight. Kids remember when their parents fight, always. Eileen and I hardly ever fight in front of the kids. It would make them edgy, unhappy. Not worth it."

She stared at him. He was sitting up now, his head against the ring of moon like an inlaid stone. "Arthur, I'm telling you something really important about me."

"You're telling me something that seemed important, but you must realize how little that incident really was. It's good you talked about it, let go of it. That's why people go to shrinks and pay someone else to help them decide what their memories are worth. I mean, do you suppose you would want your kid to be exposed to political danger? Boy, in the last few years I've known parents who have nearly lost their minds over that subject. You remember Kent State? Well, what about parents whose kids were defying guardsmen? They would do whatever they could to keep their kids from being involved."

"Arthur, that's different."

"Not so different. You must have known it. You say you never got very political in college, though the times were already political."

"I didn't like the surface of the political kids. They were smelly sometimes, and the boys always looked scruffy. But I used to wonder if they didn't have a point, and by the time I got out of college and the war was getting worse, I really agreed with them about that. What put me off was their style."

He moved toward her and unhooked the top of her bathing suit and drew it out from between her breasts and her knees, which she still hugged. Her breasts, lighter than the rest of her skin, seemed luminous in the moonlight. He came behind her and moved his hands down her hips to push her bikini pants down, though she was sitting. "You have to look beneath the surface, yes indeed," he said.

She stood up and stepped out of her bottoms as he pulled off his trunks, and together they walked holding hands to the edge of the water, lukewarm against their toes. She glanced at him and thought he had a nice body, really, a firm hardly haired body, just sprinkles on his forearms, and the sandy cluster below. She wanted to embrace him but without their bodies blending into the inevitable tryst, so she stood still in the water and let him go on ahead. He shrugged and walked forward, splashing her a little by pushing the soles of his feet backward, and as he receded, she stood as though minute, suspended in her own skin. The moon hovered, reflected in the water, and, faintly, the distant sound of steel drums from the terrace of the hotel reached her ears. She stirred at the gold reflection and it broke into navy ripples as Arthur, now up to his waist in water, turned and called, "Come here, puss. You do look gorgeous in that outfit." She followed him in.

Later, lying in the sand, wrapped together in a beach towel, she said, "I love you, Arthur," trying it on, depending on the moment and their languor after sex to keep him from understanding what it was she meant.

*   *   *

On the plane home in a two-seated first-class row, they necked quite a lot, even while dinner was being served. Less than an hour outside of New York, Miriam went to the toilet to restore her make-up and came back to find Arthur sitting up reading a magazine, his features reestablished in the angularity of his public business self. She squeezed past him to the window seat. "All fresh and ready."

She was mocking the words and tone of a man with thick sensual lips they had met on their last day while taking an excursion boat to St. John. He had been accompanied by a manikin-thin woman with incredible henna-colored hair and heavy green eye shadow, who cracked chewing gum perpetually and punctuated everything he said with a breathy exclamation, "Oh! Clever! Clever!" "That one," he had said to Arthur and Miriam as if she were one of the boys, "that one is always fresh and ready." Her name was, implausibly, Lilac, and when he said "Lilac, bay-bee!" she would clap her palms together, spreading her fingers with their many rings back, and squeal, "He's so clever! So clever!"

Arthur twisted his mouth up in an ironic smile and waved his hand as if to dismiss the memory. "Clever!" he said and then with a flash of vituperativeness out of character, "Fool with his kept woman!"

"I'm a kept woman," said Miriam, leaning back in the seat. "Just not so showy!"

"You're damned well not!"

"What am I? A wife?"

He turned toward her unsmiling, his lids heavy above his green eyes. "You keep yourself. Support yourself. If I give you gifts, it's because I want to. I'll tell you who's a kept woman. My wife. She's more like that cunt than you could ever be."

Miriam turned that phrase over in her mind, looking at him and his unaccustomed grimness. "She keeps your home. Don't you think that's service?"

"That's her diadem. A hundred-and-fifty-thousand-dollar house, clever, and a maid and a gardener, clever, and two strapping boys."

"Kept women don't get their diadems for nothing."

"She'd bleed me for every penny if I ever left her."

"And if you ever left me, you wouldn't owe me a thing — at least, nothing I could claim."

"Miriam, you don't want that from me." He was solemn, his tanned cheeks showing little lines in the artificial light.

"How do you know?"

"If you wanted to take me, you could have done it long ago. Blackmail, threats, insisting on undeliverable promises. Men in my position don't get involved with women without worrying about that. You have never laid that on me and I don't think you're going to now."

She closed her eyes and waited until the pause seemed elastic, stretching to New York. The stewardess brushed by, offering to give them a last drink before landing, and Arthur took a Scotch.

"You?" he asked and she shook her head just before the stewardess rolled the bar farther down the aisle. "Are you still peevish?"

"Arthur . . ." She stopped, not knowing what to say.

"Maybe you're making the mistake of comparing yourself to that ding-a-ling."

"No. I know I'm not that far gone. Maybe I'm comparing myself to Eileen. Maybe I'm wondering why we both accept you so readily on your own terms. Eileen may not know about me, but she must surely know you two are not connected quite right."

"She probably has her reasons for going on. You've told me more than once you're not sure you ever wanted to get married. That's at least one of your reasons."

"I don't have any very good models," said Miriam, her shoulders falling perceptibly forward. "But I find myself now looking at all that differently. I've put up all my defenses for a 'nice' world and now I suspect that I'm just shredding my brother's composition." She shifted slightly in the seat and took his hand, which did not turn about hers. "Here we were, in a beautiful place for five days, able to be open about what we have together. In New York we burrow down in my apartment like it was a hole. If what we have together isn't anything then why were we so glad to get away and let it see sunlight? Maybe it's just a glittery surface that looks better in the sun, but now for months, ever since my cousin ran off, ripping away the cloth over my family's life, I've had the feeling it isn't this, it isn't this. If it isn't this, what is it? Does that make any sense?"

"No," he said, and she could see him retreating.

"Do you love Eileen?" She had never asked him that.

"In a family sort of way."

"And me?"

"You know the answer to that."

"Well," she said, and let go of his hand.

*　　*　　*

They landed in New York in the midst of a spring rain. In the apartment they opened windows to let in the fresh smell, but not enough to wet the sills. Arthur offered to go down for milk, bread and orange juice, cottage cheese for the morning, and then said offhandedly, "Have to call Eileen tonight at her brother's. Of course it's three hours earlier in Seattle."

"Of course," said Miriam.

She watched him go out the door, went to her own phone in the kitchen and tried her parents' number. It rang seven or eight times before she hung up. She dialed her brother's number in New Jersey.

"Hello?" said David.

"Hi, it's me."

"Mimzie! How were the Virgin Islands?"

"Beautiful, really beautiful. I got a nice tan." She gulped a half-swallowed laugh. "My new bikini got used. Everything was just ducky. What's been happening with all of you?"

"The kids are fine. We went to Anita's mother for the Passover seder. It was very nice for the kids."

"Um," said Miriam, aware she had not even thought about the holiday of unleavened bread while celebrating her own exodus with French loaves in the Caribbean. Well, it wasn't the first time she had forgotten. "Any word about the family fortunes? Our cousin hasn't turned up, has he?"

"No one's called to say so."

"I thought about you, David, while I was away."

"Nice thoughts, I hope." He was smiling, she could tell from his voice.

"The nicest." She struggled against a habituated reticence to express her deepest feelings, but flipped into a different kind of habit. "You're a doll and your kids are dolls, and your wife's a doll. Hey, I bought you all presents, those funny straw hats they wear down in the islands, a whole family of hats." Her mind buzzed against her own chatter, then suddenly, "Hey, do you remember that essay you once wrote about Grandma, that Mom ripped up and made you rewrite?"

"Sure. Why?"

"I don't know. I just thought of it."

"Mom probably was a little overanxious, but maybe she was right. Who knows what kook might have gotten a hold of it and made trouble for Grandma."

"You think so?"

"Those were strange times."

She nodded sagely into the phone. "Yes, they were. How's Anita?"

"Not great. She's got her nervous stomach back."

"Too bad. Tell her I hope she feels better."

"Thanks. Well, I don't want to keep you, Mim. The phone bill!"

"Thank you, David. Goodnight."

"Goodnight."

She padded in bare feet into her bedroom and began to put the things from her flowered straw purse into her black leather pouch, which was filled with papers. "My file box," she would say, affectionately patting it. Too full. She sorted out a welter of junk mail and assorted letters, and from one corner the wad of leaflets she had been collecting for months from the red-bearded Hasid at the office. He had only once more tried to engage her in conversation, unsuccessfully, but generally seemed satisfied to give her leaflets, which she stuffed unread into her pocketbook. She stacked them on her dresser, the top one with the word RETURN in white letters against a blue background, and red Hebrew letters she could not read just below. Emptying the rest into the wastebasket, she rearranged her bag.

Arthur came back, carrying a large brown paper bag and a dripping umbrella, which dribbled across the floor near the door.

"Hey, puss, I was thinking we really had a good time, didn't we? I think that's the longest we've ever had alone together." He came over and kissed her on the nose. "Put everything away and fix us a nightcap, and when I get finished with Eileen and the kids, we can take it easy."

He emerged from the bedroom ten minutes later and stretched sleepily. "The family survives. She tried to call from Seattle, Saturday. I told her I went to dinner with a business acquaintance. She's going to call tomorrow so I can talk to the boys, who were away skiing. On Easter, can you imagine?"

Miriam stretched out her hand with a drink in it and said, "How was she?"

He took the glass. "Oh, misses me, she says. Hogwash!" He sat down in the sling-back chair and propped his feet on the glass table.

"Maybe not," said Miriam. "Maybe you're reading her all wrong."

"It seems to me pretty nervy of you to defend her. You've never even met her. What's more, it belies your business sense. It is, as they say, against your interests."

"Maybe I ought to meet her. Maybe I'm beginning to wonder what it would be like to be your wife." Miriam leaned back against the doorjamb of the kitchen.

"Miriam," he sounded genuinely surprised, "are you proposing to me?"

"I don't know."

He turned toward her by sitting forward in the chair and shifting weight at his knees, a faint smile playing across his lips. "Oh, love, I'm flattered, I am really flattered and if I weren't married, I'd take you in a minute. You know that, don't you?"

"No," said Miriam. "I think you think that. Am I supposed to thank you for thinking that?"

"What's going on with you today? Are you playing with me? I don't like to be played with. We just had a good and rather expensive holiday together and it seems to me that you're misusing the feelings that prompted me to take you on that trip."

"I thought I wasn't a kept woman."

"I don't mean *that*. If our relationship is going to last, and I hope it's going to last, we can't make unreasonable demands on one another."

Miriam turned to the kitchen and switched off the light. She swirled the liquid and ice around in her glass and looked through the amber color toward the round hanging lamp just above Arthur's head. For a moment it appeared whole as the yellow moon at St. Thomas, but hazed.

"What is it going to last for?" she asked pensively. "I'm beginning to wonder if all I have to look forward to is life in a secret hideaway with occasional trips to break the monotony — the mystery woman weeping in the back of the room at your funeral. Isn't there anything better for us?"

"Well, I see." He cleared his throat. "When my boys are through school, or at least Bruce is through high school and away at college, I might be ready to consider a divorce, or at least a separation, but now it doesn't seem a real possibility to me."

"You probably would be able to see the boys just as much as you do now. I'd kind of enjoy being a stepmother."

He was staring at her, critically, she could tell, not just

thinking about humping her, and she felt a ball of heat move with his eyes across her forehead, the bridge of her nose, her breasts, and she returned his look with the same sharpness.

"Without sentimentalizing it, I've invested twenty years of my life with Eileen and she hasn't given me cause to divorce her." He rolled the glass between his palms.

"Just to be unfaithful to her, without sentimentalizing it." She met his eyes and held the stare until he turned away.

"You gave me that cause," he said, the words coming out slowly for emphasis.

"Baloney!" she said. "There were women before me, and I don't doubt there will be others after."

"Only if we break it off."

She didn't say anything but sipped her drink and ran her tongue back and forth along the rim of the glass. They stared, each into private space, waiting.

"Do you believe in God?" she asked abruptly.

He was startled and nearly fell forward off the sling-back chair that tilted, pitching him slightly in the same direction. "Are we about to consider the theological implications of our affair?"

"No. I just wondered."

"Why? Do you?"

"Sometimes, but I can't hold it steady," she said.

"Why do you want to know about me?"

Her eyebrows circumflected and crinkles appeared at the corners of her eyes. "Curiosity. Just that. Neither of us takes divine retribution much into account. You still haven't told me."

"Not much," he said.

"Is everything going to explode between us?"

"That's up to you."

She tried not to look at him when she said, "I keep thinking about my cousin who's run away. He exploded because he couldn't help it, and since he's gone I keep feeling empty, as if the fuse he had that made it possible for him to get up and go, to say 'no more,' is missing in me. I think maybe I'm too willing to let things remain comfortable and uncomplicated even if they're imperfect, to stick with a relationship that may be better than my parents' comfortable, uncomplicated and imperfect marriage *only* because it isn't binding. I guess I'm beginning to think there are all kinds of confinements and the one you don't know you're choosing may be worse than the one you select; that maybe there are confinements that are actually good, secure — like a bunting."

"None of that makes too much sense."

"Neither does anything else," said Miriam. "Let's drop it."

They slept together without touching that night, and the next morning on their way to work, Arthur said, "I'd like to get some fresh clothes from my apartment tonight. Maybe a day apart at this point will do us both good."

She nodded, struck, almost pleased, that she felt mild pain.

She had dressed in white that morning to show off her new tan at work, and was about to pull off her raincoat for full effect before she entered the building when she was stopped by her red-bearded nemesis. He thrust another blue pamphlet with its white RETURN, and the red Hebrew letters, a regular Rorschach test, at her and said, "*Hag sameyach.*"

"To you too," she said, "whatever that means."

He shook his head and whispered, "Pesach — Happy Holiday. You don't know even Passover?"

"I know Passover."

"Do you read what I give you?"

"I take them. Why don't you ever look at me?"

"Why do you never look at yourself?" he said, his voice husky. Crowds swirled around them in waves, a river almost of people. The question struck her like a slap, and her cheeks stung.

"If that were a problem for me, your little pamphlets wouldn't help."

"*Ha-Shem* accepts the prayers and supplications of Jews wherever they are. We offer an opportunity to live for a time in a world suffused with the sanctity Judaism gives to our lives. To learn." He held out the pamphlet again, letting it drop before she actually touched it.

She turned the first page over and saw the face of a young woman, younger than herself, with her hands spread above candles, a look of placidity and joy on her face; the third fold opened to a picture of a young man whose head and arm were strapped with leather ties and small boxes. Beneath the pictures was the phrase "It is a tree of life . . . ," and two columns, one entitled "For Women," the other "For Men," which gave accounts of possible study programs, a chance to live among Hasidic Jews, to learn Hebrew, Scriptures, Prayers, Law. She squinted her eyes and closed the pamphlet.

"I'll read it later," she said, "but I don't think I really need this."

"The Talmud says, 'If one says, "I have not searched but found," don't believe him.'"

Miriam put the pamphlet in her purse. "O.K. Just keep in mind that not everybody is searching for the same thing." She began to walk away.

"But the same Lord looks at us all," he called, "and asks whether we have lived up to our covenant."

"Gentiles?" she said, turning. He for this one moment looked directly at her. She shivered at the intensity of his eyes, a deep blue almost the color of her holiday seas. "They must answer to Him in their own ways."

She went into the building, her back to him, feeling his eyes upon her, like the eyes of the men in the restaurant at St. Thomas, only now eyes looking past her clothing through her skin, looking not at her breasts but beyond.

She shut her eyes and stood in the elevator surrounded by people, feeling the world ascending against the soles of her feet.

*　　*　　*

That evening since she did not expect Arthur, she brought home a TV dinner and ate it while watching the news. She had spoken to her mother, during the day at work, and then on impulse called her grandmother, to whom she bubbled on at great length about a possible promotion in the offing at work.

"When women will be in positions of authority, the whole world will be better off. You would treat people who had to work under you kindly, I know, care about their needs, their personal needs."

Miriam, who at that time could see from her office door a woman berating a typist out in the secretarial pool, said, "Idealism, Grandma. People are people, men and women, and some of each stink."

Now she watched the television shows slide into one another, feeling an unfocused rage. It gnawed at her, cut into her skin from underneath. Laugh at yourself, she ordered her mind. Rule one for healthy functions. Aren't you a stupid girl? That thought filled her with pathos, not laughter, the sad clown, and she tried to focus her mind on the really lovely moments of the trip: dancing in Arthur's arms on a terrace overlooking the sea, swimming together, having sex in a pool of sunlight across their bed.

She shut the television off and went into the bedroom where she finished unpacking and considered that a lunchtime trip to Bonwit's to buy some soft-fabric spring dresses might be in order; she ran her hand over the garments hanging in her closet as if they were human and contact might offer some comfort. They hung in the still dark, keeping their secrets.

Suddenly Arthur's phone on the night table rang, startling her so she slapped her hand to her chest. She stared at it as it rang a second time, then abruptly moved to the table and waited for it to ring again. Her mouth was very dry, her ribs rising and falling as if they, not her lungs, breathed the life-giving air. On the third ring, she picked up the phone, hardly breathing, and heard Arthur's voice saying, "Hello?"

She dared not move a muscle.

"Hi, sweetie." The cigarette-laden voice of Eileen crossed the wire.

First the boys had to talk. Bart, whose voice was already a man's, answered his father's questions about Seattle and the family in monosyllables but gave a strangely Arthur-sounding account of skiing with "a dumb broad who was afraid of heights." Bruce, his voice still nasal and changing, was more informative about how his cousins were and how great it was to see Gram and Gramp, his mother's parents.

Then Eileen returned to the phone. "Art, what's the city like now?"

"Oh, very springy. Rained last night, but today was lovely. How are you getting on with all the reunions?"

"Fine," she said. "I wish you were here though. My mother isn't well at all, I told you last night, and Dad seems unable to handle everything by himself. Today Warren and I were discussing the possibility of putting them in one of those homes, sort of apartments for older people where there's always medical assistance and social workers available. Not right away, but soon. It costs though."

"Sorry to hear that," said Arthur. Miriam could just see him, distracted no doubt by something else: a newspaper, a silent flickering television. Her shoulder hurt from her lack of movement but she did not even twitch. "We'll talk about it when you come home, I'm sure. Are you planning to take that flight on Wednesday, the one you asked me to meet?"

"Yes. Arthur." Her voice got softer as though she were trying to speak without being overheard. "Do you suppose you might make a little room on your schedule for us to get away together? It's been really shocking to see so many divorced friends here. At home divorces happen one at a time, you have a chance to get used to them. I came here and found seven marriages that were still together the last time I was in Seattle have gone pfft."

"You think we're going to go pfft?" Arthur's voice had a lazy disinterested roll to it as if he were asking her what team she thought might win a ball game.

"No," she said, but Miriam sensed her uncertainty.

"Pfft would certainly be bad for the boys, and it's much cheaper for two to live together than apart, you know."

"Not when you keep an apartment in New York anyway," said Eileen coldly.

"We're not going to get into that *again*, on the long-distance telephone, Eileen. You're a hell of a woman. I'm proud to have you for a wife, but I don't like being picked at for something we worked out long ago."

She cleared her throat, and coughed, phlegm rippling somewhere deep in her chest. "Yes, we did, and I must admit the house runs more smoothly when you're not there seven days a week."

"Maybe hot-pants is what's troubling you. We can fix that when you come home."

"As ever, quick on the draw — sex can solve everything," said Eileen venomously. "Obviously now is not the time to have this conversation."

"No. Love you, doll," said Arthur, his voice lifting at this phrase that always closed their phone calls.

"Better!" said Eileen. Her voice softened. "Love you *too*, Mr. Clean."

Miriam nearly burst out laughing and, struggling not even to move, stopped breathing altogether.

"Night, doll. Best to everyone."

"Goodbye. See you Wednesday."

They both hung up, Miriam waiting long enough after the second phone clicked down for the dial tone to resume before she hung up the receiver and started to gulp for breath, laughing hysterically and panting, "Mr. Clean! Oh, too much!" Arthur did resemble the bald-headed male logo atop a plastic-bottle body, muscles filled with golden cleaning fluid. She laughed until she was half crying, unbidden tears spilling down her cheeks. She calmed down gradually and lay back on the bed, squeezing a crumpled Kleenex as she stared at the ceiling.

"Not this," she said aloud. "It isn't this."

7

Gershom — Rachel won't be only child. We are though. No one can replace us. — Johanna.

*T*HE DAY BEFORE, the window washer had come for his semiannual visit, and with his straps fastened to the hooks set in the brick frame of the window, hovered four stories above the ground squeaking his rubber-bladed squeegee against the glass. Now, the light poured in through the clean uneven panes, a beam of clear sun reflecting on tiny particles of dust in the air for the short daily time the light came directly through a corridor between the tall buildings to the south. It rested like a warm plate on the dark red of the carpet, a worn imitation oriental rug.

Celia was seated in her rocker, wearing a copen blue rayon robe, with a wide lace border protruding from between the fabric and the facing. It was a gift from Leah. Her tight curls, dark ringlets, hung limply down to her shoulders. She rocked intermittently, pushing the floor gently with the ball of her foot. She had prepared their lunch, but left the dishes for Sam, a recurrent alteration in a long pattern. Sam had just finished washing them and was rolling down his shirt sleeves as he came back to the living room where the Sunday paper lay spread about in white heaps. He collected the sections in a neat pile on the mahogany table. He handed the arts section to Celia, who looked away and did not accept it, so he added it to the pile.

Gershom's picture, taken before high school graduation, sat in a glass casing without a frame on a shelf before some books bound in dark colors. His eyes seemed to look above the stream of light cascading through the washed windows. Sam barely glanced at it. He took the book review and sat back on the couch, catty-corner against the arm rest, noticing the way the light struck the colored clear strings of the harp, making them luminous lines in a golden curve. He folded back the first page and read a short review of a novel about a woman dissatisfied with her marriage, then turned the next page. Celia rocked, the rocker crackling slightly, but he did not look up.

Outside, a whooping siren on a police car or fire engine sounded from blocks away, becoming ever more distant as it traveled toward its destination. The street was quiet otherwise, Sunday having stilled the garbage trucks and occasional rattle of a grocery delivery cart on the residential block. Nearby Sam could hear the throaty rumbling of pigeons, and the scratching of their thin red feet on the wide windowsills. He glanced at Celia to see if she noticed, but she had her eyes shut and rocked with the same frequency, no differently than before. He folded back another page.

The sound of the downstairs bell resonated through the room. Sam got up with a slow certainty for what was an expected sound. He checked his caller through the intercom and opened the door for Gabriel, who, dignified in a dark suit, carried a small paper bag which he gave to Sam.

"My friend, beautiful strawberries. I could not resist them. We must give some to the lady. How is she?"

"As always," said Sam.

Gabriel rubbed his hands together and went into the living room, where he greeted Celia — "My dear Celia, an exquisite day!" — while Sam put the bag with the strawberries in the kitchen. He looked down into the shallow brown well at the red berries in a green box. A sweet smell rose from them that made him think of summer woods. He rocked slightly above the bag, smiling, his round face resembling a whimsical artist's conception of the sun in a child's picture book. "Wonderful," he said, and took the box out of the bag.

He came back to the living room, where Gabriel was describing to Celia the way the park looked on this warm rosy day with the last semblance of winter gone, vanished into an all absorbing spring: children, their limbs bare, running along gray paved paths; dogs on leashes; a soft green arch of trees above the walkers. As he spoke, his hands shaped what he described though his thin shoulders maintained their firm line.

Sam went to Gabriel's side. "Sit down, sit down. We have had our lunch, we have read the paper and we have had a quiet morning, absolutely undisturbed."

Gabriel sat on the couch in the very corner where Sam had read the reviews not long before. "Can I hope that you will join me for a walk in the park later?" Celia continued to rock evenly.

Sam went to her and took her elbow. "Celia, darling, go, dress, and we can go out in the sunshine. I'll help you choose some clothes."

He disappeared with her into the bedroom and returned minutes later alone, shaking his head.

"She will take her time. She pauses over every piece she has to put on."

Gabriel raised one leg across the other, and shifted to look at Sam, who was seated near the hall leading to the bedrooms, as if alert, a sentry awaiting his call. "Do you ever speak about the boy to her?"

"I used to talk about him all the time, but so often she seemed in pain when I did, to really suffer, that I stopped. What's more, I don't know what to say. She never could let go of him when he was here, I see that clearly now. Maybe he *had* to leave. I think she may feel that too, no matter what she imagines is happening to him. Malraux says 'To recognize the freedom of another is to acknowledge his right to it even at the cost of suffering . . .' Ah, Gershom says — said — I shouldn't quote so much." He shook his head as if trying to clear it of some encumbrance. "I suppose if that is what is going on in her head, she must feel a sense of responsibility, just as I do for Gershom's pain — whatever it was that got too much for him to handle."

"He bears his own responsibility too," said Gabriel. "We all make choices, even in childhood."

Sam stopped and held out his blunt-fingered hands, the edges of nails cut straight across. The palms were up in a gesture of supplication.

"Yes, but it is easiest to accept the role that's thrust on you. Sometimes I feel such rage at him — that he didn't do something sooner, something that could have been dealt with and finished, that I didn't do something sooner. And then I don't know who I'm angry at. Even sometimes at her. What can we do?" He paused, the silence highlighting the cooing pigeons. Then he began again. "When you first advised she stay here, I was so glad, glad that professional opinion didn't go against my own inclinations, but I thought then it would only be a matter of weeks, that he would come back, that she would come back, if you know what I mean. Now I see the thing has no boundaries. Even if he comes back now . . ." He did not continue.

"You still want her here, yes?"

"Of course, but I've learned I can't console her, perhaps that she doesn't want to be consoled — I've never been able to console her about anything really, and I've tried. I have to struggle just to console myself. And then, Gershom's going has" — he searched for the right word — "disrupted all our lives. I feel as if we're all flying through the air like cannon shot and I hardly know how we're going to land."

"For example?" said Gabriel.

"You know about Leah and Harry?" Sam gestured vaguely in the direction of downtown. "You see she's living at your son's." He laughed nervously. "I shouldn't say anything to you about your son's mother-in-law, and don't misunderstand, I'm grateful to her for everything, but sometimes she seems so angry at Gershom, I half believe she wishes she were the one who left — or was left — at the center anyway."

"So she has imitated your son? An interesting idea. Maybe it is her way of assuring herself that her daughter won't do a similar thing. She can be very difficult with Johanna."

Sam stirred. Gabriel did not often state judgments, and he waited to see if more would follow. But Gabriel was looking at Sam now expectantly, a look that seemed capable of holding forever.

"Then," said Sam, "it may be unrelated, but since I've been seeing her every week, I suspect that my niece, my other niece, Miriam, isn't happy. She has such a reflective attitude these days. It's not like her. And she's quite sensitive about the fact that her mother never comes here. You know Emma. She calls but never comes. She cries at sentimental movies but has trouble with real emotion. I think she half believed Celia that what she and Seymour said . . . I'm ashamed to say I've had some of Leah's sort of nasty thoughts myself. Miriam must know that. She seems to be trying to make up for her mother, almost to perform an obligation, a family penance. Lately, she comes every Saturday with lunch and sometimes a plant." He gestured toward the plant stand overflowing with green, the tiny purple heads of African violets peeking up amid the leaves. "A few weeks ago, she went to the Virgin Islands and couldn't come, but the next week she came one evening and took us out to dinner downtown. Insisted."

"It's probably important to her to be able to do that for you — as important as it is for you to receive her generosity."

Sam sighed and rubbed his forehead. "Maybe, but it isn't

enough to make her happy. Besides, Emma's misbehavior isn't her fault."

"We are part of our seed. We do bear some burden for the sins of our fathers and mothers."

"Ach!" Sam's exclamation was gutteral, a sound emanating from deep within him. "I used to believe once upon a time that man could be relieved of that by education, by psychological insight, by social change, by, you'll forgive me, what we used to call social justice. I believed that each individual started out his life with a tabula rasa, especially in this land, this America. Celia's father, *alav ha-sholom,* the short time I knew him used to talk a great deal about the fresh start everyone could have in America."

"And now you think something different?"

Sam nodded, a meager nod but unmistakably assent. "I now think life is an individual journey that we start carrying the debts you call the sins of our fathers and mothers, but also bearing the damage done by the sins committed against our fathers and mothers. And who knows what other debts." He leaned toward Gabriel as if to confide a secret. "I was never a very political man though many of my friends were. Bernard Katzman writes all about that. Even so, I believed in social change — still do, that's why I teach — but I see that what happened before is disposed of only at great cost, great personal effort."

"Can be though," said Gabriel. "Prayer helps."

"Not everyone. I pray. Maybe I'm praying for the wrong things." He was startled by the downstairs bell, leaping out of his seat and rushing toward the bedroom. "You all right, Celia?" Then, having determined she was, went to the intercom, which rang again.

"What will my beloved girl be when she comes through this?" he said, not really addressing his question to Gabriel. "Hello," he shouted into the intercom.

"It's Rafe," said a man's voice.

"Oh, come up," he buzzed the button furiously, and went to open the apartment door.

"Gershom's history teacher. Have you heard about him from Seth and Johanna? He comes very often now. He was here yesterday too. A good man, a good man. I'm really moved by him."

The elevator in the hall opened and Mrs. Appel rushed out, clutching a plastic laundry basket, followed by Rafe. She eyed Sam standing in the doorway with the tall dignified Gabriel coming up behind him, and back around at Rafe's slight figure.

"Oh, he's for you, Mr. Lazarus. I'm so nervous. Didn't know him. He got into the elevator with me on the first floor when I was coming up from the laundry room. Forgive me."

"I'll introduce you," said Sam. "Raphael Toledano, our neighbor Mrs. Appel."

"I'm sorry I scared you," said Rafe, fighting a turn at the corners of his lips as if the idea he could be thought dangerous amused him greatly.

"Terrible times, terrible times. Who knows what can happen! A woman in the next building was nearly raped. Only screaming saved her. The super heard her and came out with his dog. Believe me, I wouldn't want to meet that dog — a German shepherd. The super has to hold him on a short chain right to the collar. He kept the rapist against the wall till the police came. Thank God!" She panted, waving a small change purse in front of her face.

"It's all right now," said Sam. "I'll wait till you get inside your apartment."

"He'll probably go free with a suspended sentence." She started to sort a welter of keys. "How's poor Celia, Mr. Lazarus?" She was calming and able to focus the beam of her terror freshly. "No words still? Will she ever speak again, poor woman? My heart aches for her." She began to unlock the chains and bolts of her apartment. The door opened with the effort of a drawbridge and she slid inside. "G'bye, g'bye. Nice to meet you."

Rafe stepped in Sam's doorway. He had no jacket and wore a cowboy shirt with a row of gamboling kids embroidered along the yoke, above jeans supported by a blond tooled leather belt. He carried nothing and thrust his hands into the back pockets of his pants. "Hello, I hope I'm not intruding at a bad time."

"No. This is Seth's father, Gabriel Rosen. Dr. Rosen."

Gabriel came forward and put his right hand on Rafe's shoulder. "My son has told me about you. I have wanted to meet you."

Sam hurried to the bedroom, as he gestured his guests toward seats. "Celia, Celia! Rafe is here to see us."

He returned. "Now that you're here, she's hurrying."

"That woman in the hall," said Rafe, "might as well be a prisoner — she's so frightened, she's in chains. I feel sorry for her."

"A good heart," said Sam, "but she collects unhappiness."

"Because she's afraid of it. I can see she thinks talking about the things she fears will keep them away from her. I've known others like that."

Gabriel cleared his throat. He did not take his eyes from Rafe. "You and I know, I think, that the worst we fear is not the worst that can be, and yet the worst that has been is even worse in the imagination."

"If we let ourselves relive it in the imagination. To feel it. I try not to do *that*." Rafe smiled ingenuously. "But you know, I study history and I'd like to think that even the worst can be examined coldly, understood. But it takes a little distance. Sometimes the farther away you get, the clearer things become." He turned toward Sam. "How is our little Mother today?"

"She's the same, but she'll be glad to see you, I think."

Rafe slid down in his chair, graceful and boyish, his back

an arc where the chair angled into a seat. The three men sat
silently staring off in front of them as if they did not dare to
venture toward the subjects that weighted the air in the small
living room.

Sam stood. "I'll go wash the strawberries. We can all have a
bowl and then go out for a walk."

"Great," said Rafe. "Yesterday, when we left, Miriam and I
walked for a long time. It was a lovely evening."

"I'm surprised Miriam was willing to walk. She's a taxi-taker,"
said Sam.

"Well, she may be used to doing that, but she didn't seem
at all put out by walking." Rafe chuckled as if at a secret pleasure remembered. "She was a good walking companion. All
the way downtown, she told me stories about growing up in
Queens. Go to your strawberries, Sam, I'm just babbling."

Sam stepped back to the kitchen and heard Gabriel saying,
"I understand you lived in Illinois when you first came to this
country." He could hear their voices from the living room, the
flow of conversation. At first he tried to listen but could catch
only phrases which became increasingly isolated from one another as he was again absorbed by his own preoccupations,
the focus of his mind now wandering away, now returning.
He put the strawberries in a colander and ran the cold water
from the kitchen faucet over them. He had a student this term
who showed promise, a boy from a black Puerto Rican household, whose interest in poetry and language came out of his
attempts to write songs. He had handed in a ballad to Sam
just the week before with the refrain *Strawberries, strawberries,
sweet taste of summer coming*. Reading it, Sam had felt a quiver
of joy run through him he recognized as his own boyhood joy
at possibility. The poem stirred something long buried in him
and he had said enthusiastic things to the boy, tried to encourage him to persist with his writing. But a shy embarrassment inhibited them both, as if this abandoned pleasure in
the natural there in the littered school building with its

treacherous uriny-smelling johns and peeling walls, surrounded on all sides by grim and graceless city streets, was
the grandest frivolity, something worse than frivolity — self-
indulgence, maybe. He hardly knew. Since Gershom had left,
after a lifetime of faith in the solace of words well-used, he
found with pain that their capacity for comfort and cure was
sometimes an illusion. Then again, the berries were real. He
reached down into the colander and raised a fat flat one to
his mouth and bit into the exuberant sweet red, tempered with
tartness. He put the remaining berries in a Pyrex bowl and
brought them to the table where he set four small bowls,
spoons, sugar and milk. What would Celia think?

She was already in the living room when he came back,
seated between Gabriel and Rafe, who held her hand in both
of his. She was dressed in the pink dress Sam had chosen for
her, but had not buttoned it properly. He no longer stayed to
supervise her dressing, depression at that task having overwhelmed him. When he had to remain with her and help, he
felt an unreasoning fury, as if this imposition was the one
among all the others that would break him, and as she began
to leave him more tasks to do in the kitchen, she seemed willing, though clearly distracted, to dress herself again. He wondered why she seemed ordinarily efficient doing the chores
for him that she had made her life's work, but so inept about
the equally familiar concerns about herself.

"Celia, dear," he said, "strawberries." And as she and their
two guests got up in one movement to come to the table, he
said, "Your buttons."

She glanced down and stepped back as Gabriel and Rafe
started for the kitchen, waiting, it seemed, for Sam to come
and do them.

"Fix it yourself," he said and watched as she did, saying,
"Good, good."

"Here, little Mother," said Rafe, moving a chair out from
the table for her. She flashed a look of gratitude toward him,

and sat down but then immediately stood up, took the bowl of strawberries to the sink and plucked all the little green leaves off their tops.

"I forgot," said Sam sadly. Celia's back straightened and she paused before turning to return the bowl to the table. Sam watched her and suddenly his life as a novel, often silent now, often unwritten, began to hum in his head. "For her it was a moment of understanding. She saw her efforts at perfect care, rebukes." Could Celia really feel that? Could he? Were in fact her life-long attentions to the details of his life now buried by her silence like growing grass beneath an avalanche of rock and sand, really rebukes? For what? He would have to try out some other explanations.

She was seated again, and looking at him, her eyebrows lifted slightly. He sat down and sighed.

"Little Mother," said Rafe, "we're going to eat to spring and to better things."

"I commend that sentiment," said Gabriel. "Whatever the value of understanding the past, Rafe, the future is what we must turn our hearts toward."

They each scooped their plate full of strawberries and passed the milk container from hand to hand. The white grains of sugar fell from the spoons over the fruit, and they began to eat, the rough outer texture turning soft in their mouths, and even Celia smiling slightly as her lips became red with the juice of strawberries.

8

ᔓᔒᔓᔒᔓᔒ

O N T H E S A M E afternoon on the patio of the cafeteria in
the Museum of Modern Art garden, Miriam sank her spoon
into a mound of strawberry ice cream as she licked the sweet
stickiness of the last mouthful off her lips. Her friend Cynthia
Levertov had chocolate and Margot Levin Rheinlander, a
friend of Cynthia's, sipped iced tea while so obviously envying
their indulgence that Cynthia, uninvited, took a spoonful of
her ice cream and dropped it into the iced tea glass.

"That was another thing," Margot said, spooning up the
chocolate lump. "He never appreciated how hard it was for
me to keep weight off. He has this iron-will mentality. If you
want to be thin nothing fattening should ever touch your lips
again." Margot's marriage had just ended after nine spiteful
years and two children, who were with their father for the
weekend. "He's that way about everything. 'I'm not going to
wear anything made with synthetics anymore.' " She mocked
his voice in a tone that made Miriam laugh and nearly choke
on her ice cream. "So who has to iron the all-cotton shirts?
They say all-cotton can be permanent press, but I'd like to see
it. His whole wardrobe out in one giant sweep! He did things
like that about the kids too. 'It's about time Lisa took music
lessons. This is the voice of your leader speaking.' So who's
got to cart her, sit with her while she practices, and who's got
to take the rap that the kid has no talent?" She stirred the

iced tea, now cloudy from the last streams of chocolate ice cream. "It isn't that I didn't try," she said, dully hitting the ice against the sides of the glass.

Miriam scooped up the pink liquid remaining in her plate, and watched the Sunday crowds passing along a hall inside the museum through a glass wall. The garden itself with its giant sculptures was filled with visitors but, despite the noise of voices and the clatter of trays and glasses on the restaurant patio, it seemed an oasis of companionable quiet.

"You're better out of it," said Cynthia.

"Don't I know it!" Margot sipped the tea violently through a red striped plastic straw.

Miriam considered Margot, a plump, dark-haired woman with curved shoulders and square features. She looked dismal, Miriam thought, but then she had observed before that getting divorced was like having an operation. The real benefits to your well-being didn't show right away.

Cynthia leaned back on the metal chair and put her hands behind her head, her elbows stretching out like misplaced wings. "Marriage is a dying institution anyway. It's clear in another generation or two only the plebes will marry, but most people will be part of collective households of some sort. Better for the kids, better for the parents."

"We fought such a lot toward the end, the kids were really relieved when we split. At least I would have been if I were them." Margot, finished with the tea, was now chewing on her straw.

"I can't speak for parents, though Arthur says fighting is bad for kids . . ."

"Her sugar daddy," said Cynthia with a wink in an aside to Margot.

". . . but when I was a kid, I used to sometimes wish my parents would get really angry because there was always this feeling of something about to go off in the house. But when it did every now and then, I just hated it." Miriam closed her eyes and her father's face came into hazy view. "I doubt my parents would have even gotten involved with each other if my mother had felt it was at all respectable not to have a man. It's odd. My grandmother pushed the idea that her daughters should be independent and marry late, but she didn't make much of an impression on my mother. The times were against it, I guess."

"My mother's all broken up about Jerry and me, though so many of her friends' children have gotten divorced lately, I think she feels it's to be expected, even fashionable." Margot blinked. "Sometimes, though, I feel like an emotional sandwich: children on one side, mother on the other."

The May sun slipping west left them in shadow looking down toward the east end of the garden still painted with light.

"Well, there's this to be said for divorce," said Miriam, "when it's over, it's over. None of this hanging on, trying to work things out."

She had confronted Arthur shortly after their return from St. Thomas with her feelings of dissatisfaction. With what? She really couldn't tell him although he defined it as an urge to get married newly coming in her late twenties. "Maybe you're feeling the side effects of living in the shade," he said, and observed that while their relationship had many homey, even dull, qualities of a marriage, it was spiced by its clandestine nature. Each time she tried to explain, as much to herself as to him, he interrupted, assuring her he loved her more than ever and even offering to approach Eileen on the subject of a divorce sometime soon. *Pfft,* thought Miriam, but said nothing. He tried to please her by bringing her gifts, and several occasions when the ongoing discussion had reached the shouting stage had ended in nights filled with extraordinarily passionate, affecting sex. She began to anticipate the erotic side to their fights, all the time watching herself like a visitor from the outside observing: This isn't going anywhere. Why are you doing this?

A peculiar shame clouded her vision, preventing her from sharing this problem with anyone who might advise her. To talk about it would be to acknowledge that she felt trapped, and her "freedom" was the distinction she wore like a rose in her family, and with her friends too although in that circle, married and unmarried, everyone claimed to be free from the old confinements. Regularly she was visited with examples like Margot, women who, having thrown their lot in with old-fashioned expectations of marriage and children, surfaced after years with the discovery that they had been in pain. Often, to add to their misery, they found that professionally they were light-years behind their college classmates who had worked since graduation. She didn't think her discomfort could possibly be as severe as that of these poor bedraggled refugees. But when she tried to imagine her life without Arthur, the same smartly decorated apartment, the same well-paying job creating or maintaining demands for things that seemed increasingly useless to her, the same parade of men she had dated and slept with before she and Arthur had discovered what a bond mockery could be, she experienced a secret dread that the possibility of a relationship more meaningful, more honest, permanent (so much for "freedom"), had slipped beyond her reach.

She found herself flirting even more intensely with the men who serviced her life — cab drivers, delivery boys, the janitor — and felt exhausted by what that demanded of her. In what she dimly recognized as compulsive behavior, she spent lunch hours shopping fitfully for clothes and records. The only relief from her own crazy patterns were the times she spent in Washington Heights with her silent aunt and enduring uncle.

Her so-called devotion to them had caused some tension with her mother, who clearly felt it a judgment of her own absence, but who, at the same time, was eager that Miriam be seen as her representative to Sam and Celia. Let her have that!

Sam's and Celia's sometimes seemed like the only place in the world where she could be simply the little girl from Queens who had liked to read Nancy Drew mysteries and draw Romance comic strips that her uncle affectionately now called the "forerunners of Andy Warhol."

She realized abruptly that she had tuned out Margot and Cynthia, who were now staring at her expectantly.

"*Do* you want to go?" Cynthia asked, clearly for a second time.

"I guess so," Miriam recovered her smile left hanging, invisible like the Cheshire Cat entirely gone. "Sorry, I was just lost."

"I hear," said Cynthia as they got up, pushing their chairs back, "that this is still a good place to meet men. On weekdays, of course, when it isn't too crowded."

"I used to come here in high school," said Margot, uselessly trying to smooth the back of her short white pleated skirt that rode up over her hips. "I once met a Yalie who invited me to New Haven for the weekend." Her lips trembled slightly with recalled pleasure. "How nice it would be to be that innocent again."

"Beware innocence," said Cynthia. "It always gets you in trouble."

They were the last people on the patio as the cafeteria was closing. They entered the museum and descended briefly to the ladies' room to repair for the evening, then walked back through the museum toward 53rd Street.

On Fifth Avenue the sun from the west cut through the cross streets like petals of a giant flower. They walked uptown slowly, enjoying the gradually receding warmth, just walking, headed toward a destination Cynthia had promised: an early-evening cocktail party in the Seventies.

"We could take a cab," said Cynthia, "though we'd be too early."

"Walking is good for my figure," said Margot, a little desperately. "I need exercise. I don't get enough exercise. The doctor I'm seeing wants me to go jogging — says everything will tighten up."

"I'm in condition," said Miriam. "I walked all the way from Washington Heights to 96th Street last night." She paused, thinking about that walk, the curious stillness of it, through blocks she would normally have felt uneasy passing.

"You don't need to worry about your weight," said Margot, obviously angry it was true.

"It wasn't planned," said Miriam. "I was visiting an aunt and uncle of mine . . ."

"The kid's not back yet?" Cynthia interrupted.

"No, they're still having trouble. My cousin is a runaway — eighteen years old," she said to Margot, "and my aunt's a little crazy. Anyway, there my cousin's professor was visiting, and we walked downtown together." She paused. "He told me something so sad about himself. When he was a very little boy, around six, his parents and sisters were taken off by the Nazis, but he hid out on this roof among a lot of chimneys and when he got down he set out to go back to the city in Italy his family came from. They were living in Yugoslavia. He walked across Europe, I mean *really*. It took more than a year. It's hard to imagine! When he got there his grandparents had disappeared, so a neighbor took him to a convent where he spent the rest of the war even though he was Jewish. His family all died, but he only found out years later when he was brought to this country by an aunt he'd never seen. He said he's never really mourned for them because they were just cut out of his life when he was so young he hardly feels he knew them."

"It gives me chills to talk about the Holocaust," said Margot. "I don't usually feel very Jewish — only my father is Jewish — but when I think about that I feel so vulnerable. That's another thing Jerry and I had some big to-dos over. I wanted to give the kids some kind of background. I would have accepted anything — really anything, but since he's Jewish, a temple seemed appropriate. But oh no, he wasn't going to have his children 'brainwashed.' He said, 'What kind of God lets six million, no twelve million, go up in smoke? My kids can do without Him.' "

"I agree with him," Cynthia stamped her heel into the pavement with the force of her feeling.

"Maybe Ethical Culture," said Margot sadly.

Cynthia started to add something, then stopped and turned toward Miriam. "He sounds like an interesting man, your professor. What does he teach?"

"History. American history. At Columbia."

"Married?" Cynthia always liked to establish people's marital status first off, a nervous tic, Miriam thought, like wanting to know where someone was from before finding out anything else about them.

"I don't think so," she said. "It has never come up."

*   *   *

The teak cabinet full of liquor was covered with South American Indian heavy woven mats, an odd mixture of orange and gold. The doors were open and as bottles emptied on the top, a blond pony-tailed boy in a violet jacket earnestly crouched amid the knees of guests and brought forth, like a sorcerer, new fluids to be mixed and iced. Much of the crowd was gathered around a table spread with delicacies: cheeses, salami slices rolled around gherkin pickles, water chestnuts wrapped in bacon, hot sliced French bread with butter and garlic, and caviar, red and black. Beyond the dining room, French doors opened to a terrace on which dwarf orange trees in green wooden tubs and spindly avocado plants edged the eastern wall. Below in the dusk, blue the color of flame, the street and traffic lights spilled liquidly into air.

Miriam, holding a paper plate filled with crackers spread with cream cheese, each topped with red caviar, and a mound of guacamole in which were stuck some dip-sized Fritos, sipped Scotch on the rocks, and leaned against the building wall just outside the French doors. She was standing with several men who were exchanging investment tall-tales. She was not really listening to them, none of them interested her, but her eyes appeared to glisten with amusement by force of a stiff squint she had learned in college. One of her companions had turned out to be a classmate from: "My God, can you believe grammar school? Do you remember that old fart, Mrs. Brenner?" She was totally taken by surprise and avoided admitting she could not quite remember his name, which was something like Roger or Reggie, sure that someone else would address him directly and she would be able to pick it up. She was aware without looking directly at her that nearby Cynthia was talking in an animated way to another woman and a tall black man in a green suit. Although she could not see Margot, she could hear her somewhere behind her in the dining room, laughing nervously.

"Excuse me." Miriam put her paper plate precariously on the top of her glass. "I need a napkin and a fresh drink." The men looked politely sorry and she moved back into the warm crowd.

Margot was standing in a corner, looking up at a dark-haired man with broad uneven teeth, much taller than herself. She had drawn her shoulders back and held her glass just under her chin while she pulled persistently down on a loose strand of hair with her other hand. The man stood in front of her so that she was caught in a triangle of space and when she laughed she seemed almost to flutter against the walls of the confining V, like a captured moth beating against the inside of a box.

Miriam watched her as she walked around the table to the liquor, and when their eyes met she raised her brows as if to indicate approval. A small mustached man, an inch or so shorter than Miriam, eyed her plate of food as she passed, and fleet-fingered, pulled a Frito free from the guacamole;

she looked back at him with mock horror and then put her head back in laughter that grated her throat. He threw her a kiss from the end of his fingers and kept walking, looking at her over his shoulder.

Margot, having found a way out of her angled prison, came leading the warden toward Miriam. He had strange large features, overdrawn, like a suggestive caricature.

"Miriam, let me introduce you to Peter. I want you to meet Miriam Miller, a friend of mine."

Fully six-feet-four, he leaned over her as she turned and stuck out her glass. "Get me a drink, Pete. Then we can get acquainted. Scotch, please."

He looked startled but obliging and retreated to the bottles.

"Interesting?" whispered Miriam to Margot.

"Not very." Margot pulled her hair again. "I'm so nervous, just don't know how to go about presenting myself as a single woman. I keep bringing up my husband." She pushed the hapless strand behind her ear and stood up straighter as Peter came back with Miriam's drink.

"Now you owe me," he said and his lips curved in an extreme smile, almost a sneer.

"That's not a gentlemanly thing to say," said Miriam, beaming. She loathed him already.

"It's not ladylike to ask someone you've hardly met to get you a drink."

"I'll remember that. Sorry." She laughed again, the same grating sound she had produced at the man who had stolen her chip.

"Lady Liberation!" he said with no trace of humor. "Wants men to serve but not to demand. Right? Margot says she also thinks women ought to have the opportunities men do to look over the line. Whatever happened to the old chase?"

"It's gone. May it rest in peace. Are you a lawyer like our host?"

"He's a computer programmer for a brokerage house," said

Margot, opening her eyes wide. "Doesn't that sound interesting?"

Cynthia had come in the doorway. She looked around the room and made her way directly toward them. "Hello, Peter," she said, "haven't seen you for an age."

Another man, wearing an orange shirt, turned as Cynthia spoke and put his arm around her shoulders. "I'd love it if you'd be that pleased to see *me.*"

She glanced at him and lifted his arm off her. "I'm not likely to be."

"Oh, oh, the lady's getting tough." He moved away amicably.

"Is Harriet here?" Cynthia looked up at Peter.

"No, it's been over for a while now."

"How did you get rid of her? She was glued fast the last time I saw you," Cynthia asked, as the man in the orange shirt made his way around the table and stood eating a piece of salami next to Margot.

"Want one?" he said to her and raised one off the plate to Margot's mouth, which she opened cautiously.

Peter seemed buoyant. He bent slightly at his large knees again and again. "When I wouldn't set a date, she went off to teach in Virginia. Not so long ago, she called and announced she was going to marry a guy . . . Paul somebody. I said, 'Don't get the idea you're robbing Peter to pay Paul. I'm delighted to be let off the hook.' "

"Oh, I'm glad you said that to her," said Cynthia enthusiastically clapping her hands. "That was the best thing to say!"

The man with the orange shirt had put his arm around Margot. "Isn't that nice, she's going to be Mrs. Somebody," he said. He was very high.

Cynthia glared at him, eyes becoming narrow as she pursed her lips. "If she likes being chattel. That's what 'Mrs.' actually means," she said. "Marriage is greatly overrated."

The orange shirt rocked forward and said in a husky voice,

"How would *you* know? Let's ask this little lady." He turned toward Margot.

"Well," she said, her voice squeaking, "I'm just getting divorced, so I'm probably not representative."

The orange shirt stood straighter and hugged her toward him. "Obviously, the man was a lout and a fool to let a diamond like you go."

"Thanks," Margot clucked, looking miserable.

They had been joined by a couple: the woman, rather dark, in a dress made of shimmering turquoise sari material; the man with wide shoulders and a forced smile. He pounded Peter on the back and said, "What's all this talk about marriage? Who's getting married?"

"Not me," said Peter. "I can't say I've ever seen a good marriage. The best are just tolerable. Do you know anyone whose marriage is really happy?" He addressed the question to no one in particular.

"Hell, no!" said Cynthia. "It may start out looking snappy, but then after a while people just age. Even couples who have lived together before. And it's always the woman who finds that she has to limit her own life, that her interests are less important, less vital. No! No!" She raised her glass to her lips and drank the remnants.

"Listen! Here's a *man* who got out before he was used up. People stay together, but the years tell on them." The broad-shouldered man was caressing his companion's upper arm. "Especially once they have children and they are forced to arrange their lives around getting home to release the babysitter."

"No one should have more than one child anyway," said the dark girl. "There are too many people in the world."

"You have children?" The orange shirt leaned over Margot and dropped his hand on her hip.

"Two," she said. "They're good kids."

"You should have your tubes tied," said the dark girl. "In

twenty-five years the world will be so crowded no one will be able to lie down without permission."

"Hyperbole!" yelled the orange shirt.

"Only mildly." She looked down and put one well-manicured hand on the back of her neck.

"One *good* marriage? Notice no one has even offered their parents as a grand model."

"Even if one wanted to say that," said Cynthia, "the expectations of that generation were so different. I don't see how they can serve as models for a contemporary couple."

"I have a cousin," said Miriam in a small voice, "who I think has an O.K. marriage." Everyone looked at her. She thrashed in her mind for the appropriate thing to say. "I mean they seem happy."

"*Seem, seem,*" hissed the broad-shouldered man. "My ex-father-in-law met me for lunch after Dawn and I split and kept saying, 'But you always *seemed* happy!' "

They had actually collected a ring of listeners, drifting in from the terrace, and the host, an exuberant fellow with steel-framed glasses, urged them to take more food and go sit down in the living room, where low black couches and large cushions covered in African prints dotted a white furry rug.

The orange shirt now arranged a cushion for Margot and himself to sit against on the floor, and the violet-jacketed bartender went around refilling drinks. A woman with a black feather in her hair said softly to Miriam, "It's nice to hear there's at least one good marriage in the world," and sat down on the floor at once almost by way of punctuation.

"The only way you can explain marriage at all," said Peter, "is that we're always too optimistic about our futures. We think we can make the world go the way we want it to go. If we knew what was in the cards for us, we'd probably commit suicide."

The tall black man in the green suit Miriam had seen with Cynthia on the patio began to laugh. "We can know what's in the cards," he said in a soft Jamaican accent, "just by reading them."

"Yes?" asked Peter, his elastic brow pulling together. "I'd like to see how much longer I could go on without things getting bad enough for me to cut out."

"Well," he said, trilling his L's, slightly, "if I may have a pack of cards, I'll tell your future."

"Ezra, you old scoundrel, I've seen you do this before," said the host. "He's very good."

People began inching forward on the floor as Ezra sat down cross-legged and took the cards the host handed him.

Miriam sat down, thinking obliquely that she had spoken to no blacks on St. Thomas except for bus boys and entertainers. Jamaica was close, she thought, in the same chain of islands. One more jarring sense of the unreality of that trip to file with the others. She hardly noticed her grammar-school classmate, still only initialed in her mind, sitting behind her. "What do you want your future to be?" he said. "Back to good old Rego Park?"

She shuddered inadvertently. "Why, just that! Baby carriages in the hallway. I can't think of anything sweeter."

Ezra had begun to shuffle the cards. He had long dark hands and a long rectangular face to match. As he rippled the cards into one another with thumbs that stood at right angles to the cards, his brow wrinkled above his glasses, and he laughed.

"All right, who will be first?" He looked at Peter, who drew back and said, "I think I'll wait, thank you."

There was a momentary hush before the mustached thief of Miriam's Frito slid into the circle and said, "I will."

Ezra closed his eyes. "All right." He shuffled the cards once again and asked the subject to cut them. With his eyes still shut, he laid out eight cards, face-up, in two rows of four. Then he opened his eyes and looked intently at the rows. He lifted the first card from the pack and placed it on the card in the top left corner. "In your house of life, I see many years.

You have a family who live long lives, uncommonly long, and . . ." He picked the next card from the pile, "you long for fame which is always just out of reach. You can see — the red queen on the two of hearts." He stared at the man. "Am I right so far?"

"Well, I have a living great-grandfather ninety-five years old and his sister is alive too. She must be ninety-seven or ninety-eight. As for fame, I could do with some."

Ezra shut his eyes again and lifted the next card, which he laid on the third card in the first row.

"In an art," he said staring at his subject. "Some art. You long for fame in some art. It will come, but late, perhaps after your death." The subject nodded. "But you want international fame. Someday it will be yours."

"Amazing! And I'll have an early Alfredo Walman," said the host, pointing to a canvas of green and blue resembling oil slick, on the wall between two windows.

"Just a stroke of good luck," whispered Miriam's grammar-school classmate. Had he ever put gum in her hair as some boys in that class had? "If he sold insurance, it could be called an art he wanted international fame in."

"Are there internationally famous insurance salesmen?" She opened her eyes wide and forced a smile.

He shrugged and said, "Why not? Must be some, if you're into that."

Ezra had selected a fourth card, which was now largely covering the last card in the first row. "You are looking for the woman to share your life. The lucky lady is someone you already know, perhaps very well." The subject raised his eyebrows but said nothing as Ezra took the fifth card. "You will father a great family. Little ones will pat your knee, and . . ."

"How many?" said the subject.

"I see at least," he paused, staring at the cards, "five, but the exact number is not clear."

"Ah," said the subject.

"He'll be too busy to paint," said . . . could it be Roddy? Yes, Miriam thought, that's it.

Ezra had the sixth card, "You will leave them a good fortune, but it will not be so easy in the beginning."

"Did you ever see a fortuneteller who said, 'You'll be grubbing for every cent all your life?' " Roddy put his hands on Miriam's shoulders and began to rub her back. It felt very good, and a tingle from her shoulder muscles coursed down her spine.

"I do not see great travels in your future, but you have already seen much, especially recently."

The subject rubbed his hand across his forehead. "I just came back from Japan, Korea, Australia. Say, how do you do this thing?"

"It's probably set up," said Roddy, "just to convince everyone."

Ezra did not answer. "Last card: always a surprise. You will meet a man soon who will do much for you, but who will also cause you great anxiety. You will know him by the resemblance he bears to a political figure you do not admire."

"Nixon's double," yelled the man in the orange shirt.

"Anything else?" The subject looked interested.

"No. But you will be a famous artist as I have already told you."

"Perhaps you could let a gallery know that," said Alfredo. "Can I have a notarized statement to that effect?" Everyone laughed and there was a ripple of voices.

"Who now?" asked Ezra, shuffling the cards.

Margot uncomfortably rolled from her position against the cushion, where the orange shirt was trying to kiss her neck. "Mine," she said, her voice strained.

"Oh do keep on," said Miriam to Roddy, who had stopped massaging her shoulders. "I'll even consider inviting you to have egg creams in my neat Rego Park apartment." He resumed. She looked across the room at Margot, whose skirt hiked up to expose her heavy thighs, as she pulled away from the orange shirt into the center of the circle to cut the cards. The cards went out again in two rows of four, the same pattern. "A normal life span with no suffering at the end. Always concern with the heart. You will be famous among your friends. 'A good woman' — it will be said of you. Already you are known for your patience. Even in your profession," he was pulling the third card for matching, "you will advance at a natural pace for you are practical but not overly ambitious. Am I right?" He rubbed his hands together and smiled at her.

Margot got up on her knees and sat back on her calves. "Well, I haven't worked for a while, but I've just begun a job as a buyer — it's only temporary — so I can gradually get back to what I used to do."

She's bound to run into Mother, thought Miriam.

"Love," said Ezra, holding the fourth card. "You have been unlucky in love." Margot was nodding her head violently. "A man who did not appreciate you, but soon one will come who will open your heart, who will give you what you need, who will be good to your children."

Miriam pulled forward and pushed Roddy's hands away. "He is saying some things about her I know are true."

"You have children already, yes?"

"Yes, yes!" she was shouting. "I do, I do!"

"You will have money from different sources to make your living, but when you are older and with a new man, you shall together enjoy financial comfort and travel together to many places you have not seen before. The surprise card: you feel the need to make changes and you will visit a country setting soon, to reflect on your life and change your ways."

"Unbelievable," gasped Margot, getting to her knees again. "How could you know about the fat farm?" She blushed. "I mean the health spa. I am scheduled to go to Vermont at the end of the summer for a month, to lose weight and get in shape, to be free for a while to think things over. That's one of the big reasons I haven't taken a permanent job." She was visibly agitated. "Do the cards say it will be good?"

"I think," Ezra stared at the cards, "yes."

The orange shirt leaped up and yelled "Yaahoo!" with a piercing western movies' screech as she rocked back. "I'm glad for you, baby!" He pummeled the cushion into a slot for her body and sat down next to her, his arm draped over her shoulder, his hand flapping just above her breast.

"Who now?" asked Ezra again. He had everyone's attention. Peter put his head down as Ezra glanced around the room. His eyes met Miriam's. "How about you, my lady?"

She stared at him, and felt breathless with a sudden wave of fear. "All right," she said, wondering if the quaver she felt in her throat was audible in her voice.

"Here comes Rego Park," whispered Roddy behind her.

She had only to scoot forward a little in order to reach the deck of cards he held out toward her. She took them and cut it with only about ten cards in the top cut. She handed it back and looked directly into Ezra's eyes. They were dark and gentle, and he smiled pleasantly at her.

"Eight cards, now the ninth to match the first. Your life is just beginning," he said, "and you will live long like the oldest person you care about, although your life will be different." Naomi, her feet bursting in her space shoes, walked through Miriam's mind.

"Your fame will be like the character in a novel who alters in midlife — those who know her are amazed and even changed by what she does, but her fame depends on the reviews of others."

He drew a third card. "You will weary of your work, although you do it well, and you will find some other. The ten of clubs makes that clear."

"Love."

Miriam looked away from the cards.

"There is a man in your life, but he is not as interesting as he once seemed, and yet you care for him still. There are other men, another man who is close by but you cannot see him yet."

"I don't know him?"

"Perhaps, perhaps not. It is not clear."

Her mind ranged dispiritedly over the various men she knew, flirted with, lunched with from the office. Maybe someone from the past. Roddy? She did not glance back at him.

Ezra was going on. "You will have children who will give you much joy." Could that be? She put her hand on her abdomen right above her womb and thought of her nephews and niece, especially Brian, the oldest, who was at a comic age, a round-faced little boy.

"They shall be your gold. You will not be rich or poor, money will be sufficient, and as for travel," he said and laid the seventh pair together, "you come lately from a sunny place." (My tan, thought Miriam, dismissing the impact of his knowing this.) "And you will soon travel to a familiar place. Now the surprise."

He raised the eighth card and did not speak immediately. She felt struck with terror; what dreadful thing could that perfectly harmless queen of hearts falling on its own ten mean? Why didn't he say?

"This is truly hard to read. It suggests recovering something lost, something precious whose value you have overlooked that will make order out of confusion. You must search for it."

Miriam became aware of her heart beating. "Where?"

"I cannot tell that, but it can be found."

"Oh damn, damn!" she said. "What the hell do you do for a living? Are you a witch doctor?"

He slapped the floor in front of him with a good-natured pat. "I am a graduate student of business administration and economics. Financial witchcraft only. Who is next?"

"Peter, you ought to go. You started this. I think you're really scared of him. Go on. It's just a game." Cynthia pushed Peter forward, his excessive lips bill-like as he took the cards. "I don't know if I want to do this," he said. "The fortune is not fixed. It is what we do with the fortune. Some men spend their fortunes like spendthrifts — others hoard them like misers. The same dollar can be invested, or spent unwisely. It is the same dollar."

"How can you change how long you are going to live?"

"If I say to you, you have an illness that will kill you soon, you can go to a doctor, or you can get in bed and wait for death." Ezra held out his hand and took the cards. "I only do this at parties, so don't be afraid," and he laughed an ingenuous and redeeming laugh. The room remained hushed.

Miriam had gone back to her place beside Roddy. He patted her affectionately. "He seems to have shaken you up. What have you lost? No!" He feigned mock horror. "Not *that!* How can *that* be regained? An operation? But what a nuisance."

She did not respond, and he tried another tack. "Rego Park, that's it! Back to Queens Boulevard on the BMT. Are you really going to be so serious?" He put his arm pleasantly around her.

Her bladder began to ache. She needed to go to the bathroom terribly. "Excuse me," she said, and got up.

In the bathroom, she stood and looked at herself in the mirror over a white marble sink with gold fixtures as she washed her hands. She had never thought of herself as pretty, although people told her she resembled a currently popular front-page model. She had a hazel-reddish hue about her, her hair, her freckles worse than ever through her tan. The face she saw looking back at her was squashed orange.

The fortune repeated itself to her. What was the relation of the pieces? Who was the man she couldn't see? What was lost? Roddy's silly answers came to mind, surprising her with nausea, and she felt as if she was really going to be sick. She bent her head over the sink, but the sensation passed and she stood straight and smoothed the royal blue sleeveless dress on which hung an enormous silver necklace of balls and petals. It was American Indian, a fashion just becoming popular, and she knew Arthur had spent a lot of money for it.

Get a hold of yourself, Miriam. She was baffled by her own apprehension, as she struggled to change her expression to lightheartedness, a habit of advertising to order looks to match the occasion: *Woman frowns with dismay when she reads price on vacuum cleaner.* Yuck! Sooner or later someone else is going to have to pee and you're going to have to get out of here.

She stepped outside the door and went to the edge of the living room, where Ezra was now telling the fortune of the girl who advocated tube-tying. She wondered how rude it would be to leave without saying goodbye to Cynthia, who had brought her, or to the host. She waited through that fortune and the next. The guests were getting restless and so was Ezra. He scratched his head and said, "I think my powers are waning." There was a little round of applause. "Oh, just one more, mine." A lanky girl rushed forward. He laid out the cards, but this time without an audience as people wandered back to the table and the bar while he told her fortune privately.

When he came to the dining room after a few minutes, Miriam came along his left side as he took an ouzo on ice from the bartender. It misted white. In the background the party rhythms of speech and laughter had been restored. Some people were leaving.

"Listen," said Miriam, hearing an urgency in her own voice that amazed her. "Listen. Can you tell if somebody missing is going to ever come back?"

He turned and looked at her, his mouth opening, a pink anemone as he laughed. "It is the only way of reading cards I know. I can't tell a fortune about someone whom I can't see."

She stared at him, silent.

"In my experience," he said, still smiling, "people generally return if they believe they will be welcome. Does that help?"

"Thank you. You're very good at telling fortunes."

He cocked his head to one side. "I hope I will be even better at making my own," and he jingled some coins in his pocket.

A man had come up to him on the other side and he turned away. Miriam looked around and found the hall leading to the bedroom, where a few bags, stoles, and light jackets lay across the low bed. Before the window was a pole plant-tree from which full pots of fern and philodendron leaned toward the dark glass. She took her bag and put on her white jacket with blue lapels, buttoning it and noting that it comfortably covered her necklace. She did not like to wear ostentatious jewelry when out alone at night. It was asking for a mugging.

She bid the host goodbye — "Thanks so much for having me" — and found Cynthia and Margot in the thinning crowd. The orange shirt was drinking a fresh drink while still hugging Margot around the shoulders.

"I'm going to have to leave soon myself," said Margot forlornly.

"Not before a late supper with me. Come on. Come with me."

Miriam looked hard at the orange shirt and decided that sober he might not be too bad. She slipped into the hall and rang for the elevator. She would find out from Cynthia tomorrow how Margot had fared.

Outside the night air was cool, even a little chill. She walked several blocks east, letting the air break over her face. On Lexington Avenue she hailed a cab and climbed in the back seat without paying much attention to the driver. Sitting back as the cab made its way downtown, she saw the green and red traffic lights sparkling in a clear night, rare for New York, like sequins on a dark shirt. What was their meaning? An empty sensation in her stomach reminded her that she had not had a real dinner, but it was not this hollowness that troubled her. As she paid her fare to a dark-skinned man who thanked her with a heavily accented voice, she realized she had not said anything to lighten his night's work, the function she often ascribed to her flirting, and she began, but found the effort too great. "You're welcome," she said flatly and got out.

She took a TV dinner from the freezer, set the oven to heat first, and went into the bedroom where Arthur's robe hung empty just at the opening of the sliding closet door.

"What have I lost?" She spoke aloud, but nothing in the room answered her. She took the necklace off and laid it on the dresser. In the dim light the little pile of pamphlets, the one with the printed white letters RETURN on the top, made a thick stack at the back of the dresser. Another inch and they would fall between the chest and the wall. She reached out for them and carried them back to the kitchen and put them on the kitchen table as she put the TV dinner in the nearly heated oven.

She went over to the garbage can with the pamphlets and started to look at them one by one before she dropped them into the waste. "How to Keep Kosher," "How to Keep the Sabbath," "The Holiday of Purim." One by one they fell on the pile of cans and coffee grounds.

Lost, something lost, she shook her head to clear it. If Arthur were here . . . Arthur was just something else lost, an idea perhaps. And Gershom was lost. She remembered Gershom backing out of Harry's and Leah's apartment, yelling about celebrating Christmas, *Not our salvation.* There was nothing wrong with that. It was just a pagan holiday anyway. *A man you cannot see yet.* Someone unlikely. The red-bearded distributor of these pamphlets in his smelly black coat? God Forbid! "Passover — Out of Egypt," "RETURN."

She turned back the flaps of the last pamphlet to see the two faces: the young woman still serene over her candles, the young man with his prayer boxes, *tefillin* said the text. It was a pamphlet aimed mostly at college students, encouraging a month's Encounter at the end of the school year with a list of studies offered. They could use some layout advice, these people. More white space. "Live for a month among Hasidic Jews for whom every moment is imbued with their Judaism. Discuss subjects with scholars: How to find G-d; What does it mean to be a Jew? What has been much overlooked by Jews in contemporary America? Theme: 'It is a tree of life to them that hold fast to it and all who uphold it are happy.'" The text described living arrangements, separate dormitories and classes for men and for women, the fee, tiny for four weeks — she read it twice to be sure — and a reference to Proverbs with what appeared to be the continuation of the theme, " 'Its ways are ways of pleasantness and all its paths are peace.' "

Ding! The oven bell rang, the TV dinner ready. She held the leaflet precariously over the garbage . . . *Whatever is left of your Jewish blood that hasn't been diluted by life in the outer world.* Why did Arthur say that?

She waved the pamphlet but it would not fall from her fingers. Who would care? Arthur? A month without him should finish it off. All we'd do is fight and fuck, or worse, fight in order to fuck. Her employer? She had some vacation time still coming; besides after seven years' employment it would be difficult but not impossible to arrange for extra time.

This is crazy! she told herself. Miriam Miller, are you going to go off to Brooklyn to live with people like that loon who scares the hell out of you? She waited for reason to take the upper hand.

Then: Why not? If it's really awful you don't have to stay. Why are you doing this? I'm not doing it. *Something lost.* Gershom running. *Maybe because we're Jews . . . we don't know mercy . . .* Could that be? *Alters in midlife.* Not yet. Twenty-eight isn't midlife. Why do I keep thinking of Gershom? His poor teacher, Rafe, to lose a whole family. Six million Jews too hard to imagine, but one person makes it real. Six million others too.

Not much mercy there. Why? Why not do it? Maybe it's crazy, but my kind of life is crazy too. Certainly not pleasant and peaceful. Maybe the cab driver was glad I was quiet. Sometimes there is something positively restful about Celia these days. Madness! You're really crazy. I'm doing it, I think. No. What did he say? *"If one says 'I have not searched but found,' don't believe him."* I never claimed I found anything. How can you find something without searching for it? *Lost, value overlooked, makes order* . . . not lost. Never even knew you had it. Maybe with you all the time.

She turned back to the oven still holding the pamphlet and took out the pan of food.

*   *   *

It was easier to arrange things than she could have ever imagined and reassuring to find that the woman she dealt with on the phone had a calm, youthful voice. A week later, carrying only one suitcase, she entered a small dark building in Brooklyn, less than six blocks from her grandmother's house.

9

Sunday, June 3, 1973
PUBLIC NOTICES

Gershom — Miriam gone away to study orthodox Judaism. Rafe Toledano comes frequently. Silence continues. — Johanna.

"WELL," SAID LEAH as she let herself in the door of Johanna's and Seth's apartment, "have I news for you! Guess who showed up today?"

Johanna's palms began to itch. "Gershom?"

"Oh, of course not. No! Another reprobate! Your Aunt Emma."

Johanna had been arranging pots on the tables in the living room in preparation for a sale she planned to hold the next day. She wiped her hands on a little towel that hung from the side of one of the tables and backed up to sit down on the couch.

"Can you imagine?" Leah patted her hair into place while looking at herself in a small mirror in a gold frame hanging just by the door, one of several decorative additions she had contributed to their household since coming to stay. "It was just after lunch when she came with no warning — the first time she's been in that apartment in six months." Leah was facing her daughter now and took a seat nearby.

"She calls regularly." Johanna heard her own voice sticky with apology.

"Calls, calls! The phone isn't flesh!"

"I hope you didn't say that to her," said Johanna, shifting. She was beginning to show her pregnancy beneath her maternity smock.

"Why did she come?"

Leah leaned forward and pursed her lips. "What do you think?"

"Mommy, I don't want to play games with you. Tell me, please." Johanna's voice was weary. She waited for her mother to go on through a pause delicately calculated for dramatic effect.

"Well, first off, Miriam has been coming in her place, so to speak, and she liked that. It's the appearance that concerns her, and as long as her daughter was willing to be her substitute, even unwittingly — I give Miriam more credit than that, I think she really comes out of the goodness of her heart — Emma could salve her conscience. But now Miriam has gone off for a month and she can't find a replacement." Leah nodded as if in agreement with her own analysis. "But that's not the main reason, and despite everything, I must say I sympathize with her. She is sick about where Miriam has gone off to."

"I'll bet she is," whispered Johanna.

"Of course! Well, apparently, when the chips are down my sister comes running. She just needed to get things off her chest. But it's really outrageous for her to come to Celia's house sniffling about her daughter's departure. At least she knows where Miriam is. Not that knowing is very comforting in this case. Emma says things that are absolutely true: that these people she's gone off to are lunatics, that they're leftovers from another century, that she might imagine someone who was really desperate doing something so irrational, but that she can't understand what a sensible, fastidious girl like Miriam would want among those dirty people with their innumerable outdated customs. She said she was positively sick to her stomach when she heard."

Johanna stared at her mother, trying to imagine the moment. Their eyes met and Leah began to laugh, an embarrassed little giggle. "Emma's right about *this,* you know."

"I don't," said Johanna, "but anyway what did Miriam say to all that?"

"I don't know. I gather she announced she was going in her usual headstrong way and went off without discussing it."

"What about her boyfriend? Did he have anything to say about it?"

"Another unknown, but Emma said she thought that Miriam was getting tired of Arthur . . ."

"Ah so!" Johanna laughed.

"Now look, I know what that's been and I don't approve, never did. She's something of a slut . . ."

"Oh, come on! There's no need to call her names."

Leah pressed her lips in, and the lines along her nose stiffened. "You take that tone with me no matter what I say. Her own father called her that when she started this affair. She's been living with a married man who's rich enough to buy her what she wants. What do you call a woman who does that?"

"I don't," said Johanna. "Each person does things for his or her own reasons and I'm not willing to pin some label on her. People are like pots, you know. If you make things hot enough they harden."

Leah sniffed, and for a moment they sat silently. "Well, whatever Arthur thought, Miriam packed her bag and went anyway. The only other person she told as far as Emma knows was Uncle Sam, and you know he would never argue with her."

"Probably if she had called me she wouldn't have gone," Johanna smiled wryly. "I would have told her I thought it was a great idea."

"You've got to be fooling!" Leah shook her head violently. "You can't believe that for a moment."

"I do believe it, Mommy. Look, I don't think she's going to become a Hasid, but the truth is she's been racing her life along a shallow course even though basically she's not a shallow person . . ."

Leah gave a stiff artificial laugh.

". . . which causes her a lot of problems. Maybe she feels now she needs some roots."

"Damn, Johanna, you are infuriating. If she wants roots, to learn about her Jewishness, if that's what you mean, she could join a regular temple, or take a course, or do any number of other things that would be quite acceptable."

"Maybe." Johanna lapsed into a reflective pose.

"Well, anyway, I feel sorry for Emma. I can imagine how she must feel, but now, I told her, she's going to have to take some of the responsibility for Celia. I said that to her, and we agreed to meet at Mamma's on Sunday. She would have come here, but I said, 'My daughter is pregnant, she has a young child, she's selling her pots tomorrow and I will not impose on her.'"

Johanna gazed at her mother who had been living in her studio for nearly three months. She weighed what she might say about the subject of imposition, but folded it all neatly into the back of her mind. Lately, she had felt like screaming — no words, just a violent body-rending shriek, but that was not a real possibility for her.

"I appreciate all your consideration."

"Don't get snippy." Leah's face turned fierce. "I'm very concerned about you. That's why I'm arranging with Elise to take care of that fool dinner party your father asked you to hostess. He shouldn't have asked you to and you shouldn't have accepted. But you're a grown woman and I can't make your choices for you. I told your father when I spoke to him the other day that I thought his lack of consideration for you was just one more example of the total abandon he's shown making this decision of his — it must be a sort of male menopause, really, but that's *his* problem. *Yours* is something else."

"And yours?"

"I have mine, but if anything it's that I'm too easily enlisted by the people I love."

Johanna stood up and began to rearrange the pots. "I understand that." She turned away.

Leah paused, recovering bit by bit her placid beauty; then she said, liltingly, "Where's the darling?"

"She's at Rita's. Seth will pick her up on his way home."

"And how's the other darling, the one we don't know yet?"

"Fine."

Leah looked at Johanna, and her eyes warmed, a pained tenderness in sharp contrast to the judgmental screen that had passed from her face. "And you, my poor tired darling? I'm sorry, Johanna. I'm sorry you have to be mixed up in all of this."

* * *

Although her mother never said as much, it was clear to Johanna that she, Seth and Rachel were expected to attend her Sunday confrontation, to be her loyal and devoted seconds. It was the role for which her mother had long tried to groom her father and which he tacitly accepted, but had never embraced with fervor. As a child, Johanna had heard her parents through the darkened hallway of the night apartment arguing, not violently but obdurately, about her father's reticence, reluctance perhaps, when her mother longed for a hero, someone to defy those who would/could/did not adore her. She had lain awake, her head propped up with her chin against the pillow and listened to their voices, her mother's tones chiding and lachrymose though rarely slipping into the indignity of real tears, her father's voice strained and even bored. Of course he heard what *she* (his sister, her sister, his mother, her mother) or *he* (father, brothers, brothers-in law) said; of course Leah was in the right. But what did she expect him to do?

It was, Leah said, a matter of loyalty. And loyalty was to love as the flower was to the seed.

In adolescence, Johanna had recognized loyalty as a matter worthy of her close consideration, for her mother's loyalty was sometimes stifling, even dangerous. Because her mother assured her that no voice could be as sweet as her own, she blithely neglected paying any attention to the volume, and was consequently told, truthfully, by a succession of teen-aged friends that she talked too loudly. Because her mother assured her that such artistic talent in one so young was a rare gift and something that singled her out, she felt no need to seek a teacher who would push her to do those things she could not do. In fact, she avoided the one art teacher she had had in high school who had suggested that her craft was somewhat sloppy, feeling freshly wounded each time she saw the lady thereafter. "Insensitive!" Leah declared. "You need a teacher who can appreciate your work." It was much later, when she was out of college and struggling to come to terms with her art, that she began to understand what Mrs. Donado had been trying to do for her, and nearly despaired of making up what was by then nearly eight years of poor work habits. In the wake of that despair, she had abandoned painting and taken up potting, as if by starting fresh she might overcome her disorder. If someone had told Seth too early that he played the cello like an angel and not made him drill the endless scales and exercises, he probably now would be selling insurance or teaching mathematics.

Now that her father had been dismissed as disloyal, and abandoned to his own entertainments (in a limited way of course — for her mother kept track of him by phone daily, issued strict orders to Elise, and wandered around the apartment at odd hours), Johanna was called upon to demonstrate her loyalty and bring to the meeting with Emma the entourage her mother perceived only as her due. Well, Johanna had learned what *not* to do. Seth's loyalty was being asked enough of. He need not come to Brooklyn.

"I want to," he said.

"Why? You know what kind of a routine it's going to be."

"I heard her say that Seymour is going to be there and it would be difficult for her without your father, and you may think you're sparing me by telling me I don't need to come, but if you're going to be swept up by her needs like always, I'll lose some more of you. Worse, you'll lose yourself."

She was lying on their bed, her hands crossed over her round belly and she felt the early feather-twitch of movement within. A catch in her breath introduced the threat of tears, but while she could recognize the symptom, she could not assign the cause to either pleasure at her blossoming baby, or pain at her own ineptitude.

"Seth, I will ask her to go home if you really are finding her being here too unpleasant. I never expected her to stay this long. And she may be pig-headed but my father certainly isn't much better. They circle each other like sparring partners. He hasn't made any concessions to her, not one."

"And she hasn't made any to him." He sat down on the bed and took her hand. "You can't remake either of them, but you can step back, even while your mother stays here."

"I try."

"No, Johanna. She's your obsession." He stroked her hand.

Johanna turned her head away, "I'll ask her to leave if you want. I've told you that."

"And become a martyr just like her? No thank you. Her being here is only a nuisance to me. To you it's much worse, and the problem won't end when she goes home unless you get to the point where you can say to yourself, 'This is bad for *me*, not Seth, or Rachel, or little X in there,'" he patted her belly, "'but *me*, Johanna.'"

She looked at him and smiled faintly. "I'll go by myself on Sunday."

"Forget it. Consider me merely the livery."

"Who's being a martyr now?"

He stood up and smiled down at her. "I'm no martyr, I told you, I'm protecting my interests. And Rachel's."

She stared at him. "God damn it! Sometimes I wish you would just get furious and scream at me if that's what is really on your mind."

"You're not that lucky," he said, and leaned down to kiss her forehead. He went out of the bedroom, humming a theme from the *Trout Quintet*, which he had been working on for a concert next week.

Johanna stared at the ceiling. She felt helpless, a lethargy of limbs, an absence of bones as if her flesh hung on nothing, as if her tibia had been drawn out her big toe.

*   *   *

Her grandmother's house was brick, set close to its neighbors with a patch of lawn between its enclosed porch and the sidewalk, on a shady tree-lined Brooklyn street.

Naomi and Frank had lived in this house more or less continuously since 1926. Frank had spent time away in the service, and on an occasional vacation without his mother, but since taking over the Liberty Press just after his father's death, he had made 1412 his home by choice and, with a more domestic sensibility than his mother, cooked wonderful dishes for family get-togethers, repaired aging window frames and arranged for rooms to be regularly painted and repapered with fresh, if unimaginative, materials.

Naomi, until her sight had begun to fail, had braided rag rugs and a number of these dotted the floors, small ones over blond carpets with pale orange and brown flowers on twisted green vines around the edges. In the dining room, a large braided rug, her largest, lay beneath an oval table and six dark chairs with green-striped seats.

From the living room where Johanna was sitting, she could see Leah and Naomi setting the table for eight. They were talking constantly and quickly to one another, their speech flowing like a river without shoals of silence. Johanna heard the rhythms and was struck that neither her mother nor her grandmother seemed to wait until the other stopped talking to answer, but rather wove response into one another's conversation.

It was very hot for June, and Frank, Seth and Rachel had gone off in Frank's red Thunderbird to buy ice cream while Leah and Naomi, in deference to Johanna's pregnancy, had urged her to rest while they took charge of setting up. Though their voices reached her dimly, she let her mind go free. In the corner was the china-faced doll with golden curls sitting on a red rocker with which she had played as a child and in which Rachel now showed great interest. She looked at it fondly and then turned her eyes to the photograph of her grandfather, Max, which sat to the left of the mantel, where it had been since her earliest childhood.

He had been a thin-faced man with high cheekbones and dark thinning hair. She vaguely remembered that when she knew him, his hair was thinner than it appeared in the photograph, but her memory was amended by the story that had been told repeatedly about how she had described him as having a "high forehead," having no other term in her child's vocabulary for his receding hairline. She had a visceral memory of sitting on his bony lap, smelling the starchy smell of his clothes, and touching the calloused dry fingertips with their short stubby nails. He had been very fond of her, she supposed, because he always brought her trinkets bought from sidewalk vendors near "the place," his beloved press, and oranges, but as she stared at the photograph, she noted how her memories were ultimately irretrievable from the body of impressions and stories she associated with this man through her mother's perceptions.

"He was very strict about some things," her mother would say, "and not always warm. I was his favorite because I was a good student and I liked to talk about books with him, but he gave his approval in discrete packages. What I would have given to have had him hug and bounce me, or later stroke my hair," and at that moment her hand would fall on Johanna's head, heavy with longing, filling Johanna with guilt that she did not sufficiently appreciate the loving gesture. "He showed his approval by letting me keep the books for the business, by encouraging me to go to college, and finally by letting me know I was marrying a man whose family he considered 'first-rate.' Ha! But kisses or praise, not for me."

Johanna thought she remembered her grandfather kissing her. Did she? He didn't smile a lot, she thought, but she did remember some occasion — Fourth of July? V-J Day? something around the end of World War II where she had stood with him, their hands over their hearts, while the national anthem was being sung, and seen his eyes fixed on the flag and swelling with tears. She had had no idea until that moment that grown men were capable of crying. The vision of his emotion, which he had patted away, without explanation, with a neatly folded white handkerchief, remained with her.

She remembered only one other occasion clearly — his sitting reading to her and her cousin David from *Winnie the Pooh*. David, who was always skinny and shy, had sat in his grandfather's arms and she had sat beside him on the very couch she was sitting on now as his deep voice, scratchy but basso, intoned on Pooh, Piglet and Christopher Robin. Christopher! she thought. A beautiful name. Too bad it's impossible to give a Jewish child. Would her grandfather have thought that? What would he think of a great-grandchild named Christopher? Just an American/English name? A name taken from a children's book that had become a classic? But then would she consider naming a child Charlotte after the humane spider in *Charlotte's Web*?

Her thoughts were interrupted by the doorbell and she got up to let Emma and Seymour in. Emma looked older, indefinably so, an extra line here perhaps, a gait. Johanna could not quite fix on it. She had always felt a special affection for her aunt because when she and David were small and still good friends, and Miriam just a baby, Emma had done all sorts of gay things with them. She saved and studied government pamphlets on things to do with children on rainy days, or recipes appropriate for very young cooks, and was willing to spend afternoons playing games with them that her own mother found tedious. Once David had had a hamster named Brownie, of whom Johanna was very fond. One day on a visit, she asked about Brownie and was told by Emma, David nodding in agreement, that Brownie had, the day before, gone on a long trip to Hamsteria to see his brother Twinklenose and might not want to come back. "Lies," her mother had said on their way home. "You know, of course, Brownie died, and it's very sad. You mustn't tell David because his mother doesn't want him to know. The truth is so much better, but she doesn't understand that." Johanna had felt a pain in her chest at the thought of Brownie's death and wondered, treading a six-year-old's balance between desire and disbelief, at the scrawled letter David received from Brownie several days later apologizing for not telling David he planned to go but assuring him he was well and happy in Hamsteria with his brother Twinklenose. The letter skirted the issue of his possible return and shortly after that David was given two green turtles with flowers painted on their shells. *Voilà* Aunt Emma.

Her Uncle Seymour was heavier than when she had seen him last and looked tired too. He and Emma kissed Johanna.

"How was your sale, dear? Good?" Emma asked casually, and assured, turned to greet Leah and Naomi, who had come from the dining room.

"What do you think about Mimzie?" Emma asked Johanna as soon as they were seated.

Johanna paused, selecting words carefully. "I think she probably will get a great deal out of the experience and will do something useful with whatever she learns there." How formal!

Her aunt's jaw stiffened. "This group she's gone to is crazy. What can she learn from Hasidic lunatics? I know her religious education was limited but I could never have guessed she would do something so extreme to make up for that."

"Sick," said Seymour, "the girl's sick. First she's with this high-powered exec who takes advantage of her for a long time. He doesn't plan to marry her, you can be sure. Then she turns around and goes off with the craziest religious nuts I can think of." He was sweating profusely.

"It could have been Hare Krishna," said Johanna. "She's no fool. Think about this as a kind of experiment."

Naomi was sitting in a blue chair just in front of a shelf of porcelain knickknacks: *chotchkies,* she called them. "This is what we left in Europe. Always crazy, those people. Even the orthodox — my father was orthodox — even they wanted nothing to do with them. And now Miriam, an independent girl with a good education, a good job, modern, goes to live with them. They don't even speak good English. I can't understand. If your grandfather knew it would kill him."

"Do you know what her boyfriend thinks about all this?"

Emma's eyes became slits. "I hope he told her she was out of her mind! But it's possible he didn't make much of an effort to stop her. Mimzie hasn't said exactly, but she's hinted that the relationship is not what it once was. Maybe that has something to do with it. You know Arthur, don't you?"

"I've met him," said Johanna.

"And *that,*" said Naomi. "What did she need *that* for? All that hiding. They have to hide all the time." She shook her head and her thick glasses slipped down her nose. "I love that girl, but I don't understand what's going on in her mind."

Seth, Frank and Rachel had just come in the back door with the ice cream. Rachel, shy, held her father's hand tightly.

"Well," said Frank, "it's O.K. Rachel chose our flavors. You want to tell what you chose, Rache?"

"Chocolate and peppermint stick," she whispered into Seth's hand, then buried her face in his side.

"Peppermint stick wasn't her idea, but she had a taste and

decided she liked it," said Frank. "Hey Rache, come sit with me." She turned from Seth and went to him instantly.

"He's so good with children," Leah said softly to Johanna as they went into the dining room. "I think he would have been a fantastic father."

After ice cream and drinks, Leah washed Rachel's sticky fingers with a wet cloth, and coaxed "a kiss for Grandma," before she let her pad off to play with the golden-haired doll on the red rocker and a pile of old magazines.

"A sweet child," said Naomi, sighing and leaning back. "And bright. A good mind."

Leah's face flushed with pleasure, a personal triumph. "What do you think, Mamma? With her parents, her genes, how could she be anything but brilliant? Darling!" She beamed toward Rachel. Then her glow faded.

"Well," she said, turning, "we must discuss Celia's situation. Now that it's summer, Sam will be home most days starting in another few weeks, but he needs support. He can't handle the house and her without help, and more than help — encouragement, which means someone has to be there." She looked around the table sternly. "I have been there every day during the week since January and I think I'm entitled to a respite. Emma, I don't mean to pick a fight with you, but you have not offered, even offered, to relieve me. And worse, you've avoided her and Sam." Her voice was becoming brittle.

Emma raised her eyebrows and leaned forward on her elbows. "I did not go to see her because in the beginning it was clear she blamed me and Seymour . . ." Seymour shifted slightly in his seat and mumbled "crazy" to himself. ". . . for the disappearance of her boy. She was abusive of me and when she went completely crazy, I felt, and Seymour agreed with me — didn't you, Seymour? — that she would be disturbed by seeing me. It isn't as if I haven't stayed in touch, and of course Mimzie was going regularly too . . ."

"That had nothing to do with you," interrupted Leah.

"What do you know about what it had to do with? She's my

daughter and despite this current foolishness, we're usually very close." She glanced around the table at Johanna and Seth. "What's more, Leah, I have to work for a living as you well know, and lately I've been going out to New Jersey to help poor Anita. She's a very nervous girl, David's wife. And with what her nerves do to her stomach, and three little ones, someone is needed there. Your life is a lot freer than mine."

"Have David and Anita asked you to come to help?" Leah was pointing at her sister with a spoon.

"Do children have to ask for such a thing?"

"Maybe then, they could manage without you some of those days."

Seymour crushed his napkin into the tablecloth and breathed heavily as he glared at Leah. "What the hell are you suggesting? She's needed there! And what would you know about having to work? Your husband can tell you the state of the business, if you're still talking. As a tax lawyer he hasn't been a great help."

"He's not willing to do anything dishonest!" Leah was beginning to puff up.

"What's more," said Emma, hurrying to restrain Seymour, her dangerous ally, "I don't think I would be very good with Celia. Her condition would just grate against me. I can't imagine having the patience to set her hair and make sure she's dressing."

"She does more of that herself, now," said Leah.

"Well, all the things you do. You're very patient. You've always been able to calm her. Even when we were girls and she would get all fluttery, you had a good effect on her."

"Do you know, when she was a child she used to hold on to my skirt if I wanted to go anywhere and cry until she turned purple. Terrible! None of the rest of you ever did that. A colicky baby." Naomi's face wrinkled at the unpleasant memory. "Born with a burden, that one."

Leah shifted in her chair and stared at Emma. "Don't try to get out of this by flattering me. Do you think I've enjoyed these six months? It's been very hard on me, and on Harry too." Her look was charged.

"I don't flatter you. I'm just saying what's true. I don't have your patience."

"If you weren't so intent on getting out of things, you would find some other description, probably not so nice. Frank, don't you think she ought to give a little time to Celia?"

Her brother, amazed to be consulted, turned pale. "Lee, don't ask me. I told you I'd give you some money to hire a nurse. Maybe that's the best thing." His voice trembled slightly, the youngest, an only brother, always terrified of and courted by his sisters.

"Frank is right. We've all said that," said Emma quickly. "A nurse would do it."

"Damn it, a nurse can't give her what she needs — family love," Leah was raging. "And as for whether you would 'disturb' her, at first perhaps that was true. You did, after all, betray her confidence that afternoon though there's no telling what Gershom would have done anyway. But the other day when you came, she didn't seem especially upset to see you."

"Nor especially glad. She hardly noticed I was there."

"She doesn't notice me either when I go," said Naomi. "She ignores her own mother. I did something wrong with that child. It's not just the circumstances. Always I tried to be fair, to raise you to be independent."

"Fair!" said Leah. "Fair meant the three of us went to bed at the same time, and even Franky when he got to be bigger. Older children are entitled to privileges, Mamma."

Johanna was startled. She remembered her mother telling her when as a child she asked for a brother or sister, "You don't have to compete for your rights, darling, or my time. You are my treasure!"

"Well, how I could possibly do her more good than a nurse is beyond me. Besides, as you say, Sam will be there regularly in a few weeks. When Mimzie gets back," she stopped, as if thinking of something else, "I'll go up with her."

Leah banged the table with the palm of her hand. "Do you have any idea what I've given up to care for her? All the time I've been there when I might have been looking to my own concerns. You talk about work and your daughter-in-law, but when you wanted to pour your heart out about your daughter then you managed to find time to come up. My life hasn't been the same since that charming scene in my living room when that inconsiderate brat practically stepped on his own mother to get out. You want to know the truth? If I never see Gershom again, it won't trouble me. My husband has had to do without me, which has caused some difficulty between us, I might add. Mamma and Frank have spent parts of every weekend there. Johanna and Seth, as if they didn't have enough to do, go and visit. Your own Miriam comes. Even the brat's history professor, a lovely man. Oh, I'm forgetting Seth's father, and many days, one or another of her neighbors stops by. But her youngest sister?" She was panting.

"Mommy, calm down." Johanna touched her mother's arm, but Leah did not seem to notice.

"Leah, I'm not saying she shouldn't go at all, but it's not like she has your time or money. During the week she has to work." Naomi turned to Seth sitting quietly beside her. "She works and works as if they could get rich in that store. What do you think?"

"Nothing for publication," said Seth. "I reserve my opinion."

Seymour, who had been staring at Leah throughout her tirade, suddenly stood up. "Miss Smarty Pants here doesn't understand things like that. A patron of the arts yes, a philanthropist yes, a do-gooder, but to sweat out a living? Faah! What does Harry think about all this, Leah? What does Sam feel? Does he even want you there? How come he hasn't been invited to this confab?"

"Pig! Sam is very grateful. Sam is a real human being — compassionate and brave."

"And Harry?" He smiled and made a broad gesture.

"That's none of your business!"

"Leah," began Emma, "Seymour, sit down. Leah, I think you're overreacting. I have my own problems, as I know you have yours, but I'm sure you will work everything out. With Harry too!"

"I wouldn't have any problems with Harry if you had carried some of the load till now."

"I've told you why I haven't."

"You've told me you don't want to. And I tell you if you hadn't been desperate to talk to someone we *never* would have seen you. Harry has asked me, he has asked me why you haven't done your part."

"Fair is fair, Leah," said Naomi sadly. "People can only give what they can give. She has her own tsoris."

Leah turned to Johanna and said sharply, "Do you have anything to say?"

Johanna put her head in her arms on the table for half a minute as they all looked at her. Then she sat up. "Why don't we talk about this summer," she said. "Obviously, it would be nice if you could have some time off. Maybe, Aunt Emma, now that you feel that Celia's not so angry at you, you'd be willing to drop in occasionally. I think Mommy is upset because of the strain she's been under . . ." She looked up at her mother and could see from the line her lips had formed that she had failed.

Emma studied Johanna's face and Leah's. "I think this summer will take care of itself. Sam will be home. I'll come when I can, though if Celia's hostile, I'll have to stop. But Leah, I don't like being pressured into things. All our lives you've held yourself up to me as if you were some sort of saint. Whatever I've done, it's never been as good or pure or selfless as what you do. When I didn't work at Papa's in the afternoons because he wanted *you*, the smart one, to do it, you reminded me every day I was just wasting my time with my friends while you helped out in the place. I remember once you found Seymour and me necking and you told me with such self-righteousness that you would tell Papa, as if you wouldn't let Harry do anything more than give you a peck on the lips goodnight. Such virtue! I had to practically swear my life away to keep you quiet."

"It was more than necking," muttered Leah. "Harry and I were engaged."

"Do you remember that, Seymour? No matter what I do, I'm sure I can never be good enough for you."

The creases on Leah's face beneath her make-up filled and grew like tiny welts. She sat back. "I have nothing more to say to you," she said stiffly.

"Sometimes I wonder why I had children," said Naomi. "Maybe in a different world, not so grabby, children would grow up kind to one another. When I was a girl I thought a home where boys, girls, young, old were equal, children would come out of that able to give something." She covered her eyes with her hand.

"Come on, girls, let's make it up," said Frank, stretching his hands toward them, but they were beyond his reach.

"I'll help you clean up, Mamma," said Leah, getting up and taking some of the dishes to the kitchen.

*   *   *

After Rachel had been put to bed that evening, Johanna lifted the rock that had been clamped down upon the subject by Leah's heavy-lidded looks and excessive attentions to domestic detail.

"I'm sorry it turned out the way it did."

Seth, who was reading the newspaper in the far corner of the living room, looked up. She could tell he thought she should remain silent, not unstop her mother's anger, not offer this opportunity for recrimination, but the weighted air was oppressive, strangling, and he could sit outside that miasma, she thought. It was different having to live under it.

"You weren't much of a help for someone with such sympathies." Her mother gave a forced little laugh. 'Let's talk about the summer.' That's how that bitch has gotten away with everything."

"She's not a bitch, Mommy. Besides what's the point of going over and over the past?"

"Perhaps if you really understood what she's done, you would understand what the problem is. Do you want to write it down so you'll get it straight?"

"No, I don't. I . . ."

"Well, I'll tell you. I've kept very clear records. On December twenty-sixth she called and heard Celia say some unpleasant things about her and that fat dummy she's married to. Did you hear what *he* said about your father who's given him years of the finest legal advice — all for free? So she declined to make her appearance. A good excuse. She would have found another though. Until January twelfth she called every day, though of course she didn't speak to Celia, not even to say she was sorry. After her attack on me January first, which I'm overlooking — lovely New Year's greeting — she expressed her regrets, whatever they're worth, that I was stuck with it by suggesting Celia ought to be put away. On January thirteenth she didn't call. The next day she gave a sob story about the business to Sam, and from then on until the first week in February she called every other day. Your father was beginning to get edgy just about then and I would have welcomed a little help. On the weekend of February third, Miriam came up for the first time and after that . . ."

"I can't stand this," said Johanna.

"You listen."

"I know all these facts. You've gone over them with me too many times already."

"Perhaps if you really understood them, you'd understand my point of view." Leah's voice crackled.

"You think that if everyone had the same information, they would come to the same conclusions. That's not so. Facts aren't truth, you know. It's the way they're interpreted that counts and I don't agree with your reading. That's the problem you've had with Daddy too."

"You talk to me about him! He certainly has ignored the facts."

"No. He's just interpreted them differently and, Mommy, you can't force people to think what you want them to think just by repeating yourself. Emma and you are slaves to an old pattern and no matter *what* happens you manage to slip into your appropriate roles."

"There's isn't one person in this world to take my part, is there? My husband wants my undivided attention. My mother wants to be fair. Now my daughter wants to interpret facts. What about *me?*"

"Why have you made yourself the issue instead of Celia?"

"That's no answer, Johanna. I know how far I can count on you. Well, I will have nothing more to do with my younger sister and I already accept the fact that your 'reading' is such that you won't consider continuing your relationship with her as disloyal to me."

"God, I wish I knew how to explain to you . . ."

"Don't explain, thank you. Some women are lucky enough to have daughters who support their mothers. Miriam takes her mother's part, I'm sure."

"Right or wrong," said Johanna miserably.

"Wrong," said Leah, "though I know you don't believe it." She stood up and walked over to the doors leading to the studio. "It's been a long day. I think I'll go to bed. Nothing I can say is going to change your mind. That, at least, is clear. I hope your daughter won't have occasion to do to you what you're doing to me."

"Isn't that just another way of saying you can't wait?" said Seth amiably over the paper he had put down across his knees.

"Seth, please . . ." Johanna began in a little voice lost in the boom of Leah's firm, "Certainly not! The last thing I want is to see Johanna hurt."

Seth cocked his head and glanced at Johanna, who sat shaking her head almost uncontrollably, like a doll with a spring in its neck. He turned back to Leah. "I realize it's very hard to see this situation clearly but consider that all the circumstances are different than they were in January. Something as basic as how many hours Sam needs to be away from home is going to change in a few weeks. Maybe if you sleep on it, you'll have a different perspective in the morning."

"Nothing is changed, Seth," said Leah dryly. "I know you mean well. Just take care of my daughter. Goodnight." She disappeared inside the curtained French doors.

They sat in silence for a few minutes, Johanna covering her face with her hands. She felt Seth's arm go around her shoulders as he came beside her. With a gentle pressure he raised her up and faced her. "Lady," he said, kissing her nose, "lady, how would you like to go to bed with me?"

She stared at him and put her finger to her lips. He went about the living room turning off the lights and returned to steer her gently down the hall toward their bedroom. He closed the door behind them and pulled her against him. She felt his warm breath on her ear.

"I don't get you," she said, still distracted. Her body was wooden. It would take months to get the blood flowing again.

"I have a fetish for pregnant women," he said, "especially when they look beaten."

She pushed him away suddenly, stepping backward. "Stop it! I don't exactly feel sexy and that makes me want . . ."

He reached for her hand and pulled her back toward him. "To go sleep in the studio? It's already taken. Give me a kiss instead." He stroked her chin and she reluctantly put up her mouth, her teeth clenched together. He met it as if unaware of the barrier and then kissed her eyes. "You know, lovely lady, when I first met you, you were attracted to me because you thought your mother wouldn't approve. Remember? Musician. Foreign-born. 'Exotic background,' wasn't that her term?"

"That's not why I was attracted to you," she grumbled.

"Let's just say it was a fortunate coincidence." He was grinning. "I remember the first time I met your parents very clearly. Your mother eyed me as if I were a side of beef she was buying. If she had found me tender and juicy right off, you would have wondered what was wrong with me."

"She doesn't like most people right off. That's one of her problems."

He was moving, pulling her with him toward the bed. "Johanna, you worry a lot about your mother's problems. And her opinions. Do you know that?"

"So you've told me." She was feeling sad, even tired.

He began to unzip her dress and she felt his hands fumbling behind her, undoing her bra. "Do you think she has an opinion about our sleeping together? I think you must. Let's see. Your version goes something like: 'How can Johanna think of a thing like that when I'm in pain. When I told you to take care of my daughter, Seth, I wasn't thinking of her sex life.' " His hand had come around to her breasts and she felt her nipples tingle slightly under his fingers.

"It's not like that. Damn!" she said. "Why are you doing this?"

He kissed her again, his tongue coming just inside her lips to touch the tip of hers. Despite her annoyance, she felt herself opening up and the stifling sense of guilt lifted slightly in the night air. She put her hands against his chest. "Why?" she whispered but it was without urgency.

"Just to remind you," he said, as he pulled her dress at its sleeve and raised it over her head, "that she *really* says to herself now, 'Johanna didn't do so badly with that foreign-born musician.' Even I know that. That should give you some confidence in your judgment."

Her lips crept up into a smile as he kissed her neck. "You're smug," she said. "It was just blind luck, I've told you, and you're stuck with me now because I wouldn't want to take my chances again." Her fingers under his pants grazed the little raised birthmark on his hip, as familiar to her as her own skin. She felt comforted, relaxed by their closeness.

"And here I thought what held you all this time was my charm."

"That too," she said.

10

~~~~~~~~~~

Sunday, July 1, 1973
PUBLIC NOTICES

Gershom — Dad on vacation. Emma visits Folks. Miriam due back soon. How about you? — Johanna.

A GRAY DOOR swung closed behind her as Miriam stepped out into the warm summer air, blinking in the sunlight as her eyes adjusted to the glare. Her new friend, Ginger, a thin young woman with stringy blonde hair, stood beside her clutching a battered black suitcase and squinted, her free hand shadowing her eyes. It was Sunday and the streets were quiet; a few children played at a house about a block away and their laughter carried through the still, hot street. Miriam heard their voices as if she had never encountered such sounds before, another sensation to define the new world she entered just as the sun beating the pale cotton sleeves of her blouse made her aware of her arms, two fresh appendages to be discovered and explored.

"Maybe I'm making a mistake, maybe I should stay," Ginger said tentatively. "I don't know what to do." She put the suitcase down and turned to Miriam. "I really envy Sheila staying. She seems so sure."

"Let's go," said Miriam, picking up her own suitcase. It was heavy and really too big for her to carry comfortably.

Ginger and she started to walk toward the corner nearest

them. Several blocks beyond they could see the traffic, a Sunday leisurely traffic, along a broad street. "So, what are you going to do now?" she said to Ginger.

"Get on the subway and go to my father's apartment. What else can I do?"

"And then?" asked Miriam.

"Then, then, who knows! That's the problem. Get a job. Make a life. It all seemed easier in there." She gestured back at the building they had left. "What about you?"

"Right now," said Miriam, stopping for a moment to transfer her suitcase to the other hand, "I'm going to go to my grandmother's house. She just lives a few blocks from here. My uncle can drive me home."

"But then what?"

"I have a life," said Miriam softly, "but it has to be changed. Everything has to be changed, but I do have a place to live, and a job I can keep on doing till I find one I like better."

"If I'd had all that, I don't know if I would have split. Like I'm glad now I didn't. I mean it's not hard to give up everything because there's not much to give up."

"Despite the job and the apartment," said Miriam, "and even a man, I felt just that way — nothing to give up, just a hole to fill."

"It would be easier to stay here if you want a real orthodox life. I mean I keep saying that to myself."

They had reached the corner and stopped, their bags on the ground.

"You're probably right. I'm just going to have to see what kind of changes I can make in the life I had — adapt it, I guess. I kept thinking the whole first few weeks we were there that Judaism ought to have something like convents, but then I began to see that the message was to live in this life, make the world holy. It would be easier to go off away from it, but I think I would get tired of a convent."

They looked at each other and smiled a little.

"Aren't you going to walk me to the subway?"

"I won't make it back to my grandmother's in this heat." Miriam shook her head. "I've got to go this way now," she said, pointing, "but I'm on your side. You have my phone number and I have your dad's."

"Don't mention him! I'm so scared to see him. He's gonna make fun of me." Ginger sucked in her breath. "Pretend it's like my Zen-macrobiotics phase."

"Maybe not. I'll bet he'll be glad you're going to stop wandering around and do something more orderly."

"Yeah. He wasn't big on my going from pad to pad, just coming home when I needed bread. I hope I don't do that again." She wrinkled her brow.

"Call me if you need encouragement. It's the first step that's the hardest. I'll need support too, I bet. We'll talk soon, O.K.?"

They hugged each other, pulled back, then hugged each other again.

Miriam picked up her bag and started down the street, turning to wave once at Ginger, who had crossed to the other side. Alone, the heavy bag whacking at her legs, she looked up through the leaves of trees, rich summer green, and she began to walk quickly. It seemed a thousand years from May to this first day in July. She felt transformed in some way, strengthened, but at the same time, panicked by her own fragility. Dangers awaited her everywhere — in the bare arms of girls who passed, in her hunger, which could now be satisfied only in prescribed ways, in her family and their opinions. Were joy and terror to be her lot? She felt the rhythmic beat of the bag against her legs and in her mind began to recite in Hebrew, the entire Shema. It was appropriate here in Brooklyn on these streets, but how would it be in Manhattan, or even in the house she approached, her grandmother's? Outside a house on the other side of the street, she saw a bearded young man, a yarmulke on his head and the fringes of his ritual undergarment hanging from beneath his shirt, putting out garbage in the cans along the driveway. They rattled like any garbage cans.

Her grandmother's house, an ocher textured brick, appeared like an apparition; she stopped, noting the red car just beyond the shared driveway before the garage. Frank must have already gone out for the Sunday papers, she thought. She put her suitcase down and looked up at the door. Then she took the bag and went up three steps through the first door onto the porch and rang the bell.

Frank, wearing bedroom slippers, baggy slacks, and a plaid shirt open at the collar, came to the door. He looked at her almost without recognition, then said, "Miriam, oh Miriam, come in, come in."

She put her suitcase down just inside the door. "Hello, Uncle Frank," she said. "How are you?"

"I'm fine. How are you?" He emphasized the last word, and grinned.

"Better."

"I hear you spent a little time nearby. Are you finished?"

"Finished, and starting."

"I mean you're not going back there?"

"No." There was a strained silence. "Where's Grandma?"

"Inside, in the kitchen. She'll be glad to see you. You worried her. Do you know that? She worried about you even worse than about Gershom."

"Has he turned up?"

"No, no. I don't think he is going to come back."

"And Celia?"

"Still quiet." He passed his hand over his lips, then smiled broadly. "Come on in. Hey, Ma, look who's here! Miriam!"

Her grandmother appeared in the doorway of the kitchen, her white hair radiating out of its tight pull. She reached out toward Miriam.

"You come here. I'm glad to see you. Oy, am I glad! Are you done with this crazy thing you do?"

She went forward and hugged Naomi, who kissed her

cheeks with wrinkled moist lips again and again. "It wasn't so crazy," she said, and hugged her tighter.

"Miriam, come in. You sit down, have some coffee, some Danish. Tell me what!" She was beaming, the rims of her eyes red with pleasure.

"What do you want me to tell you?"

"Everything! What else? Why did you go with those fanatics?"

Miriam did not answer at once. She considered she could not really say why she had gone in the first place, although she could explain easily why she had stayed. Her perceptions were so altered it was hard to get the old time back in focus. "It's not easy but I'll try to tell you." Frank brought a mug of coffee to her and they sat down at the kitchen table surrounded by newspapers. Her grandmother pushed the plate with pastries toward her.

"Your mother has been upset like I've never seen her. She usually covers up, but not this time. A woman of passion she's not, except that you really got inside her. I don't blame her. Hasidim, they're just meshugga. A sensible girl, free, like you, what are you doing with them?"

Miriam looked at her grandmother and began to laugh. "Can I tell you, or are you going to tell me?" She patted Naomi's hand. "They don't seem so crazy anymore, but they did to me for a long time. It was just that everything about my life seemed so meaningless, so really stupid. And I kept asking myself why I couldn't stop seeing Arthur, why I was playing around thinking about marrying him when I didn't understand why I got involved with him in the first place, why I was writing advertising copy to sell things I didn't care about, why I felt as if I wasn't attached to myself. It doesn't sound sensible, I know, but I felt as if I were hollow and my insides were somewhere else. First, I was just annoyed by this Hasid near my office who kept giving me pamphlets, even a little scared of him, but I couldn't stop thinking about him, the way he looked, the things he said to me. It was unnerving, and then one day I decided I had to look for something — my center. You'll laugh. This man doing fortunetelling tricks at a party told me that." She stopped and waited for her grandmother to respond.

"What a place to look," said Frank with amusement. "Who would think you could find anything in Brooklyn."

"Why not?" Miriam smiled. "What's wrong with Brooklyn?"

"So you come and you live with them, eat their food, say their prayers, and did you find something out that way?"

Miriam hesitated, staring straight ahead. "That I can't go on living my life the way I was, that I need some order, something bigger to plug into. I don't think any of the things I've done in the last five or six years have come close to giving me the satisfaction I've felt lighting the Sabbath candles in the last few weeks, or saying the blessing over the bread at each meal."

Her grandmother rocked forward. "So, what are you going to do? Be an orthodox Jew, even more than orthodox, like one of them? I see your long sleeves on a hot day in July. I know what they mean. You want to leap back to the shtetl. That's what those people do."

Miriam touched her long sleeves, crossing her arms as she did so. "No, I don't think I'm going to wear long sleeves all the time. But they do mean I'm going to be — what? more modest. I think I have a lot to learn about modesty."

"Modesty, peh! Modesty like this is a leftover of shame. You feel ashamed?"

"No. Modesty is just showing respect for your body."

"You see the children, the little girls in hot summer, all covered up, sweating, and you tell me that's respect?"

"Grandma, I don't want that, but I can't ever again put myself into a dress that shouts 'Look!' I've done that, even when I thought it was clever, and I ended up feeling like a fool, or worse."

"You're going against the tide of fashion: less fabric for a higher price," said Frank.

"So what else?" Naomi's lips were pursed.

Miriam paused, her mind flashing. This was the question she had been posing to herself for days. "I think I want to live as an observant Jew. I think I believe there's something more, and we're taught" — funny phrase, she thought — "that we should perform the rituals and that then we will understand. I think I want to give that a try — to keep a kosher house, to observe Shabbos, to go to synagogue, to think about what I do, even the simplest things, to think about that something more."

"And that man? Arthur?"

"He had to go anyway. I knew that even before I was calling our affair adultery. I'm just as much to blame for that as he is."

"If he didn't have a wife, there wouldn't be all these lies. That's bad. For the rest, it doesn't matter if you give yourselves to one another without compulsion. When I was young, idealistic people believed in free love like that."

"A nice theory," said Miriam. "Anyway, it's not what I want anymore."

Naomi thrust out her hands, her cheeks hollowed. She looked suddenly older. "Miriam, you make me so sad. Three daughters I have, and two granddaughters. I believed always in freedom for women. I know the orthodox in Europe and those women were slaves not even able to perform services, no matter how pious. Slaves! I said when I was a girl I wouldn't be a slave. I wanted freedom, a world where men and women would be equal, comrades. Bolsheviks talked about it. So they didn't turn out the way they talked! I believe it anyway. I come to this country — didn't want to, I want to stay in Russia to bring the revolution, but my brother comes with a ticket and my sister and I go with him on a boat to the new land. And in a place I can't speak the language, everything's new, I meet and marry your grandfather. Don't misunderstand. He was a good man, but about lots of things we didn't agree and he insists we speak only English. I didn't argue so good in English in those days. But I have three daughters. I say they are going to be free. Your mother, Emma, you know how she got her name? We want an English name after my father, Emanuel, and two years before when Leah was born, Emma Goldman, the anarchist, a great lady — she had courage, I used to read her *Mother Earth* then — was put in jail for talking about birth control. In those days you didn't talk about it. So I say let's call this one Emma, she's going to be my last. Your grandfather, who thinks another way, says, 'Emma — Emma Lazarus, the great American poetess, Jewish, who writes a poem on the Statue of Liberty — a good name.' He's happy. I'm happy. Your mother, she doesn't write poems or have courage! What a namesake for that lady who fought all her life for freedom, who was willing to pay whatever price for what she thought!"

"Does mother know you named her after an anarchist?"

"Not from me. Of course, I tell her about Emma Goldman, your grandfather tells her about Emma Lazarus, but she hardly knows what we're talking about."

Miriam smiled wistfully at the thought of her mother's bafflement.

"But at least you, I thought. Not Celia, not Leah, not our brave Emma, not even Johanna, who tries but is blown like a leaf by her mother, but *you* I thought, at last a girl like the girl I would like to be, at last one of my own."

The telephone rang and Frank got up to answer it, drawing the receiver with its long cord off into the dining room.

"So Mom was going to be your last, but then Franky came along, or did you plan that he was going to be a boy?" She was teasing, choosing not to acknowledge what she knew to be her own closest family bond.

Naomi's face clouded; she glanced at the dining room door, then drew closer to Miriam, her voice very low. "I tell you something I never told anyone but my sister before. After Emma, three little girls in four years, the first so whiny, the second so clingy, I didn't want any more. When I got pregnant with Frank, a mistake, I try to get rid of him: drank things, fell down stairs. But he was meant to be born, no question. I'm glad, but a strong man he's not."

Miriam stared at her grandmother. "If he hadn't been born, you'd probably be living with one of those little girls now. Lucky you weren't successful. God was watching over you." Her heart was beating rapidly.

"Not *so* orthodox, she speaks the name of God. Well, maybe. After that I learned how not to get pregnant."

They sat in silence for a minute, not even looking at one another.

"Maybe Gershom is your free spirit," Miriam said softly, "even if he is a boy."

"The end isn't written to that story yet. The question is can he be free and with his family both. I worry where he is, what he's becoming. You're a smart girl. Do you think running away makes you free? Nah!"

Frank, the survivor, dispassionate heir to Max's precious Liberty Press, came back into the kitchen and hung up the phone. "That was Hy Berman. The combo got a last minute job to play at a twenty-fifth anniversary party tonight." He rubbed his hands together in delight. "Someone in the band that was supposed to had a death in the family. You knew I play trumpet with a little group, Miriam?"

"That's nice, Frank." She smiled at him, ashamed she had forgotten.

"Ma, if you want to go to Celia's we got to go now. Miriam, I'll drive you home, or to Aunt Celia's if you want."

"I think I'll go home," she said. "I have to make some arrangements."

"Let's have lunch first," said her grandmother. "What do you want?" She started for the refrigerator.

"Some fish," said Miriam. "Have you got some herring, or tuna?"

"A pot roast sandwich? You'd like maybe some cold

chicken?" Naomi continued to peer in the refrigerator, her back to Miriam.

"You know the answer. An egg would be all right."

Frank looked puzzled, then recognition spread over his face and he grinned. "You are really going to eat kosher? Even out of the house?"

She nodded once and lowered her eyes. "Do you have fish, Grandma?"

"I didn't hear you."

"I'm just exercising my freedom."

Her grandmother turned to look at her, and shook her hands at Miriam. "You call this freedom? Do eat this, don't eat that, not those two together. Pots. Plates. This is not freedom."

"I've never felt so free." Standing, she walked forward and put her hands on her grandmother's shoulders. "I'm telling you the truth."

Naomi leaned against Miriam, as if listening to her heart. "Truth," she said sadly. "I always wanted to say what I thought. I named your mother for a woman I admired most because she never said what she didn't mean. Even later took on the Bolsheviki. Ah — that's another story. And your mother doesn't know the difference. Lies, truth — they're all the same to her." She stepped back. "Miriam, I'll give you fish, but I'll pray just in case there *is* somebody listening, you come to your senses."

"I have," said Miriam, feeling her smile rising to her eyes. "I think maybe I have."

* * *

Frank left her in front of her apartment building and she made her way upstairs, pushing the big bag along the floor of the hallway. It scraped against the tiled floor with irregular little bumps. At her apartment, she paused and sighed, then took out her key and unlocked the door. Inside everything was still, as if the very air had not moved since she had left. She shut the door behind her and leaned against it, looking into the familiar living room. She felt her old life coming toward her, ready to engulf her. It seemed so natural, this homecoming. She shut her eyes for a moment, then laid the suitcase down in front of her and opened it. In a side pocket, she found a little packet wrapped in paper. She unwound it and took out an enameled metal mezuzah with the Hebrew letter *shin*, dark blue against gold. With it was a little card of instructions. She turned to the closet near the door, in which there was a small unpainted dresser. In the top drawer there was a hammer and a few nails among a small assortment of hand tools. She opened the door again, measured a hand's breadth from the top on the right side and then placed the mezuzah at an angle against the door frame, tapped nails into the holes at the top and bottom of it, and hammered gently. The nails were too long for the shallow wood and would go no farther when they hit the wall. They protruded slightly, and Miriam considered them, frowning. She would have to get the super to put it up properly, but it would do for now. She read the appropriate blessings from the card aloud softly, put her fingers on the mezuzah, then kissed them and closed the door. "Jewish space," she said.

She put away the hammer, stepped over the suitcase and walked into the kitchen. She switched on the light and looked at the silent counter. Opening the cabinets, she glanced at the dishes. There were already two sets, one for good and one for everyday, four place settings each. Would God forgive her if she simply declared them meat and milk without going through the elaborate or time-consuming processes of koshering them? Maybe she should get new ones. Was "Waste not, want not," a Talmudic lesson? Was the spirit or the law more important? So many things to think over. She opened the refrigerator and was struck by its sour smell. It needed cleaning anyway.

In the bedroom, Arthur's clothes still hung in the closet. Weeks, and he had not needed anything. She had been herself, she could see, a wild extravagance, nothing necessary. She looked at the bed. How to kosher that? She opened the drapes and the window, before moving on to the bathroom where his funny shaving mug, the fat round-cheeked face of a Dutch burgher, still sat on the shelves above the padded rose-colored hamper.

He had made her laugh and she thought of that with appreciation, but of something finished and remote.

She returned to the kitchen and called her parents.

"We'll come right away," said Emma. "You probably need things."

"Don't come," said Miriam, "I'm not ready. I have a lot to do, and as for what you can bring, I'll have to do my own shopping."

"You aren't going to keep kosher, are you?"

"Yes."

"Miriam, what kind of madness has taken hold of you? I thought living that way would cure you."

"I'm sure we will have lots of conversations about it," said Miriam as she turned the revolving can shelf in the corner cupboard and noted the things she had that she could keep.

"Celia and Sam have missed you." Emma's voice stiffened as she thrust about for words. "I went to see them several times while you were away. Celia actually smiled when I mentioned you. That man, the history teacher, was there. He asked about you too."

"Rafe?" she smiled. "I look forward to seeing him. He's very nice. A really good person."

"He was very curious about what you were doing. I wouldn't have told him, but Sam did. I think it surprised him, even shocked him a little. That's the reaction you're going to find."

"I'll just have to find it," Miriam was still smiling. "I don't think Rafe will be unsympathetic, at least."

"When will we see you?"

"Soon," said Miriam. "In the next few days. There are just some things I have to do first. I'll be out for the Fourth of July — that's only a few days away. I know Daddy's watching baseball. Don't disturb him. Just give him my love." She noted that only a few of her canned goods were still usable.

*   *   *

Several hours later the kitchen was done. The cans and boxes that could no longer feed her were in a paper bag and she had divided the kitchen goods and marked some of them with adhesive tape and a letter M or D for meat or dairy. The refrigerator smelled fresh again. She looked over the one blender she owned and after some consideration dubbed it dairy. As soon as she could, she decided, she would buy a second, and some new dishes too.

Evening was falling. She took a frozen package of macaroni and cheese from the freezer and set her oven to heat it. A fortunate leftover from the old days, she thought, and pushed the question of whether the cheese was kosher from her mind. While it was heating, she went down to the delicatessen-market, a block away, open twenty-four hours a day, and brought back milk, a few vegetables, fruit, rye bread, corn-oil margarine and farmer cheese. She also got some olives, kosher salami, a jar of herring, and a blue and white box with red letters containing short white Sabbath candles. Once back at the apartment, she touched her mezuzah and her lips, then took a deep breath. It was going to be possible to live.

After eight o'clock, she decided to try Arthur, although she thought he might still be in Connecticut. She dialed from the kitchen and heard his phone ringing in the bedroom. There was no answer. Thinking about him as she passed back through the dining alcove, she noticed the glass decanter and brandy glasses that were his and lifted them off the shelf to put near the bag of canned goods.

*   *   *

The first day back at her office was startling. The walls of the advertising agency, a pastiche of posters and magazine pages seemed frenetic as women with dewy lips and big eyes gazed at her from every direction.

"What happened to you?" demanded Cynthia. "Where did you go?" She eyed Miriam suspiciously. "Are you O.K.?"

"Why? Do I look as if I'm not?"

"Hell, I don't know. You went off so suddenly, I thought something — an abortion maybe." She paused as if requesting permission to go on. "You are all right, aren't you?"

"I'm fine." She gestured toward the chair by her desk. "Sit down. No abortions, but something is different. I went to Brooklyn to live with the Hasidim — the group that guy with the red beard belongs to."

Her friend beamed. "Wild! Boy, I bet you can write a brilliant exposé. Have you got a market yet? There must be plenty."

"Cynthia, would you believe I went because I needed to? I don't have anything ugly to expose about them." She could see Cynthia trying to process what she had just said.

"They're dirty people living in another era!" Exasperation. "They say their prayers and rock while they do it like some sort of primitive tribe. At the same time, they act holier than thou. I can't believe you don't see through them."

Miriam shrugged, spreading her hands. She had played this scene over and over in her mind during the last week, rehearsed it, but when she began to speak she was almost whispering. "They have their idiosyncracies, and like most people, they sometimes do things out of habit that don't mean much, but even so they taught me a lot. I was just casting about trying to be up-to-date, really flip and clever about things, but I kept feeling there was something missing, or so well disguised it was unrecognizable. I used to tell myself that living with Arthur was O.K. because, his presents aside, I paid my own way and if he wanted to wander it must be his wife's fault. But when I let myself think about what he really wanted from me,

and worse, what I was willing — no eager — to take from him,
I wanted to run like hell . . ."

"So," Cynthia interrupted, her voice edged with sarcasm,
"you got tired of being his fancy lady. There are easier ways
of getting rid of a man than plunging headfirst into orthodoxy."

Miriam ignored her. "I'm not blaming anyone but myself. I
knew what I was getting into. But once I was there, and Gershom left, I began to feel I needed something, not just different, but — how can I explain? I decided I didn't like what I
was. Then we went to that party and my fortune told me what
I already knew — that I had to find the thing I'd lost, never
valued, been afraid of. I used to be so afraid of that red beard,
but it wasn't him. It was me I was afraid of."

"You are out of your mind. That fortuneteller is just a business student. I've seen him do it before. He sizes people up,
says a lot of very general things . . ."

"I know. Maybe he doesn't have any special powers. It's just
that by chance, perhaps, he said things that, despite myself, I
wanted to hear. I had to do something."

"And now that you've conquered your fear, Queen Esther?"
She leaned forward and stared hard at Miriam.

"I guess I'd like to be able to take myself seriously some of
the time, and to live by some rules that I can count on not to
pass into yesterday's trivia as soon as I've gotten used to them."

Cynthia shook her head. "You absolutely flabbergast me.
Why did you come back to modern America if you feel this
way?"

"I don't want to abandon everything. I know if I stayed,
after a while I'd see nothing but the idiosyncracies and I'd
hate it." She paused. "And then, even if I wanted to, I'd have
a hard time arranging a marriage, and unmarried women
don't have a real place . . ."

"Charming!" Cynthia was almost screaming. "How can you
accept the values of a world that thinks you're shit?"

"I'm trying to explain. I couldn't hack their kind of marriage anyway." She closed her eyes and began very deliberately. "I know they have feet of clay, but they also have real hearts, and I want to take mine and live with it the best way I can." Now she was staring at Cynthia. "There must be other people like me." Her voice fell.

"Sure, the world is full of crazies," Cynthia snapped. "Exactly what do you think is going to happen now that you've made your decision for Moses?"

Miriam blinked, then beamed. "Hey, that's pretty good. I'll have to remember that." Her face became sober again. "Nothing miraculous. I just want to try Jewish life. After five thousand years, it must have something to offer."

Cynthia put her face in her hands, then looked up. "We'll have lunch later and I'll have my rebuttal prepared." She got up. "No more shrimp salad, dope! Did you think of that?"

"I'm sorry I didn't study debate," said Miriam. "I can see defending myself is going to be the hardest part — a lot harder than giving up shrimp . . . and I like shrimp," she called as Cynthia disappeared around the corner of her door, moaning.

Miriam dialed Arthur's office. "Would you ask him to call Miss Miller at Brown and Bernstein Advertising when he has a chance?"

* * *

When Arthur returned her call, she asked him to come by after work and when she arrived, he was already in the living room, the air-conditioning unit on, a bottle of champagne in an ice bucket and Frank Sinatra singing softly on the stereo. When she came in, he got up from the sling-back chair and held out his arms. "God! I've missed you."

She stopped and looked at Arthur. He was not handsome in any traditional way and yet he had sharp charm, as if amusement had cut lines in his brow. He could, she knew, with just the slightest movement of his lips or forehead dissolve her into laughter at certain moments, or excite her erotic fantasies. But she had rarely, it suddenly struck her, felt real tenderness toward him and that former omission of feeling seemed gaping. What had it all been about? Yet seeing him, she felt the old attraction.

"Have you really?" Her lips formed a small tentative smile.

"Of course. Listen, we were having problems but there's nothing we can't work out." He paused abruptly and said, "Hey, puss, put down your stuff and come here," and he patted his chest.

"No," said Miriam.

His face clouded, his lips becoming unnaturally thin, and he put his arms down, waiting for her to continue. She had stopped at a kosher meat market and she was carrying a large bag which she took into the kitchen. She carefully placed some of the meat on the right side of the refrigerator and some in the top freezer, having divided each shelf in half with a little adhesive marker. She returned to the living room and sat down facing Arthur, who was seated now on the couch.

"This isn't the greeting I expected," he said, leaning toward her.

"I'm sure."

"Tell me what's on your mind."

"I'm glad you want to know," said Miriam. "I'm about to."

"Shall we have a drink?" He gestured at the champagne.

"Not just now, and I won't have that anyway." She looked at him and chuckled at his impassive expression, a studied look she knew hid bewilderment, anxiety. "Arthur, for no good reasons, I like you."

His lips curved slightly as if trying to repress whatever surged within him. "You certainly have an odd way of demonstrating it."

She got up, turned off the music and, for a moment, continued to stand with her back to him. Then she returned to her seat.

"I've composed a lot of speeches to you in my head, and letters too, these past weeks. I thought first if I never saw you again it would be better, but then I thought there would be a lot of misunderstanding so I decided we should talk, and I hope you'll listen to me first."

He raised his brows, then nodded. "Go ahead."

Given the floor, she closed her eyes and collected her thoughts. "It's over," she said, her eyes open again. "It's not your fault. You lived up to the terms we started with. If I were still willing to go by those rules, we could go on. It's not marriage either, though the last month before I went away I tried that idea out. I really don't think you're a good marriage risk. After all, I know how seriously you take your vows and if I ever marry I think I want a different kind of marriage. Certainly, I want one in which I don't have to cover up or underplay what's on my mind, because I've come around to valuing my feelings."

"Of course." He leaned forward a little more.

"Oh, don't play the understanding lover! What you want is a woman who always seems happy, and around whom everything is always 'nice,' no matter what she has to plow under. It's ironic: that's the quality in my mother that nearly drove me crazy when I was a kid. But I guess it was habit forming." She stopped and looked off toward the wall.

"Your habits the last few months would never suggest you were so well trained," he said dryly.

"Let's just say I've been going through a debriefing period." She was looking at him again. "Anyway, that's hardly all of it. I've been trying to figure out what kept it together. Excitement. Money. I blush to say that, but you have given me a lot of gorgeous things. That you're so successful and you're funny, that you're older — I've always liked older men. The fact that you aren't Jewish because most of the Jewish men I knew were dull and flabby like my father and I always found non-Jewish men sexy and sort of exotic. About Eileen, I kept on telling myself that if the marriage were any good you wouldn't need me and that your kids were all right anyway so I didn't need to feel any responsibility. And of course, I liked you, even occasionally loved you."

"And you don't love me anymore!" Arthur's voice clicked as he stated this like the closing of a drawer. He drew back and folded his arms.

"I don't even ask myself that. It's just that my rules changed. Even before going to Brooklyn, I guess when Gershom went away, I began to think about myself and the sorts of things I'd been running away from. There was this awful emptiness, as if I couldn't feel anything very deeply . . ."

"Nothing?" he asked. "Not even wanting more of me? I can hear you . . ."

She was shaking her head and waved her hand in front of her face. "No, I don't mean it that way. I mean, it was as if whatever is — shall we call it God? I suppose that's as good a name as any — was so far away." She hesitated again. "I went to Brooklyn to look for it, and while I was there I looked at myself too, and at you, and at us. And I thought about Eileen. You know, I wonder if we have really fooled her. I bet she knows. I said and you said she had her own reasons for going on. I wonder if one of them might not be that she loves you, figures she can outlive any affairs you might have and grow old with you."

"You are generous in your estimations, my dear." His voice was curt. "And so sympathetic now that you claim to have given up on the idea of replacing her."

"I didn't say that to make you angry, Arthur. Please. The three of us share the past whether we like it or not, but the most important thing that has happened to me is that, as Cynthia says, I've made a decision for Moses." She giggled.

"I can't believe it!" He looked as if she had delivered a true blow. "Those proselytizing Jews really took you in! You think you're going to be cleansed of your sins and stand before the holy throne all dressed in white? What crap!"

She felt as if a tiny bird fluttered inside her chest. "I'm not thinking about what comes later. Jews stress living in *this* world and I know I need to feel differently about myself *now, here.*"

"I can just see you, now, here. A married lady with eight little ones clustered around your knee. Be fruitful and multiply! And what else? I did a little research. They chop off their hair and wear wigs."

"That was good of you to find out!" She blinked, momentarily shaken. "Don't think I haven't considered that. No, I know I can't go that far. I don't know yet what my limit is but I do know something. All those commandments are there to keep you from having to fool people, or lie, or deny what you are. From one point of view, they're confining, but from another, they set you free." She could feel blood rising in her cheeks and she beamed at him feeling supremely happy.

He stared at her for a few seconds, then got up and stood in front of her.

"You have never looked so beautiful," he said gruffly. "You make me want you so badly, I can barely stand it. If it weren't like desecrating a nun, I swear I'd rape you."

"No you wouldn't. Violence is not one of your faults."

He hovered uncertainly above her as they looked at one another. Then he shrugged and said, "Lucky for you! Regret isn't either."

"I didn't think it was."

A slight smile turned up the corners of his mouth. "We are friends, I hope."

"Of course."

They walked into the bedroom, where Arthur took a heavy brown suitcase from behind his clothes in the closet and laid it on the bed. He opened a drawer and started to remove his underwear and socks, but stopped.

"Maybe I'm giving up too easily. There isn't some romantic rabbi behind this, is there? Someone else?"

"No, no one else."

"What if I were to undergo the surgeon's knife? Convert!"

He looked so fierce saying this that she began to laugh an

ecstatic, rippling laugh. It was so good to know she could still do it. "I would like to hear you explain your 'conversion' to Eileen." She patted his arm. "I'll help you with your things. You don't have to do that for me."

He had relatively few things left there, having sent his winter clothes to the cleaner and not yet brought in a supply of summer ones, but they filled the large brown suitcase and a little bag of hers. In the dining area, she offered him the sack of canned goods, and wrapped the brandy glasses in newspaper. "Don't throw out the brandy," he said as she took up the decanter. "Will you have a drink with me now?"

She bowed her head and took two juice glasses into which she emptied the remainder of the brandy — was this brandy made from grapes? She couldn't remember. Then, she rinsed out the decanter and wrapped it and its stopper in newspaper.

"To your new life," said Arthur, raising his glass.

"And to yours," said Miriam, raising hers. The brandy burned her tongue in a pleasant way.

"You know where to reach me if you ever want to — if you ever need me," he said.

She nodded. "Thank you. By the way, do you want the Bonwit's card or shall I just tear it up?"

He looked genuinely surprised, then grinned. "I trust you to get rid of it in an honorable manner. But I hope you'll keep everything else." He reached in his pocket and put her keys on the counter.

They sipped the brandy in silence, but before he was finished he put down the glass. "I'd better go. I find staying here with you is very difficult. May I give you a last kiss?"

She reached up and kissed him gently on the mouth but withdrew before he could press her to him.

He picked up the bags, his hands full, and moved to the door, where he put the large one down. He turned to face her.

"Oh, Miriam, darling." He had never called her that before.

He touched her cheek. "You know we had more than just a cheap affair. What I loved in you was what we could have had together if we had met in another time, in different skins. I always had the sense everything was possible with you."

Tears filled her eyes, and she gave him an impulsive hug, then waved him out, and leaned her face into the wall, swallowing her sobs.

*   *   *

Later she prepared her meal, said the *Motzi,* the blessing over bread, ate a roll, chicken and peas, a pear, and after the *Birkhat ha-Mazon,* the prayer to conclude the meal, cleared the plates. Yellow sponge for dairy, she used the blue for meat. Then she called her parents and told them about Arthur.

"I'm not sorry to see him go. He took advantage of you. He may be rich, but you can do better."

"A nice Jewish boy," said Miriam with amusement. "It's all right, Daddy, I'll make you proud."

After that she called Celia and Sam.

Sam was effusive. "Miriam, your grandmother told me what a change you've gone through. I know you're going to meet with a lot of family resistance, but be strong. It sounds good to me."

"Uncle Sam, you are dear! Those are the first kind words I've heard. How's Aunt Celia?"

His voice fell. "The same, more or less. Now that I'm not teaching days, I take her to the park, sometimes Leah comes with us, sometimes Rafe, and she responds more. But the same."

"I'll be up on Sunday. I can't come on Saturdays anymore."

"Do you have a shul to go to?"

"I have to look for one in walking distance. There are a few around here."

She heard the muffled sound of a hand cupped over the mouthpiece of the phone, and then Sam said, "Rafe would like to say a word to you."

"He's there?" She was surprised.

"He does so much for us."

"I'd like to talk to him."

There was a pause and she heard Rafe's warm inflected voice on the phone.

"Hello, Miriam."

"Rafe."

"I want to hear about your adventure. I'm eager to see you and hear everything."

"I look forward to telling you," she said and felt her breath lift in a sure surge of joy.

II

Sunday, July 29, 1973
PUBLIC NOTICES

Gershom — We are all changing, even in silence, as
you must be. Don't misjudge us. — Johanna.

M IRIAM WAS standing in front of her building as Johanna
drove up in her blue Volkswagen. "Your timing was perfect,"
she said as she got in. "I just came down."

Johanna turned to look at her cousin, thinking that with
her own swelling belly she appeared much changed from their
last meeting but that it was Miriam who was truly altered. "You
don't look any different," she giggled and felt instantly stupid.

Miriam reached over to kiss her cousin on the cheek. She
slammed her door and fastened her seat belt. "Just goes to
show, looks don't mean much. How are you?"

The car started off slowly and Johanna responded with the
reserved speech of an intent driver. "I feel fine. I've started
to feel the baby move a lot recently and that's lovely, the best
part of pregnancy." She hesitated, wanting to say more but
uncertain how to begin. A hush, no more than half a minute,
pervaded the car as she slowed and stopped for a red light.
She glanced at Miriam and murmured, "Celia's certainly taught
us silence speaks." She could see Miriam nod once. "Other
things in my life are not so great. My mother is still staying
with us."

Miriam's eyes opened wider, her brows rising slightly. "I've heard. All the time?"

"Most of it, but she likes to keep a foot in both worlds. My father had two dinners recently for his political friends. Each time, she refused to have anything to do with them so he asked me to serve as hostess. Then, just before I really had to start doing anything, she decided to take over — for my sake. Of course, she stayed there afterward, the second time for several days. I hoped . . . 'For my sake' I wish she'd move home permanently."

"I'm sure," said Miriam.

"I'm not being nasty. It's just that I find it very hard to work with her around, even when she's not actually in the house." She bit her lower lip. "And I think Seth must hate what our life is like these days although he's too polite to really say so."

"I don't really understand what happened between your parents," said Miriam.

Johanna shook her head and shrugged. "Neither do I. Maybe we could talk about it sometime. Right now, I want to hear more about you. What you're doing seems amazing to me. Not only to me."

Miriam considered this as they headed west toward the parkway, struck that the momentary lulls in their conversation did not frighten her as they once would have. "I really didn't anticipate the reaction I got. In fact, this whole thing has been as much a surprise to me as to everyone else. I only went to that Hasidic Encounter because I needed to go somewhere to think things over."

"You've always been more of a rebel." Johanna was shaking her head. "I wouldn't have had the courage to go in the first place for any reason. And then to face them afterward! I can't. I'm such a doormat."

Miriam was startled to hear the tension in Johanna's voice — a little crack. She searched for the right thing to say to her family's model of virtue: happily married, accomplished and devoted. She reached out and patted Johanna on the arm.

"It's a nuisance always having to worry about what the family thinks, isn't it? My folks used to give me a hard time about men, particularly Arthur in the beginning, but after a while they caved in — at least Mom did. Daddy always grumbled. But on the whole, they took that easier. I think my affairs actually were exciting to my mother, what she wished she could have had — especially the freedom to walk away." She thought for a minute, struggling to get back on the track. "They're finding my new lifestyle very difficult because they see it as some kind of judgment of them, I guess. It's so silly. I'm not out to convert anyone. The first time I saw Rafe and told him about what happened to me, he said he was struck by that. We've talked a lot about it. He's usually at Uncle Sam's and we walk at least part of the way downtown together. I think he'll be there today."

Johanna had turned on to the West Side Highway. "I like Rafe," she said, but it was clear that she was not really thinking of him.

Miriam continued cautiously, "I don't think you can just take a position for the sake of taking a position. Unless something matters very much, it's always easier to give in, to let the family tell you what to do or not do. Or if not the family, the people you're friends with and, Johanna, believe me, I didn't stay in Brooklyn among the Hasidim because they would have been the same. Worse maybe. If you really worry about being — what did you call it? — a doormat, you have to ask yourself if there's anything that matters enough to you to support your pulling out."

"Doesn't sound like you."

"I'm not the same me."

They drove again in silence for a while, the sun hitting the water and making it sparkle, little gold lights on blue edges. In the distance, closing, the George Washington Bridge stretched weblike and magnificent across the river. The day was clear and every steel cable etched itself against the sky. It began to loom larger, making it harder to take in the whole.

"I used to think my marriage and my art were that important, and I'm sure if I felt Seth's and my relationship was going to be permanently harmed by this — interlude — I'd be able to stand up. Oh god damn, it's more than that!" She half turned toward Miriam, "I'm sorry I said that."

"Come on," said Miriam. "Only some of me isn't the same."

"Well, I've always known how weak I was, how everything I value privately could be submerged by the family. It's still true but now I'm worried, not because of what I'm doing to Seth, or to Rachel and somebody else soon, but because I can see how even those people can take me over, how easily I can just be consumed by their activities and needs. All my life I've been trained to do enough to stand out without taking any leap that would separate me, endanger me." She had started out the exit at the bridge. "Originally, when I heard about what your orthodoxy would involve I got very smug. 'I can just see her sitting in a synagogue balcony. I can just see her pouring water ritually over her hands before meals . . .' "

"I don't do that," said Miriam. "Just wash, like always."

"You know what I mean. I wanted to put you on the defensive . . ."

"You're not alone," laughed Miriam.

". . . because you had the strength to do something I couldn't do. I don't want to be orthodox, but I'm talking about choosing."

"I know."

A shadow passed over Johanna's face, then lifted. "Are you happy?"

"Wow," her breath came out in a puff of laughter. "That's quite a question. I used to think I really knew what it was to be happy. Remember?" She stopped, trying to recall how that felt.

"You put on a good show of it at least," said Johanna.

"You want an honest answer? Yes? I think I'm happy, although in such a new way, the word I used to use doesn't apply. There are a lot of things that haven't fallen into place and I keep discovering new things — that part is really great . . ." She made no effort to repress her delight but as quickly again became serious. "What I really need is a community, which is why it was so tempting to just stay in Brooklyn. I'm kind of lonely and that scares me. I've been going to shul in a little synagogue where I seem to be the only woman over eighteen or under fifty. Very few women come anyway, maybe because it's the summer. The people who *are* there don't say more than Good Shabbos, if that, though the rabbi's been nice. And I have trouble following the Hebrew, though I try. I'm going to have to study it just to keep up with the prayers, and I'd like to understand what I'm saying. And then, I want a different job, one that I don't find so meaningless. I guess I need to reorganize my life, the way I've had to reorganize my kitchen but the rules aren't so clear." She hesitated. "And I'm afraid about men."

Johanna looked startled, then began to laugh. "You?" She stopped. "I understand. Everything is different."

"Everything!" Her lips tightened slightly. "I don't want to have to play games anymore and I can't be with the sort of men I've been with before. I hardly know what other men are like — and now he's got to be an observant Jew . . ." She stopped, the sentence hanging as if she could not think of what else to say.

"Do you miss Arthur?"

"Sometimes. Not him really. The company, sex, who knows what? It wasn't the kind of love that shares much." She realized this articulately for the first time as she said it. "We laughed a lot together."

"That's not so bad."

"Depends on why you're laughing."

"I hardly ever laugh at all," said Johanna grimly. "At least at the moment."

"As a former Giggling Gertie, I advise you not to overrate it. But then you've never thought of laughter as a patent medicine." Miriam pursed her lips as she said this.

Johanna had turned into Sam's and Celia's street and found a parking place nearly in front of their door. "Luck," she said and pulled the car into it. She turned off the motor and sat staring straight ahead. The sunlight hit the windshield at a certain slant and rays of yellow seemed to pour across the front seat into their laps.

"I don't think you can imagine how relieved I would feel if I didn't take things so seriously. I'm either frantic because of my mother, or about my child, and then about avoiding being the same kind of mother. And while I'm busy being the good girl who wins gold stars, the artist in me, and the lover — the parts of the wife that aren't all dutiful and basically dreary — are locked up. I'm scared that one day I'll find they have vanished altogether — that *I, Johanna* will be gone." She paused, still staring straight ahead, then said almost in a whisper, "The only one who'll notice will be Seth; and what will he do when the part of me he loves the best has been killed off, *kaput?* "

Miriam reached across the warm light for her cousin's hand and held it affectionately. She had never once had a conversation of this order with her cousin who was older and, if anything, wiser about most things. At least Miriam had thought she was. Not without resentment either. Oh Lord our God, King of the Universe, be good to my cousin. Help her.

Johanna pulled her hand away and smiled at Miriam, looking at her directly. "Let's go up," she said.

Although they had no air conditioning, Sam's and Celia's apartment was cool compared to the heat out of doors. The pale light and the brick walls conspired to soften the temperature, mold it. Sam had made a large pitcher of iced tea, which was on the coffee table when Johanna and Miriam entered, a few empty glasses by it. Celia, a glass in her hand, was sitting as usual in her rocker and nearby, Rafe sipping tea and smiling. He stood as Sam brought the women in and held out both hands to them.

"Johanna, Miriam, I'm glad to see you." He gave them each a flying handshake, his white teeth gleaming.

Miriam smiled back, feeling her ears tingle with the force of her own smile. He always had that sort of effect on her, she noted, an openness still unfamiliar and refreshing as a cool breeze. Johanna was smiling at him too, as if released from the weight of her reflections.

Celia was looking at them and nodding slightly as she rocked. They each greeted her with kisses and questions that had to bear their own answers, then stepped away. Celia watched them, her eyes darting from one to the other as they sat down, accepted some tea, and filled the shade with pink gingham and lilac.

Sam, his short-sleeved white shirt open at the collar, gray hairs from his chest and neck spilling out wildly, beamed at them.

"So, Johanna, you're feeling well? Yes? Miriam, is your religious practice coming more easily?"

"Not without snags, but I'm learning."

"How are you doing with your Hebrew?" asked Rafe.

"I work every day on it, but I wonder if I'll ever be able to read anything without stumbling." Her mind bounced to this newly learned alphabet that required all her concentration. "In English to see is to read for me. In Hebrew seeing is just the beginning."

He leaned toward her, his dark eyes sparkling like black jewels. "If you want me to, I could find out about classes at Columbia or maybe Jewish Theological Seminary — Conservative, you know. For the fall?"

"Please," she nodded again, her lips slipping into an effortless grin.

Johanna turned her glass, looking first at Sam and then at Rafe. "You two are both on vacation. I bet that feels good."

"For me, very good," said Sam, "but Rafe is writing a book.

College teachers don't get to use their vacations the same way."

"About what?" Johanna bit.

"Developing political patterns during the period immediately after the Revolution. Doesn't that sound deadly?" Rafe chuckled.

"No. Is it?"

"I like it," he shrugged. "And the library is very cool. It's not a subject for everyone."

"I wonder," Miriam trilled, "at the kind of discipline it takes to write a book." She heard her own voice bubbling unnaturally and tried to subdue it. "I do a lot of writing, most of it idiotic, but I could never go on for a volume."

"A book has a way of making its own life. Can't stop." He took Celia's hand and said, "Little Mother, maybe you ought to write a book and speak your heart."

Miriam was startled by the frankness. No hidden meanings here. Celia looked back at him expressionless. She seemed not to have understood.

Sam sighed, his round cheeks falling. He spread his short fingers as he reached out toward her almost in the posture of a benediction. "Sometime, it will all pour out. Sometime soon."

They sat quietly for a minute and he continued. "I think you're right, that once you start, books must write themselves. It's the starting that's the problem."

"Starting anything is hard," Rafe looked at the two young women. "What about starting a pot or a piece of sculpture, Johanna? What about what you've started, Miriam? Hard, but hard to stop once it's going."

"Why don't *you* use the summer to write?" said Johanna to Sam. The words came out of her mouth before she could stop them and she gasped slightly, realizing she was opening an old wound. "What I mean is, I've always thought you could write something wonderful. You used to tell such fabulous stories."

Damn! That was the sort of thing she always hated her mother for doing.

"The best," said Miriam. "They were a highlight of my childhood. I still remember some."

Sam's square shoulders took on a curve. His life as novel, started long ago and hard to stop, surged forth in his mind. "He longed to be honest with them, to speak of that which undone remained the burden of his life. But how to begin?" His head bobbed slightly and he parted his dry lips. "I thought about doing it only when I was young and had more optimism."

"The proletarian vision, Sam," said Rafe affectionately. "That's optimism for you."

Sam nodded. "That's right. I saw the world through a haze of youthful enthusiasm: Just set mankind on the right path and all will be well. So I read the novels of social change and managed to overlook what all those authors, and others too, knew and said — that sometimes what one does in the name of a good cause is brutalizing, does something to the spirit, may even do something to the nature of the cause. I began to understand that myself in France, during the war. Anyway, the novels I wanted to write changed even without my setting pen to paper. I began to understand how petty daily concerns can wear people down even when they're not living in poverty, how, quite apart from social issues, most people struggle with forces inside themselves that they don't understand fully. The more I understood how hard it is for the best to surface in man — in any particular person — the more I despaired of writing. I felt like Robert Jordan — Hemingway's American fighting in the Spanish Civil War — who wanted to write a book later about what he knew but felt he would have to be a better writer than he was because what he had come to know wasn't simple." He blushed, a ruddy flush coming up from his neck to meet his eyebrows.

"Look at me," he spoke with a new huskiness. "I can't even rely on my own sense of that to explain it to you. I have to call on someone else, a character in a book. I despaired because I was afraid I couldn't make it true enough. That's what Gershom would call copping out, isn't it? Well, I'm not proud of it, but then if I had had the talent I think it would have spilled out anyway." He stopped, gazing off toward the window.

Celia had begun rocking again, nodding, whether at what Sam had said, the mention of Gershom, or some vein of personal reflection was unclear. She turned and stared at Sam curiously.

"Talent is as much obsession as anything else," said Rafe, "probably even more for artists than scholars. If you're obsessed it's like having someone shake you by the shoulders."

Johanna crossed her legs. "Sometimes," she said slowly, "I think it's the obsession to get lost in something — really absorbed. It's hard to sustain when it doesn't work out." She smiled as if remembering some warm moment. "Now, when I give Rachel some clay to work with, she hits it and pulls it and whatever comes out she loves. Calls it *gorgeous* — that's her favorite new word."

Celia stopped rocking and smiled slightly. The conversation turned to Rachel, to little children, and from that to politics — the peculiar rumblings about Watergate. Sam made more tea and brought out cookies as they passed an hour and a half in the changing light, the brief pool of sun coming and passing.

Johanna glanced at her watch and stood up. "The time has come." She turned toward Miriam. "Would you like a lift home?"

Miriam hesitated. "Uncle Sam, are you tired?"

"Stay if you want," said Sam. "Aunt Celia and I are happy to have you."

"I'll walk with you later, if you'd like," offered Rafe. "We could even go to dinner at a vegetarian restaurant I know in honor of your new dietary habits."

"Thank you, Johanna. I'll call you this week." She reached her hand toward her cousin and whispered, "We'll talk."

"Seth sends his love to everyone," said Johanna, moving toward the door. She turned to Celia, who was staring at her hands. "Aunt Celia, I hope you're going to feel better soon." Celia lurched forward slightly as if startled and accepted Johanna's kiss. She reached out, put her arms around Johanna and her face against the gentle swelling.

"Babies *are* nice," said Johanna tenderly and she bent to hug her aunt. Celia's eyes were moist. "Oh," whispered Johanna, "it will be all right."

At the door Sam said, "Do you think running those ads is really serving any purpose?"

"Yes. He probably sees them. It's a kind of contact. At least the possibility."

Sam cleared his throat. "Unsatisfactory," he said, "but better than nothing, I suppose."

He returned to the living room after seeing her out. Miriam and Rafe were now seated together across from Celia, who watched them intently.

"Miriam is telling me about what *this* week was like with all the new habits she has got to form." Rafe winked at her.

"I told you. Habits are things you never think about. I always have to think about what I'm doing, at least somewhat, for the rituals to really have meaning." She sounded irritable.

"I'm teasing," chuckled Rafe. "I'm surprised you can't tell."

She saw her uncle sit down and laugh too, and wondered for a moment at the wall that had been raised within her to cut her perception of tone, of playfulness. It was troubling.

"I'm sorry, but I haven't been able to figure out just how to fit the new parts of myself together with the old." She blinked, a shadow of her old coyness. "We don't want me falling to pieces, do we?"

"Never," Rafe's eyes were twinkling. "Maybe the missionary zeal is catching," he added. "Despite all the changes you've undergone, can you imagine yourself playing the part of your red-bearded friend?"

Miriam shuddered slightly. She had not seen him for a while. "No, but I'm grateful to him nonetheless." She laughed freely now. "I wanted to thank him but he's disappeared. Maybe I made his quota from that corner."

"Well, he started the process, even if he's not the end and that's good." Rafe reached toward her with his voice.

"There's a blessing you can say when you meet someone who really knows Torah," Sam offered. "I have a siddur. We could look it up." He searched briefly on the bookshelf and found a small white book. "A wedding favor," he said in an embarrassed tone and flipped through the pages. *"Baruch ata Adonoi Elohenu melech ha-olam . . .* Who hast imparted of Thy wisdom to them that revere Thee.' Will that do for your friend, Miriam? That's an expression of gratitude."

"He wouldn't even look at me if I said it right to him. So it's probably better for me to say it here in secret though it would be fun to see if he'd be flattered, for just a moment to turn those fierce eyes to mush." And she chortled with mischief.

"Every man needs to feel his work is a blessing," said Sam almost to himself. "I hope you have a chance to tell him."

*   *   *

Miriam and Rafe had walked downtown several miles from Washington Heights to the Columbia area and had dinner in a roughly decorated vegetarian restaurant. She had a cheese and spinach pie, and explained at some length her conflicts about whether to give up nonkosher cheeses, an aspect of kashruth she hadn't quite come to terms with. Like nonkosher wines, or wine vinegars. "I mean a grape, after all, is a grape. Out in Brooklyn, all those things seemed very clear. Do it all. But since I'm having to work it out in my own style, I find it isn't so simple."

"I'm sure." He seemed preoccupied.

They were walking again down Broadway, past the little

shops and bars near the university. Miriam looked at him. He was only a few inches taller than she and the darkness of his mood seemed to meld with the olive tone of his cheeks and dark hair. He looked delicate in the twilight hanging on in the summer evening, and buffeted by some inner storm.

She put her hand on his arm for just a moment to catch his attention and he glanced at her, a wan grin coming up. "Sorry," he said. "Thinking."

"Of what?"

"About being Jewish."

"Me or you?"

"Me, though I don't really know what I am. I mean I know what I was born but a lot of things have happened to me and I hardly know what I believe."

"After what happened to your family, how can you have any doubts about what you are?"

"Not what I am. What I believe. They're not necessarily the same thing. You should know that. If I had asked you three months ago what you were you would have said you were Jewish but it wouldn't have been the same as now."

They walked a while longer not speaking and then he said, "Would you be willing to come into a church with me? I want to show you something."

"Of course," said Miriam, wondering if "of course" was the appropriate answer in spite of her instinctive feeling it was.

He led her downtown a few more blocks and then onto a side street where a small church, its outer stone darkened with New York grime, opened its doors to the night.

"It's always open," he said. "At least, I've never been here when it was closed. Catholic churches are like that, I think. How's that for a generalization I can't prove?"

Inside, the church smelled of sweet spices, sticky pine. It was lit by a few bronze-colored chandeliers of many small low-wattage bulbs and the light of the votive candles. The stained-glass windows were gray with night coming through and only the vaguest outlines of figures appeared, suggesting the reds, blues and greens that awaited the sun. They were quite alone in the building and the stillness pressed against them.

He led her to a small side altar before which the votive candles flickered and splashed in the dullness. Her eyes were becoming accustomed to the shadow and as they stood in front of the altar she could see with surprising clarity what he was pointing to.

It was a large wooden crucifix, Jesus wracked with pain. The head was crowned with long pointed thorns, some of which dug into the wooden flesh from which droplets stained red ran across the forehead and, like tears, down his cheeks. His head was lowered to one side so that a bulge in the back of his neck, the top of the spine, appeared beside the cross. His arms, which seemed to support his weight, were lined with ropes of tendons, strained with their burden, and hollow cups formed at his underarms. The wound beneath the right breast bled almost to the gold cloth that wrapped his wooden loins. Where his hands and feet were fastened to the cross, his fingers and toes pulled back in anguish. There was nothing tranquil about this figure, nothing that suggested knowledge beyond pain except for his eyes, which were shut as if to welcome blackness.

Miriam stared at it, chilled by its brutality, the mercilessness of the artist, and the tingling pine scent in her nose. She turned toward Rafe, who stood gazing beyond it, his own face drawn and grim, and she touched his hand. He looked at her abruptly as if surprised by her presence, then began to speak very softly. Even the breathy words seemed to echo in the empty chamber.

"This cross is very like the one in the chapel of the convent in Verona. Every morning and evening for more than two years I stared at that cross and listened to the mass, you know. Sometimes I would squint my eyes, and the body would seem to writhe with pain. He seemed to suffer unendurably and when the nuns told me he suffered for me — so I would not have to — I believed them. It was safe in the convent and I had had a hard year walking and stealing and doing other things I don't want to talk about. If he was going to suffer for me I was going to let him. That place, which belonged to him, was comfort and all the nuns asked of me was that I love him. In his pain he became a kind of protection. Do you understand? It's hard for me to explain now. Then much later, when I was with my aunt in Springfield and began to understand what had happened to my family, to me, I used to think about that crucifix and hate it. Christ turned into a devil who pretended to suffer, but who got people to do evil things that way, who demanded human sacrifices. I hated him. You can't imagine how I hated him — or at least the deceitful vicious demon I believed he was. But I'm not a good hater. It wearies me, and after a while that passed too." He stopped as if lost in the cave of his memories.

"And now?" whispered Miriam. "What do you think about him now?"

At first she thought Rafe had not heard her for he seemed possessed by his own thoughts, but then he continued, still staring off, his voice rising slightly. "For a long time I didn't think about him at all, but then he would work his way into my consciousness and I began to see him as the Jew he was, the quintessential Jew, the Holocaust victim turned into something he never intended to be, and then finally, because it seemed to me others suffered too, as a symbol of man, of every man's and woman's suffering, especially the kind we inflict on one another. I come here and I look at this cross, this Jesus, and I see Sam and Celia, I see Gershom and I think of friends I've had, of my family and everything seems very sad. Here's the symbol, the emblem of that sadness."

He turned to look at her and as their eyes met, she reached out and took his hand in both of hers unable to speak. They stood there in the dim light for a time longer, then turned to leave the church, her right hand still clasping his left.

Outside the air was still, hot and smoky red with the neon
lights shining on Broadway. They walked along, holding hands
but not speaking until the traffic rattle reached inside their
cocoon. He said in a less strained manner, "Now you know
my dark side," and he grinned. "We've walked enough. Let's
get a cab. I'll take you home."

In the cab she tried to sort out her impressions.

"You're overwhelmed," he said gently. "I can see that. I'm
sorry."

"No. I just have to put all the things you said in some order.
I guess I don't always think of life as being sad. In fact, often
it's wonderful. And I liked the things I learned in Brooklyn
that seemed to say 'Life is good. Live it. Appreciate it.' For
instance, there are lots of blessings like the one Sam read you're
supposed to say when you see beautiful natural things. Real
suffering is horrible, of course, but if it's sadness you're talking about, I think it's just as bad to live without feeling anything, to never know real joy, to never try to make life better.
I think that's a Jewish position." And she laughed with embarrassment. "Don't I sound scholarly?"

"You sound nice," he said. "It's a good position whether it's
Jewish or not."

"Did you ever learn anything about being Jewish? I mean
you started out this evening telling me you didn't know what
you believed, and I know what that feels like. When you came
to your aunt, to Illinois?"

"Well, we didn't even really talk about what had happened
until I was in high school, but when I was thirteen, my aunt decided I should have a bar mitzvah. We had nothing especially
Jewish about our lives, though she belonged to a Reform temple and we went on the High Holidays. She also belonged to
Hadassah and socialized a lot with the ladies. Maybe she felt
obliged to pay back some of their weddings and bar mitzvahs.
I don't know. Anyway, the Reform temple only had confir-
mations for children who had gone through the religious
school and since they weren't usually confirmed until they were

fifteen, the rabbi tried to persuade her to enroll me. I didn't want to go to Sunday School and she didn't care so she took me to the Orthodox synagogue — there was one in Springfield — and the rabbi there agreed to get someone to teach me everything in about eight weeks. I memorized my haftara perfectly, but I could barely read Hebrew. The chanting reminded me of the masses in the convent. It was strange. Anyway, my aunt invited some friends and a few of her husband's relatives and one Saturday morning I stood up, apostate that I was — I hadn't gone into my hating phase yet — my new suit from Myers Brothers covered with a prayer shawl and sang my portion and the blessings the first and last time." He paused as if momentarily reliving the occasion, and sighed as he continued. "Then we had a party with bagels brought down from Chicago, lox, all that. But, Miriam, what should have stretched back like a bridge over those years in the convent, back to my parents, back to my grandfather, whom I could vaguely remember making the blessing over the wine, jumped up like a wall, and I felt cut off from both my pasts — the Jewish and the Catholic. I sometimes think that's why I studied early American history. It avoids them both."

She looked at him sideways, his profile framed by his full beard, feeling stirred by his story. "Eight weeks," she said. "You had about as much training as I have."

"Except you know what and why you are learning, or at least you have the illusion you do." He shrugged as the cab pulled up before Miriam's apartment building.

He let go of her hand to reach for some money and she felt strangely bereft. They had been holding hands without stopping ever since they had left the church. She looked at her hand like some new organ she had discovered, sensitive to sensations previously unimagined — an ability to feel life and death.

He paid the driver and opened the door to get out, helping her out after him. She fished for the key, unlocked the lobby door and they were in her building. She felt terrified. Of what? They went up in the elevator, her hand hanging coldly at her side. Ninety degrees and she was freezing. They walked down the hall to her apartment door and she turned toward him, then changed her mind and took the key to unlock the door. Nothing she had to say could be said in this hall.

She touched the mezuzah and then her lips as they entered and he shut the door. They were still standing by the doorway beside the closet when she turned around and faced him. Her skin was tingling all over, even the soles of her feet, and she backed up slightly from the black into the gray frame of light from the living room windows. She reached for the light switch but flashed it on only to flash it off again, then just stood there helpless.

He came forward and took her face in his hands and kissed her on the mouth with such tenderness she felt as fragile as the most delicate crystal, so light she could fly. She did not stir and only waited, breathless for a moment. Then, as if impelled by some part of herself not truly part of her pulsing body, she gently put her hand on his shoulder and pressed away.

"Rafe," she whispered, "Rafe, I need to tell you something. I want you to understand. Please. Right now you excite me very much. Is it a shame for me to say that? I lost my virginity years ago, and men, there have been a lot of men in my life. Too many, some without any feeling at all, except fun maybe. Now I promised myself I couldn't do that anymore . . . if I should marry . . . that sex is going to have to have a different kind of meaning." Her voice cracked and she could feel the threat of tears, a vibration across the bridge of her nose. "Do you understand what I'm trying to say?"

"Of course," he said, stroking her cheek with one finger. "Of course. There's no need to say it."

A flood of foolishness washed over her. It wasn't what his kiss had meant. Even in the gray light she felt her face, burning from the inside, must be brilliant red. He continued to stroke her cheek and then he said, "You're lovely," and smiled so wistfully she felt her heart would break. He might understand her but she was sure she didn't understand him. "I mean . . ." she began, breathing rapidly. He interrupted her. "I don't often offer as much of myself as I have offered you. To women especially, although there have been too many of them the other way and some without any feeling at all. Not even fun! Let's not be afraid, either of us." He put his arms around her and they stood quietly in the darkness, her heart beating like an African drum; she felt as if she could stand there forever but she drew back.

"Rafe." She was startled at the pleasure she felt saying his name. "Rafe, would you come on Friday night and have Shabbos dinner with me? If you remember how maybe you could even say the Kiddush." She heard the words stumbling out of her mouth without her usual ease of speech.

"I'd like to come," he said solemnly. "I don't know if I believe in a God who gives us things and demands that we bless them. I don't know if I believe in God at all, but I'll try to say Kiddush."

"It's really a man's prayer. I mean, women are only supposed to say it if there is no man to do it."

"Do you buy that?"

"I don't know."

He put his hand on her cheek again and smiled at her. Then he asked, "If I come another evening before Friday, can we take a walk while you teach me to say it properly and tell me what else we'll be doing and what it all means? I'll buy you a good glass of iced tea. O.K.?"

She nodded.

"Tomorrow?"

She could hardly wait. "Tomorrow."

He moved back and opened the door to the hall and the light glared in. She stepped toward him almost against her will and he reached over and kissed her forehead. "You had better turn on a light," he said and she obediently switched on the overhead light again. He closed the door behind him.

Even after he had gone, she continued to stand there, trying to plumb the depths of the mysterious sea that had opened up within her.

12

Sunday, September 16, 1973

PUBLIC NOTICES

Gershom — New term begins. Miriam/Rafe study Hebrew. Dad back teaching. Where are You? — Johanna.

THE YEAR HAD gotten off to a bad start, Sam felt. The whole school was restless; one could sense it while walking down the halls even when the students were in class. The first assembly, led by Mr. Borghese, the principal, a short, nervous man, had deteriorated rapidly. Several girls came in late and, finding themselves abruptly the center of attention, minced toward empty seats in exaggerated imitations of beauty queens, causing a hullabaloo of catcalls, whistles and shouting. Only when Mr. Borghese threatened to lock the canteen machines in the student lounge for a week did a restive quiet settle in the auditorium. Although optimistic speeches by teachers and student leaders followed, outbursts of giggles and stamps punctuated them, and Sam reflected to himself that something about the atmosphere that could have been deflected into humor if caught at the right moment had turned menacing.

Like so many things. The moods and circumstances of his life seemed to hinge on just such miscalculations. This word or that said at the right moment or, conversely, the wrong one could alter the course of a life. He had always believed, sometimes against his own desires, in the power of words, and,

looking over his present sensibilities, that seemed to stick. Or
the power of no words. He knew that now too. *In the beginning
. . . God said . . .* Wasn't that the ultimate creative act? Could
words withheld explode with their own energy? The Bible
never says if God spoke before. Perhaps He was silent until
the Word burst forth, driven forward by its long unsaying.
Words: the spoken questions, threats and statements; or the
little messages like smoke signals: the public notices in the
Times, the written word, permanence.

He had turned his hand to writing children's stories — his
first attempt on paper in many years — after Johanna and
Miriam had remembered his tales with such affection. A gift
for Johanna's new baby perhaps, since Celia would not be able
to buy one and no longer knitted. A gift for himself? Occasionally, rarely but occasionally, he would begin the process
and get entirely lost in a world of knights and ladies, of awkward creatures with loving hearts who performed unexpect-
edly heroic acts or gave unusual assistance. Sometimes they
needed help too. Wasn't that it? To strike the balance between
giving and receiving? He loved the stories and wondered what
Gershom would say if he knew about them though he thought
less about Gershom these days.

He *had* wondered uneasily if perhaps the start of school, the
academic year, would bring him back. It was, he realized even
while hoping, a perception colored by his own inner calendar
and by his memories of Gershom as a little boy, all dressed up
in corduroy pants and a carefully pressed plaid shirt, ready
for the first day with a new pencil case and a fresh notebook.
If he was to come back, it would be on his own terms and in
keeping with a system that he would have to make clear. Would
Columbia accept him back, he had asked Rafe recently. After
his inexplicable departure? "Probably," Rafe had said, "if he
wanted to go back." If. Parents always wanted their children
to be happy but almost always in the way they themselves
would be happy.

Rafe and Miriam — that was another story and one that he was careful not to disrupt with his words. It was clear their friendship had become a profound one and perhaps more than friendship, but he did not dare ask or state it as fact. Even with his silent Celia (What would the force of *her* silence finally bring forth?), he kept his counsel. Rafe had joined Miriam's quest in some way of his own, at least apparently so. He went with her to synagogue, he brought her books which they both read and now he had begun to study Hebrew with her. They no longer met in Sam's living room but came together, looking flushed from walking and easy with themselves. What if a word, a speculation, a rumor to travel the telephone circuit of Miriam's family were to disrupt that ease, complicate it, even destroy it? He said nothing, not even in response to Leah's questions and occasional innuendos: "I would have thought with this new religion of hers she would restrain herself. I've wondered about that Hasid she met too — all that talk about his eyes." Oh well, Leah!

What about the word for Leah? *Go home and stay with your husband;* or *Leave your poor daughter in peace;* or *Don't use your sister this way?* Would that word also have to come from somewhere else or did he have some rights there? It was an area of danger.

Danger. He was sitting that afternoon at his desk in the English Department office, where for the past two years he had been Acting Chairman. Not out of any recognition of ability, he believed, but merely because he had outlasted everyone else. Under new school regulations issued on the first day, office doors were to be kept locked at all times and students had to knock to obtain admission. A bad rule. How can locked doors achieve anything? But he shared the office with two other teachers and so he obeyed. It was now after the last period bell had rung in the afternoon, but someone was knocking now and he got up to open the door . . . for Elvira Moore, a small black girl from his senior English class. Elvira was one of the students he loved best. She had been in his junior class last year and lighted his life through that grim time with her modest manner and absolute commitment to the books she cared about. She wrote proficiently although not in an exciting way and one of the things he and she were planning to work on this semester was to enliven her writing so that she might do well as an English major at Hunter College.

Elvira was very dark and tiny, and today she had her hair braided in tight little rows across her scalp, which made her face look smaller still. She was wearing a green skirt, slightly longer than the average school-length miniskirt and a neat yellow blouse. As she came in she smiled shyly at Sam.

"Hello, Mr. Lazarus. You got time for me today?"

"Of course, Elvira. What can I do for you?"

"The paper you assigned about the Langston Hughes poem? I wrote a first draft. Could we go over it?"

There was a student! That first paper wasn't due for another week. Probably very few others would even be handed in on time.

"I'd like to. Did you like the poem?"

"Oh yeah! That 'raisin in the sun' line is good."

"Image," said Sam. "It's a simile really. What sort of feelings did the poem create in you? No, don't tell me; first let's look at the paper and you see if I'm responding the way you want me to to what you've written. If you tell me what to expect, I won't be able to read it the same way."

"O.K." She reached into her notebook and fished out three sheets covered with penciled writing and many crossed out words. "I kept thinking like you told me about how I got to choose just the right word and I used my dictionary a lot. Sorry it's so messy."

"Do you have a thesaurus?" asked Sam, smiling at her. "If you don't you ought to get one."

"The library has one. I think they — I mean they're expensive."

"Paperback ones aren't bad. I think I might have a second-hand one for you. Will that do?"

She seemed genuinely eager. "Yeah, thanks. I be . . . I've been making my own list." She fished out a small notebook from her purse, in which rows of words filled the first pages. "Some words sound so good. Like this one — 'emphatic' 'em-*pha*-tic.' It sound just like it means. Strong. I use it in my essay." She glanced down at the essay pages. "Here —'Hughes makes an emphatic statement about what despair that comes from having unfulfilled dreams can do to blacks.' How's that?" She was beaming.

"Good sentence. Not just to blacks though. To anyone."

Someone was knocking at the door. He stood up and went to open it. Outside were two boys, one a black student named Johnny Lee whom he had had last year in his remedial sophomore level class and the other a tall boy of indeterminate race whose name he did not know but whom he had seen snaking down the halls. Johnny Lee glared down at him, the whites of his eyes quite red. He was smiling in a sardonic manner, the corners of his mouth twisted up.

"Mist' Lazarus, I got to see you."

"I have another student with me now, Johnny Lee. Unless it's something I can answer right away, can you wait about twenty minutes?"

Johnny Lee leaned against the door pressing it slightly farther open. "Can't wait, Mist' Lazarus. Jus' can't wait. Me and my friend Martin here jus' can't wait." He pushed the door forward shoving Sam into the room and the two boys entered the office, a longish narrow room crowded with desks, chairs and file cabinets.

"You will have to wait," said Sam firmly. "I told you I'm busy just now. If you can't stay around this afternoon, we can make an appointment for tomorrow." He felt uncomfortable, a familiar fear that haunted the school, a shadow riding to work on the subway with the teachers each morning.

"I be here now and I stay," said Johnny Lee. "Girl," he

looked down at Elvira, whose eyes were wide with awakening terror, "you jus' get your ass ou of here."

"But I . . ." she began then stopped as Johnny Lee put his hand on her arm and pulled her up.

"My business come first, hear me, girl? You be good or you get your face pushed in. Now get."

She was backing toward the door, clutching her purse and notebook to her breasts. She looked desperately at Sam, who nodded reassuringly at her. Why hurt Elvira? "We'll talk about the paper another time," he said, hesitating to tell her when to come back. Offer her the protection of anonymity. No one should know where she was, when, or with whom. Get help? No. Disappear, Elvira! She backed out the door visibly shaking.

Johnny Lee closed the door behind her and leaned forward over Sam. He was wearing a blue bandana around his forehead and his hair bushed up in an Afro above. In the middle of it was stuck a heavy red plastic comb like the crest of a cock.

"Martin, this here Mist' Lazarus. Now I got sompin' to tell you, man. Las' term you give me lots of trouble and I get a D in your special ree-mee-dee-el talk-like-the-white-folk class." Sam could see the boy was not entirely in control of himself, high on something. Liquor? Pot? Uppers? Horse? The symptoms weren't quite clear. He moved back alongside his desk, the first one against the wall to the left of the door, as far as he could get from Johnny Lee and, still standing, found the backs of his knees pressed against the seat of his swivel chair.

"You got a D because you didn't work very hard. You're bright enough to get A's if you wanted to. I told you: standard English is a tool to help you get ahead. Nothing more."

Johnny Lee seemed not to be listening. "Now, man, I wants to play basketball this year and the coach he tell me I can't play regular till my grades is higher. He tell me my average go down too low. Got one D too many, he say."

"So it's not only English, then," said Sam, struggling to keep his voice steady. "Anyway, that's the school's rule, not the coach's or mine."

"Whitey talk. You want me to make like a mother-fuckin' Tom. You say I be smart, you go change my fuckin' grade so's I looks as smart as I be."

"I can't do that," said Sam. He glanced over at Martin, who was pressing his palms together, passing fingers between the fingers on the other hand and out again. His face was impassive, a terrifying boredom waiting to be moved. Sam wondered half-heartedly if he should ask Martin to leave. "If you work hard this term, you'll be able to play next term." As soon as he said it, he knew it was not going to work.

"If I don' play till nex' term, won' be on the firs' team," hissed Johnny Lee. "No startin', just substitutin', fillin' in." He moved closer and Sam fell into his seat.

"Maybe you could arrange to play after midterms if you do well enough." Why me? he was thinking. Why not one of those other teachers who found you wanting?

"Yes, Massa, I done hear that from the coach but I not waitin'. You big man. You chief honkey-talk man. You jus' find my card and change that grade pretty-like. You jus' made a mistake — got me mix' up with some other black boy." He leaned over Sam so closely his breath stung Sam's nostrils. It smelled acrid.

"Tell you what," Sam decided on a new approach. "You go home and sleep off whatever it is you've taken, and tomorrow you come back and we'll discuss it again, maybe with the coach. I won't change your grade but perhaps we can work out some program of extra work . . ."

Even before Johnny Lee's hand struck his mouth, he knew what was coming almost without fear, with the surety that must precede death. He put up his hands to shield his face as the blows fell one after another, Johnny Lee beating the heel of one hand, the other a fist, against Sam's cheeks, neck and mouth. A gray mass turned light to red shade and one eye began to throb upward. Then suddenly from behind he felt

Martin strike the back of his head and knock him forward out of his chair. He landed on his knees and struggled to his feet only to receive a blow to his belly that bent him double. Hands grasped his jacket, pulled him straight and thrust him back across the desk, sprawling, papers and journals flying across the floor. Though his vision was hazy, he saw Martin flash a knife and thought, Not that, oh Lord, not that! He felt his sleeve pulled away from his right arm above the elbow and heard the slashing of the knife through fabric while Johnny Lee pinned his left arm and leg to the desk.

"That jus' a promise of what be comin', Mist' Lazarus, Suh! Jus' a promise. Nex' time won' be jus' cloth." He heard Johnny Lee's voice at the same moment he felt himself thrown to the ground, where he lay still in hushed relief that it was over. "Tomorrow we be back." He felt them stepping over his prone feet and heard the door slam as they left the office.

He could hardly move. He was bleeding from the mouth and nose and from a cut on his forehead just above the eyes. His right eye was swelling and he could see only hazily from it. For what seemed a long time, he lay breathing rapidly and, gradually, became aware of a noise he realized was his own moaning.

A frantic knocking started at the door and a voice, Elvira's voice, "Mr. Lazarus? Oh, Mr. Lazarus? It's me, Elvira. Are you all right? Please, Mr. Lazarus, you all right? Please! Please!" He struggled to turn and raise himself so he could reach the doorknob but at first only managed to hit the door with his hand. He lay quietly for a long moment, then tried again. This time he gave the knob a slight turn and the lock gave way but since he was lying on the floor blocking its path, the door only opened a crack. He could not see her, although she apparently could see him. "Oh, dear Jesus! What they do to you? I'm going for someone. Mr. Lazarus, I'm sorry! Oh, I so sorry!"

*　　*　　*

At first he felt nothing, not even real pain, just a deadening numbness. Sensation only slowly began to return as he lay on a cot in the nurse's office where he had been brought by Mr. Borghese and Dunn, the maintenance chief, each supporting him on one side. The nurse had already left for the day and they had had to wait outside her locked door while Dunn went to get the passkey. Elvira had rushed to a nearby classroom to get a chair for him to sit on and staunched a new flow of blood from his nose with a wad of tissues from deep within her pocketbook. Once inside, Mr. Borghese and a music teacher, Mrs. Holland, had cleaned his wounds, put a towel wet with cold water over his eye, and sent Elvira to the counseling office for a cup of coffee. She brought it back and, looking worried, handed it to Sam as Mr. Borghese and Mrs. Holland helped him into a sitting position. The heat of the coffee stung his swollen lips and a wave of nausea rose in his chest. He fought it back, aware gradually that he was hurting — hurting and wretchedly sad. He looked at Elvira, who stood in the corner awkwardly clutching her purse, and said, the words coming out slightly slurred, "Elvira, thank you very much. You're a fine girl."

She whimpered slightly and whispered, "You're O.K., Mr. Lazarus? Are you O.K.?"

"Will be," he said, breathing heavily, although he wasn't sure. "Thank you."

Mr. Borghese patted Elvira on the shoulder. "Why don't you go home now, Elvira. You did a very good, very brave thing and we'll talk more about it tomorrow. It ought to be noted on your records. I think Mr. Lazarus will be all right. Mrs. Holland and I will stay with him." He looked at her and smiled his stiff thin-lipped smile. "Did you see anyone who might have been responsible for this? Do you know who it was?"

Her eyes lowered in a frightened glance at the floor but before she could speak Sam intervened. "Leave her be. I know who it was. He was high, I think. Go on home, Elvira. Do you feel safe going home alone?"

She bobbed her head once in an uncertain nod and backed out the door after grabbing her notebook from the chair.

"I'll call the police," said Mr. Borghese. "Can't have this, so early in the term especially."

"No," said Sam, feeling nauseated again.

"Yes," said Mrs. Holland. "For all our sakes."

Sam bowed his head and waited.

*   *   *

He told the police the story twice, the second time in a nearby hospital emergency room where they had taken him, while he sat dressed in a humiliating backless gown, as a disinterested intern tended to his wounds, and his swelling lips slurred his speech. Now he feared the end was going to be dreadful: a scene in juvenile court, weeping mothers for whom his heart could only ache, a police guard in the school, an uncertainty in the future about whether or not to grade honestly, fear. "The only thing we have to fear is fear itself" — the ringing catch-phrase of his youth, the phrase of hope.

Worse than fear, he realized in the cab going home, was the sense of failure he suddenly felt sharply and more bitterly than the pain that now pervaded his body. For every Elvira, there were ten, no twenty, Johnny Lees — resentful, angry, doped up past reason. It was useless to explain the causes to himself, to hope that the spark he carried from his books would settle and fire them to greater effort. With his white man's skin and his white man's tongue, how could he hope to persuade them that he understood the cost of change, had paid it when he left behind the Yiddishisms of his childhood, his parents' habits from a shtetl Europe, so many things. He could speak to no one except those few willing listeners. Not to most of his students, not to his son, not even to his wife. And maybe what he had to say was wrong. Maybe hope and confidence in ideas really *were* chimeras, and despair the great leveler after all. He felt enmeshed, and despite himself, lines from Whitman pressed forward in his mind: "O cruel hands that hold me powerless — O helpless soul of me! O harsh surrounding cloud that will not free my soul." Despair, but despair that found catharsis in glorious words. No, this time was different. He despised himself as Gershom would despise him. He could feel the metallic-tasting raw inside of his lip with a tongue he only now realized was bruised as well. His right eye was swollen nearly shut and the back of his head was pounding. The place where he had received a blow to his stomach ached with an acid, grating pain. He glanced at his watch and realized with a receding wave of nausea that he was more than two hours late coming home, that he had never called and prepared Leah to warn Celia about how he must appear. It was too late. The cab was stopping in front of his house and he could not possibly muster the energy to walk to a pay telephone. He paid the driver and painfully, slowly, withdrew from the cab, steadying himself on the open door.

The lobby was gray and cool, and none of his neighbors whom he often met coming home from work were near the mailboxes or elevator. The hall was still and smelled of cooking odors.

He got in the elevator and for the first time caught a look at his face in the small mirror on the back wall. His right eye, swollen to a mere slit of an opening, was discoloring already to the shade of chopped meat. His lips were distended in an irregular bumpy fashion and to his surprise there was a large lump on his left cheek, shiny and still flesh colored, which hurt only dully when he touched it. The cut above his eyes was now stitched and bandaged, and so were the two on his neck. His shirt and suit jacket were slit on the right arm from elbow to collar seam and then slightly down at an angle into the chest. He put his head against the wall and closed his eyes. For several minutes the elevator did not move and finally he reached out and pressed the button for his floor.

Before the apartment door he assembled himself as best he could and took out his key. At the first jingle of metal, the door sprang open and Leah, looking quite frantic, peered out. When she saw him her face hardly changed but the lines hardened.

"Oh!" She swayed unsteadily against the doorway. "My God! Sam! I was afraid. You were so late and I'd been waiting . . . What happened?" She put out her hands to him and took him by the elbow.

"Wait," he said, noting his speech was still thick. "Give Celia a little warning. A student. I'll tell you later." He stepped inside the vestibule. Leah just stood there as if unable to move.

"I've been waiting," she said again. "I had something to tell you. Important. I don't know now." She closed her eyes and opened her lips but nothing came. Then: "Are you all right? Oh what a stupid question! I mean is it any worse than it looks?"

"I'm not in a hospital," said Sam. "Please go warn her."

"I need to tell you first." Leah looked around desperately but Celia was nowhere in sight. "Today," she whispered, "she sat down at the harp and played — just a few bars of something. That's the first time. I'd almost forgotten she did that. Sat there for a long while after."

Sam leaned against the door. He was feeling nauseated, but at the same time airy, floating. His head was pounding; he could hardly tell from pain or hope. "I have to sit down please," he said and she led him into the empty living room where no Celia waited. He took a chair and breathed deeply, trying to quell the temptation to retch. "I want to hear. Every bit. But first please go tell her."

Leah nodded and backed to the kitchen door. "Celia," he heard her saying, "dear, Sam is home but he's been hurt a little. He's all right but he looks rather bad. Don't be upset."

Celia came to the door from the kitchen slowly and stood staring at him. Although her mouth opened, she did not cry out or moan, just stared for a long moment. Then she came toward him and, stopping just before him, looked down at his face. He tried to smile but his lips simply would not go. "I'm all right, darling, really I am. It's nothing," he whispered.

She was standing beside him in a hush that made even these many months of silence reverberate with sound, a closeness like the walls of a prison cell covering her, enclosing her. Then she reached down, took his hand and raised it to her lips, palm up. As she kissed it, he could feel her tears silent as soft rain. After a few moments she hit her chest gently twice with her other hand and, letting go, turned away. She walked across to the hall and into the bathroom, where they heard her turn on the water. Sam felt his breath quicken when she returned with a wet towel, neatly wrung out and folded, and placed it against his eye. Then she turned again and disappeared into their bedroom, closing the door behind her.

After a minute of silence, Sam and Leah both began together, "Tell me . . ." and stopped.

"You need to be taken care of," said Leah. "Let's go in Gershom's room. You can lie on the bed there. Has a doctor seen you?"

He nodded. "Police wanted a report; they took me," he said and leaned on her as she helped him up and they walked in a crooked line to the long-unused room.

Leah turned on the light and helped take off his jacket. "You're not cut under there, are you?" she said with more calmness than she normally showed.

"No. Only a threat."

"I'm glad you got in touch with the police."

"I'm not."

"You know who?"

"Yes."

"Why?"

"Bad grade, drugs — he needed drugs and a friend who likes violence to do it. Don't want to talk about it now. Police know." He sat down on the bed with effort and raised his legs onto it, lay down and closed his eyes. Leah replaced the cold wet towel Celia had brought to him and covered him with a blanket. Carefully she removed his shoes.

"Do you want some tea? Some soup? There's soup for dinner. Toast maybe?"

"Hard to eat yet," he wheezed. "I was hit in the stomach. Makes me feel sick."

"You need a good doctor to look at you." She was regaining the Silverstein urgency in her voice.

He shook his head slightly. "No. I've had enough." Then he opened his eyes. "Tell me about the harp."

Leah sat down in a chair beside the bed. "She had been sitting for most of the morning in her rocker, reading and rocking. During lunch, I talked to her about the house and what we needed to buy. I said I heard Rafe and Miriam came on Sunday again and she beamed. She really likes them. Then she went back to the living room. I was going to wash the lunch dishes but before I could get started I heard this plunk. I was afraid maybe she had fallen against the harp so I came in, but she was sitting there behind it, looking at it. She didn't see me, I think, she was staring at it so. Then she tipped it and played, it couldn't have been more than ten bars, waited, then played again, the same thing and a little more. I don't know what it was. That was all, but after that she sat at the harp for a long time and ran her hand along the strings without making a sound. Then she just sat and after a while got up and went in the bedroom. She was dressed when I went to get her for our afternoon walk. She hadn't been before and usually I have to remind her, though not always. That's all. We went down and the rest of the day was the same as usual." She hesitated. "She didn't even seem especially agitated by your being late. Of course I tried to make light of it though I was worried."

Sam had heard Leah through a web of pain but every word

was embedded in his mind. "How long altogether did she play?"

"Really play — only about four or five minutes, maybe less — but she was there for nearly half an hour."

"Did you say anything to her about it?" Leah did not answer immediately. When she spoke her voice was very soft and uncertain. "No. I was going to say, 'Play some more,' but I couldn't. It seemed so private — as if she had to be alone with it, alone with herself." Then, sounding more like the Leah he knew, she said perkily, "I feel certain it's a good sign, that it means something has changed, that she's getting better. Don't you?"

"I hope." He realized the nausea that had been washing over him had stopped. "Leah, would you get me a little tea with milk and honey? Nothing else."

"Of course." She slipped from the room. He felt grateful to be left alone.

In the stillness, he tried to reconstruct the moments of Celia's playing; what they had been like; what her fingers had looked like, her body leaning against the spine of the harp; what the stroke of music on the ear sounded like. His imaginings played against his pain, the sore lips now swollen into stiffness, the throbbing place at the back of his neck, and new aches catalogued as they unfolded. The room was hung with ghosts. In the shadows he could see the face of Johnny Lee, his hand raised, his blue bandana wet with sweat. And Gershom too, looking away, turned away. All the books falling out of shelves, falling to the floor as he had fallen to the floor. How could he, with his stiff lips and sore body, move past them, be alive with promise he knew could flower into something better? Promise! It screamed its unbirth through his pain and yet, now, for the first time in months, he felt a surge of fresh shoots. Restoration. Of what? Anger? Possession? — the things in Celia he had chosen to overlook. Or the delicate, beautiful, to him beautiful, woman he had fallen in love with long ago, he had wanted to strengthen with his own strength. Had he actually, should he believe he had, glimpsed the lamp of rescue on this night when he could barely see through the slit of one eye? He rocked in the stillness, pulled between the shadow and the light.

Leah returned to the room with a cup of tea. "I'm going to stay tonight. I can sleep on the couch." He hardly understood what she meant.

He let her help him sit up and took the tea. "Leah," he said, his voice cracking as he spoke, "in the living room there's a little white book on the shelf by the plants. It's a daily prayer book. Favor from my nephew Ira's wedding." He was panting from the exertion of speech. "Could you bring it?"

She looked surprised but said nothing and went to get it.

"Put it on the night table," he said. He handed her the almost empty teacup and lay back against the pillow, half-propped against the head of the bed for a few minutes. Then he struggled to sit up again.

"Sam," said Leah urgently. "I could call Gabriel. He hasn't left for his trip yet. I know he'd come. You really need better medical care than you got."

He shook his head. "I'm just bruised. If my eye isn't better tomorrow I'll think about it. Help me up. I just want to go to the bathroom."

She got him to his feet and he shuffled to the other room. In the medicine chest mirror his face was more discolored than it had been in the elevator. How long ago was that? He had no idea.

He opened his pants and pulled up his shirt to where the fist had hit his stomach. There was a large red bruise swelling beside his navel. He touched it charily. An ugly feeling. He opened the medicine chest and found the aspirin bottle. He took out three pills and stared at them absent-mindedly before swallowing them with a swig of water.

When he returned to the bedroom he removed the slit shirt

and asked Leah to get him his pajamas. "I don't want to upset her by going in," he said.

Leah came back a minute later with his things. "She's asleep. Didn't even stir when I went in. This whole day must have worn her out. So much. She never had dinner. Do *you* want some now?"

"No," said Sam. "Let me change."

He had more trouble getting his pants off and his pajamas on than he had expected. The aches now pervaded his consciousness entirely but without their earlier sharpness.

He called Leah softly and she came back in and pulled back the covers of the bed where fresh sheets had long been laid for Gershom. She helped Sam in and said, "Don't hesitate to call even in the middle of the night if you need me," and her remark about staying on the couch began to register.

"You don't have to stay."

"I want to," she said.

He did not protest but closed his eyes. After she left, he switched the bedside light on and took the prayer book. With his weary left eye he found the prayer: *Hide not Thy face from me in the day when I am in trouble; incline Thine ear unto me; in the day when I call answer me speedily.* He made no attempt at the Hebrew, but closed the book and replaced it on the night table and turned off the lamp.

At first, sleep would not come. He could not get into a comfortable position and everything hurt, especially his head. But, after a time, the aspirin began to ease the throbbing and he fell into a troubled slumber, dreaming of violences, waking to sobs he heard distinctly in his sleep but which faded like echoes as his mind revived. He slept again and dreamed again. When he would awaken he was aware of the pain, now sore in a new way. Once he thought he heard the harp playing but it was just another dream.

In one dark hour he thought he awakened to find a woman standing by the bed. Leah to see how he was? His one eye was puffed almost entirely shut and sealed with a stiffened secretion. With the other he could see only dimly in the dark. In the quietness, he felt Celia's hand, its tiny calluses unmistakable, stroking his temples. He reached out his hand to her and she took it. He tried to speak but his lips and tongue were set. She stayed holding his hand and stroking his hair until sleep overcame him and he fell into a deep unimaged dark. When he woke again he was alone and the room dusty with a vague light. He lay for a long time in Gershom's lonely bed, thinking without words of his son.

After a short time he became aware of a slight sound at the door. Celia pushed it open, carrying a tray with a cup and a covered plate. She set it down on the chair beside the bed, then stood looking at him.

He struggled against the swelling and stiffness to form words that would not come clearly. "Where's Leah?" There was no answer. He didn't expect one. Then her voice (Could it be her voice?), thin and unnatural but her voice (Was he dreaming?) came. "Sam. This is breakfast, Sam." Unbidden, a prayer from his boyhood filled his head briefly, obscuring the pain, the blessing said at all beginnings: *"Baruch ata Adonoi Elohenu melech ha-olam — shehechianu, v'kimanu, v'higianu lazman ha-zeh —* Who has kept us in life and preserved us and has enabled us to reach this season." She had already turned and left the room when his mind cleared enough for him to feel his hopes plunge deeply beneath the hurting and to remember the night with its dreams. Uncertain of whether she had really been there, he reached out. His hand grazed something. Yes. The tray remained.

13

Sunday, October 14, 1973
PUBLIC NOTICES

Gershom — Dad's teaching again. Mother much better. Quartet touring. Israeli war troublesome. Gabriel's there. — Johanna.

October 9, 1973
Jerusalem

*D*EAR SETH AND JOHANNA,

I realize you must be very concerned about me but I am well though very saddened. Who could have imagined the holidays in Israel would turn so bitter? Hannah Eckstein had described Jerusalem on Yom Kippur as an Eden — a place where one could be purified and reborn as on the day of creation. She said this only the day before, when I visited with her in the morning. It was hard to have to remember that afterward. I was in shul when the sirens began to sound. Then a truck came with a loud-speaker blaring for people to listen to their radios. On Yom Kippur there are usually no radio broadcasts. It was chaos. The young men ran out of the synagogue without even waiting to take off their *talaysim*. The rest of us old ones stayed to finish without knowing everything but knowing enough. Within the day — twenty-four hours — the young men were gone. They have disappeared from the streets and the shops. It is as if they have just been lifted away. Except, of course, for the ultra-orthodox with religious dispensations, who are preparing now for Sukkot almost as if nothing had happened. I see them in Machne Yehudah buying the four species, examining each *lulav* to make sure the fronds are evenly spaced, the *etrog* to be certain it has no deformities. But even their calm concern with ritual is altered. Many leave to go do volunteer service, especially in hospitals. Today, I watched from my window a sukkah being built on the balcony of an apartment nearby. There is already at least one sukkah in each of the courtyards I can see and this is by no means the most orthodox part of the city. I am surprised myself at the comfort I find in knowing that the order of the year goes on regardless and that the festival will be observed.

I hardly know what to say about the great deformity: this war. If only it could be laid aside as one may discard the imperfect fruit! The Israelis seem confident but one cannot be sure with enemies besieging them to the north and south. I am grateful that, so far, Jordan has remained out of the battle. The news on the radio is unclear and depends, too, on which country is doing the reporting. I will write more about this soon and about the volunteer service I do. I would like to be able to promise that I shall be home by November for the birth of the baby, but if I feel I am needed I will stay as long as I can. Although the Israelis talk about a victory in six days as if it ought to be expected, joke about taking Damascus, there is no way of knowing how long the fighting will go on. It's not what I would have chosen, but since it has happened, I'm glad at least I have an opportunity to serve. I am sure you understand.

I rejoice that Celia continues to improve (your letter arrived just before Yom Kippur) and that you and Rachel are all well. Greet Miriam for me and wish her Happy Holidays for Sukkot and Simhat Torah. Greet Sam — I trust he is well over his mishap, Celia and, of course, your parents, Johanna. Our good Raphael too.

Love,
Abba

"Well," said Leah when Johanna finished reading the letter, "I'm glad to hear Gabriel is all right. Sam's 'mishap' — that's an understatement. It would be very unfortunate though, if he couldn't get back in time for the baby. The war isn't over yet and you're due in less than a month."

"Sad for him," said Johanna, "but I bet he stays because he will find ways to help."

"It's important to help your family too," said Leah, "though you're fortunate to have your own parents nearby. I'm sure as an American citizen, he would have no trouble getting out if he really wanted to . . ."

"I wouldn't bet on that," murmured Johanna.

"I hope nothing happens to him. It would be very bad for Seth and his sister. For you too, I suppose. Who's this Hannah Eckstein?"

"An old friend from Europe. She was here but made *aliyah* a few years ago."

"Crazy," said Leah, "to give up America for that. I bet she's having second thoughts now. Married?"

"Widowed."

"Maybe that accounts for Gabriel's interest in staying there despite the baby."

"I think he just cares very much about Israel. So . . ."

"The drama of the situation certainly affects people." Leah had interrupted her. "Even your father. He said he thought maybe we ought to join a temple again when he heard the news. It's been years! After all, Israel's bound to be an issue in the next election."

"I can't speak for Daddy's motives," said Johanna, "but I

understand why Seth's father wants to stay and I'm sure if we were there, we'd feel just the way he does."

Leah laughed an artificially hearty laugh. "Oh, Johanna, darling. I'm glad you're sitting in your New York apartment, where you can afford to be so sentimental." Her voice was chiding, as though speaking to a naughty child.

"Sometimes," said Johanna, "I don't feel we communicate."

"Whose fault is that?"

"I wasn't blaming anybody."

"It sounded awfully like blame to me." Leah turned away. She was sitting at an ironing board in Johanna's kitchen, ironing pillowcases, something Johanna herself never did. She folded a white case with a sprinkling of wild flowers printed on the border and she took the last one from the pile, which also included tablecloths and a few of Rachel's dresses.

"I wish you would let me have Elise come just once every few weeks." She pouted at the pillowcase. "She could make fast work of all this and do a far better job than I can."

"No," snapped Johanna, wondering as she did why she objected so much to her mother's repeated offer. Having a maid in now and then would be nice. "You don't need to do these, I've told you. The wash-and-wear finish is fine with us."

"It's better when they're pressed. I like to see to it that you have a little ease in your life. With the baby due to arrive so soon, it's a good thing Celia and Sam don't need me as much."

"What about Daddy?"

"I've been doing plenty for him," Leah pronounced each word deliberately, "and, as he knows, not all of it with my heart in it. He's another one who tells me we don't communicate and now, with all this Watergate business . . ."

She had been spending almost every night at home with Harry, only staying with Johanna a day or two a week at the most.

"When you saw Aunt Celia this morning, how was she?" Retreat to a neutral subject. Well, not *so* neutral.

Leah smiled. "Remarkable. She's able to talk about how she is feeling and how Sam is doing though she doesn't seem to understand how depressed he is with the court case still hanging over him. I think he doesn't confide in her. I think he talks to Rafe Toledano about it though because he said Rafe might go to the preliminary hearing with him. I'm glad he's sparing Celia."

"Does she sound like her old self yet?"

"No. She's still speaking less, more softly, more slowly. I'm surprised about how calm she's been about Sam going back to teach. Not just what she says. Her whole manner. There's been quite a change in her. Perhaps she still doesn't feel comfortable talking."

"Gershom? Does she mention Gershom?"

Leah looked up at Johanna with anger, folding her lips together. "She's mourned enough. If he had actually died, the grief might have been easier for her to deal with." She shook her head. "I would never bring him up and if she did, I'd try to change the subject as soon as possible. But," her voice became sprightly again, "she tells me she's been practicing the harp. That shows you what a little loving care can do. Now it's you I worry about, my darling, with Seth on tour especially. Are you exhausted?"

"Fine," said Johanna firmly. "I'm fine."

* * *

In the late afternoon, her mother left and Johanna dressed Rachel for a romp in Riverside Park. They walked out into a bright four-thirty, Rachel running ahead, her red jacket bobbing like a lively apple.

"Wait for me at the corner," she called ahead to her daughter, wondering, as she said it, how it was possible to protect a child and at the same time let her go. She remembered her own childhood with a wave of claustrophobia. Everything conspired to keep her from making any mistakes that could not be easily corrected. She had sometimes felt, especially in adolescence, that a plan for her future lay folded and ready in some cupboard, allowing her all sorts of gracious progresses, like a princess, but closing off the route to the real world with its risks. She dreaded the thought of imposing such visions on her own child but, at the same time, found herself quickening her step as Rachel ran fully to the curb, where she stopped abruptly without having slowed down first.

"Darling, you have to stop a little before you get to the street or you could trip right off the curb."

Rachel looked at her mother with curiosity. "But I didn't. I stopped," she said with a three-year-old's sense of justice. "I waited like you said."

"Yes."

They walked across the Drive in silence and once on the promenade above the river bank, Rachel, swinging her arms and singing, bounded toward the sandbox area where they usually joined other mothers and children. Johanna walked alone slowly behind, the new child bulging out before her. She could not move quickly any longer, a part of pregnancy she didn't like. Resented, in fact. Resented not being able to find a comfortable position to sleep in; resented not having enough energy for her own work; resented the invasion of herself. And yet she wanted this child. At her insistence, she and Seth had waited seven years to have Rachel, pushing off the moment when yet another person would entwine her life. And that, despite the fact she had not imagined just how absorbing that tiny being could be. This baby was different. She had fewer fears and she had always known she would not have an only child, for the sake of the child as much as for herself. She was getting older — thirty-two nearly, and if they ever chose to have a third child, it was wise to have a second now. Did she want another? She couldn't say. Children were delightful and demanding, a dangerous combination that she alternately treasured and disliked. Above all, she hated herself for being unable to love and yet retain her distance. For being sometimes so very like her mother.

Inside the sandbox area, she saw only a few people she knew, but one was her friend Rita, knitting an enormous red and gray scarf and wearing a tweed jacket with a plastic button on one lapel. The button, a leftover from the days of Vietnam, had the word *peace* in heavy blue letters on a white background. Johanna sat down beside her and glanced at the button questioningly.

"If I had one that said *shalom*, I'd wear it, but this will have to do. Have you heard from your father-in-law?" Rita kept on knitting.

"Yes. He's fine and doing some sort of volunteer work. He didn't say what."

"Good," said Rita. "Bastards!" Then she looked at Johanna's middle. "You haven't dropped yet, have you?"

"No."

"Soon," said Rita, and she turned the knitting to purl.

In the sandbox, Rachel had found the Holseizer's youngest, Linda, and was building a sand tower in a nearby corner. The light was changing, the sun a heavy gold over the Jersey cliffs.

"Did you ever feel sort of desperate just before the kids were born? As if you were being taken over?"

"Well, you are in a way. But no, I was taken up with the romance of it all. That's why I haven't finished my graduate work, and being a biochemist without a Ph.D. is like being a tightrope walker without a sense of balance. So much for romance!" She turned toward Johanna, smiling. "Hey, did I tell you there's a possibility I might have a part-time research job after the first of the year?"

"That's great! Where?"

"In Ralph Corman's lab — you know, my friend from graduate school. Well, it's only a possibility but I hope it materializes. For one thing, we could use the money."

"I wish I felt a little more romance these days." Johanna

leaned against the back of the bench. "Mostly, I feel terrified
that I'm going to disappear into the nursery, sucked into the
wallpaper. Flat Mommy permanently carrying her buckets of
milk up a green hill."

"Not you! You've really managed to keep up your potting,
your painting. Not many people can do that. You'll be all right."

"So much of the time I feel like I'm not doing my work out
of love so much as desperation," she snickered, a wretched
sound. "To keep me from sitting in twenty-five years with
Rachel and her children, hovering over them because they're
the investment I made and they had better pay off."

Rita turned her knitting again. "Living so close to your
mother lately has thrown everything out of focus."

Johanna sighed. She felt exceedingly dull. "If I say one more
thing about that matter, do you think you can bear it?"

"Of course." Rita looked up from her knitting, her hands
still moving.

Johanna said nothing.

"Well?"

"Just, I've asked myself over and over what's created this
'yucky,' to quote one of our favorite programs, situation that
doesn't seem to have an end. What I keep coming back to is
the picture my mother's painted of herself as a talented girl
going off to college on the subway each morning, studying
education instead of art because it was practical. It's ironic,
she's never taught. Then, meeting this paragon, my father,
whose background and promise were so great she was willing — get that — to throw away everything for him. Goodbye
to her practical career. It must have been nice not to have to
keep books anymore for the family business, to indulge her
interest in art. But no! She doesn't see it that way. Because
anyone she loves has to be the most! The best! Worth the
sacrifice of her whole life. Him! Me! Me, at least as she presents me to the rest of the world. As a daughter, of course,
I'm not so good but you should hear her carry on to other

people about my brilliant marriage, my husband's magnificent career, 'if only they had a little more money,' and my talent."

"I've heard her," said Rita, crinkling her eyes, "and I always agree with her."

"Well, it's damned easy to get like that. When Seth has concerts and there's a party for the quartet afterward, people are always coming up to me and saying, 'Oh, you're the cellist's wife. He was wonderful!' And even while I'm hating it, hating just being a wart on the master's hand, I can feel myself giving in to it. It's like trying to walk on whipped cream. You don't want to sink in, but it tastes good when you do. Am I making any sense at all?"

"Perfect. Last night, in fact, I went to one of those engineer shindigs of Oren's. I was having a conversation with that woman Oren works with who has always made me feel she thinks my brain dissolved when I gave birth. Somehow we got onto the subject of the research I'd done on plant viruses and do you know what she said?" Rita's eyes were wide and she stretched her mouth into a clownish frown. " 'I had no idea you were so interesting. Oren should have told me.' I wanted to smash her. I wanted to smash him. I wanted to bash their heads together. I was speechless, I was so angry." She sounded gleeful, chuckling with an embarrassed satisfaction as she practically shouted the last phrase. "But when we got home, I wasn't speechless. I really laid into Oren and he said I was overreacting, that she treats everyone that way, even the guy she lives with."

"As if his brain dissolved giving birth? My! My!" Johanna was giggling.

"She is pretty cocky! Say — do you suppose . . . ?"

They looked at one another and exploded into laughter. They laughed until tears were running down both their cheeks.

"Damn it," said Rita, wiping her face. "But even though I can't stand that, when we went to Amsterdam for him to give that talk, I basked in the glory. And all the time people were telling me how brilliant he was, I *knew* the implication was that to have such a man, I must be brilliant too: in bed or with the quiche pan — certainly not in the mind."

"You do make pretty good quiche. Tell me, is it the buckwheat crust or the touch of dill in your mushroom quiche that turns Oren on?"

"It's the dill, it's the dill," rasped Rita in her best vamp voice and they were laughing again wildly.

"Oh, I'm going to wet my pants or have the baby here if I don't stop laughing." Johanna gulped as she began to regain control. "I haven't been this silly in months."

They sat back quietly, nodding at the dropping sun, until their amusement passed.

Johanna, her passages tightening again, felt suddenly cold in the shadows the trees cast. "Sometimes I'm afraid," she said.

"Me too. Afraid, most of all, that when I do climb off the merry-go-round of raising children, I'm not going to have anywhere to go. Most of the skills I had before I had kids weren't strongly enough established in the first place and the few I did have under control are atrophying fast. Especially since I'm a scientist. I haven't kept up the way I should."

Johanna stared out across the sandbox into the colored fall leaves. "Do you know any woman — I mean someone our mothers' age — who ever really got it all in order? Was happily married, had kids and kept her own identity?"

"I know a few married women who've had careers but whether they're happy, whether their daughters are any better off than the rest of us, I don't know."

They sat quietly for a few seconds watching the children.

"Do you ever," Johanna was speaking so quietly, her voice was almost a whisper, "do you ever lie awake at night and look over at Oren, or hear the kids breathing, and think to yourself, 'Where am I? How did I get mixed up with those people?'"

"Sure."

"I never think that about my mother though. Better for me if I did."

Rita folded her knitting and put it into her sack at the back of Linda's stroller. She called to Judy, her five-year-old, who was playing hopscotch with some bigger girls on the far side of the sandbox. Then she turned to Johanna. "Maybe it's you, not your mother, who has got to let go. If kids are independent enough, there's not much you can do but say Godspeed."

As if in confirmation, the baby gave her a forceful kick. "I've told myself that a hundred times."

"Well, maybe on the hundred and first, it will take." She walked to the sandbox to collect Linda, a lively two-and-a-half-year-old covered with sand. "Even in her hair," said Rita with distaste as she put her, squealing with protest, in the stroller. "Say, how's your uncle who got beaten up?"

"He's better physically but he's pretty unhappy about his teaching now. It kind of knocked the good spirits out of him. He's a lot happier about my aunt though."

"Great," said Rita. She put up her hand in an affectionate wave. "I'll see you soon. Take care."

*   *   *

"I'll wash myself," said Rachel, sitting in the bathtub looking fresh and shiny from the water. Her hair was piled on top of her head and hung down in little curls over the top of her forehead. Johanna felt the warm aura of loving the child seep up through her chest and throat. She found her remarkably beautiful, by far the prettiest little girl she had ever known, wanted to tell her, but guarded her tongue. There's nothing wrong with praising a child, expressing admiration, love. No child psychology book would fault a mother for that; yet, she remembered feeling special embarrassment when her mother would praise her, especially when she was naked, as if something was being violated. And what is Rachel going to think about me while she's looking at her child? she thought.

"I'll wash myself," said Rachel again. She was already doing it.

"O.K.," said Johanna. "Do a good job." She leaned back against the wall and closed her eyes.

"Don't go to sleep," said Rachel. "It's not polite."

"I'm not sleeping. People don't sleep standing up like horses or elephants."

"I do when I'm an elephant."

"Well, you aren't one now. You could never fit in the bathtub if you were. And I'm never an elephant."

"When Grandma is here, she pretends to be an elephant. But I'm really one."

Johanna laughed, half charmed. "Make sure you're a clean one." She waited for Rachel to step out of the bathtub to be wrapped in a towel.

"Where's Daddy tonight?" asked Rachel.

"In Baltimore." Seth was on the last week-long tour his quartet planned until after the birth of the baby. Touring was one part of a musician's life she hated and he tolerated merely. She had spent more than a month alone once, early in Rachel's life when the quartet had gone to Europe, and their phone bills had turned astronomical.

"Baltimore," the child said it slowly, trying out all the syllables. "Did I ever go there?"

"Not yet."

"Sometime will I go there?"

"I expect."

Rachel sighed. "When I grow up I'm going to go to Atlanta, Charlotte, Durham and Baltimore," she said, naming all the stops on Seth's tour so far.

"And what will you do there?"

She considered. "Say 'Hello, I'm Rachel' to everybody."

Johanna smiled. How to keep that spirit alive? "Are you finished? You did a good job except for the spot on your chin."

Rachel rubbed at it fiercely with the washcloth. "A very good job," she said. "I did a very good job." She stepped out of the bathtub ready for the towel. Johanna wrapped her up and rubbed her back, feeling overcome with love.

"Are you ready for bed?" she asked tenderly, putting Rachel's nightgown over her head.

"No, I'm going to stay up till Daddy calls."

"That's too late. He's planning to call early tomorrow to talk to you."

"I'm going to talk tonight."

"Not tonight."

"Yes," Rachel's voice was becoming petulant.

"It's been a long day," said Johanna, trying reason. "I'm tired. I think you probably are too. I'll read to you."

"No," said Rachel. "I don't want to go to bed." She backed into the hall.

"Where are you going?" Johanna could feel the joy slipping away from her.

"Inside." And the child skipped down the hall.

Johanna, heavy, followed her. "If you don't go to bed now, Rachel, I won't let you watch Mr. Rogers tomorrow."

Who is that going to punish? she thought.

"Yes, Mr. Rogers," Rachel's voice was rising.

Johanna went to pick her up and the child began to cry, flailing her arms and legs.

"Don't kick! You could hurt Mommy or the baby."

"I don't want to go to bed. I'm not tired."

More flailing.

"No, Rachel." She had not realized the child was so strong. She could not carry her and put her down on the floor and tried to push her toward the bedroom. "Rachel," she said, her voice coming louder than she intended, "when Daddy calls, I'm going to have to tell him you weren't good. You promised him you'd be good."

She only knew she was weary and, when she had to return to the bedroom for the third time to the sound of a small voice calling, "Mommy," she said, "I won't come again, Rachel," and sat in the living room, listening as her daughter cried herself to sleep.

It was with a sense of loss that she finally sat down at the high desk in her studio.

She was working on plans for a punch bowl and cups that had been commissioned by someone she had met, ironically, through her sandbox associates. The woman, too old to have little children to bring to the park, was the good friend of a younger woman who did and, after meeting Johanna and seeing some of her work, had asked her to create something suitable for parties of thirty or forty people — a piece that would decorate her table as well as be functional. It was an interesting project that had her considering designs and glazes, that absorbed her as she rocked into the pleasure — the inner silence her work brought, a stillness sometimes rich with flashes of insight, actually erotic when things were going very well. She usually reserved this work for the hours Rachel went to nursery school but with Seth away and the apartment silent, the designs that had been floating before her inner eye all day demanded her attention and, on impulse, she tried sketching them on paper before attempting a clay model. She drifted with them into a sweet restorative time in which her tiredness and irritation lifted like smoke.

The phone rang, startling her, and her heart quickened as the stillness fled. She stood up to go and answer it. It was, she knew in some instinctive way even before she picked up the receiver, her mother.

"Is everything all right there? I worry with Seth away. He really could have chosen a better time for the tour."

"Everything's fine. I'm doing some work."

"Oh, I'm sorry I disturbed you." There was a brief pause. "Johanna," her voice was a little softer, "I'm going to take a cab over. I think I'd like to stay there tonight."

"Why?"

"Well, your father is involved with his political cronies. They're talking 'strategy' all the time now that Agnew's out and there's this special prosecutor business. He's so wrapped up, he won't even notice until later. I'm leaving a note, as if he would worry!"

"I wish you would try to resolve your problems with him."

"Try! Of course I've tried. Do you think he's made the slightest effort?"

Johanna's head began to ring with the conversation she had already had numerous times. "All right," she said and hung up without saying goodbye.

Rage rocked her. "I hate that woman," she said aloud between clenched teeth and tingled with the shock waves of her guilt. "I hate her. I hate her. Why does she do this to me?" She struggled to regain the calm destroyed by the sound of her mother's voice, but it was dissipated, blown to dust. Her agitation was in her feet and she began to pace the living room back and forth, pounding her fist into the palm of her other hand and muttering, "God damn, god damn!" The pacing continued until she stopped, alarmed by the thought of her studio, and rushed in to gather the sketches, which lay abandoned in the room her mother would occupy. Sirens sounded in her head and inadvertently the image of the Israeli young men racing from the synagogue pervaded her mind. In this moment of panic, Leah was quite the enemy come on a sacred day, her apartment, marriage, even her child, the land she occupied uneasily as a defense against invasion. It was territory she had won painfully and with each sheet she caressed into the pile her outrage quickened.

The downstairs bell buzzed and her mother's voice said, "It's me," over the intercom. Well, she didn't really hate her, did she?

"I'm sorry to trouble you so," said Leah, putting down her traveling make-up kit, her only luggage. "I just couldn't stay in that house a minute longer. I despise that big Ornstein woman — she's really vulgar, and Edward Gregor with his obsequious manners! I believe the man is a fairy. They take your father over and he expects me to serve them and greet them as if they were worthwhile human beings."

Johanna felt a familiar cringe as she took her mother's coat and hung it in the closet.

"Aren't they?" she said.

The corners of her mother's mouth dropped and her eyes clouded. "I wish you would spare a little of that universal understanding for me," she said slowly, and with her chin up, walked over to the couch.

Johanna came into the living room after her and sat down. She had played this scene a hundred, two hundred times and every time she ended badly. Shuffling possible responses, she found she had used them all at one time or another to no avail.

"I know you," continued Leah, patting her hair back in place. "You like everyone. Just like your father. It doesn't matter to you what sort of shenanigans they indulge in. Well, character counts, I think."

"One of these days," said Johanna dryly, "Daddy is going to tell you not to come back at all."

Leah looked shocked, her lips parting slightly. "So you think his politics and his disregard of me are justified. That none of what has happened is his responsibility."

"I think you are knocking yourself out and aggravating him for no reason whatsoever. You no longer go to Celia's for whole days at a time. You claimed you objected to all this political activity because you felt you couldn't be expected to take time from helping her. Now she's helped. I mean she may not be altogether well but she's on the way and so that's not the reason anymore . . ."

"Now you need . . ."

"Cut it out! I can do very well by myself. There's something much more basic going on and if you don't see that, I assure you Daddy does. And I do."

"Well, I can see we don't understand each other on this

point." There was a brief silence. Then Leah pointed to the sheets of paper on a small table and, in a completely different manner as though she were talking to someone new, asked, "What are those drawings you have there?"

Johanna looked down at the pile of sketches she had left when she went to answer the door. "What I was working on when you interrupted me."

"May I see?" Leah's face shifted from an aged heavy look to one of youthful interest. She reached over, took the pile from the table. As she began to leaf through them, she said, "I'm just curious. Did you actually make those candlesticks for Miriam?"

"Yes."

"I hope she was properly appreciative. She didn't offer to pay you, did she?"

"They were a gift. To celebrate the change in her life."

Leah laughed a pointedly artificial laugh. "We'll see how long that will last." She returned to the sketches, flipping them and holding an occasional one out at a distance as she viewed it through squinting eyes. "They're fabulous! You really are a genius. This one with the petals that come out of the design is extraordinary. A third dimension growing out of two. Look what you could do with the leaf here. Do you have a pencil?" She searched the table.

The rage Johanna had pushed back out of old habit surfaced. An occasion in her adolescence: her mother insisting she change the sorrowful face of a child to a happy one flooded her memory with a cataract of anger. Anger. "Put down my drawings, please! I'm working on them. They're not finished. I'm not the least interested in what you would do with them. If you want to make your own designs, I'll be glad to give you some paper." She heard herself shouting.

Leah turned, her mouth open with genuine amazement as Johanna continued.

"And don't tell me how marvelous they are. They're in process. I know my limitations and strengths and when I think I've got something workable I'll do it."

"But they're good. I didn't mean anything . . ."

"God damn, yes you did mean something. You praise me the way you used to praise Daddy, but just let one of us venture out on our own and you can't stand it. Have you ever thought about that? Have you ever asked yourself why you do that? Maybe if you found something of your own to do you'd let us go free."

"Go free? My whole life has been dedicated to your freedom — making sure you felt secure enough to be able to feel free — and to supporting your father." She spoke with a hint of a quaver. The tone was uncertain.

"And you want us to pay a price for that which is to give you freedom to meddle. I was just thinking of that time I made the poster for that UNESCO competition and you fiddled with the face on the child. I was just a kid and didn't know what to do about it then. What the hell right had you to do that?"

"I thought it was better. That's so long ago. I'm sorry . . ."

"What kind of reasonable woman does a thing like that? What kind of reasonable woman leaves her husband because he's involved in something that excludes her for a while? I used to think you were someone who cared about interesting things. I hardly think so anymore. You're so busy praising or condemning us, the rest of the family, it's not possible to care about anything else." Never in her whole life had she felt so angry. It was pouring out of her as water from an unruly hose, even as her other self watched her, whispering, You're going to regret this.

"Johanna, truly I'm sorry. I see I've disturbed you very much." Leah's face was aged with sorrow. "I know this is a difficult time for you . . ."

"This has nothing to do with it's being a difficult time for me. Do you honestly think that Daddy cares anymore whether you stay there or come here? You've played that card into the ground. He has to do what he has to do exactly the way I do. Or Seth. You'd have me arranging his schedules to suit your sense of what should or shouldn't be. And as for my work, over and over you've disrupted it more than any baby, any tour, anything else in my life — even before Gershom decided to drop out. Sometimes I wish I were either weak enough or strong enough to do the same."

"Johanna, that's sinful!"

"Is it? Well, let's get something straight — my work, my successes or failures, aren't yours. They're mine. They are more mine than anything else in the world. They have to do with who I am and that person is not your daughter. In fact, she's not Seth's wife or Rachel's mother. She's herself."

She could see Leah shrinking, the carefully made-up face no longer hiding distress, and she stopped because, although there were vast storage bins of words, the rage had peaked. They sat quietly for a few minutes, Leah looking at her hands.

Finally, she began to respond, softly, slowly, not looking up. "I'm not going to defend myself. You have the luxury I don't of knowing you're adored."

"Shit," said Johanna.

"Let me finish. Your husband admires you and accepts your family. Your father-in-law accepts you. Your parents have both never given you anything but their support and love. That's your good luck and I don't want to take it away from you. You and your family give me a great deal of pleasure and your talent gives me pleasure. Believe me. Sometimes I think about what you're doing, what you have, and I feel that you are the one contribution I've ever really made to the world. But for just that reason you look at me and despise me . . ."

"I don't despise you."

"Well, let's just say you judge me the way you accuse me of judging people. I could never have dared say the sort of things you've just said to me to my parents. My father was an unusual man, but he favored me only so long as I followed in his footsteps. And what did that mean? When I was a girl, in my sophomore year of high school, I started going to the press each day and for years I did his bookkeeping and some proof-reading and checked all the mail that went out for grammat-ical errors. His precious press! He wanted to eventually pub-lish books. Did you know that? English books — the doorway to America! When I read all the things he suggested, and did well in school, he was very solicitous but when I wanted to study art — paint still lifes — he considered that an indul-gence and said so. He loved me in his way but he wanted to conquer the new world and I was a foot in the door from his point of view. My mother, who loves the world but not the people close to her, used to tell me my interests were either too much like Papa's or else too bourgeois. Same thing — painting was an indulgence to her too in those days though not for the same reasons. I should join the Communist party. Everyone I went to college with flirted with that idea, but paint or study art? No! A new woman, they didn't talk about libbers then, tried to change the world, was free in her relationships with men even if it loused up her marriage chances. And it did, you know.

"Sometimes you say to me, 'We don't communicate,' like this afternoon. Well, I never felt I communicated with anyone until I met your father. We were really able to be open with one another. In those days he treated me as if I were someone quite special." She looked down at her hands and stretched the carefully manicured nails before her briefly: a diversion. "I remember trying to talk to my mother about the way I was feeling, changing, when I was thirteen or fourteen and all she would say was, 'If you could talk Yiddish, I'd tell you a thing or two, but in English?' Well, my father didn't allow Yiddish at home, except sometimes if guests came, and I couldn't speak it. Yiddish! He was right, of course. Better to get rid of that hybrid."

They sat in a hush, Johanna weighing her frenzy. She was surprised by how relieved she felt, released, though still cautious. She took the pile of sketches, which lay now in a disorderly pile on the little table, and straightened them. "I don't question your feelings, Mommy. I'm sure you felt the way you say you did. You have told me that many times. But like about so many things, I question the way you interpret what happened. Your feelings may have been based on some kind of unreal expectations. Nobody in the whole world besides you is ever as certain about what other people mean when they say things, what they feel. You tell me lots of times what I feel or what I should feel, which is even worse."

Leah did not answer but continued staring ahead, her face twitching slightly as if she were repressing tears at great effort.

Johanna continued. "Grandma may consider art a kind of bourgeois indulgence but she has never given me the feeling she considered my work useless. I don't expect her to jump up and down about it though. They let Celia play her harp. That wasn't an indulgence?"

"Sometimes I think you purposely misunderstand me. More than thirty-five years have passed, nearly forty, and Grandma has changed some, and so have her attitudes. Communism didn't pan out quite the way she expected. Not that she was alone in that madness. Communism! The Messiah! Stupid! As for Celia — they always pampered her anyway. Besides, music was different from art. It's very Jewish to make music but not to paint."

"But a harp . . . ?"

"Do you know how she got that harp? When my father came to America, after he lived with his cousin for a while, he moved in as a boarder with an old couple from Hungary, who had once had some money. Unusual. They had the harp. They brought it with them from Europe. Nobody played, however. The old man died but my father kept on living there. He studied English while he worked as a typesetter for a Yiddish newspaper. Then he got a job on the *World*. The old woman he lived with was convinced he would succeed in America. When my parents married she presented them with the harp as a wedding gift — a great honor. It's not so extraordinary that if Celia was going to have music lessons, she should play the instrument that was collecting dust in their living room. She always complained that she really wanted to play the piano."

"I've never heard that."

"She never says it now." She shrugged.

"The lesson to be learned from that, it seems to me, is that nobody gets exactly what they want, that you have to make your own opportunities. I mean praise and support from family aren't the only sources for people. Besides Daddy supported you. He liked the things you liked. You've filled the house up with art that has cost lots of money and he has always let you, even been enthusiastic about it. Maybe you should open a gallery."

"I've thought of that. Also I've thought of setting myself up as an interior decorator. Of course the women in your father's family don't do that kind of thing. They are gracious hostesses and devote themselves to charity, if any activity. He wouldn't like it. And don't tell me he's encouraged *you*. You're his daughter, his only child, not his wife. Anyway, Johanna, do you suppose I'd love you and your father — despite everything I love him — any less if I were a busy business person?"

"Maybe you'd have less time to dwell on what every little blink of our eyes meant. Love is very complicated, and expressing it all the time is unnatural, if you don't mind my saying so."

"So, I'm unnatural in addition to all my other sins!" She looked up and sneered at Johanna. "How unfortunate you are to have such a witch for a mother." Her old offended voice was returning. It signaled a response in Johanna as instinctive as the migrations of birds: apologize, explain she didn't mean anything so dreadful, assure her mother of her love. Restore her childhood.

She decided to say nothing, closing her eyes. Her baby stirred within her and she laid her hand on her swollen belly.

"Maybe you would have been better off with a mother like your dear Aunt Emma who manipulated her children without really encouraging them and now has two rare birds to show for it. David is an unsuccessful milktoast like his father, with a demanding, unattractive wife who bosses him around, and Miriam is a whore who has found religion. Like a character from a bad play."

The rage, stilled briefly, rose up in Johanna precipitously. "Miriam is not a whore! That's a hideous thing to say. I've told you that before."

"Well, I don't know how else you would describe her sexual habits — especially this last affair. Do you think this religious phase she's going through is going to change her basic nature? It's clear she's now trying to latch on to that history teacher. He seems such a decent man. I thought he would know better." Leah's voice had taken on an almost gay, spoiling-for-a-fight tone.

Johanna took a deep breath. This too was an old pattern: deflect their differences with one another to differences about a third party. How could she handle this without abandoning her cousin? She thought of Miriam with a kind of admiring tenderness she felt for no one else, now especially.

"I won't discuss Miriam with you," she said. "Her life will speak for itself." She looked at her mother and smiled sadly.

"I don't discuss her with anyone but you! I mean Uncle Sam and I occasionally mention her but that's it. I thought it was possible to say things to you that I wouldn't say to anyone else, but I can see I was wrong."

An untried courage rose in Johanna. Her voice trembled slightly. "Mother, go home. I don't think you should stay here anymore. I haven't done the right thing in letting you come.

From the beginning, it was bad for you, for Daddy, for me and Seth. I don't want to have to go on absorbing your anger. All my life, I've listened to you about the failings of other people. I've never liked it, you know that, but there was a time when I thought of my listening as a kind of safety valve. I don't have the strength to be that anymore and, what's more, I think maybe by letting you go on this way, I haven't helped you. Not at all. Go home. Talk things out with Daddy once and for all. Hear what he has to say, and when he's finished think about what he feels. You can't expect to change him really. You can only change yourself."

"Of course your father has no need to change. He's merely the injured innocent." She looked out under half-closed fluttering lids. "Johanna, it's nearly eleven. I don't feel very comfortable going out and getting a cab now. You may have a point but I'd like to sleep on it."

"In your own bed. I'll have someone go down with you and get you a cab." She stood up and tottered slightly, looking down from a height that seemed vertiginous. Then she walked to her mother, leaned over and kissed her on the head.

"Don't try to make up to me," snapped Leah.

"I'm not," said Johanna. She went to the door of the apartment and started out into the hall. A smell of onions lingered in the air.

"Are you going to humiliate me? Come back." Leah's voice was high-pitched from the doorway. She reached toward Johanna and grasped the edge of her maternity top as Johanna stepped entirely out of the door. Now, standing in the public safety of the hall, she turned slightly toward her mother and pulled the hem of the top to her belly.

"No one is going to be humiliated," she said quietly and continued to walk. She knocked on the apartment door at the far end. A young man in jeans and a workshirt opened the door and from behind came the sound of rock music on the record player.

"Hi, Johanna," he said pleasantly. "What's up?"

"Billy, my mother needs someone to help her get a cab. Would you or Jeff mind very much? I know it's late." She was astounded to hear herself sound calm and reasonable.

"It's fine. I'll just put on my shoes and be there. How's Seth's tour going?"

"Good. Good audiences. He'll be calling soon." She returned to the apartment where her mother was already in her coat. "One of the students down the hall, Billy, will go down with you."

"Hnh." Leah looked away.

Here begins my punishment, Johanna thought. "I think this will be best for both of us," she said, meaning it. "Tomorrow things will seem better."

Her mother closed her eyes, a gesture intended to shut her out.

"It's going to be O.K. I still love you."

Billy, in an Irish fisherman's sweater, arrived at the door. "Hi, Mrs. Seligman."

Leah opened her eyes and said limply, "Hello, Billy. Thank you for coming." She stared at Johanna for a moment, then without saying goodnight, she slipped out of the apartment and closed the door.

"So be it!" said Johanna. She laughed aloud, trembling inside. A drunken euphoria took hold of her, but it passed quickly and she began to speak aloud to herself: the internal interviewer.

"Did you do the right thing?"

"Absolutely!"

"What do you think she's going to do now?"

"She's going to be hurt and offended and unwilling to talk to me for a while. But she'll get over it."

"How do you feel?"

"Powerful! Free! Maybe grown up at last."

Later, on the phone from Baltimore, after she told him what had happened, Seth asked, "How do you feel?" and she said, "Awful! But I think I'll be all right if I can just stick to it."

14

Sunday, November 11, 1973
PUBLIC NOTICES

Gershom — Joshua Adam was born November 7. His *brit* is 4 Thursday at home. — Johanna.

*A*FTER THE FIRST Shabbos he spent with her, every Friday evening Rafe would arrive at Miriam's with a hallah and a bottle of Israeli wine. They would stand together while she lit the candles and he blessed the wine and bread, and then sit down to eat the festive meal. Sometimes they tried to sing a few of the songs Miriam had sung in Brooklyn, but they were not all firmly fixed in her mind and so they developed a repertoire of only three. After dinner and the singing of the final blessings, they stacked the dishes in the dishwasher and sat talking. Each Saturday morning, he would come back early and they would start the day by going to the synagogue she had found in her neighborhood, where she sat upstairs in the balcony and he on the main floor to the south of the reader's platform. On the first Saturday he had been approached by one of the older men in the synagogue and invited to make the blessings before and after the reading of a section of the Torah. He had declined, glancing up wryly at Miriam, who sat on the north side of the balcony, looking down at him. Over the week he practiced with her and, on the next Saturday, accepted the offer. She listened to his voice, shaky, repeating the Hebrew that turned on his tongue in an uncertain pattern, and thought he sounded heroic. When she greeted him after the service, she had giggled conspiratorially and whispered, "Good show," as he closed his eyes in mock modesty. That evening as they made *Havdalah*, smelling the sweet spices and plunging the twisted candle into wine to mark the conclusion of the Sabbath and the beginning of the week, they had kissed one another with the tender little kisses they now frequently exchanged. *"Shavuah tov* — have a good week," she said softly. "I was proud of you today." He kissed her hair and gazed affectionately at her. "Thank you," he said with a shy pride she recognized as genuine.

They bought a copy of *The Jewish Catalogue* and spent several evenings reading it to one another almost as if it were a novel. He borrowed a theoretical book of Buber's on Hasidism from the Columbia library and they tried that, discovering quickly that they needed more basic texts, but thoroughly enjoyed the Hasidic stories in his *Tales of Rabbi Nachman.* They bought an Orthodox prayer book with English translation and began to read and discuss it. One day, he arrived with registration forms for an introductory Hebrew class and said, "I want to take it too." They started in September on Tuesday and Thursday evenings, arriving always together holding hands like children, and, sitting beside one another, struggled with the startling letters in words read from right to left. One night after a particularly grueling class session, she said, "Why are you doing all this? I can see you were curious in the beginning but do you believe anything? Are you doing it just to humor me?"

His face had grown serious though as open as ever, and he had said, "Not to humor you. I don't know why but it feels right. If it doesn't, I'll stop."

Just before Rosh Hashanah, which came in late September, he told her that a friend of his from the math department had invited them to come to dinner on Shabbat — they pronounced it with a *t* at the end now that they were learning Israeli Hebrew — and to attend a Saturday morning service in a home, conducted by a *havurah,* an unofficial synagogue formed by a group of people, many of whom, like Miriam, had discovered their Jewish lives as adults. Since the dinner and the service were both near Columbia and she wasn't willing to ride on the Sabbath, he invited her to stay at his apartment. She hesitated and he took her hands in his and kissed them. "Properly, I promise."

With a family of four and another single man, they had a Shabbat meal similar to the ones Miriam had loved in Brooklyn. And when, afterward, they had sung and even danced a little, she had watched Rafe's eyes shining like dark jewels between his tousled black hair and beard and thought he looked beautiful. It was not a word she had ever applied to a man before.

They walked back to his apartment through a warm clear night, their arms around each other, singing new songs to fix them in their repertoire. In the apartment, he had put a vase of yellow and white chrysanthemums in his bedroom and she laughed, "Are those for me?"

He looked embarrassed. "Well, I don't often have a woman sleeping in my bed these days — even when I'm staying in the study."

Her body quivered with longing. Just his words fired her desire for him. She stepped away and turned her back.

"Miriam, don't be a goose. I'm not propositioning you."

"Have you ever lived with a woman?"

She heard him shuffle slightly. "Yes," it sounded stifled. She turned and saw the sparkle had faded. He looked drawn. "Only one for an extended time."

"Tell me about her."

"Why?"

"I want to know. You know so much about me." She stopped, realizing how many things she had told him.

"Can you have tea even though we sang the *Birkhat?* I'll light the stove."

"Sure."

He went to the kitchen and put on some water. It was an old apartment, all the rooms off a long hall and the kitchen at the very end. She followed him, feeling netted by the darkness that had come over him as he stood tapping his fingers against the stove. She could feel his discomfort vibrating across the room and felt her throat tightening. They did not speak to each other until he had poured the water over the tea bags into battered white mugs and had turned toward her. Impulsively, she came forward and put her arms around him and felt him turn his about her. They stood in that loose embrace for minutes. He seemed released and pushed her away gently, handing her a mug. They sat down at his kitchen table, a pine butcher-block, and he put his hand over one of hers across the top.

"Well?" she said.

"I cared a lot about her at the time. It's quite a while ago. We talked vaguely about getting married but there was always something in the way."

"Was she pretty?"

"Yes."

He was quiet again.

She began tentatively. "What kinds of things?"

"None of them was really an impediment. There was something holding us both back. She was extravagant and kind of silly, you know, and she thought I was moody. I guess I am, though less now than I was. Anyway, she traveled a lot for her work and we got used to a part-time romance. Maybe if she had been here every day, the relationship would have ended sooner. I had a friend from graduate school who was living in Philadelphia and once, when I went down to do some research there, I took her with me and introduced them. After that, whenever she was in Philadelphia, which was fairly often, she would call him up and they would go out to dinner. Eventually, they went to bed too. I didn't know it for a while but I began to suspect something, although not that exactly. Then one day I came home and found the two of them sitting in my living room waiting for me. They were both very embarrassed and dreadfully sorry but things had just gone too far and they had to have each other as well as my blessings." He took a long sip of tea.

"Did you kick them both out?"

"No." He smiled sadly. "I understood everything. In some sense I think I was relieved and I liked them both. I thought I loved her at one time but our relationship had become mostly sex and habit. I went to their wedding but at least was spared being asked to be best man."

"Do you ever see them now?"

"Occasionally, but our friendships have suffered some." He looked at her, his mouth twisting up slightly in a self-conscious deprecating look.

"Hurt?"

"My pride was. Humiliated — that's more like it." He cocked his head to one side. "I felt like an awful fool."

"You felt used," she whispered.

"Yes."

"I know what that feels like, though sometimes I've used people."

Rafe paused before continuing. "In the long run, he really bothered me more than she did. In graduate school, he and I had been sharing an apartment with a good friend of mine from college, who committed suicide. We had both suffered when Richard died — felt guilty that we hadn't really seen what was coming and done something to prevent it. That had been a kind of bond." He looked off above her head. "Sometimes I feel that kind of guilt about Gershom although I knew him much less well." He raised his eyebrows and small wrinkles twisted above them.

Her heart fluttered slightly and she raised the cup, no longer really hot, along her cheek, before drinking the last drops. "I used to feel that way about him all the time when I let myself." She looked across the table directly into his dark eyes. "Is your friend Richard the reason you've cared so much? Sometimes I've wondered why."

"Probably one." He was gazing back at her and she could see questions, a great depth of field, behind his long lashes. "There are others. Some I hardly know myself."

The air was still and warm in the room and Miriam felt the waves of his presence washing over her. He was not like any other man she had ever known: filled with mystery and yet exposed. She sensed a great vulnerability close to the surface and yet each time she approached it, it turned away, twisting like the lip of a giant cup. They had recently begun their Hebrew classes and always met for a vegetarian dinner before. When she would come on the bus or subway and meet him at their designated place, she would sometimes see him from a distance standing against a stone pillar, looking sad and preoccupied. When he smiled at her, the sadness vanished, replaced by a caring strength.

"You know what I liked best tonight?" he said suddenly. "The blessing over the children. If I ever have a child, I'd like to be able to bless him in such a public way."

"Me too," said Miriam. "If I ever have a child."

They sat silently and she added, "There was so little blessing in my family. Blessing a child is putting him in God's care, isn't it? You have to trust that he will be watched over. Sometimes I think that one of the things that drove Celia crazy was that she never trusted anyone to watch over Gershom. She was the same way about Sam and maybe she was right about him. Look what happened this week."

"But they're both getting better. I called today again to see how Sam was and she got on the phone and said, 'Thank you, Rafe.' I was really thrilled." He let go of her hand and picked up both their mugs but continued to sit. Then he said softly, "I think if I believed, I could almost see the hand of God in that."

"Really? I think I'm beginning to believe but I don't see that. Just meaningless suffering."

He shrugged and got up to put the mugs in the sink, his back curving slightly. Miriam stood up behind him and said, "Too late for theology?" in a piping voice she hardly recognized as her own. He turned around with surprise and she blushed. "It's a voice from my past," she laughed, and he laughed with her.

In his room, the flowers welcomed her. She changed into her nightgown and robe and went down the hall to his bathroom. Coming out, she met him wearing a blue-and-white-striped terry cloth robe. He looked boyish in the dim light of the hall, despite his beard, and shy. She was filled with a sense of how important he had become to her in a very short time, and a warm wave of familiar sensation throbbed low in her.

"Sleep well," he said and went into the bathroom without touching her.

She watched the door close, feeling a twist of pain. In his bedroom, she sat down on the bed and considered. They often kissed, fondly, their mouths meeting and parting. Nothing more. Why didn't he kiss her now? She wanted his kiss and his arms around her desperately. No. What she really wanted was to lie in his arms all night long. Her nipples were taut. She took off her robe and lay down in his bed, her heart racing. "Damn, Miriam," she said to herself, "you think the only way to relate to a man is through sex. Cut it out." But it didn't help. She said the prayers to be said before sleep although she was not standing and facing east, and then appended a codicil: "Oh Lord our God, King of the Universe, help me to be quiet. I have never had a friend like Rafe. I care about him very much. I think he cares about me. Help me to do what is right for both of us." Weariness took hold of her and she relaxed, drifting into stillness. "Thank you," she whispered as she fell asleep.

In the morning, they attended services in a West End Avenue apartment with a large living room. A screen had been set up between two banks of chairs that faced a small portable ark and the women sat on one side, the men on the other. Unlike the women in the synagogue she had been going to, the women here did not talk to one another during the service but paid close attention, singing the responses and following carefully. They stood and *davened* during the Adoration: the prayer that spoke of bowing the head in reverence and bending the knee before "the King of kings, the Holy One, praised be He." Their hostess from the night before, Elana, sat next to Miriam and helped to guide her through the service when she stumbled and lost her place. There was also a bit more English in this service than the ones she and Rafe had been attending and she found it easier to keep up. Gradually, this world was opening up, she could feel it, but it was still touched with uncertainties.

When the service concluded and the screen was withdrawn, she saw Rafe sitting, talking with several men, and resisted for a while the desire to rush to him and receive his Shabbat kiss. Elana was introducing her to the other women and one, whose name Miriam had not quite caught, said, "Oh, you came with Rafe. My husband has been after him to come to a service for a long time — ever since he discovered he was a survivor — but this is the first time. You must be having a good influence on him." Before she could respond, the woman moved away to help set the table for a buffet meal. "A genuine *cholent*, a stew that cooks all night, you know," said Elana. "Usually, we just have herring salad but this week we were ambitious."

She moved toward Rafe and he stood up, beaming at her. He introduced her to the two men he had been speaking with and said, "We've been talking about the meaning of the passage that was read today." He was excited, a kind of intellectual excitement she had seen radiating from him when he talked about his work and, lately, about some of the ideas in the books they read. He cupped her chin in his hands and kissed her lips. "Shabbat Shalom. Did you enjoy it?"

"Best service since Brooklyn," she said and started to explain to the others about her Encounter with the Hasidim. Everyone gathered about the table, where one of the men said the blessings over wine and bread, and people began to take paper plates full of stew and salad; discussions were going on in little groups about the meanings of passages and prayers; a man stood up and spoke about the way in which the scriptural section related to the Torah portion; someone responded. Then singing began. They sang many songs Miriam had heard and sung before and more new ones. The children all sang, their voices sweet and certain. A joy pervaded the apartment as, after the dessert, they all gathered to sing the grace after meals.

Miriam watched people departing now and felt deflated, which must have shown in her face, for Elana, her long dark braid bobbing, came over to her and took her hand. "I know," she said. "You wonder why Shabbat can't go on forever. That's why I always put off making *Havdalah* to the last possible minute. Most of us here are like you. We didn't grow up with Judaism intimately. Our parents were too busy trying to be American. A few did though, and they help the rest of us a lot. But listen, Judaism is a well of all sorts of strength and joy. Once you begin to drink from it, you find it's an endless source. And best of all, it allows you to do all sorts of things to make your life richer. You don't really miss the things you give up because what you get is so glorious."

Miriam stared at her. "How do you know so much about me? It's like you're talking out of my head."

"We come from the same place," said Elana mysteriously.

Rafe had come behind her without her realizing it. He put his hands on her shoulders and she turned to look at him.

"You look happy," he said.

"So do you."

"It's been a good Shabbat."

Outside the air smelled sweet, the fall beginning. She took

his hand and said, "Let's run." They raced down the street, laughing together.

That night, after *Havdalah* and a light supper, as he was about to leave her at her apartment, they stood near the door, a place she had grown to hate because it meant his leaving, and he said, "I'll come and get you early, say about ten, tomorrow and we can go to Sam's and Celia's. I bought some books I thought he'd enjoy while he's recuperating. I said I'd go with him when he has the stitches out on Monday but I think he'll be home at least another week. And I got Celia a new recording of Mozart's flute and harp concerto. A very good one."

She put her hand on his arm, which was thin, she thought, though wiry. "You're so good, Rafe. So good inside," she said, her voice trembling. "I don't think you need religion to teach you that."

His lips twisted up in the same self-deprecating look she had seen before. "I have a lot to learn," he said softly.

She tried to speak, to find the words to tell him how fine he seemed to her, but abandoned the attempt. After a minute she said, "It's terrible you should have to go up and back again. Do you want to stay here? I'll give you my bed if you want. I don't mind taking a turn on the couch."

He smiled again, this time wistfully, and rubbed the side of his finger along her cheek. "I don't think I could manage two sleepless nights in a row," and he kissed her. "Goodnight, sweet girl," he said and, aching, she opened the door for him to go.

*   *   *

After lighting the festival lights in beautiful new blue candlesticks Johanna had made for her, they had spent the first of the two days of Rosh Hashanah, the New Year, with the *havurah* and the second in the synagogue where they now knew a number of people and were greeted with cordiality.

"We missed some service last Saturday night. At midnight,"

Rafe whispered to her in the lobby, where they met during a break in the service. "*Selihot*. Didn't we read something about that?"

She tried to remember. "It wasn't on my calendar. I don't even know what that is." She shook her head despairingly. "I wonder if it's possible for me to get it all straight."

"Take courage. It's always like this when you start a new subject. We'll look it up later."

Miriam gazed at Rafe. As a New Year's gift, she had given him a bag with a prayer shawl and an embroidered blue velvet yarmulke. The skullcap, with its design of silver thread, sat on his dark curls like a crown.

A week later, on the evening of Yom Kippur, they attended services at the synagogue but wished to join the *havurah* for the morning services, which were to be held in an apartment on West 110th Street. She spent the night of the Day of Atonement at Rafe's apartment again after walking several miles uptown following the evening service. She thought, as she lay alone in the dark, of the appropriateness on *this* night of lying chastely in Rafe's bed and she turned her mind from him as certainly as she turned her mind from food.

In the morning, they walked to the service not even touching hands. In the living room, the screen was already in place and people were seated before the ark. They began the service with a quiet solemnity and moved into the morning. "Our Father, our King, we have sinned before Thee . . ." Off in the recesses of the large apartment, a phone began to ring and finally, in desperation, the woman whose apartment it was got up and went to answer it. She came back minutes later, quite white, and whispered to someone just behind the screen on the man's side. He stirred violently and got up. Miriam could see the man with a crocheted white and blue skullcap whispering in the ear of the rabbinical student acting as rabbi, who was standing to one side as the cantor, a member of the *havurah* with a beautiful voice, chanted the service. At an appropriate break the young rabbi came forward. "Ladies and gentlemen," he said, "my fellow Jews, I must interrupt this service to tell you that Israel has been attacked on this most sacred of days." A gasp went up from the congregation. "We must pray for our people in Israel and for Jerusalem." Almost without a break, the cantor intoned a prayer Miriam recognized as one for peace, which was not what followed in the prayer book.

Miriam was not altogether sure of the significance of what she had heard. She tried it over in her mind and then abandoned it, beginning to feel her hunger. It was the first time in many years she had fasted and her head was starting to throb. I've wasted so much, she thought, put so much energy into making myself feel good without caring about anything more. I'm sorry, God. And she let each throb remind her of the things she wanted to put behind her.

After the morning service, although the cantor continued to chant, people gathered as far to the rear of the room as possible, whispering about Israel, debating if the circumstances were such that they could permissibly turn on a radio. She looked for Rafe and saw him sitting against the wall, quite alone. He looked pale, almost ill.

"Are you all right?" she whispered, taking his hand and dropping it again.

He nodded slightly but she could feel herself shut off from him.

She stooped so that she was looking into his eyes. "Maybe you should take something to eat."

He shook his head and whispered back, "I'm all right."

She stood up, looking down at his head and the blue skullcap with its silver stitching. He had closed her out again and a catch in her throat surprised her. Oh God, she prayed, take care of my Rafe. She was startled by her own thought. Was he hers? Would he ever be? She knew she was his. What if he tired of this religious quest? Oh no, she prayed again, please, I need you both. What presumption! God and man. She could feel tears smarting in her eyes and she turned away from him so he would not see.

The next service was the memorial service, and she was told by Elana that, since both her parents were living, she should not attend. She watched Rafe go forward to sit among the men, his shoulders bent with an inner anguish. They began to intone the Kaddish, the prayer for the dead, which she followed in English, noting, not for the first time but with the first real wave of understanding, that it did not mention the dead at all but was, finally, a testament of faith. She looked toward Rafe's back. He was suffering, she could see, and every fiber in her body strained toward him. He had aged that afternoon, she thought. From the back of the room she watched him in the company of men, standing sometimes but never straight, and her headache disappeared into another kind of ache. She reflected on the fact that she was too concerned with him. It was her own atonement that needed seeing to and she thought perhaps she understood the value of the separation of men and women.

The afternoon services wore on, evening came, and the tea, apples, honey and hallah were brought out to break the fast. Never had tea tasted so good to her. Radios were turned on, and the TV, so they might hear the world's news of Israel attacked while at prayer by Egypt and Syria. She took Rafe's arm and said, "Do you want to go? We could get something to eat — some eggs or a tuna salad, or some fish — somewhere around here." He nodded grimly but said nothing. They left, saying goodbye to very few people.

In a restaurant nearby, they ordered fish and ate in odd silence. *Celia's certainly taught us silence speaks,* she remembered Johanna saying and tried to hear Rafe's eloquence. For the first time silence between them seemed frightening. "I should have prepared to have a meal to break the fast. Next year I'll know," she said tentatively, but he did not respond. Finally, she said in a strained sort of moan, "Let me in. Please."

He looked at her, startled. "I'm sorry. Today was very hard."

"Why? Why *so* hard?"

He pushed his plate back, "I don't want to talk about it here. Can we walk? Please?"

She got up instantly, her plate nearly empty. Outside, New York night was red and white lights against an almost entirely darkened sky. She reached for his hand and felt it was cold in her own warm one.

"Today," he said, his voice sounding quite unnatural, "I thought about my parents and my sisters. Also my aunt. I said Kaddish for them. I've never done that. There are some other people too but that was enough. I don't think about them very often." He sounded almost strangulated. "I've told you I've never wept for them. It all happened so long ago but hearing about the war in Israel and feeling I need to make up for the way I've chosen to forget, neglected . . ." He stopped in mid-sentence, panting.

"Are you O.K.?" She was terrified.

"Physically. Listen, Miriam. You are the first person I've ever asked to listen. I don't like to talk about this." He started to walk faster and she almost had to run to keep up. "Before the Nazis came to our apartment, we knew they would come. My father kept telling us that if they came we were to hide — we all had hiding places — and that if any of us managed not to be found, even if the others were, we were to try and go back to Verona, where his parents lived. My mother's parents were from somewhere else. I think Rome. He told us that even if that happened, if we went to Verona we could all find each other again. He put some money under a board in the floor. Some Yugoslavian, some Italian. It was so stupid, so hopeless. He was a very gentle man. Never hit me. Kissed me a lot. My mother too. We had Shabbats in our house, but you know, I'd forgotten till lately. When the Nazis came, they all were found, my sisters — one was older, one a little younger. Only me. I don't know how they didn't see me. I was skinny even then and I was too scared to move. When I came off the roof, I sat

in that apartment even more frightened for a long time. I
wanted to follow them but I didn't know how. Then I took
the money and went to the railroad station but it was full of
soldiers and freight cars. I don't like to think, but today it ran
over me like water, that my parents and sisters may have been
in those freight cars. Oh God, I'm going to be sick." He was
panting and stopped walking, unable to breathe easily. He
looked sallow and clutched his stomach.

"Do you want to throw up?" she asked, her own heart
pounding. She was quite ready to hold his head even if it
meant vomiting with him.

"No. It's better." But he was perspiring. He looked around
somewhat frantically. "Will you come with me to the church?
It's near here."

"Anywhere you want," she said.

They were walking now quite quickly again toward the
church he had taken her to before.

"I didn't wait in the station. Probably a good thing. I started
to walk. I don't want to tell you about that trip. I was with
Gypsies. I solicited men for a girl — she couldn't have been
more than fifteen. She was very kind to me. I stole. I did
things all the atoning in the world can't wash out of my memory. I never cried. Not even when I got where I was going.
There were Italian police and soldiers everywhere. No one I
knew, no place I knew. I never cried. Not in the convent, not
on the plane to America, not when I heard finally that they
were dead, never." They had reached the church.

Standing in the doorway, looking down the center aisle, his
face contorted, he looked almost wracked himself. Inside, there
were a few old women near the front, and one old man kneel-
ing and saying a rosary. Rafe stood silently, rocking on the
balls of his feet for a few minutes. Then he whispered, "Not
when my aunt died, the only other person in my family. Not
when Richard died. It's like a shell around my heart."

She was looking at him, buffeted by his story, wishing that

she knew what she could say to comfort him. But nothing she had ever articulated before began to approach what was needed now. She just touched his hand with her fingertips.

He stood quietly for a long while, staring down the aisle and shaking his head, then turned and, without having actually entered, went back into the street.

She followed him, cut off still, despite the deluge of words. Outside, he stood waiting for her. "I'll take you home."

In her apartment, after a quiet cab ride, she brought him an apple and pared it for him, something she had no memory of doing before for anyone, not even herself. She cut it into small pieces and offered them to him one by one. He ate them, while sitting silently on the couch.

The phone rang and she went to answer it. It was Ginger, her friend from the Encounter, eager to share the experiences of their High Holidays, to grieve over Israel. She was gone perhaps ten minutes, during which she anxiously watched the back of his head from the kitchen, but when she returned, she found him asleep sitting up on the couch. For a long while she sat near him in warm silence, free of thought until it occurred to her that Arthur had often slept like that on that couch. When she thought of him, the shallowness of that time appalled her. Forgive me, God, she thought. Forgive me, Eileen. She looked at Rafe and marveled at how the sight of him warmed and consoled her. She went into the bedroom and got a blanket, which she brought to cover him, but as she spread it over him, kissing his head as she did, he started to awaken.

"Miriam," he was fairly shouting.

"Yes?" she said. "What?"

"Are you here? Really here?"

"Really."

He pulled her down on the couch, holding her arms, and kissed her mouth, parting her lips with his tongue desperately, eagerly. Then he pulled back and started to laugh a little, more himself. "I'm sorry," he said. "Sometimes I dream you're with me and I wake up and find you aren't. I'll go home now."

"Stay. You're so tired."

"No," he was shaking his head. He stood up. "Please forgive me for pouring all that out on you. You really have to suffer my moods. It's terrible."

"Rafe, I don't think it's terrible. It's terrible when you don't tell me." She could see him withdrawing. "Tomorrow we're supposed to take Sam and Celia to visit David. We have to study our Hebrew. We'll be together. Tomorrow we'll be together."

He nodded.

"Will you call me when you get home?" she asked.

"Why? It's late. Go to sleep."

"I won't be able to sleep if you don't."

He was ready to leave.

"Rafe, it's all right now. Really all right. I'm with you."

A wan smile crossed his lips and he touched the side of her face. As he lowered it, she caught his hand and kissed it.

Half an hour later, he called. "It's your boor," he said, "safe at home."

"Goodnight, my boor," she whispered into the phone and, after he had hung up, "My sweet boor, my precious boor, God bless you."

*   *   *

After the holidays of Sukkot, Shemini Atzeret and Simhat Torah, toward the end of October, the *havurah* began an adult study group to discuss Torah. It met on Wednesday nights and they began to go to that as well as to their Hebrew classes. About the same time, Miriam began a new job in the public relations department of a large publishing house. It came with a nice raise and a sympathetic boss, not Jewish, who listened to her explanation of why she could not work most nights and might have to leave early on Fridays as the days grew shorter, and said, "Good for you! You do your work well and I don't care when the hell you do it." He was slim and blond, with a shock of hair that kept falling over his eyes, and she realized that she once would have dubbed him very attractive and flirted with him. Now, he was nice, pleasant, but a chasm existed between them that neither was likely to try to leap.

One Monday evening (the only free day in the week), she and Rafe went to visit her parents. "When can you come?" her mother had asked after she had explained their schedule. "Can't you come alone one night? Do you go everywhere with him?"

Miriam's breath caught. She had not spent one full day without him in nearly three months and she considered the possibility of spending one day away from him now. Her parents had had Friday night dinner with them on one occasion and seen them at her grandmother's house one Sunday when she and Rafe had brought Sam and Celia there. They were reserved about her religious practices now. She thought it possible she could go without being attacked. But Rafe. What about Rafe? They ate together every day. (He had recently asked her to help him kosher his kitchen so he could prepare proper meals for her there. "Are you sure you really want to?" she had asked. "I'm willing to eat eggs and fish in your house." "It's a kind of discipline," he had said. "Good for me to take on.")

"I'll discuss it with him," she said to her mother, "but we do usually eat dinner together."

"What's going on between you?" Her mother sounded quite eager, the edge of condemnation softened by her own excited fantasies.

"Nothing sexual, if that's what you mean."

"I can hardly believe that," said Emma crossly.

"It's much too complicated to explain." Miriam wanted to hang up. She couldn't explain entirely. "Be sure you make fish."

At her parents', she and Rafe sat together and she clasped her hands in her lap, feeling the palms perspiring as they talked about their celebration of Simhat Torah.

"I was given a chance to carry the Torah," Rafe was saying, "in one of the processions, and Miriam pelted me with candy from the balcony." (They had gone to the synagogue for the evening service.) "I could see her aiming right at me," he chuckled.

"Does a smart guy like you really buy all this garbage?" asked Seymour, scratching his head fiercely, "or are you just going along for her sake?"

Miriam held her breath.

"It means a good deal to me on its own. I keep finding things in it that speak to me and the fact that Miriam and I can talk about what we're learning makes a great difference." He was not looking at her.

"I don't know," said Seymour. "It seems like a lot of mumbo jumbo to me. Once in a while, it's nice to do something Jewish: I have a box to collect for Israel in my store, for the war; lox and bagels on a Sunday morning. But all this other business!" He stared at Rafe. "I hope you're not sucking her further into it."

"We're doing it together, Daddy," said Miriam, angry.

"Neither of us is doing it out of any obligation," said Rafe.

"You mean, I assume, that you're not obligated to one another." Emma was smiling her broad let-us-have-amplification-and-clarification smile.

Rafe did not answer immediately and Miriam's stomach began to hurt. She tried not to look at him as she began to say, "This is a silly discussion . . ." but he had already spoken. "She isn't obligated to me." Stung, she found herself staring blankly at her hands.

*   *   *

The first Saturday evening in November, they were invited to a party at Cynthia's.

"Bring your friend along," Cynthia had said breezily. "You are still seeing him, aren't you?" Since she had started her new job several weeks before, they had not talked.

She had been to no such party since that time long ago when the fortuneteller had brought her his messages. She looked through her wardrobe in search of an appropriate dress. Many of her clothes hung unworn these days, no longer a part of her life. She found a black mini, cut in a low V in the front but with long sleeves and a sash, and put it on, squinting at herself in the mirror. On one shoulder, she put the topaz and pearl pin Arthur had given her for Christmas. She brushed her reddish brown hair until it shone and colored her lips a pale coral. A touch of perfume on her ear lobes, and all this as a dress rehearsal.

When the day actually came, they had spent the morning in worship, the afternoon talking and walking, and eaten dinner in his apartment from his new Corningware plates for meat. She went into the bathroom to change and came out resplendent. She could see him looking at her but he said nothing.

"Shall we go?" she said offhandedly, thinking that, in his tan corduroy suit, he was splendid.

The party was already crowded and smoke-filled when they arrived. Some people from Miriam's old office and a few familiar party-going friends of Cynthia's greeted her with enthusiasm. She introduced Rafe to several of her old coworkers and then left him with a drink in his hand talking to an advertising design director to go and talk to Margot, who was there with the man they had met drunk in an orange shirt. "Hello. How *are* you?" She threw her most vivacious voice into play. "You look great! So thin!"

"It was the fat farm," said Margot, blushing. "But I'm working to keep it off. John, here, keeps an eye on me."

"Not just on what she eats," said John and he patted her backside affectionately.

Cynthia came over and examined their glasses. "Everyone have enough to drink? Oh Miriam, as ever with Scotch. Religion hasn't changed that, has it?" She put her arm through Miriam's arm. "Would you excuse us just a minute?" she said and pulled Miriam off to a corner.

"He's gorgeous! Why didn't you tell me? How can you stand not going to bed with him?" Miriam's heart sank and she regretted more than she could ever have imagined having confided this fact to Cynthia.

"Our relationship is different," she said, swallowing some liquor.

"Are you sure he's straight?"

"Of course," Miriam began to feel slightly, safely high as she gulped down another mouthful.

"Is he up for grabs then? I mean is it anything more than platonic?"

Miriam felt chilled. She could hardly speak. He was so much at the center of her life now that she could no longer separate the strands of where her feelings began and his ended. The thought of his having another woman burned her to the core. Yet, despite their long hours together, their intimate and endless conversations, their frequent kisses, they had never really touched one another, never allowed tenderness to flow into pure physical pleasure, never even necked — that inadequate form of sex play from her high-school days. She blamed herself for having made chastity a condition at the beginning, still knew the reasons, but now, back in her old world however briefly, she looked across the room at Rafe and felt betrayed.

"It's more than platonic," she said coldly, "but it's very private."

"Well," said Cynthia. "I'd be careful. Some girl is going to come along and cuddle him and it'll be goodbye religion and all. He is absolutely adorable." She drifted off among her guests.

A man she vaguely recognized from some of Cynthia's other parties came up and put his arm around her shoulders. "You are looking fabulous," he said. "How are things?"

"Great," said Miriam, swinging gaily around though she felt

miserable. Well, he had said she wasn't obligated to him. "What is it you do again? Is it the law?"

Music started loudly from the record player. "It's the law," said the man, "and I'll have the law on you if you don't dance with me."

"Not in public surely," she trilled and put her glass down on a convenient table. They moved into the middle of the living room, where a tiny space was now being used as a dance floor. Even as she moved with him, she could see Rafe standing with a group of people including some women, talking as if he were unaware of her and she felt herself a knot of pain. Dancing violently relieved it slightly and as the first number finished, one of her former colleagues cut in and took her from her partner for a second dance. "So this is what you do after Shabbos," he said. "I don't think my grandfather would have approved."

She laughed coyly and whispered, "It's all in the intent," into his ear. When the dance was over, he got her another Scotch and told her religion had not done her a bit of harm, she was as pretty and sexy as ever. From the corner of her eye, she could see Rafe dancing now with a small woman in a one-shouldered blue mini, so short her matching blue panties showed at every turn the dance took. She started to chide the man on her right for not paying any attention to her, even though they had never met, and soon was out on the dance floor again, near Rafe and his partner. As she passed him, she stuck her tongue out at him and he smiled at her.

"Food!" called Cynthia and the music stopped, as people began to gather around the table. The girl in blue had taken Rafe's arm and they were walking toward the spread. Miriam took her own partner's arm and sidled over to the canapés. She looked down at the array of things she mostly could not eat and charily took some bread smeared with cream cheese and smoked salmon.

"Is that all you're going to have?" said her partner, who was filling up his plate. No wonder you've got such a great shape," and he slipped his arm suggestively around her waist. She turned toward him to beam up at him and suddenly saw Rafe beside her.

"Oh," she said, "I must introduce you. Rafe Toledano, this is . . . why, I don't know your name. It must be a nice one."

"Tom. That's enough," said her partner. He was tall and stocky. Beside him Rafe looked finely chiseled. They shook hands. "What's your business, Rafe?"

"I'm a college teacher," he said, smiling.

"Are you *really?*" The girl in blue was standing just behind him. "Oh, I knew you were a brain."

Cynthia came by and peeked her head in. "Mix it up now, mix it up. Hey, I made the salmon for you, lady," and she handed Miriam a plate with three canapés and a few pieces of herring.

"Where are you from originally, Rafe?" said Tom, his arm finding its way around Miriam's waist again. "You don't sound like a New Yorker."

"Springfield, Illinois," said Rafe.

"Oh. Will it play in Peoria? That part of the world." Tom gave Miriam a little squeeze. "How are things in Springfield?"

"I don't know," said Rafe. "I haven't been there in years."

"What? Don't like the Midwest?"

"The Midwest is fine. I just don't have anyone there anymore." His answer stabbed her.

His dancing partner rubbed her bare shoulder with her cheek and ran one hand down his back. "I feel the same way about Sandusky, Ohio, where I grew up."

Miriam had put down the plate just as some slower music went on. Tom started to pull her toward the center of the room. She had wearied of the game but now found herself being pulled against the body of a man she didn't know or like particularly well. Always before, she had found a satisfaction in the reflection of her own attractiveness when men pressed her in intimate dancing that suggested future pleasures however remote, but this time she felt mildly ill. She was wretched as he tried to tuck her to his groin and kept pulling herself back from him only to feel his arm tighten around her. She could not see where Rafe was and, for one panicky moment, feared he had left even as she realized with her rational part that he would never do such a thing.

The song ended and another was beginning. Rafe was tapping Tom on the shoulder. "You can't keep this pretty lady to yourself all evening," he said firmly but amicably to Tom. "I'd like this dance, Miriam." And he took her hand and led her to the edge of the dancers.

No sooner had his arms gone around her than she began to tremble violently, flooded with shame. She pushed her face into his shoulder and felt him stroking the back of her neck as they danced.

"Sh, little one. Sh. It's all right. It's all right."

"Oh, Rafe," she whispered, embarrassed because here, of all places, she was crying.

"I'm here. I'm holding you."

She saw the room behind him through a blur of tears. "Can we go?"

"We can do whatever you want," and he kissed her ear, "if you'll dance with me first."

She looked up and saw him smiling a crooked smile at her. He kissed a tear off her cheek and she put her face down in his shoulder again, grateful the room was dimly lit. They danced through the next two dances until she had composed herself and they went to say goodbye to Cynthia.

"How come you're going already? You've hardly been here. Rafe, I haven't even gotten to know you. I hope we'll meet again."

"I'm sure we will," he said and shook her hand.

They went out into the hall and down the elevator. Outside he hailed a cab and they got in. She was still trembling and silent and he sat with his arm around her, rubbing her shoulder through her coat. She said nothing. Out of the cab, through the hall, up the elevator to her door. Nothing. At the door, she touched the mezuzah and kissed her fingers and so did he.

Inside, she let her coat fall to the floor as she began to cry hysterically, sobbing and hiccuping while he held her, whispering, "It's all right. It's over."

"You don't understand," she sobbed.

"Yes, I do."

"No."

"It's your old life. It took you over."

"No."

"What?" he said, stroking her cheek.

"It's you. I wanted to make you jealous but I felt jealous of you — that silly woman you kept dancing with. I feel so stupid. It's because you don't really think I'm attractive."

He was silent for a moment and let go of her. When he spoke, his voice was husky. "Miriam, I think you are the most beautiful woman I've ever seen. Just looking at you gives me pleasure."

"Don't you ever want me?"

Again he did not answer right away and finally said in a very low voice, "All the time. I can't believe you don't know that. There is hardly a night that goes by that you don't parade through my dreams. I hardly sleep some nights. If I had just met you at that party, I would be scheming right now how to get you into bed."

Her voice cracked. "Is it because of what I said the first time you kissed me that you don't ever touch me?"

"I touch you."

"I mean . . ."

"I know what you mean. If I were to touch you like that I wouldn't stop and neither would you. What you said in the beginning you meant and you still mean it. It goes for me too. If I took you inside now we'd have a very sweet night but a very sad morning. And then what? For us I think right now sex would create a barrier, a wall, because we wouldn't be able to consider everything else clearly. That would be pretty bad," he put his arms around her and kissed her eyes and the corners of her mouth, "because when we begin to make love, I want it to really join us, not divide us."

She had started to tremble again, and he took off his jacket and put it around her.

"Oh, I'm sorry I acted like such a fool . . . I'm so ashamed of myself," she whispered, still close to tears.

"Sh, sh. It's over." He sat down in the sling-back chair, pulled her down on his lap and stroked her hair.

"I used to act that way all the time." She pulled at her pin. "Arthur gave me this pin and he liked this dress."

"You look beautiful in it."

"I once wore a see-through dress with him. In a restaurant. That's the only time I felt as dumb as I do now."

"I wouldn't want you to wear one, at least not in public, but if I had seen you in it I would have wanted to take a good look." He was kissing her hair. "You smell good," he said. "Is there a blessing for that?"

She turned her face so she was looking right at him. "Rafe," she said, "I need you very much. I've never said that before to anyone, but I need you."

He kissed the palm of her hand. "I need you too," he whispered, and after a minute added, "and that's something I don't usually allow myself to even feel. It's dangerous for me."

She took his face in her hands in the same gesture he often made to her and kissed him at first very gently but after a moment her lips parted and she felt his arms tighten around her as she put her hands behind his shoulders. His hand slid down along the outside of her thigh. Then he pulled back, looking at her from under half-closed lids. "Miriam?" he said. Half a question, half a request. And she got off his lap.

*   *   *

The next week he took her to a small party at the home of one of his colleagues, where for most of the evening she sat next to him, smiling and talking about the Mideast crisis, rising prices, and university politics. It was clear those people liked him, thought well of him. When the food was brought out, the wife of the man who shared his office sidled up to her.

"I'm awfully glad to meet you," she said. "Rafe has been so changed since he met you."

She felt at once alarmed and pleased. "How?" She smiled at the woman, whose eyes were big with the look of someone wearing contact lenses.

"Oh, Leonard says he seems much calmer and happier and I can see he looks comfortable. Sometimes he used to come to parties with graduate student girls and play the grand professor with his little protégée. There wasn't anything in it of course but he would look triumphant and miserable at the same time. It's very clear he trusts you enough to be himself." She put her hand on Miriam's arm. "I like you for that." And they both beamed.

She saw Rafe across the table laughing with a friend and her skin prickled with pleasure. She looked back at the blonde wife whom she had just met and, taking advantage of the freedom she felt in their new acquaintance despite the lady's indiscretion, or perhaps because of it, said in a flood of feeling, "He is the kindest, most understanding person I have ever known. I've never felt so close to anyone before."

*   *   *

On the evening before Joshua Adam's *brit*, the study group was to meet, but before going, Miriam and Rafe stopped at Johanna's and Seth's to deliver their gift and to see the baby. "Tomorrow will be really hectic. I'm so glad you came tonight," said Johanna.

In their bedroom was a small mesh crib and in it a tiny

baby. Miriam had forgotten since her niece was born just how small a newborn baby was. She reached down and touched the baby's hand with a single finger and it pulled into a little fist.

"He's lovely," she whispered. "Rachel, you were that little once. Can you believe it?"

"I was even littler in my Mommy," said Rachel with authority. "So was Joshua."

Rafe's hand had slipped in hers and she felt his thumb rubbing the top of her knuckles. She turned toward him and saw his eyes on the baby, clouded and tender. "May I hold him, Johanna?" he said.

Johanna lifted the baby out of the crib still sleeping and placed him in Rafe's arms. He gazed down at the small face with its clenched shut eyes and watched until the baby yawned a great yawn and turned his head. Rafe put the hand not supporting the baby on the baby's cheek and the little head turned again toward the finger, lips parted and pursing.

"He's looking for food and you can't provide it," laughed Johanna. "In a while he'll be awake and howling."

"He's marvelous," said Rafe. "I can hardly believe him. I don't get to see too many babies. He's like a little miracle. Look, Miriam, how his eyelids flutter, how soft his breath is." He was looking at the baby, not at her.

"Yes," she whispered, her own breath short, having discovered a new longing in herself. She watched Rafe put the baby gently down in the crib. He didn't stop looking.

"Come, let's go inside," said Johanna, "and open your present." Miriam began to follow her and Seth, who had been standing in the doorway, Rachel running along beside. With a sixth sense she knew Rafe was not with her and she turned back for him. He still hovered over the crib, his hands gripping the side. "Rafe? Rahfee?" It was the name an Israeli member of the *havurah* called him. He looked up at her and held out his arms. As she came into them, she could feel his heart throbbing and she touched the back of his neck just where his hair began to grow. "He *is* marvelous," she whispered. "A perfect little boy! Come inside. Come with me." She could tell he was too moved to speak.

In the living room, they watched Seth open the box in which were a small silver Kiddush cup with an engraved Jewish star and a small yarmulke in white velvet with gold stitching. "This means a lot to us. He will use them. I promise."

They had also brought a little gift for Rachel, who opened her box and found a tiny necklace of pink and amber beads.

"They are *beau*tiful. I can wear them tomorrow, Mommy. Yes?" She put them around her neck and whirled to see if they would stand out.

"Is your father back?" Rafe, recovered, asked Seth.

"No. He's staying on in Israel. When we called to tell him about the baby he said he hoped we would forgive him, but that he felt he could still be of service and that at a time when the Israelis felt so isolated, the presence of Americans, people like him who stayed voluntarily, offered some comfort. He'll have to be back in a month for some professional obligations but for the moment he wants to stay."

"He must be sad to miss the *brit* though," said Miriam.

Seth smiled. "Yes, and I'm sad too, but in some sense he's living the covenant that the circumcision — the whole occasion — represents, so I can't be too upset."

Johanna started to go into the kitchen to get some tea and the nurse, who was staying with them for a week, bounced up, saying, "Sit down, Mrs. Rosen."

"I'll help her," said Miriam, getting up to follow Johanna. She felt Rafe move toward her slightly and said reassuringly, "I'll be right back."

In the kitchen she put her arms around Johanna. "The baby is beautiful! Really! Is everything all right with your mother?"

"She's coming round though it's not over," said Johanna. "She insisted on my having Mrs. Ryan but she hasn't come herself except to say hello and see Joshua. When she comes she's friendly but proper. I knew once the baby was born she wouldn't be able to sustain her anger at the same pitch. I get the feeling she and Daddy have been talking about everything, maybe even that he's getting his licks in but I don't know. At the moment, they aren't confiding in me. Would you believe I'm stupid enough to have mixed feelings about that?" She stepped back from Miriam so she could look at her. "And you? I've never seen you so glowing."

Miriam felt the blood rising in her cheeks. "I feel good," she admitted.

"Jewish life or Rafe? When he looks at you, you can see the sparks!"

"Can you?" She bit her lip and closed her eyes. "I'll help you get the tea," she said. "We have to go to our *havurah* discussion group."

"You didn't answer," said Johanna playfully.

"I can't. It's kind of a package. Both. Johanna, you once asked me if I was happy and I couldn't answer that either but that answer at least I know now."

"I don't need to ask that anymore. It shows!"

"Go sit down," said Miriam. "I'll get the tea."

They ran, after leaving, down West End Avenue to their meeting. Near their destination, he let go of her hand and ran ahead, then turned to catch her with an agitated exuberance, laughing like a child. A child with his face, she thought, or a father laughing with his child.

That evening they were discussing the Torah passage concerning the sacrifice of Isaac. It was a portion that gave everyone a great deal of trouble, especially the parents of young children.

"I mean," said Elana, pulling on her long hair, "even if God appeared to me and I knew without question I wasn't being fooled, I don't think I could take one of my babies to slit his throat. I think I'd rather suffer whatever punishment was given. It couldn't be worse."

"But don't you see?" her husband, Robert, was saying, "It's a question of faith. When Isaac goes up to Mount Moriah with his father, he asks him where the lamb for the burnt sacrifice is and Abraham says, 'God will provide Himself the lamb for a burnt offering, my son.' We can say he was just trying to reassure Isaac, but I think the real sense of that passage is that Abraham does believe that God will protect Isaac though he can't say how, that there is a reason for what's happening and that there will be divine intervention. Most important, Isaac accepts that. You might say he receives a gift of faith. That's our end of the covenant. We do it for children all the time. The first time a child crosses the street by himself, or takes a bath alone, the parent has to have faith that the child will be protected and the healthy child takes on that faith, although we don't always call it faith."

"But that's different," said another woman, the mother of two. "It's one thing to let your child go in the normal way of growing up. It's quite another to do something you know could cause him harm."

"I don't think it's always so clear. Parents constantly make choices for their children where they take some plan of action that doesn't have a clear end. The fact that they're not usually life-endangering is just the good fortune of our circumstances."

A man from the back of the room spoke. "I agree, Robert. Some of us are thinking of making *aliyah*. What about the sons we take with us to Israel — and the daughters? We would go with the faith that in their time, there would be peace in Israel even though over two thousand young men have just died there. Some of the reasons for choosing to go are like Abraham's. They have to do with a sense of God's will and confidence in His compassion."

The discussion went on with Miriam paying close attention, looking over her Bible to really master the passage, when she looked over at Rafe. His eyes were closed, but he did not seem to be asleep, and she touched his hand. He opened his eyes and stared at her, the corners of his eyes crinkling up. He took his pen and wrote the word *faith* in big letters across the top of her notebook and a big question mark. Then he closed his eyes again.

After the group disbanded and chatted over coffee and cake, they came down into a cold street. He said, "Do you want to walk for a while?"

"Do you know how much of our life we spend walking?" she said mischievously. "Before I knew you, I hardly walked anywhere."

"It just helps make the trip home longer," he said, putting his arm around her, "but I shouldn't do that. I have a lot of work to do tonight. My book is in total disarray but I can't let my teaching go."

"I could go home by myself," she said, sensing his anxiety. "Then you could go work."

He stood still, staring off across the street. After a few seconds he said, "Will you stay with me tonight, Miriam? Please. I need to work but I want you to be with me." His voice was thin.

She reached for his hand that was resting on her shoulder. "If you want me to. Why?"

"All that talking about faith . . . Isaac. I was thinking about Isaac. It just made me feel very strange — especially after seeing the baby. I want to go home because I have to work but then I'd like to talk. Would you mind that?"

"Do you think I can wear what I'm wearing to the *brit* tomorrow? I won't be able to change."

His eyes met hers, gray in the odd streetlight. "You will look lovely. You do look lovely, so lovely." Ever since the night of Cynthia's party, he had made a point of telling her every day how nice she looked.

"So do you," she said. "You look like a lovely little boy with a beard in that pea jacket."

They turned and started to walk along Broadway toward

his apartment. There were many students out even though it was already ten-thirty. One hailed Rafe as they passed with good-humored camaraderie and she leaned against him, in the curve of his arm, feeling safe. She realized that she had not often felt safe in her life although with no reasons comparable to his for sensing danger and yet, now, she recognized that for most of her life she had been hiding from something. Was it God Whom she believed in with less reservation each day? Herself? She didn't know.

Inside his apartment, a small light burned to scare off potential burglars. His living room was still full of record albums. He sat down without taking off his coat, then stood up to take hers a little roughly.

"I have to go to work. If you want, you can get in a pair of my pajamas and go to sleep. Or if you feel like it, play some records. Just don't go away."

"I won't."

He nodded and virtually ran out of the room down the hall into his study, carrying her coat. She sat down on his couch, a nubby gray-blue, and looked at a magazine from the table nearby. Then she went to the record player and put on a stack of records, enough for several hours. Sitting back on the couch, she closed her eyes and, after a few measures, fell asleep.

It must be, she realized only very slowly, the early morning hours, two or three, the records all played out, when she felt him near her, kissing her, whispering, "Please, Miriam, wake up. Can you wake up, sweet girl?" She opened her eyes and saw him in the dim light looking at her, his face drawn as if he were in pain. She put her arms around his neck and felt him relax slightly. "Please can I talk to you?"

She pulled him down beside her on the couch and moved to turn up the light on the table beside her to be able to see him better, but he stopped her.

"Miriam. Miriam. Miriam." He said her name as if to gain his balance.

"Did you finish your work?" she asked, stroking his hair.

"Yes. But all the time I was looking at it, I kept thinking how strange it was I knew so much about the past but not really the past that was mine. And that bothers me. I saw the baby tonight and I thought I must once have been a baby but I knew nothing about it. No pictures — well, my aunt had one blurry one that had been sent to her before the war — no stories. It's all gone. And that's just my life — my own lifetime. I know so much about America but it's taken me till the last few weeks to ever hear about the covenant. It just passed me by. I wonder what it was in me that didn't, sometime before now, say, 'Stop! You're whole. You can't drop off a piece of yourself as if it didn't exist.'"

"It hurt. It's easy to want to forget things that hurt."

"Probably." He stopped and stared off into the dark end of the living room. "One of the lessons of history that historians usually ignore is that even in the midst of terrible troubles most people continue to live their ordinary lives. They eat and sleep and love just the same while wars rage, while treaties are made, while governments rise and fall. That doesn't mean they are never touched by these things but what really dominates their lives is their own feelings, and only when the 'history' they live through gets in the way of those feelings do they care about it or study it or try to rescue themselves from its force." He turned toward her, his eyes hollow tunnels. "Doesn't that tell you something about me? How I've been avoiding this rendezvous even as I've been preparing for it? I've been such a good history student," he stressed the word *good* sarcastically and pounded his palm into his fist, "diligently read Thomas Paine and Henry Adams but went out of my way to avoid European history or Jewish history that would help explain what happened to me. Even avoided the Bible, which is really an unnatural omission for an American historian. And there it was: the story of Isaac . . . my story except Abraham was himself the ram with his three poor sheep . . . My parents tried so hard to offer me a kind of faith . . . hope that . . ." His words, which had been coming faster and faster, skidded to a halt.

He was shaking, she thought, even more upset than he had been on the night after Yom Kippur. She tried to put her arms around him but he pulled away. "Do you pray, Miriam? I mean when you're alone."

"Yes," she spoke in a breathy voice, quiet, "but I'm still learning how."

"But do you believe?"

She thought how to answer that. Saying prayers she had learned had opened some valve that now allowed her sometimes to say her own; to pray for him among other things. "I think I do," she said. "Yes I do. I couldn't explain it all to you, but I believe there is some force we can reach out to, that helps us, maybe even guides us."

"I think maybe tonight I do too. It's like a little plant. I hardly can breathe without disturbing it. Miriam." He turned to her quite desperately and she reached out to him with her heart, aware that her touch would only distance him. "Miriam, I've spent my whole life asking myself why I climbed out on that roof and was saved. I've never been able to know why the others were taken and I wasn't. That's the answer I've been looking for. Now I think maybe I was saved because I was capable of faith."

Miriam sat forward abruptly. "What about your sisters? What about your mother and father? They were capable of faith. What about all the people who survived who have no faith?"

He stared at her, his large black eyes inky with tears. "Oh, I cannot speak for them. I cannot judge them. I have waited so long just to be able to speak for myself. Just to be able to mourn." And the tears spilled down his cheeks as his body began to quiver with small spasmodic silent sobs.

She took his head in her hands and he lay down willingly to let her cradle it against her breasts, the vibrations of his weeping passing through her, shaking her, her blouse and skirt becoming damp with the dammed flood of thirty years. They stayed together so for an immeasurable time.

After a while she began to rock him, to kiss his hair and neck, and, as the sobbing slowly stopped, to kiss his eyes and cheeks. She could taste the salt of his tears on her lips and feel her cheeks wet with her own tears. He lay against her, breathing heavily, sighing and then turned his face and kissed her breast solemnly, tracing the curve with his finger. She quivered, unable to contain the love she felt for him. It was spilling over in her tears, in the moisture between her thighs, displaced in the desire she felt to contain all of him, even his grief. He sat up and they began to kiss each other's faces, eyes, ears, their lips grazing one another's like birds feeding, to touch each other's arms and necks, finally to hug one another wordlessly. Never in her wildest fantasy had she ever imagined feeling so much love.

Suddenly he let go of her, stood up and walked away, his back to her. He stood at the window, staring past the curtains into the ebbing night.

She wanted to run to him, to touch him, to beg him to love her even half as much as she loved him but she stayed on the couch.

He turned around after a long time and their eyes met. In the shadow, his face was gray, lines accenting his thinness, the black of his beard paling his skin. He held out his hand to her and she leaped up and rushed to him. He took both her wrists and held her back.

"Miriam." His voice was thick from his tears. "Miriam, I am nearly ten years older than you and they are an unnaturally long ten years."

"It doesn't matter." There was a catch in her voice as she struggled to find the words. "We are being born together for the first time now. We are the same, like twins."

"Too close, perhaps?" It had a hard sound.

"No!" She was desperate.

He let go of her wrists and gazed past her. "I have lost everyone I have ever loved, one way or another, and I have never loved anyone the way I love you." His voice dropped and she shivered.

"You won't lose me. Never. We're part of one another. I love you so much, Rafe, more all the time. I'll always love you." She reached toward him and his eyes filled with tears again. She put her arms around his neck and kissed his shoulder and ear, feeling his cheek and beard wet against her face. "God will protect us. I believe it, my sweet love, I believe it."

He rocked back and forth for a moment, then put his arms tightly around her and, for the first time, their bodies pressed hard together, her breasts coming home against his chest. She felt him stir and swell against her and she clung to him, holding him as close as she could, whispering, "I love you, Rafe, I love you," like an ecstatic incantation in which every word was a unique invention of her own.

When they parted, he took her face between his hands, and after looking at her for nearly a minute with so much love and longing, she felt quite weak, he said, "I suppose we must first get a *ketubbah,* a beautiful one, so that after the wedding we can hang it in our house, in our Jewish home, my beloved, my bride."

To her own amazement, she began to sob with relief and joy, and she leaned against him, repeating, "Yes, oh yes, my love, yes." She stopped, laughing as she cried, and wiped her eyes with her hands. "I was so afraid you weren't going to ask me."

His somberness melted in his look of surprise. Then he began to smile his old open smile, hugging her, hugging her, and saying, "Oh, little one, Miriam, my wife, my blessing, forgive me, forgive me, but I never dared before to be this happy."

15

SAM HAD arranged to leave school early in order to have time to collect Celia before the *brit*. He noted with a twinge of sorrow that he now felt relieved whenever he left the old building that for so many years had seemed if not a sanctuary at least the repository of an old and noble idea. That was how he phrased it in the novel of his life, a habit he did not give up easily.

Celia awaited him, her tight curls gracefully in place, wearing a new dress, a soft green, and seemed wistful and younger than she had for years.

"You look wonderful," he said and she smiled shyly in response.

The apartment was already fairly crowded when they arrived and put their coats on the pile rising on Seth's and Johanna's bed. Sam glanced in the empty mesh crib and away toward Celia. "You think we can see the baby?"

They found Johanna in Rachel's room with the baby asleep in his carriage. Rita Holseizer and Seth's sister were with her, all kept at a respectful distance from the baby by the stolid, imposing baby nurse.

"We wanted to take a look at him," said Celia softly, handing Johanna a box with blue ribbons. "It's a big size. Oh, he's darling. Don't disturb him."

Sam offered a manila envelope he had been holding behind

him. "This is also for when he's bigger. A little something from me," he said, handing it to her.

Johanna began to open it expectantly.

"No," said Sam. "Save it to look at later. It's just a few stories." He turned toward the carriage and peered down at the sleeping baby, avoiding Johanna's eyes.

After a few minutes of conversation about the baby's sleeping habits, they returned to the living room, where, in a corner near the window, the *mohel,* who was to perform the circumcision, was preparing a table and laying out his instruments. Celia stood still for a moment, glancing around and blinking like a person long confined in the dark who has just emerged into light. It was the first time in nearly a year she had been surrounded by so many people.

Sam suddenly became aware of Rafe standing across the room at the entrance. He was opening the door as each new guest arrived, nodding, in some instances directing them to the bedroom, but it was clear he was waiting for someone particular. Each time the bell rang, his face lit up expectantly. Sam could see him quite clearly through the sea of heads and felt no surprise when he opened the door at last to Miriam and beamed. But the way they embraced, as though oblivious of anyone else in the room, startled Sam. Something had altered between them, he could see, and he felt that perception confirmed when they passed within a few feet of him unaware, on their way to the back. He put his hand on Celia's shoulder and began to say something but she stopped him.

"I saw."

"Since she has been friends with him," said Sam, picking up a conversation they had been holding off and on for several weeks, "she has seemed so much more like the bright, cheery little girl she used to be. I can't imagine her being so unselfconscious, even a few months ago."

"One of these days they are going to find out that they're in love with each other. Maybe they have already." She leaned

toward Sam and said in a loud whisper, "I said that to Leah
the other day and she called me a romantic like it was a dirty
word. Look, there's Mamma."

Sam did not think again of the scene he had witnessed at
the door until, just before the ceremony was about to begin,
he saw Rafe in his blue and silver yarmulke, standing beside
Seth and Seth's brother-in-law near the *mohel's* table. Miriam
had just come to join the family group that had formed around
Naomi.

"Johanna's not coming out," she said and looked away toward Rafe.

"Sensible," said Leah sternly. "A barbaric custom really,
though I don't suppose you see it that way now."

"No," said Miriam, although she seemed unable to see anything in the room but Rafe, on whom her eyes were fixed.
Then, she pulled back and smiled softly, momentarily shifting
her glance toward Leah. "It's the sign of God's special relationship to the Jews, even, I'd say, our special responsibilities . . ." She stopped midsentence, coloring slightly as the
mohel began to chant the blessings and the baby was brought
in. She looked toward Rafe again and Sam noticed that when
he started as the baby began to cry during the actual operation, she twitched sympathetically with him.

The baby quieted as a piece of gauze soaked in wine was
placed between his lips. Leah looked quite pale and said against
the background of the blessings still being read, "Oh, I'm glad
Johanna stayed inside." She peered at Celia. "Was it too much
for you?"

"No, I'm fine." She took Sam's arm as the ceremony finished. "He should have a long life — a good life."

Emma, standing to one side of her mother and brother,
said breathlessly, "It's just as well Seymour couldn't come. He
always feels faint at these things. He really wanted to but when
you own your own business it's not so easy." She exchanged a
look with Miriam, whose attention was briefly focused on the

family. As Rafe came toward them, Miriam turned and reached out to him.

Seth called everyone to join him around the table before an enormous braided loaf of bread as Elise, in her black and white uniform, passed trays of wineglasses among the guests. Johanna had spirited the baby back to Rachel's room to be nursed and the atmosphere was now wholly festive. Seth raised a wineglass and the party guests became quiet as he said Kiddush. A plate with broken pieces of hallah was passed to all the guests as he made the blessing over the bread, breaking off an end of the uncut loaf before him on the table. Everyone ate their bit of bread. Then he held up his wineglass a second time and waited until the renewed conversations stopped, silenced by a few attentive friends who hushed the others, "Sh, Seth wants to say something."

"Today is a very special day," he said, "a day of double joy for us. Not only do we celebrate Joshua's *brit* but also a happy event — a *simcha* — in the lives of two people who are very dear to Johanna and me. I ask you to join with me in drinking long life and happiness to Johanna's cousin, Miriam Miller, and Rafe Toledano, who are engaged to be married."

Sam felt Celia tugging on his arm as she squeaked, "I knew it. I just knew it." He turned to look at the couple as words of congratulations rained over them and saw them clinging to one another, beaming. After half a minute Miriam put her face against Rafe's shoulder. As she raised it, their eyes met for a moment before they let go to accept the kisses and handshakes. Never, Sam thought, had he ever seen love as exposed as in that brief look. It thrilled him. Other people pressed toward the couple and by the time he and Celia reached them they looked almost giddy.

"You've made us very happy," he said emphatically. "We're not surprised though."

"No one seems to be," said Rafe. "I think we're more surprised than anyone else." He had his hand on the back of

Miriam's neck and Sam could see his thumb stroking her beneath her ear.

"I'm just surprised it took him so long," giggled Miriam with a touch of her old bravado. A slightly surprised, indulgent smile brushed across Rafe's lips as she put her arm back around his waist in an apparent gesture of apology.

"A mensch," Naomi was saying to Emma. "She got herself a real mensch, your daughter. He's a good human being, which counts for everything."

"Did you know, Em?" Frank asked, thrusting his hands down into his jacket pockets, as though to put away his obvious discomfort.

"Yes, they called us this morning. But she's a cagey one. I asked her just a few weeks ago if anything was going on between them and she said, 'No, no!' Well, I told her and Seymour too, he's a good man. Of course, she won't be able to live in the style she was used to before she started all this religious business, but they'll never starve."

"Money is at the root of most of the world's troubles," said Naomi. "She needed the jewelry, the clothing, like a hole in the head. And if they insist on living like orthodox Jews, with a man like him, at least she won't have to worry he'll stick her with the children while he goes off to be a big so-and-so in the synagogue."

"You forget what it's like not to have enough money," Emma replied bitterly. "Well, no more of that. This is a happy occasion. I wish Seymour could have come, or David."

An animated Celia brought Sam a plate of deviled eggs and cake from the buffet, and turned immediately to Miriam and Rafe, who were talking with Harry. Johanna appeared from the back of the apartment, the baby now sleeping in a milky dream perhaps, unaware of his soreness, and in the chatter of the next hour, people departed, heading home to their dinners, as Rafe and Miriam did, regretting that they had to go so soon but explaining that they wished to get to their Hebrew class on time.

Sam and Celia remained, invited to go to dinner later with Leah and Harry.

"How is the baby, poor duck?" asked Leah as Johanna returned from checking Joshua.

"Fine," said Johanna. "It was good he slept through the party. I actually got to talk to people."

"A lovely party," said Leah enthusiastically.

"Especially because of Rafe and Miriam. They made us so happy."

Leah's eyes narrowed, Sam thought, like a bull at the flash of red cloth. "They timed it well enough to get full exposure. Well, she's her mother's daughter."

Celia's voice, shocked, sounded, "Leah!"

"Let's start again," said Johanna gaily. "Rafe's and Miriam's engagement made us very happy."

"He's quite a young man," Harry interjected. "After all I'd heard about him, I wasn't sure he could live up to his reputation but I was impressed. He must really know his stuff about American history to have tenure at Columbia. I could probably learn a lot from him."

"Leah," Sam was struggling to keep his words from betraying how angry he felt, "they have been working at changing so much about themselves, it's beautiful. This engagement didn't come lightly, you can be sure."

"Miriam is so much softer than she used to be . . ." Johanna was speaking.

"It's going to be a joy to have Rafe in the family," Seth said. "He gets better and better."

Leah looked around at them, her lips folded together. She sighed. "I never would have picked them as a couple but I may have been wrong. I wish them luck. They're a little crazy about religion but that's the way they want to live. Mamma had to promise to make fish for them for Thanksgiving. Can you imagine? You would think they would bow to convention at least far enough to eat her turkey."

Johanna put her hands together and said smoothly, "They're

following a set of conventions." She was sparring with her mother, Sam could see.

Leah glanced around, clearly about to take her daughter up but after a moment seemed to reconsider. She patted her hair back and reached for her purse to retrieve her compact and lipstick.

"Like most converts," said Harry, "they're more holy than the holy. With a little luck they'll get over it. Listen, have you told them about your design yet?" He nodded appreciatively at Leah. "Let's talk about something else for a minute."

She beamed back at him, her eyes crinkling at the corners. "Oh, yes," she said. "I've designed a campaign button for Harry. Really striking, we both think. People won't forget it once they've seen it, I can assure you."

*   *   *

Before Miriam and Rafe were to go to Queens the following Sunday to spend the day with her parents and her brother and his family, they called to ask if they might stop by. Sam did not speak to them but got the message from Celia, who insisted he go down to get onion rolls from a nearby Jewish bakery.

"And cream cheese," she added as he went out. "They like that."

She waited for them, preparing plates and napkins as if they were coming for a feast, and rushed to greet them when they arrived, kissing them at the door before they had even come inside. Sam stood behind her, feeling his smile elastic and unrestrained. The scar on his forehead where he had had stitches, still a bright pink line, prickled. Apart from that, all visible evidence of his beating was gone.

"You have made us so happy. We have been feeling warmed by you two for a long time," he said when Celia finally released them.

They were seated in the living room when Miriam said, "We

have a date for our wedding," and she and Rafe both began to tell them, interrupting each other, laughing, describing their plans for the wedding, eight weeks off, to be performed by the rabbi from the synagogue they had been attending but to be held in the home of a member of the *havurah,* which would be giving the reception to follow. Then there were their plans to live in Rafe's apartment until they could find a bigger one, also near Columbia and their hopes of finding someone to sublet Miriam's.

Sam watched them, feeling moved in ways he had not known since Gershom's departure. Despite all the pain of the last year, something good had come.

They had been talking together, quickly, happily, but became suddenly quiet.

"Well?" asked Celia. "What else? We want to hear everything."

Rafe moved nearer to Miriam on the couch. He licked his lips and sucked the lower one perceptibly.

"Sam, Celia," he began, then stopped. His face darkened momentarily and Celia, looking frightened, turned toward Sam.

Miriam put her hand on Rafe's shoulder and he pulled it up against his cheek. "I feel embarrassed," he said stiffly. "Please feel free to refuse me. I'm going to ask you for something that is perhaps beyond the pale of friendship." His speech slipped surprisingly into intonations that suggested his foreign birth.

"Something we would both like," said Miriam and she kissed his shoulder.

"It is customary in traditional Jewish weddings for the parents of the bride and groom to bring them each to the wedding canopy. I have no parents, no relatives, and though I am a man of thirty-seven, I have never been married before and I wish . . ." He looked at Miriam and she smiled encouragingly at him. He turned back to them. "I know I am not your son, I don't want to take that place, but I love you both and would be very honored if you would consent . . . agree to lead me to Miriam." He shut his eyes and held Miriam's hand anchored against his cheek.

No one spoke. Celia looked at Sam as from a great distance and Sam could see her hands quiver. She nodded once. He stood up and came over to Rafe.

"There are sons and sons," he said. "I have over many years had students I have loved as sons. We have a son, whom you know we love and pray for. To lead him to the *huppah* would be my greatest joy." He paused, thinking of Gershom as a bridegroom. "Perhaps I still may have that chance. But you, Rafe, you are a son who has given without asking anything. A most unusual son. You take no place. You have made your own. We are the ones who are honored." He grasped Rafe's free hand in both of his.

Rafe leaned forward, only releasing Miriam when he stood to embrace Sam. Then he turned to Celia and bent to kiss her. She returned his kiss and rested her cheek against his arm. "I have wondered over and over what we could possibly do for you." She stared off across the room.

"Thank you, little Mother," whispered Rafe. He passed his hand across his eyes. Then he turned toward Miriam and, sitting back beside her on the couch, put one arm around her shoulders and said huskily, "Sam, do you know you're quite an eloquent fellow in your own right?"

Sam bent his head forward. "The subject was inspiring," he said awkwardly. "Besides, I've been giving some thought to something I once read, which was that too much quotation is bad because it tends to stifle conversation since it makes people uncomfortable to feel that everything they might want to say has already been said better than they can put it themselves. George Eliot, I think." There was a pause. "Notice," he added, lowering his eyes and grinning a little, "I'm just paraphrasing."

* * *

This year the only celebrants of the Silverstein family Christmas were the Seligmans, Rosens, Naomi and Frank. The older Millers sent gifts but chose to go to David's home for a little party there. "Not really Christmas," Emma had told Johanna. "Tell your mother. Miriam and Rafe will join us. Just a family get-together." Sam and Celia did not go, but spent the day with Sam's sister and her family. They had never fully understood Celia's silence but, since their visits were infrequent, they considered it a passing malady, a sort of fit, understandable under the circumstances. Sam's sister said she thought Celia was looking well, and fed them cold cuts and seltzer through most of the afternoon while Sam watched football with her husband on a new color television.

Sam had feared it would be a difficult day for Celia, and as he watched for some sign that she might be about to break, he felt precariously close to it himself as if this day should be marked as a day of mourning. He recognized the evil of that thought. Had Gershom died? He somehow couldn't believe that. The scar on his forehead stung slightly, and he put up his hand to touch it, aware of Celia across the room. She seemed distant but not disturbed and he let his eyes return to the dabs of color darting back and forth across the unnatural green on the television screen.

He had arranged to fill the day with life for her and invited Gabriel, just returned from Israel, to join them in the evening. It was Hanukkah still and, out of deference to Gabriel's sensibilities and to minimize the anniversary this day marked, he had made sure their menorah was filled with the proper number of candles, ready to be lit when Gabriel came. But Christmas was evident everywhere else: in the subway on the way home, where they viewed fellow passengers carrying their packages; in the flashing lights in the windows of a few stores on Broadway, forming strange patterns against closed iron-grill gates; and above all, in the lobby, where the Christmas tree sat surrounded by last year's polyester snow.

"I never realized how many pro games there are on Christmas," said Sam as they entered the lobby, hoping to allay the Ghost of Christmas Past he felt awaited them. It was a literary allusion he could hardly avoid.

Celia said nothing.

"Football really has taken over as the national sport. Everyone seems to watch it these days. More than baseball, I think."

"You're making conversation, Sam." Celia looked at him. Her face was drawn. "He won't come back on Christmas. He didn't like Christmas so much. At least not since he was a little boy."

"Whenever he's ready," said Sam. He looked down at the ring of keys in his hand.

"Whenever, or maybe never," said Celia.

He stood in front of the elevator, staring at her. "Never?" His throat was constricting. "I can't resign myself to never. Have you?" His voice broke.

"No," she said, "but it's possible. Either way, we don't have much say in the matter."

He put his hands on her shoulders. "I believe he's all right," he said firmly, "that even if he never . . . he's all right."

She looked up toward him but not at him, her lips thin and pale under the remains of the day's lipstick. "I want to go upstairs, Sam," she said. "We have a guest coming."

Gabriel joined them about eight-thirty. He embraced Celia with an affectionate hug, patting her on the back. "The lady looks well. I am glad to see such improvement. Sam," he turned and extended his hand. "I'm happy there have been no serious after-effects."

Inadvertently, Sam raised his hand to his forehead.

"You can hardly see it," said Gabriel. "Soon it will fade completely, become a minor blemish."

After they lit the Hanukkah candles together, he told them about the war, the many families he knew in Israel who had lost young men. "Excruciating! One family had gone from America to protect their son from what they felt were the dangers of assimilation. On the first day he died. One cannot ask them whether they would prefer he lived, even as a non-Jew. What was remarkable, though, were the students who came to help from other countries. Not just Jewish young people either. I met a man who was a teacher at the rabbinic seminary, which has students mainly from America who were drop-outs of the sixties. He said he expected that when the worst of the troubles from the war passed, some of the volunteers — they were doing volunteer work of all sorts, especially on kibbutzim, where most of the young men had been called to serve in the army — would find their way to him."

He paused. "I thought to look for Gershom among them. That is, I half-expected he would turn up there."

Celia closed her eyes.

"When he comes, we're here," said Sam, realizing as he said it that it was not an appropriate response.

Silence enveloped the room and Sam tried to find his voice. Unable to, he glanced anxiously at Celia, whose face was a mask of pain. He leaned forward. As if conscious of his movement, though she was not looking at him, she seemed to relax.

"And you, Celia?" said Gabriel deliberately. "You will welcome him home?"

"I have nothing to say about his coming home. I've told Sam that," she said very softly. "He can't be brought. If he sees those ads, it's only with his eyes."

"How do you know about the ads?" Sam asked weakly. He had never told her.

"You think I haven't heard Sadie Appel oy-veying at the door to Leah all these months? You whispering on the phone to Johanna? I read them too while I was waiting."

"Were you waiting for him to come home?" asked Gabriel. Sam realized it was a doctor's question, not intended to receive a yes or no.

"Waiting to know what to do." She was looking at neither of them.

"And now?"

"Not sure now but I can't wait anymore." She seemed about to weep but no tears came. "Sam says he is all right. I hope so. I don't know if someone who gives up his parents can be all right. Sometime I would like to know that." Her voice was getting thick.

"He has to live with himself," said Gabriel.

"I don't envy him. Maybe Johanna should stop running the ads, Sam." She said it calmly. "Maybe if he sees them, they make him feel guilty."

"I want to give him the best chance," said Sam. "Still."

She shrugged. "Gabriel, I'll get some tea? Have you seen Miriam and Rafe yet?" She was standing, her face brightened slightly. "They are wonderful, so happy, so good for one another! And your lovely little grandson!" She went toward Gabriel suddenly, lurching a little. Sam rose from his chair. Her voice was strained, pleading, but she was not crying. "I want to come out in the air where it's fresh. I must. He'll have to understand I can't wait forever. Is it terrible of me? Am I so terrible?"

"No," said Gabriel, standing and holding out his arms to receive her. "Not terrible. Not terrible at all."

*   *   *

During the week after Christmas, while Sam was free from his teaching, they spent several days searching for the right gift for Miriam and Rafe. On Saturday, three days before the New Year, they decided to return to a Madison Avenue shop and buy the silver tea service marked down for the post-Christmas shoppers. Even so, it cost more than any wedding gift they had ever bought and Sam wondered if it was the sort of thing Miriam and Rafe would really want, but Celia was set on it. "It has grace," she said, "and they'll use it over lots of years. I always think of my cousin Hattie when I take out the silver tray she gave us. Nothing lasts like silver. Even after we're gone, they should remember us."

Sam somehow doubted that they would ever be forgotten.
"Of course, they met in our home."

Outside, the street was busy, dusk coming in and Sam
paused before a bookstore window, glancing over the display
with an accustomed expectancy. He took Celia's mittened hand
in his and began to walk, feeling the cold penetrate. They
walked close to the buildings as though the light from the
shops offered warmth. From a distance, he noticed a couple
coming toward them. The man — broad, with a brownish
beard — wore a tweed overcoat and astrakhan. His scarf, high
on his neck, was carelessly folded, one end flapping against
his coat front, but he carried himself with enormous dignity.
The woman was younger, a fragile beauty with a mass of
blonde hair under a woolen tam. She was clutching the arm of
the man, smiling and nodding toward him. He looked down
at her from a slight height, his broad front projecting forward
like the bow of a ship as they walked into the wind. Sam stared
at him. There was something familiar about this man, hidden
perhaps beneath the beard, something that went with a larger
lady, bigger boned, a young woman with kinky hair.

The man, as if in response to Sam's glance, abruptly looked
away from his companion and met Sam's eyes. He stopped,
rocking slightly and began to smile, tentatively at first, then
beaming, and Sam knew that smile.

"Sam Lazarus! My God!" He rushed forward, letting go of
the delicate girl and enfolded Sam in a great bear hug.

"Bernie," said Sam, feeling elated. "I can't remember the
last time. It must be fifteen years. It's good to see you." He
pulled back out of the embrace and thrust his hand toward
Celia. "You know my wife, Celia. Celia, you remember Bernard Katzman."

Celia hesitated slightly, then stepped forward. She stretched
out her hand and took the large one coming in her direction
as Bernard Katzman leaned over and kissed her cheek. "Celia,
as lovely as ever," he said.

"It's good to see you," she responded, and Sam could almost believe she meant it.

The slender lady behind Bernard moved closer to the buildings out of the line of pedestrians but remained in the background as if waiting to be called stage center. Her movement caught his eye and he took her hand and brought her to their circle. "This is my wife, Anne," he said, and then with a boisterous laugh, "my new wife. You might say we're still on our honeymoon. We've only been married six months. Sweetheart, this man is a boyhood friend of mine, Sam Lazarus, and his wife, Celia. God! The times Sam and I had together — high school, college, those all-night sessions talking when we weren't both working. Girls!" He winked at Sam. "He knew me when I was courting Rose. Was at our wedding."

Anne shook Sam's and Celia's hands, smiling mostly at Bernard. "We'll have to tell her." Her voice was melodic.

Sam could feel his face take on a question though he fought against it. But Bernard was prepared to answer even without having seen. "Oh, yes," he boomed. "Rose and I split several years back. She got the house and money to keep her. We see her and the kids. They're on their own anyway now. Did you know I'm a grandfather?" He guffawed, then lowered his voice in a friendly self-mockery. "Don't even mind admitting it now that I'm in my second youth."

Sam felt regret at Rose's summary dismissal. He remembered her with fondness as a girl always ready for good-spirited argument. Big-boned, yes, that was the image that had caught him. Not pretty yet compelling, warm. *She really knows what to do in bed,* he remembered Bernard confiding in him many years before.

"You've certainly become a man of letters," said Sam. "I've read most of your work and I'm impressed. Is anything new coming soon? *Accusations and Dreams* was the last, wasn't it?"

"Ah, yes," Bernard thumped him on the back, "but what's coming is just the thing for you. First volume of my autobiog-

raphy. In fact, you're mentioned briefly toward the end. It only goes through high school. But the next volume is about college and the war. You have more space in that. God! It's good to see you!"

"I remember." Anne opened her eyes wide. "Your first literary friend."

"Right!" He clapped his hands in their heavy leather gloves together. "Are you still teaching? What a lucky lot your students must be!"

"Still teaching," Sam's voice was quite small. "I try, but the school atmosphere isn't what it was when we were boys."

"And your own boy? You have a son, right?"

Sam paused long enough to hear Celia clear her throat.

"He's away right now," he said, "finding himself."

Bernard Katzman seemed to understand. "It's the age for self-discovery," he said kindly. "Lots of kids go on quests. Campuses are full of them. It took some of us into our middle age to discover the things about ourselves they know now at twenty."

Sam was suddenly aware of the cold. It cut into him with a razor sharpness.

"Maybe," he heard Celia say, "but maybe they will have to keep on searching to really be sure. Maybe each age has different answers anyway." He turned to look at her, amazed.

"Listen," Bernard was saying, "it's freezing. Maybe you and I can get together for lunch on my next trip in. That's the trouble with university life in the provinces: Anne and I both have to be back right after New Year's to finish up the term. God! I miss New York!"

"Please," said Sam. "I'll give you my address and number." He reached inside his coat for a pen and slip of paper to write it on.

"Bern loves New York," said Anne, addressing them directly for the first time, "and I'm getting to like it myself because he keeps showing it to me the way tourists don't ordinarily get to see it." She looked away again admiringly up at her husband.

They shook hands vigorously and Bernard patted Sam on the back. "Let's keep our calendars open so we can make that date, probably in June." He casually slipped the paper Sam handed him into his coat pocket. "Celia," he said and leaned to kiss her. "We must be on our way. We're already late for our cocktail party. It's my publisher's bash. Goodbye. Great to see you! I'll be in touch." And he whirled Anne away down the street.

Sam watched after him, feeling a lingering nostalgia for a time he felt the future promising and fruitful. Celia's hand slipped between his arm and side. He looked at her and she smiled back.

"You know," he said, "I could never have done what he has done. He knew, still knows, how to make use of everything. That's a special gift. Maybe that's what talent really is. Knowing how to turn all things to your advantage."

"Perhaps," she said.

"He deserves his success. It's the kind of success we both dreamed of once. Rose too." He paused waiting for Celia to speak. They had started to walk again and he felt her beside him, quiet but there. "I couldn't do what it required," he said.

"I know," said Celia, almost whispering. "It doesn't matter. You've done more good than most men."

Tears welled in Sam's eyes and he matched his rhythm to hers in time with their silent understanding.

* * *

With Sam's consent, Miriam and Rafe instead of Johanna ran the public notice every day for two weeks before the wedding.

> Gershom — On Sunday, January 13, at 6 p.m., we will be married in Apt. 7D, 380 Riverside Drive. We want you to come and share our joy. — Miriam and Rafe.

Their wedding day dawned bright and crisp. Miriam could feel the cold air through the crack between the window and the sill of her childhood bedroom in her parents' apartment, where she had spent the night. She had managed to find time to go to a mikvah, a ritual bath, during the week, an act she understood to mark the ending of one life and the beginning of a new one. And it was in that spirit she and Rafe chose to stay apart the night before their wedding and to fast. "A time for reflection," the rabbi had advised them. "A little like Yom Kippur." She lay in bed now, feeling no hunger for food, only a longing for the sight of Rafe's head on the pillow beside her, his presence. She stretched with an almost feline pleasure, thinking of Rafe asleep in their bed.

They had consolidated their furniture, buying little new except a bed, as if by this act also to mark a separation from the past. But from the first, when they had explored one another's bodies with a shy excitement she had never known with any other man, it was clear her past held no precedents. She marveled at his beauty, his narrow hips, the whorls of dark hair against his chest and belly, tapering to fullness at his penis; at how the gentleness she loved in him from the beginning translated into passion, at once tender and playful; at how naturally and quickly the habit of affectionate restraint fell from them like a shadow. Just the idea of him was enough to make her ready to receive him and in the beginning when they made love, she came, for the first time, as he entered her. They slept always touching, partly entwined.

She was filled with awe at how their trust and love had permeated everything, a completeness, the more remarkable here in the world belonging to her childhood. How many times she had lain in this same bed, fighting hot tears and feeling utterly alone!

She ate nothing at all in the morning or early afternoon and arrived at the apartment where they were to be married feeling clear, if slightly light-headed. Her wedding dress, a pale cream color, slim in an Edwardian high-necked style, had no train though Emma kept fussing about the skirt as if it did, pulling it up from the rear and cautioning her to step carefully.

She was in a bedroom surrounded by women — Johanna, her matron of honor; Anita, Elana and Cynthia, her attendants; as well as her mother and grandmother. Seated with a flurry of activity going on around her, she was uncharacteristically quiet as she found herself feeling vulnerable and lonely. Seth knocked and opened the door to bring in the flowers, which had just been delivered.

"Seth," there was an urgency in her voice that surprised her, "is Rafe here yet?"

"Oh yes, and very eager. He's signing the *tenaim.*"

She bit her lip.

Cynthia began to laugh. "I think the bride is nervous after all. You still have a few minutes to reconsider," she said, lifting a bouquet beneath Miriam's chin like a child testing with a buttercup to find out if a friend liked butter. "Are you sure you want to give up being single?"

"As fast as possible," she tried to make her tone light but felt instantly ridiculous.

"A whole life you're going to have with him," said her grandmother. "The good and the bad. A few minutes more or less won't mean anything at this end."

"Mimzie, don't lean your leg against the chair. You'll crush the ruffle," said Emma.

"At the other end is different," said her grandmother, no longer addressing Miriam, and sighed.

Once Miriam was fully dressed with her veil in place, Elana took her to the living room and seated her on a large violet chair. The guests stood to one side as Rafe, wearing a white *kitel* tied with a sash over his dark suit, was brought forward in a circle of dancing men. He stood before her and raised her veil. They neither touched nor spoke but there was a vocabulary in his eyes and the tiny upward turn of his lips and, after a moment, she looked down, shy before all these people. The rabbi was intoning a phrase she knew had to do with her becoming a mother and remembered with a rush of pleasure the first time she knew she wanted to have Rafe's children.

He was led away between Sam and Celia to stand under the *huppah,* a canopy made of a prayer shawl supported by poles held by four men, Seth, David, Leonard and Ben, another friend of Rafe's. Robert, his best man, stood beside him. It took all her self-control not to race to him this late Sunday afternoon, but to walk slowly between her parents, watching him. He had never looked so wonderful to her, and as she came beneath the canopy, her parents stepping to one side, she began to circle him seven times — to enter the seven spheres of his soul, it had been explained to her. "Bless us," she prayed. "Let us always be close and happy with one another. Please." Finished, she took his hand and they stood together before the rabbi. Everything inside her pulsed *yes.* Her hand clasping his pulsed *yes.* She felt tears welling out along her cheeks saying *yes.* The rabbi offered them a cup of wine he had just blessed. First Rafe sipped from it and when it came to her lips, the sweet wine warmed them and tingled on her tongue.

"Will you, Raphael, take this woman, Miriam . . ." the rabbi was saying and she heard his voice respond firmly, "I will."

"Will you, Miriam, take this man, Raphael, to be your wedded husband? Will you be a true and faithful wife unto him? Will you honor and cherish him?"

She felt as if she were shouting, "I will," but the sound came little louder than a whisper.

He placed the gold ring they had carefully chosen together on the index finger of her right hand. "Behold," he said in Hebrew as they had been taught, and suddenly she beheld him, wet-cheeked as herself, tears running into his beard, but his face composed and his eyes glowing. "Thou are consecrated unto me by this ring according to the Law of Moses and Israel." She placed a ring on his finger and repeated the phrase to him.

They stood, their arms linked, through the reading of her *ketubbah*, the marriage contract, which he then handed to her. The rabbi spoke briefly and kindly of their new commitment to a Jewish life and home and of the way in which their union would make them more than just the sum of their two separate souls. The seven benedictions were read by friends from the *havurah* and finally, a glass wrapped in a velvet bag was placed at Rafe's foot and he stamped on it. There was a burst of applause and shouts of "Mazel tov!" He turned toward her, a radiant bridegroom, and taking her face between his hands, kissed her once, then clasped her in his arms and kissed her again to affectionate laughter from their guests. They walked together to the back of the living room, showered as they went by candy and raisins, and into a bedroom in which some hallah and honey had been left for them to break their fast and where, for a few minutes, they could be alone.

In the stillness, they just hugged each other, clinging. When they pulled away with great effort, he took out a handkerchief to wipe her face and his own and said, "You look so beautiful," in such a sober way that she had to laugh and he began to laugh too. They fed each other mouthfuls of bread dipped in honey and licked the sweetness from one another's lips.

He took off the *kitel* and led her into the living room, where they were greeted with a cheer and everyone lined up to congratulate them.

"First time I ever saw a groom cry as much as the bride," said Seymour, good-naturedly pumping Rafe's hand, "though probably lots want to."

"You think they're all so happy?" said Rafe, patting Seymour on the back. Miriam saw surprise register on her father's face and, taking her cue from her husband, said, "Afraid to show it though, Daddy. Right?" She hugged her father.

Emma, beside him, clearly embarrassed, kissed Miriam and then Rafe. "Seymour is an old softy at heart really." She stopped uncertainly, then beamed and said, "Good luck! We're very happy."

Sam and Celia hugged each of them, sniffing and dabbing their eyes. "An honor, a joy," said Sam, although it was not clear to whom.

"A long life," said Naomi. She had taken off her thick glasses and held them in one hand. "As long as you respect one another, that's the main thing." Frank nodded at her side.

David and Anita, Seth and Johanna, and all the children except Joshua offered hugs and kisses. "I'm glad we decided to leave the baby with a sitter," said Johanna, "because this way, I can really enjoy your wedding! Happy marriage, you two!"

Gabriel came next in line. He took Rafe's and Miriam's hands and held them pressed together for half a minute. "Blessings!" he said.

Harry and Leah issued congratulations and passed Rafe an envelope. He put the envelope inside the breast pocket of his charcoal gray suit. "The most elegant suit I've ever owned," he had told Miriam after they bought it. "I guess a married man needs a suit like that."

Leah paused before Miriam. She smiled affectionately. "Your dress is beautiful and this whole occasion is in such good taste. May I see your ring?" Miriam held out her hand, the plain gold band with beveled edges now firmly on her left ring finger. "Simple," said Leah. "Nice." She kissed Rafe. "Listen, Harry can always make use of an American historian on his campaign team."

The evening was filled with a buffet dinner and dances. Friends from the *havurah* lifted Miriam and Rafe each on chairs and danced in little groups while the bride and groom held the ends of a handkerchief between them. Their wedding cake was brought to the middle of the room on a rolling teacart and they cut it and passed pieces to their guests. It was a glorious time. Only as she was about to go and change her clothes, taking her bouquet from its place as table centerpiece, did Miriam realize that Gershom had not come and whispered to Sam as she and Rafe passed, "I'm sorry the invitation didn't bring him."

Sam squeezed her hand. "It was worth trying but I didn't think he would come. Celia says we can't force him. In his own good time. Maybe he never saw it. I think we're going to stop running the ads anyway." He looked at her, considering her dress, and said, "I've never seen a lovelier bride or a more adoring bridegroom. Be good to one another."

"We will." Miriam could feel herself redden. "I'm sure of that."

Emma came up behind her. "I'll help you change, Mimzie. I can pack up the dress for you after you're gone."

Miriam hesitated, looking at Rafe. She had been anticipating being with him those few minutes in the silent room, of having him help her out of her wedding gown into everyday clothes.

He leaned forward and kissed her on the forehead. "Go ahead," he said. "I'll stay here with Sam and Celia while you change," but he put his mouth against her ear and whispered, "I'll miss you." She adored him as he sat down in a bridge chair next to Celia and took her hand in his.

Emma began to trail her toward the bedroom. Right by the hall, Cynthia was sitting with a friend of Rafe's with whom she had spent most of the evening, her face animated with a look labeled "Interest" as he spoke. When she saw Miriam coming, she put her hand on his knee by way of excusing herself and got up.

"You almost make me want to get married myself," she said gaily. "If any man ever looks at me the way Rafe looks at you, I might just do it." She kissed Miriam hard on the cheek.

Impulsively, Miriam pushed her bouquet into Cynthia's hands. "Catch."

Cynthia stepped back, holding the bouquet at a distance. "Now don't ruin things by getting sentimental," she groaned, but she didn't return it.

In the bedroom, Emma began to undo the loops and buttons that fastened the high neck and back of Miriam's dress. "Well, Mimzie," she said, "it was a lovely day, a really lovely wedding. Your friends prepared quite a feast. Everyone was so gracious to us. So warm."

Miriam felt the dress loosen and began to lift it over her head. Emma was going on. "Rafe is such an unusual person, different from anyone I've ever met. I think he'll be a good husband and that you'll be happy. You can really look up to him." She paused. Then, "You know, people always say that whatever happens during the day, a husband and wife should never go to bed angry."

Miriam could sense Emma's awkwardness, grateful that the mechanics of dressing prevented her from having to turn and face her mother. "It's all right, Mother," she said kindly. "I know. We'll see you and Daddy a lot." It was not exactly what Emma wanted, she knew, but she had no intention of sharing more.

Emma paused as she began to fold the dress. She stopped and watched Miriam putting on the wool dress of beige and gold, colors Rafe liked on her. "Daddy and I may not seem like the best example," she said slowly, "but we've lived together through some trying times and always been faithful."

"Yes," said Miriam.

"I'm not saying marriage is always easy but it's better to have someone even to fight with than to be alone. I'm glad you've settled down finally." She cleared her throat. "And your father is. He used to worry about you. Did you know?"

"Yes," said Miriam. She was brushing her hair and restoring her lipstick.

Her mother just stood behind her, looking over her shoulder in the mirror. Their eyes met in the glass and Miriam turned to look directly at her.

"It's good you're so much in love," said Emma steadily. "It's a better way to begin." She came forward and she and Miriam hugged one another.

"Thank you," whispered Miriam, surprised by the wave of emotion that threatened to engulf her.

Outside, Rafe was waiting, still with Sam and Celia, but he stood up as she came toward him and took her hand.

Seth came downstairs with them and hailed a cab about a block away, riding in it to the door of the building, where it waited, meter ticking, as they thanked Seth, both of them embracing him, and got in.

It was a big cab with a partially open glass partition separating the driver from the passengers. Rafe told him the address of their apartment, just blocks away, then sat back and put his arms around Miriam. It was the first time all day, except for the brief time after the ceremony, they had been alone.

"Well," he said, "would this be Miriam Toledano?"

She had written the name hundreds of times in the past weeks but it still came to her ears strangely. "It doesn't sound like me yet," she said softly, "but I'm your wife for sure."

She put her arms around his neck and their mouths met, his breath and beard against her skin, a sweet warmth in the cold air, as they came together.

From the front of the cab, music with Latin rhythms drifted to the back and they heard the driver begin to sing along with his radio. They rocked back against the seat and smiled at one another.

16

*T*HEY RAN the last ad the first Sunday in February.

> Gershom — We hope you have seen these notices
> but since we have had no word from you in more
> than a year, we will not run any more. We hope
> that you are well and happy and know that you are
> always welcome. Love — Mom, Dad and Johanna.

March came cold and parted warmly. It was early April and
the trees along Riverside Drive had begun to feather. Johanna, struck by the delicate textures of barely budding leaves
rising from the wood, tried to catch them in a plate she was
working on.

"Would you like to spend next summer in the country?"
Seth had asked her one evening after his October tour. "The
quartet's been invited to be in residence at a new music camp
in Colorado. We could just fit it in between concert engage-
ments. I think you'll be able to get lots of sitting help — and
I hear there's a kiln."

"Do I have a choice?" Johanna had looked at him with genuine question and a touch of amusement.

"Some. We agreed we wouldn't make any decision until we
consulted our wives. So, I'm consulting."

She thought then of a summer in the mountain air away
from the city and away from her mother, and nodded. "We'll

have to try and sublet though. We can't afford to leave the apartment empty for two or three months."

They had started to show the apartment in the last two weeks of March and had a likely couple coming to look at it a second time now that it was April. She had cleared away her sketches, made Rachel put away her blocks and put Joshua in his playpen just before making a cup of coffee for Rita, who had stopped up on her way home from the lab where she now worked mornings. They sat together in the living room, enjoying the spring light that poured through the windows and listening to a student of Seth's struggle through a difficult passage in the studio, where he and Seth had retreated.

"Do you think they'll take it?" Rita asked, flicking a cigarette ash into her saucer.

"Probably. Our setup is good for them. They have one child about Rachel's age, and he needs one more summer's residence at Columbia for his Ph.D. I do hope it works out because I'm feeling very anxious about all the arrangements I have to make.

"A summer in Colorado seems worth a lot of trouble," said Rita gaily. "How's your mother taking the idea?"

"She's so wrapped up in Daddy's campaign, she'll hardly notice we're gone. And I expect she'll have a mass of activities planned for us when we get back."

"Don't do them," said Rita. "Use the kids as an excuse." She gestured toward the playpen, where Joshua had rolled to his back and was swinging at a mobile.

"Actually, I'll have to find some potting students when we get back, and we've got to find a bigger apartment." Seth's student hit a distinctly wrong note and the music stopped to a faint buzz of voices. Johanna sighed. "If we weren't going, I'd start looking seriously now. We're feeling cramped here already and it takes a long time to find a good place. Miriam and Rafe have been looking and they tell us it's hard to find anything reasonably priced at all."

Rita raised her eyebrows. "How are they doing? The marriage working?"

Johanna beamed at Rita. "They're so happy, it's catching. Seth says its an erotic experience to be in the same room with both of them." She put her hands under her chin. "They've invited the whole family to have Passover seder with them, the first one my family has had in years."

"So the religion's stuck!"

"Oh, yes. She says they're not so orthodox: she doesn't go to the mikvah every month, they'll drink nonkosher wine, but by *my* standards . . . !" She paused momentarily. "But besides that, there's something quite special about them. I never dreamed I'd feel that way about Miriam and anyone she seemed likely to marry but she's really undergone a kind of metamorphosis."

"Ah, love!" sighed Rita.

"Don't knock it." Johanna shook her head. "Tell me about the lab."

Rita began an account of the work she was doing as the cellos began to play again, but only briefly. Seth's student finished his lesson and came out of the studio, holding his instrument in a thin plastic case ripping slightly at one end. He put it down on the floor and it glittered in the sun.

"Do you know where the plastic tape is, Johanna? I want to help Larry fix his case." Seth, his shirt open at the neck and wearing a pair of brown denim slacks, came bounding out with exuberant energy. She felt a great burst of feeling for him, exquisite and fresh.

"I'll get it," she said, as Seth introduced his student to Rita.

Rachel came out of her room, crying with a minor injury. The phone rang with a caller for Seth. Rita decided to leave and put on her coat. Johanna soothed Rachel, got the tape and started to say goodbye to Rita.

"Colorado is going to seem very calm after this," Rita mused.

"I swear if it weren't for the lab, I'd force Oren to take us away for the summer."

The downstairs bell rang.

"It must be the Howells," said Johanna eagerly, ringing the buzzer. "Even New York will seem calm when the apartment business is settled."

Larry was using the tape liberally over his cello case and Seth had just hung up the phone when the apartment bell rang.

"I hope it goes well," said Rita, heading for the door with Johanna. "Bye, Larry. Bye, Seth. Oh, Joshua, don't start crying now!"

Johanna opened the door and glanced carelessly at a man standing in the hall, which seemed darker than usual because her eyes were accustomed to the bright sun flooding the living room. "Not the Howells," she said sadly, looking back at Rita.

The tall figure in the doorway moved forward and she stepped back suddenly, clasping her hand over her mouth to repress a scream.

"Hello, Johanna," said Gershom.

*   *   *

He looked quite different, she thought, as she watched him now sitting on the couch and drinking coffee. It was no wonder she hadn't recognized him at first. He was not much taller but the gangling limbs had given way to a body that belonged to itself. He was wearing a loose turtleneck sweater knit in a coarse orange yarn and it set off his dark eyes and long hair — down past his shoulders, in fact. She was trying hard to stay calm because she was nursing the baby, as she told him what it was like to have two children, when Seth said, "I can't stand this. Where the hell have you been?"

"I wondered when you were going to ask me that." Gershom's lips turned slightly up at the corners, the barest shape of a smile. "A lot of places, but for the past year or so on a farm — a commune — upstate."

"Did you ever see the notices we ran in the *Times?*" Johanna's voice was unnaturally high.

"Some. I don't suppose all."

"The invitation to the wedding?"

"I saw that."

"What brought you back now?" asked Seth, and Johanna admired his directness.

Gershom hesitated. The empty cup rattled slightly in the saucer he held. "It's a long story. I made some deals. Wasn't sure what to do next. But the big thing is I guess I feel ready." He stared at his hands.

"Are you going to stay?"

"I don't know," said Gershom. He glanced up at them for a fleeting moment, then looked down again. "How are my folks?"

"Remarkable!" said Seth. "It's about time you got around to them. Remarkable, especially considering how they were not so many months ago. If you saw the ads, you must know your mother didn't talk for nearly a year."

"Yes," said Gershom.

"And your dad got beaten up by some punks in his school. Did you know that?"

"Yes." He was looking at the floor. "She didn't talk at all?"

"Not a word!"

Gershom shook his head slightly and continued to look down.

"Then when your father was beaten up, she started to speak again and now they are closer than I think they've ever been."

"They have Miriam and Rafe too," said Johanna, feeling instantly that that was the wrong way to present it. "What I mean is they feel very close to Rafe and Miriam, very happy they had something to do with bringing them together. And Rafe and Miriam have been wonderful to them."

"Forgive me," said Gershom, looking up at last, "public notices are fine but I have felt a little confused. You do mean my waffle-headed cousin, Miriam, and my history professor? They *are* married to each other?"

"Very much so," said Seth. He began to laugh. "Gershom, you look dazed. Did you get the message that they're practicing orthodox Jews too?"

"Is that why she studied all that stuff? Because of him?"

Johanna and Seth began together. "No!" And Johanna finished. "She did it on her own and he got interested. They'll have to explain it to you themselves."

Gershom passed his hand across his face. "You do understand I find it a little hard to imagine."

Seth looked at Gershom from an angle. "I expect we'll find quite a few changes in you once you decide to open up."

The coffee cup and saucer trembled in Gershom's hand again, clicking against one another. He eyed Seth somberly. "Probably," he said.

Seth's mouth began to form a wry grin. "My curiosity is at a bursting point," he said, "but perhaps you ought to call your mother."

"I think I'd like to wait till Dad is home," mumbled Gershom. "I know I caused her a lot of grief. She really didn't talk all those months?" He waited for their nods. "That's another thing pretty hard to imagine. She wasn't exactly silent before." He put the cup and saucer down on the coffee table. "How do you think they're going to feel about seeing me?"

"Oh, glad!" Johanna was nearly shouting. "So glad!"

"I wonder. No recriminations?" he said.

"Probably some," said Seth, "though surely not at first. It's a little unreasonable to expect them not to say anything. But they've gone through a lot and they're not the same."

"They're going to rejoice," said Johanna, raising the baby to her shoulder.

The downstairs buzzer rang and Johanna moaned, "Oh, damn! The Howells."

As Seth went to tick it, he said, "How do you feel about seeing *them*? Don't answer yet. Johanna, Rachel's being unnaturally good. Why don't you take Gershom in and see what she's up to. I'll talk to the Howells. Then you can tell us."

* * *

"I thought about showing up there, just appearing," he said, "but I'm afraid to do it that way. I'd like to prepare them first so we can meet without picking up at that Christmas dinner I still have nightmares about. God! I felt desperate. If I had stayed any longer I would have smashed something or slung food all over your mother's precious carpets. I *had* to get out! I didn't plan to go anywhere special, plan anything. Just wanted to walk it off. And after a while I found I'd walked home. The minute I came in the apartment, I knew what was going to happen when my folks got back and I didn't think I could stand it. I didn't know where I was going to go but I knew I couldn't stay there. So I grabbed a few things, some money, and left. I certainly had no idea I'd be gone for very long." Seth, Johanna and Gershom were sitting at the table two hours later, the luncheon plates empty, Rachel gone to play-group, the baby asleep in his crib.

"I ended up riding around on the subway all night. I was just lucky some bastard didn't mug me. When the train came up on an elevated track and I realized it was morning, I was scared as hell. I got off at the last stop in the Bronx, and found a place to have some breakfast, knowing all the time I should get back on the subway and go home. I sat for about two hours in this diner, trying to work up the courage but I couldn't. So I took my stuff and went walking just to clear my head. I was in Westchester, I think, before I decided to go away. First, I thought I'd go see a guy I knew from school, who had gone home for the holidays to New Jersey. I started to hitch there but after my first lift, I decided that maybe it would be better if I went somewhere where no one knew me. So, I made a sign that said 'Washington' — I thought it would be fun to see Washington — and a trucker picked me up and left me right in the city. I'll always remember that evening. It was cold and I had no idea where I was going to sleep but I felt incredible — like I'd been let out of a box. I'm sure we'll talk sometime about what happened to me but for a while, at least, things seemed to break my way and I thought if I just hung loose, I'd be all right.

"I only thought about coming back when the beginning of second semester came around. The three or four weeks I'd been gone seemed like much longer and when I thought about Christmas, everybody sitting round the table, most of all my folks, it was like looking through a long tunnel at a little speck of light. Hard to see clearly. While I was considering what to do, I happened to buy a copy of the *Times* one day and saw one of your ads. I must have read it fifty times, trying to make sure this Gershom was me, Johanna you! It's one thing to read about strangers but when it's you . . . ! When I thought I had it straight, that there was this silent lady — my mother — living in my house, and if I came home, I'd have to face her and Aunt Leah too, if I came at the wrong time, I panicked.

"I know how that must sound to you, but I thought if I came back, I'd be buried for good. And on top of that, I felt so angry all over again that it just seemed sensible to keep what remnant there was of my sanity by staying away."

Johanna had clapped her hand to her head. "If I had thought the ads would keep you from . . ."

"No," Gershom interrupted. "It wasn't just the ads."

"Would you have come back if you hadn't seen them?"

"Can't say. All I know is I decided to do something else. But for a long time I read the ads, daily, greedily I'd even say, like a secret vice, even when I was too poor to buy the paper and had to read it in libraries, sometimes a day or two late. You would run the same ad for about a week but each time I read it, it looked different — a code of some kind. I had these dreams about coming home, ringing the bell, and being greeted by *gloom,* my father bent with being noble, and *doom,* my mother with tape all over her mouth.

"Once, when I needed some money very badly, a guy I met in Cincinnati, a rabbinical student — that's a long story — lent it to me on the condition that I not go any farther away from New York than I was already — like no rides to the coast — until I had gone back and settled things with my folks. He said he knew I was an honest man and that if I agreed to that condition, 'in lieu of interest,' he said, he'd be glad to lend me the money. And he said he didn't want to see the last five until I'd gone home whenever that was. Still owe it to him though I've paid the rest.

"The girl I was traveling with at the time tried to convince me he had no right to put such restraints on me. She said I was letting myself be bought. But I had no problems with that promise except during the Yom Kippur war. I was waiting tables in a vegetarian restaurant in Ithaca where some religious Jews used to come to eat fairly often. Some of them decided to go to Israel to volunteer their services and they got me really turned on about it. I was ready to go with them. I'd learned a lot about farming, vegetables and flowers, by then and I thought I could really help on a kibbutz. Turn the desert green like the ads say. But Tracy, the guy who had started the commune I lived on, reminded me about my promise. I almost hated him when he did that, certainly hated myself for having told him. His daughter, Maura, said she knew he'd find a way to stop me. (I worked with her in the restaurant but she had just left the commune to live in town.) In the end though, it was my promise and I had to live with it. I could say to myself over and over again, 'Steve's studying to be a rabbi. He'd approve of my going to Israel.' And then, even if he didn't actually say it, I'd hear Tracy's voice, 'Not without stopping off in New York first!'

"It's funny about the orthodox Jews. When I first started to work in the restaurant, I'd just gone through a long stretch of not reading the ads. First I was greedy, then I went on a fast. I had stopped reading them when I found out that Mr. Toledano was visiting my folks. That amazed me. I didn't want to believe it because I kept thinking I couldn't ever face a professor who'd seen my parents' house — all the needle-point, the famous harp — let alone actually met my parents. It was like my head was a time machine. There I was far away — in Pittsburgh — and yet I felt as if I was going to leave the library and find myself walking down the street in Washington Heights, dying of shame because there would be Mr. Toledano coming out of my house."

"I don't suppose it makes any difference to you that he loves your parents," said Johanna.

"I don't understand all that, but I'm different in lots of ways than I was a year ago and death-by-embarrassment is not one of my things anymore."

"That's progress!" said Seth, grinning, and for the first time, Gershom really smiled.

"You're the same, at least, Seth. Well, I hadn't read a notice for nearly two months when I picked up the paper that had one telling that Miriam was studying orthodox Judaism and suddenly all these guys with those little crocheted doilies on their heads, who came into the restaurant, made sense. I mean I knew what they were but I hadn't put being kosher and eating vegetarian food together until then. Especially because the commune is mostly vegetarian. No animals are raised for slaughter. A few people eat fish and occasionally chicken but that's about it. Me too, now.

"I remember I brought the *Times* home and showed the no-tice to Tracy and he was very interested. I'd told him a lot of things but I hadn't told him about seeing the public notices. Then, of course, the whole thing came out — what I knew, what I couldn't figure out, and after that I brought the *Times* in pretty regularly. Tracy is a very sharp guy and we would look at the notices together. Some of them seemed a little ob-scure, Johanna. Did you know?"

"Gershom, up until now, I've been so glad to see you I haven't felt mad but now I'm seething. Do you have any idea how much I couldn't say? For instance, my mother and father separated for a while, which my mother didn't want made public knowledge so I could hardly put it in the newspaper."

"Did she live with my folks?"

"Only days. She stayed with us. I'll tell you about that sometime. And though you haven't asked, their problems had something to do with your mother being sick and my father wanting to run for Congress."

"You're kidding!"

"Have a button," she said fiercely and reached for one from a little jar filled with them. "Mommy's so enthusiastic now, she gives these out in quantity, but it didn't start out like that, I can assure you."

"You don't sound nearly so docile, Johanna," said Gershom, gazing at her.

"It'll save her from having an ulcer by the time she's forty," said Seth. "While we're on the subject of things that didn't get said, your aunts Leah and Emma were barely on speaking terms over who would take care of your mother. Even now they are merely 'civil.' "

Gershom said nothing. Then he shrugged. "Tracy used to say that until I went home, the notices would be like one hand clapping. But he figured out a lot of them, all the same. Like, long before the notice about Miriam's engagement to Mr. Toledano, he would say, 'I think your cousin is trying to tell you there's a romance going on.' It seemed so wild to me.

"He's an unusual man, Tracy, a stupendous man really. If you saw him — he's very big — holding a seedling, putting it in the earth . . . it's really something. For him the chief commandment is Honor Life — the growing things, people. He'll tell you that. In some ways he reminds me of Dad. When he talks about 'doing right things,' 'respecting the earth,' I can just hear Dad with his quotes and convictions that literature can save mankind. Once, actually more than once, I got into a big talk with Tracy about Dad, the great failure, the also-ran syndrome he lives with, and Tracy said he thought Dad sounded like a person who had given a lot of himself to others and that when I got home someday I ought to have a long talk with him, starting out with no prejudgments.

"When I told Maura that, she said that of course he was sympathetic with failures since he was one. They left Philadelphia and what he calls the nine-to-five-sell-your-soul race when she was twelve. She didn't want to go and even though it was six years ago, she hasn't forgiven him.

"I thought very briefly about coming back to Columbia in the fall — there are things I'd like to study now — but there was so much to do on the farm — all the harvesting, and we were adding a wing to the barn — I couldn't see leaving. Somehow that made me feel angry at Dad, not want to see him, because I could just imagine what he had to say about my screwing up at college."

"It was low on his list of concerns," said Johanna. She was aware of how curt she sounded.

Gershom hesitated, a shadow passing his face. "Don't think it ended with that. I think I can handle his opinions about school. When I read about his being beaten up, it got to me. And Mom talking again! I was cracked so wide open, when I got back to the farm, I couldn't get out of the car because I was shaking so hard. My mind was going wild: 'Old Quotation Sam, pompous ass, got what he deserved. Probably quoted *Uncle Tom's Cabin* to some black dude,' and at the same time, I was crying. I mean really! Tears all over. I couldn't calm down." He was ripping the napkin at his place into tiny shreds. No one said anything.

"Tracy asked me if I wanted to go home, but the idea of Mom clinging to me: 'My beloved boy! It took *this* to bring you back . . .' "

"I don't think she'd say that anymore," Johanna interrupted.

". . . that kind of thing from everybody . . . Old smug Seymour would pop into my head. Even Grandma!" His eyes got big. "How's Grandma? Sometimes I wondered if I'd ever see her again. Is she O.K.?"

"Marvelous," said Johanna, "as usual."

"I'm glad," he said. He moved the shreds of napkin in patterns on the table. He was not looking at either of them when he began again.

"There was part of me that wanted to get on the first bus, but part of me that wanted to slam the door forever. Maura told me I should stop looking at the notices if I really wanted that and I think she was probably right. I tried not to read them for a while but it was like an addiction. I kept coming back to them. When I got the idea of going to Israel, one of the things that seemed so great was that I could replace the past with the future, a future I could see. I'd still like that." He raised his eyebrows, small wrinkles forming on his forehead.

"My father said he looked at all the groups of American students he saw, thinking you might be among them. Did you know he was there?"

"Your father must be a mind reader."

"He's been a very good friend to your parents," said Johanna. "Did you see the announcement of the *brit?*"

"Yes. Forgive me. I didn't even think of coming. But the wedding was something else. I mean I don't understand Miriam and Mr. Toledano . . ."

"Rafe," said Seth. "He's your cousin now, almost a brother."

"I don't have a brother," said Gershom. "Have no idea what that's like. Well, the wedding invitation followed Christmas, the holiday of good cheer! And I felt rotten. Not angry anymore though. Depressed! Maura and I would go for walks in icy old Ithaca. We couldn't ever go very far. I tried to talk out everything with her. What I'd done, what the folks had done, what I felt about a world I couldn't make sense of, in which I was maybe a pawn in some sort of cosmic chess game. After all *my* talk at Christmas, there was my flip cousin, turning religious — marrying my college professor, whom she met somehow because of me while I was off the board. Or why my mother didn't talk for so long. What that must have meant to my dad. All because of a move I made. The wrong move? Once you've made a wrong move in chess, it's not always possible to recover.

"I was tempted to come but Maura and I role-played a little and I figured I'd ruin Miriam's wedding. It was really gutsy of her to ask me — Maura pointed that out — because, sure as hell, the bride wouldn't have been the center of attention.

"Then the ads stopped. They just stopped. I skipped a few weeks and when I got the paper again, they weren't there. I was surprised how much I missed them, how much I'd come to count on them. Tracy said that if I was going to stay away, I couldn't expect people to stay the same at home, care the same way, keep on issuing invitations. Maura said he was laying it on thick, but even without him, I was pretty low.

"And so was she. We were doing spring planting and Maura didn't join us because she'd had a lot of trouble. She'd been living with this guy she thought was the type to take her back to Philadelphia. That's another story. When he left her, he took all the money they'd been saving together.

"Last night we were working together in the restaurant and I told her she ought to go back to the farm. She could help with the planting and packing the roses we grew to sell to people for their gardens. She said she couldn't face everyone, especially her father. No one was in the restaurant and she started to cry. She said she felt stupid, used in fact, and I said, 'No one's going to judge you. So, you made a mistake!' And she said, 'You're no one to talk, Gershom. If it's so easy, you go home!' She didn't expect me to do it, I know, but when she said it like that, I wanted to. She cried and cried and we held each other. Finally, I said, 'I'm going, Maura. It's time. You tell your dad.' She looked at me so strangely and said, 'You mean it!' And I knew I did. Not because of her either. I really did!"

*   *   *

What would remain with Sam when he recalled their reunion was that though he and Gershom wept almost uncontrollably, Celia's eyes merely sparkled as she stroked Gershom's head. Speech receded briefly again and she was only able to whisper. But, he acknowledged to himself, words are only reflections of things that stand whether they are spoken or not.

"I'm sorry I couldn't come back sooner," Gershom had said and that seemed right. One had to do what one had to do.

"He's changed," Celia had allowed when they were finally alone. "Looks like a young man. Not a boy anymore. Even with the long hair." Her voice, small as it was, quavered slightly, but it was said with no tone of regret.

He restrained himself that night, lying awake, unable to sleep, from getting up and going in to sit by his son's bed, the bed he remembered lying in, aching to his very center. Does Gershom ache? he asked himself. What has he gone through? He closed his eyes resolutely but sleep wouldn't oblige him. As he spread the fingers of his left hand above the blankets, his mind crept toward his life as novel but he consciously called it back. If they talked from tomorrow to some undetermined time in the future, would they ever adequately describe the boundaries that now extended their worlds? Perhaps it would be a mistake to define them since they were still in the process of change. Sooner or later, he suspected, they would tell each other enough. He closed his eyes and awakened to a fresh morning in which he tiptoed out, leaving his wife and son still sleeping.

He returned in the afternoon to find them sitting before the stand of plants, now neatly trimmed, some hanging vines propped over green sticks.

"Look what Gershom did today," said Celia, pointing at the plants. "He learned about plants on his farm."

"I want to hear about the farm," said Sam wanly, fighting a wave of jealousy. What had Celia learned from their boy? He mentally slapped himself. Not theirs. His own.

"Mom told me today about going to Paris when she entered

that harp competition and going to a great park to see green-houses filled with beautiful plants . . . really lush, she said. I thought I could help make this group come closer to that standard."

"What greenhouses?" Sam looked toward Celia, surprised.

"I don't remember the name. I've always remembered them though. It was one of the most wonderful days. I was with a whole group of people, mostly harpists, some others. We sang and laughed." She pulled absent-mindedly on a curl. "That was in another time."

Her secret, he thought. Something hidden in her memory for nearly forty years, not to be shared until the right moment presented itself.

"I remember coming home and feeling so guilty that I'd taken all that money from the family to go and then, to come back without a prize — just a few certificates to show I'd been there. I tried to remember everything I saw so I could tell them, so at least they could feel they had been to Paris too but I hardly thought the greenhouses were worth mentioning. Yet they've stuck in my mind all these years." She turned to Sam. "I called everyone. They're all dying to see Gershom. I said, 'Just let him catch his breath!' Mamma was nearly crying, she was so excited. I even called Miriam at work. She and Rafe want to come and see him as soon as possible. Maybe tonight. And of course, they want him to come to their seder. Only if he wants to, though."

Sam glanced at Gershom cautiously. Another family gathering!

"The celebration of a departure," said Gershom with a half-grin. "How appropriate."

"Gershom and I have been waiting all day," said Celia. "I didn't want him to tell me anything — places, people — until you could hear it too."

"I'm ready to listen right now," Sam said, sitting down. He put out his hand toward Gershom. "Let's start."

And so, for the first time, Gershom began to tell his story.

About the Author

Elizabeth Klein was born and educated in New York, and worked as an editorial researcher for *Newsweek*. From 1976 to 1978, she served as president of Illinois Writers, Incorporated. Ms. Klein is the author of a chapbook of poetry, *Approaches*, and has published poems regularly in magazines and anthologies. She has lived in Jerusalem, Israel, and Reading, England, where a portion of *Reconciliations* was written. A recipient of an Illinois Arts Council grant for *Reconciliations*, she lives in Champaign, Illinois, with her husband, Michael Shapiro, a professor of English, and their four children. She is currently at work on a new novel.

About the Author

Elizabeth Klein was born and educated in New York, and worked as an editorial researcher for *Newsweek*. From 1976 to 1978, she served as president of Illinois Writers, Incorporated. Ms. Klein is the author of a chapbook of poetry, *Approaches,* and has published poems regularly in magazines and anthologies. She has lived in Jerusalem, Israel, and Reading, England, where a portion of *Reconciliations* was written. A recipient of an Illinois Arts Council grant for *Reconciliations,* she lives in Champaign, Illinois, with her husband, Michael Shapiro, a professor of English, and their four children. She is currently at work on a new novel.